A L I E N S ™

V A S Q U E Z

THE COMPLETE ALIEN™ LIBRARY FROM TITAN BOOKS

The Official Movie Novelizations
by Alan Dean Foster
*Alien, Aliens™, Alien 3, Alien: Covenant,
Alien: Covenant Origins*

Alien: Resurrection by A.C. Crispin

Alien 3: The Unproduced Screenplay
by William Gibson & Pat Cadigan

Alien
Out of the Shadows by Tim Lebbon
Sea of Sorrows by James A. Moore
River of Pain by Christopher Golden
The Cold Forge by Alex White
Isolation by Keith R.A. DeCandido
Prototype by Tim Waggoner
Into Charybdis by Alex White
Colony War by David Barnett
Inferno's Fall by Philippa Ballantine
Enemy of My Enemy by Mary SanGiovanni

The Rage War
by Tim Lebbon
*Predator™: Incursion, Alien: Invasion
Alien vs. Predator™: Armageddon*

Aliens
Bug Hunt edited by Jonathan Maberry
Phalanx by Scott Sigler
Infiltrator by Weston Ochse
Vasquez by V. Castro
Bishop by T. R. Napper

The Complete Aliens Omnibus
Volumes 1–7

Aliens vs. Predators
Ultimate Prey edited by Jonathan Maberry &
Bryan Thomas Schmidt
Rift War by Weston Ochse & Yvonne Navarro

The Complete Aliens vs. Predator Omnibus
by Steve Perry & S.D. Perry

Predator
If It Bleeds edited by Bryan Thomas Schmidt
The Predator by Christopher Golden
& Mark Morris
The Predator: Hunters and Hunted
by James A. Moore
Stalking Shadows by James A. Moore
& Mark Morris
Eyes of the Demon edited by
Bryan Thomas Schmidt

The Complete Predator Omnibus
by Nathan Archer & Sandy Scofield

Non-Fiction
AVP: Alien vs. Predator
by Alec Gillis & Tom Woodruff, Jr.
*Aliens vs. Predator Requiem:
Inside The Monster Shop*
by Alec Gillis & Tom Woodruff, Jr.
Alien: The Illustrated Story
by Archie Goodwin & Walter Simonson
The Art of Alien: Isolation by Andy McVittie
Alien: The Archive
Alien: The Weyland-Yutani Report
by S.D. Perry
Aliens: The Set Photography
by Simon Ward
Alien: The Coloring Book
The Art and Making of Alien: Covenant
by Simon Ward
Alien Covenant: David's Drawings
by Dane Hallett & Matt Hatton
*The Predator: The Art and Making
of the Film* by James Nolan
The Making of Alien by J.W. Rinzler
Alien: The Blueprints by Graham Langridge
Alien: 40 Years 40 Artists
Alien: The Official Cookbook
by Chris-Rachael Oseland
Aliens: Artbook by Printed In Blood
Find the Xenomorph by Kevin Crossley

ALIENS
VASQUEZ

A NOVEL BY V. CASTRO

TITAN BOOKS

A L I E N S ™ **: V A S Q U E Z**

Hardback edition ISBN: 9781803361116
Paperback edition ISBN: 9781803363035
E-book edition ISBN: 9781803361888

Published by Titan Books
A division of Titan Publishing Group Ltd
144 Southwark Street, London SE1 0UP

First paperback edition: October 2023
10 9 8 7 6 5 4 3 2 1

A CIP catalogue record for this title is available from
the British Library.

Printed and bound CPI Group (UK) Ltd, Croydon, CR0 4YY.

Did you enjoy this book?
We love to hear from our readers. Please email us at readerfeedback@
titanemail.com or write to us at Reader Feedback at the above address.
www.titanbooks.com

Dedicated to all the Castro women in my family
and my beloved daughter

El riesgo siempre vive. The guts to take a risk is the dream,
even if your corazon must become as combustible as a grenade

PART I

JENETTE

1

2171

"VAS-KEZ, you dumb fuck!"

Jenette didn't respond.

"Whatever," he continued. "Here, your name is Recruit. If you're *good enough*, that is. Now move!"

The man who assumed he was Jenette's superior flicked his eyes from her breasts to her sculpted arms, then to her face, giving her the type of look she'd received all her life.

"You won't make it."

"Who do you think you are?"

The patronizing glare rolled across her with the pressure of a two-ton space rover, bone crushing. She stepped into the elevator that would take her to the training pit. The metal doors closed, leaving her in a vacuum of silence with only her reflection staring back. Her brown skin shimmered from the sweat that managed to escape the red bandana across her forehead.

Before this moment she'd been on the scantest of MRE rations, had hiked every day for five hours, and stayed up writing a paper to the court arguing why she deserved a chance in space.

Take all those self-destructive tendencies and take aim, mujer, she told herself. The tattooed teardrop next to her eye appeared to slide in the dim light. All she had in this life was the woman staring back at her. Neto's words echoed in her mind.

"Us against the ugliness in the world. You think they want any of us to make it? If they did, we would see it. Nah, we fucking take it any way we can," he'd said. *"They protect their territory like they the gangbangers. Believe that. Put it on your waist and in your piggy bank."*

Then she thought of Leticia and Ramón.

It was as much for them as it was for her, even if she'd only held them long enough to give them names. That had been the most difficult battle she imagined she would ever face. Her Mesoamerican ancestors believed that if you died in childbirth, you would be given a warrior's welcome in the afterlife. She hadn't died, despite the agony she endured alone, bearing down with her heels in stirrups and hands tearing at the hospital bed sheets. The two babies ripped her flesh as they crowned. So many battles she'd already fought sola. The journey to that test had been worthy of the fabled underworld Mictlan.

Jenette wondered what gods or demons were left to be met in her life. She'd believed she would die in prison, but was released into service to the USCM—the Colonial Marines. In just her first trimester, it had been a machete through her guts when she signed away all rights to her unborn children. There had only been time for one final kiss and glance before they were whisked away. Then came the enforced sterilization process.

Jenette was a warrior, had walked the warrior's path, even if it was wayward at times where she stumbled with bad judgment. Now in this final test for the Marine Corps, she had to muster all the ganas of every soldier in her family who served before her. In this moment her bones weren't made of calcium and marrow, but of steel. They would be steel for as long as she needed to get what she wanted.

A second chance.

No fucking way would she die behind bars. Too many like her had lived and died there, in a fungal cocoon of hopelessness for petty shit or things they didn't do. You want to kill a soul, cage it. Want to show people their place in the world? Four bare walls without real care or rehabilitation can be as cruel as it is a statement. Monsters are created.

Don't be surprised when jaws snap your neck.

She didn't like bullfights or rodeos, but she'd studied old video recordings of both, preparing for this battle that would determine whether or not she would make it into the Marines. With matador concentration she held her pulse rifle, and cocked it.

Alright, papi, swing those balls my way.

Like any recruit, she'd had to run a gauntlet of weapon prep, marksmanship, survival skills, physical fitness, and hand-to-hand combat. Every challenge she accepted with her bandana worn low and gold cross shining. Without failing a single one, she'd moved forward in the Marines with the stealth of a dark horse—even when she received recognition in two different rifle competitions.

This challenge wouldn't be an exception. Jenette crossed her body in the shape of the crucifix and braced for the attack from an android opponent who would be twice her size and programmed to make this anything but easy. The mistake she saw time and time again in this cumbia of "win or lose" was arrogance, the lack of respect for the opponent.

No one was going to make it easy for her. No one would give her *anything* in this life.

Don't underestimate the instinct *that is survival.*

Respect was everything—getting it and keeping it. Now was her time to burst through every barrier and run hard.

The metal door opened. The training pit was dark. The silence was what she imagined space might sound like. Lights began to appear dimly overhead, and the temperature of the room increased to that of a desert at the hottest point in the day. She flicked her eyes to the top of the pit at the one-way glass in the walls, knowing every movement would be watched and judged. The scrutiny on her performance would outweigh the others. This controlled evaluation was meant to test strength, senses, and ability to think on your feet—all in the space of ten minutes.

Doors opened on the opposite side of the room. There he stood. The android was six feet one inch of pure synthetic muscle, holding the same weapon as she. His eyes remained blank, without a flicker of life or sympathy. He only knew the instinct of his programming. A timer on the wall above his head flashed a countdown in red blinking lights. As it hit zero, he would come alive with one intention, to make her fail or give up. But these assholes had forgotten that when you grow up in a system rigged for your failure or to devalue you, you replace skin with an exoskeleton of having nothing to lose.

In her mind's eye she saw the faces of those who had locked her up, of dead family members languishing in ill-equipped and overrun hospitals, the babies she would never know, the guards who had wanted to rough her up. All of it was butane for her fire-breathing nostrils.

Bulldoze him like a tank. Smoke him. Be the goddamn tank. Don't forget you come from soldaderas.

Zero.

Jenette aimed her gun with ease—as if it were an extension of her arm—and fired. The android mirrored her actions, forcing her to tumble to the side to avoid getting hit. Those suckers hurt. Many times, in afterhours training, she'd been walloped courtesy of Drake.

She kept moving and continued to fire as she ran around the circular perimeter, but *goddamn* he was fast for his size, with speed more minotaur than man. Then again, he wasn't human. There was no emotion on his face, no tell she could pick up on.

All she needed was one clean shot in the sandstorm of rubber bullets. The two of them couldn't keep running with the dizzying motion of a carousel. *They* would make sure of it, because combat wasn't no game of ring around the roses. In real combat, someone always died.

She stopped abruptly and darted toward the android while taking aim. Her shot hit his left shoulder. The blow slowed him down, with his body jerking backward, but it wasn't enough to offset his shot to her pulse rifle, which flew from her hands upon impact. It clattered to the ground. Without missing a beat, she grabbed a smaller gun attached to her waist. This time her shot hit the android in the center of his right hand. The malfunctioning digits seized, giving her enough time to take another shot.

He dropped the pulse rifle.

Jenette kneeled for the kill, aiming for the head. One huge stride toward her, coupled with a roundhouse kick, knocked the pistol out of her grip. The bones cracked and her flesh stung with the feeling of a hot iron, but she held her scream between gritted teeth.

It ain't over till it's over, motherfucker.

Without hesitation Jenette propelled herself straight into his body. The sudden impact made him stumble back.

On her right ankle she had stashed a switchblade, the kind she carried as a kid and the one grandfather Seraphin told her was the weapon of choice for the pachucos of old. Jenette flipped it open then plunged it as deep as she could in the part of his lower belly not covered by the protective vest, then swept it across. He shoved her to the ground while pressing a hand to his body where it was leaking white liquid.

Booming broke out above her head.

Then simulated gunfire.

The temperature decreased rapidly, accompanied by a simulated rainstorm. The lights strobed across the pit. This was *their* way of saying *"Are you going to win or lose? You decide… now."*

The android took the opportunity to strike again, but this time she was ready to end it. When he lunged for her, Jenette drove her boot straight into the hole in his belly. He pushed closer, ignoring the boot in the cavity of his midsection as he grabbed her by the neck. With her opposite leg she attempted to kick him as hard as she could anywhere her foot would land, trying to rupture his wiring or something. The water made her boot slip.

Thanks to the bandana her vision hadn't blurred. Her wounded hand was all but useless, however, and already beginning to swell. Jenette could feel her windpipe closing as his fingers constricted around her neck. It was now or never. No way would it end like this—nothing and *no one* could grab her by the neck. She squeezed her abdominals hard to lift her closer to the android. She still had the switchblade in her good hand, and with one hate-fueled swipe she caught him across the throat.

White paste flooded from the gash. His face contorted from the damage. His grip softened. Jenette took that moment to grab his wrist and pull him to the ground, securing his torso with one knee as he convulsed from his two wounds.

"Adios," she said as she dropped the knife and yanked out the cables inside his neck. White liquid flew into the air and splashed across her face and chest as sharp electric shocks ran through her fingertips.

The lights went up and the shower ceased. A robotic voice spoke.

"*Congratulations. J. Vasquez. You are the victor and have successfully passed your final evaluation. Please make your way through the open doors.*"

She lifted her gaze to the tinted rectangular window at the top of the training pit and nodded. With her good hand she stowed her switchblade in the left thigh pocket of her fatigues. You couldn't go wrong going back to basics, your roots.

Every muscle ached as she lifted herself from the ground. Her mouth was a cottonfield beneath the blazing sun.

Drake greeted her when she stepped out of the elevator, standing with the rest of the recruits waiting for their evaluation. A large screen in the holding area showed each showdown. He gave her a large grin as she walked out. It was nice to have a friendly face after staring down an emotionless android.

"I knew you had it in you," he said. "You made that shit look easy... I can't wait to get a crack at that dildo. He won't know what the hell hit him."

"What choice do we have but to make it?" she said. "This is it for me. No plan B and no trust fund—and careful with that 'dildo.' He has some moves. You might get fucked if you don't stay on your game." Jenette rubbed her neck, hearing her voice strained from the android's grip.

"Don't I know it, sister. You ready to celebrate tonight?"

"Hell, yes," she said. "Let me shower first and get this hand wrapped. Tell me when and where?"

"Will do. I'll send you a message later. We're gonna get lit tonight, like the good ole days."

She gave him a confident smirk. "Good luck, man." Then she slapped his hand, even if the reverberation made her want to wince. *Don't let nobody see your pain. Don't let your own sweat sting your eyes, otherwise you won't be able to see, and that's what your enemy wants. They want you to be blind. ¡El riesgo siempre vive!*

Abuelo Seraphin always had the good advice.

A commanding officer stopped her before she could make it out of the waiting area. If she hadn't known better, he could have been the brother of the android she just destroyed. "Vasquez, you did major damage to the android with that switchblade. No one knew you had it on you. It's not USCM issued."

"No one said I couldn't improvise," she replied. "Send me the bill." He stared at her without expression.

Then he reached into his pocket. "You showed creativity, tenacity, and that you're a hell of a fighter. Remarkable strength. Here." He handed her a square patch with "USCM" embroidered on it. "Welcome, Vasquez. You're going to the stars."

"Thank you, sir!"

"We are your family now." He turned on his heels to return to the observation chamber, where he would watch the rest of the evaluations.

Jenette's heart galloped. It was just a patch made from cloth and thread, yet the weight of it could carry her places she never imagined.

She walked back to her training quarters with head held high, feeling like a Roman gladiator. In the bigger scheme of things, they were all pawns to benefit the higher-ups orchestrating wars, politics, and "building better worlds," as they put it. Pure entertainment for the new gods, puppet masters stitched from the flesh of dead soldiers and colonists, the strings forged with gold coins and credits.

Gangbanger, she had been called. The whole system was rigged by a gang of suits. Everyone belonged to a gang in this world, wanting only to protect their barrio.

* * *

Jenette pressed the button to close the door to her tiny efficiency quarters. Her wobbly legs managed to make it to her single bed before giving way for her body to crumple, now that the adrenaline had faded. Her boots had to come off, but suddenly she lost all energy to move or control the sobs escaping from her chest without warning.

Eyelids fluttered, hoping they would set free the overwhelming emotions in that moment. She removed the sodden red bandana from her head, Abuelo Seraphin's bandana. She brought it to her eyes and squeezed them shut. Her hands clutched it until her knuckles went white. She had to keep her palms to her face to prevent the brown mask of bravado from slipping off with her sweat and tears. Tears and sympathy were a luxury not reserved for her type. Her injured hand didn't register the pain with the explosive fission escaping from her heart. She needed something to remind her this moment was real.

There would be nothing more to prove.

One door of destiny shut as another opened.

She had done it. No one believed she could or would— just another Brown number in a white jumpsuit when she signed on the dotted line to be released early for a murder she hadn't committed. She'd sacrificed it all and only had herself now.

Wiping her tears, Jenette exhaled. With the overwhelming emotions purged as much as she would allow, she pulled off her combat boots. There were no more tears from her eyes except the one permanently marked on her face.

Jenette removed the switchblade from her pocket. It was still wet with the white mucus from the android. Back in wartime 1940s Los Angeles during the Zoot Suit riots, you were either a zoot suit-wearing pachuco called a gangster with a switchblade, or a military man fighting the good fight. Blood from both spilled during those riots. Jenette—where she came from and who she was—possessed the spirit of both now. She was a Marine, but she also remembered that street life.

Placing the switchblade on the bed, she messaged Roseanna the good news. A photo flashed on the screen, of two small children covered in mud, playing with a litter of baby pigs.

Roseanna responded immediately.

As if there was any doubt!

Can't take it away if it wasn't yours to begin with, Jenette thought.

She belonged to the Marines now, likely the only family she would see in the flesh until the day she died. At least she had her homie Drake with her. Small blessings and shit. She stood up and ran her fingers through her short hair until they touched the nape of her neck.

Damn it felt good.

Time to shower, get her hand seen to, then raise hell—or maybe just the roof that night.

2

2166

As far back as Jenette could remember, she had always wanted to be a soldier. Her father, her great-great-uncle Roland who was buried with a Purple Heart for his service in Vietnam, her grandfather, and great-grandparents, all with roots that began as farmworkers on Earth, moving farm to farm like many Mexicans emigrating to the US hundreds of years ago.

"*¡El riesgo siempre vive!* That is what my grandmother would say to me," Seraphin told her, "and what she heard from the women before her. Did you know the military could be for you, too? You have a distant relative who was a soldadera and fought in the Mexican Revolution. Those soldaderas were a bad group with their rifles and bandoliers. Chihuahua, watch out!"

Abuelo Seraphin liked to repeat this story time and time again. "People risk their lives and the lives of their children for a chance at something more. It's a story told across Earth for centuries, and it carried people into space. There has been much tragedy, so many lost in the oceans, rivers, and deserts, but also there is hope. Never lose your hope even if you lose your way."

Her grandfather said this while polishing his old combat boots with a round black-and-gold tin of black polish and an old T-shirt made into a rag. His memories and nuggets of wisdom also were shared while he tended his garden of chilis and squash, a red bandana across his brown forehead. His pride had continued long after he retired, and he was buried with all his military gear.

Most of the men in the family joined the military to be educated through the GI Bill. The cost of everything on Earth was sky-high, even back then. Someone had to carry on their military tradition, the slow bachata toward upward mobility wherever it could be found.

Growing up in Los Angeles, Jenette had liked making forts, playing guns, watching ancient reruns of *G.I. Joe* or *She-Ra*. She'd tease her sisters, brother, and cousins with insects and small animals while the children did their homework in a silent circle at the kitchen table. She captured centipedes, and crickets squirmed in a jar as she crept up to unleash them on the table. They all roared in fright, and she with laughter.

"Jenette, I'm *telling*! You're so necia all the time!" they would whine. Her mother, Francisca, stood by, giving her a look of disapproval.

"Why can't you be like other girls?" Mother said.

"Look at Roseanna and Carmen. Come with me. If you can't behave, I'll keep you busy with the housework."

Despite her mother's protests, Jenette would run around the house, imagining new worlds with monsters to kill. This earned her the title of Disaster Master. She would walk into the kitchen to see a broken toy in her mother's hands.

"Did you do this? You want your father to work himself to death trying to provide, when all you do is cause trouble by breaking things. You will clean all the bathrooms for a month."

The only time she wanted to sit still was at Easter.

Cascarone time.

For months Francisca would gingerly break the eggs at the top end, creating a small opening to allow the slimy contents to slip out before jumping from the heat of a pan sizzling with red chorizo fat. The shells would be rinsed then placed upright in an empty egg carton. The eggs with jagged mouths lined up on the counter until there were rows and rows of them. Sometimes spiders or flies would find their way inside and crawl in and out. The sight made Jenette shiver.

A few days before Easter it would be time to dye them different colors, fill each one with confetti, and cut squares of tissue paper to be glued at the top.

The great annual Easter cascarone fight would ensue. Jenette stalked the house with a carton tucked beneath one arm looking for unsuspecting victims. The element of surprise was essential. No one was safe from having a cascarone smashed hard on the top of their head. Her victims expected to be picking confetti and eggshells out of their hair for days.

Nothing was ever safe in her wake.

Abuelo Seraphin's favorite granddaughter was shaping up to be a big bad Marine.

A quinceañera, a tradition for hundreds of years, was the last thing Jenette wanted when her mother Francisca brought it up on her thirteenth birthday.

"You are now a teen, and in two years we will have the most amazing party for you!"

"I'd rather die than have one of those," Jenette responded, "like a doll or a little pet you dress up for your friends." Her mother didn't speak to her for days after that.

To add insult to injury Jenette took her defiance a step further. All her life she had kept hair that fell to her waist. The traditional dolls she received from Mexico had two braids with ribbons interwoven with the hair, long black yarn tied neatly to the sides and wearing a traditional dress to the ankles. Her mother and grandmother loved the thick tendrils that had been a family trait for generations.

This beautiful hair was cumbersome, so she cut it all off.

Jenette did not want to be one of those Barbie dolls

presented at girl parties—the ones suspended in the middle of a pan with the dress made from cake and topped with piped pastel icing in the shape of flowers. Barbie was only released when every morsel was eaten, and only crumbs remained on her bare body.

"Jenette, por favor! Why did you do this?" The gasp from her mother's mouth, followed by a shake of her head and the pious crossing of her chest, told Jenette she would never hear the end of it. "I should have stopped Seraphin putting all those ideas in your mind." How would she ever find a husband now, her mother seemed to cry.

She didn't give a shit. She loved the feel, the same freedom as the guys.

Jenette was already at a disadvantage, being a Brown female with no family name or fortune, so why not make her life easier? Jenette wanted to be accepted as the best of the best, with the ability to smoke an enemy as fast as any of the men. And despite what her mother might have thought, the short hair looked good.

Jenette would have given anything for those harsh words from her mother's lips, because at least there would be a hug again when her mother's frustration subsided. It was better than a bunk bed in a stranger's house.

* * *

Without any regard for the small dramas in the lives of everyday people, the world came to a halt for millions.

A gruesome, highly contagious sickness raged through the population before anyone knew what was happening, and before it could be brought under control. The "flesh-eating bacteria," they called it, and the description fit. The vaccine supplied by Weyland-Yutani came too little too late for many, the priority given to anyone leaving for the most valuable colonies in space, and supplies sent to keep the colonies free from infection. She saw her father Pablo and Seraphin for the last time as they were wheeled into an ambulance, writhing in agony, knowing it would be the only goodbye they would get. No one—barely any of the doctors or nurses, even—came out of it alive or without permanent damage.

Her sister Roseanna was on the front lines of death, and when not in the hospitals she was in a bottle of booze or pills to cope with the stress and to stay awake. One evening in their mother's home she was slumped on the couch with a beer in her hand.

"Mama, it's hell out there," Roseanna said. "I feel like an undertaker and not a nurse. I need Santa Muerte's spirit to take over me. Otherwise, something else is driving me too fast somewhere I don't want to go. I can feel it."

"Don't be silly, Roseanna. It will pass, and you're an angel. No more bad talk and no more cerveza. You're saving lives. After all this you'll get into that program to be a doctor—I just know it—and then we will have a big party... since this one didn't want a quinceañera." She nodded toward Jenette. "It's what your father would want, too. He worked long hours, but it was to provide. He was so proud of you, even if he didn't say it enough."

"Maybe I'm meant for something else." Roseanna stared at the wall. There was a vacant shadow in her eye as she took long gulps from her beer. Her skin was red raw from the hot showers and antiseptic soap she had to use after a shift at the hospital. "What if I don't want to be a doctor anymore? They're just as fed up and overworked..." Her voice trailed off.

Some of the hospitals offered bonuses for taking on extra hours. Two days later Roseanna crashed her vehicle on a run to an emergency call. She was alive when paramedics arrived but placed into a coma for her recovery. No one knew if she would make it.

Jenette wondered what being heroes did for any of her family.

Before her accident, Roseanna stole a spare dose of vaccine, only managing to do so because she was a health worker. Francisca kept it safe in her bra and underwear drawer for weeks while she monitored the news of her daughter. One evening she slid the green inhaler across the dinner table, her fingers trembling, toward Jenette.

"Take it," she said with sweat rolling down both temples, her skin a plastic sheen of smaller beads of sweat.

Jenette put down her fork of twirled chicken ramen noodles.

"No. It's for you."

"Stop being so defiant and take the damn thing!" Francisca raised both balled fists to her chest and took a deep breath. "For once do as you are told. Everything I have done has been for you... *all* of you. I've tried my best to keep you, Carmen, Sandro, and Roseanna out of trouble. One day you will understand how hard it is to stay true to your roots, while trying to reach for the stars, whatever those stars look like.

"We are the people from the soil, it is true," she said, "but we don't have to stay seedlings. I just wanted you to be seen as a good girl because we are seen as so many other things. I should know. Maybe trying to keep the old traditions was wrong. I'm sorry. El riesgo siempre vive. I am risking my own life now to spare yours. You have a purpose. Live to see it through."

The flesh hanging from her cheeks and desperation in her eyes scared Jenette. Her mother had never spoken to her with such fervor—or honesty. Jenette complied, sticking the inhaler all the way up one nostril and inhaling the vaccine in an explosion of burning magma. A single tear rolled down her mother's face.

"Thank you." She clutched the hem of her blue T-shirt before running to the toilet. Jenette heard her vomiting in the bathroom, then shuffling back to her bed and the warm comforter that awaited her there.

Two days later Jenette found her under the comforter, no longer retching... or breathing. She held on to the pillow on which her husband had slept, and clutched a family photo album and rosary. Jenette turned away, left the room, and closed the door.

How was this reality?

She couldn't be left alone in this world.

When her father died, she had cried for her mother's sake. He had worked more than he spent time with her or her siblings, and always felt like a stranger because of the odd hours he kept as a foreman and lead tech liaison for the android factory. They came from generations of thinking that when times are good, then you have to take advantage of it. Surf that wave because you never knew when you might get knocked on your ass, or the work would dry up. The need for androids never relented, new models were created all the time, yet the fear of *"what if"* burrowed with the hunger of a parasite.

If Father wasn't dealing with labor disputes, then it was the day-to-day with the factory.

Now she looked around the house. Everything remained the same, but suddenly it seemed hollow, without any soul. Something had fled from this space she no longer recognized.

Her shock turned to a typhoon of rage for not having any control over any tiny crumb of what her life could or should be. Through hysterical sobs she grabbed up all the plates and glasses on the drying rack next to the sink and threw them to the floor until the shards resembled Easter confetti. Then she turned over anything that wasn't secured to the tiles in the house—which was everything. Jenette screamed and shrieked with not a soul in range to stop her. Carmen and Sandro were floating in space for the Early Learners Terraforming Program offered by their school, and Roseanna lay in a coma. All others in her family had been claimed by the spinning wheel of fate called death.

When there was nothing left for her to destroy or any voice to scream, she walked into the bedroom to remove the gold cross from her mother's neck and placed it on her own. She couldn't have the paramedics stealing it. Before calling an ambulance, she gave her mother's cold temple one kiss.

"I love you, mama. Thank you. I'm sorry if I didn't tell you enough."

What would she have left to cling to?

Nobody wanted to feed and look after a teenager. Jenette was sent to live in a foster home.

Roseanna survived the accident, but her blood work indicated a cocktail of alcohol and medication. Instead of facing any time, she chose to be transferred to Texas for rehab and a contract to work in a rehabilitation facility. Even though all the remaining family assets were transferred to Roseanna, taking care of Jenette was out of the question. She could never handle medication, would never be a nurse, but she would be trained as a counselor.

For Roseanna and Jenette, the familiar life they knew was gone in the time it took to sneeze.

If this was it then, Jenette figured, what was the point of anything? If she mattered so little in this world, what did it matter what she did?

Taking risks took on a new meaning.

She was settled in a modest home with nice enough but neglectful guardians, Timothy and Hazel Hall, who fostered a bunch of kids. There she met another teen named Liberty Love, a beautiful girl of sixteen wanting the glamour of gang life, a real buchona with impeccable makeup, thick fake eyelashes, and curves on show. When Jenette asked her where her family was, she shrugged while filling in her plucked eyebrows with dark brown pencil.

"Fuck if I know. My mom died and my dad couldn't get work after losing his business," she said. "We used to live large, amiga. He sent me to live with my cousin until he could find his feet again, but all of it fucked with his mind after a while. My cousin gave me to the state when I refused to get a job, so I could give her the entire check. If I'm going to wear some ugly ass uniform with married pervy dudes trying to pick me, then at least I get to keep my dinero. That outbreak, it hit a lot of us hard, fucked us all up gacho. People getting sick without enough healthcare."

Jenette felt like she had found a kindred soul in grief and heartache, yet they couldn't be more different. Jenette was more of a tomboy, always causing trouble, running the streets in Dickies and sometimes a slick red lipstick, if the mood struck.

A week later another kid, P-Wee, came to stay. He was a skinny half gringo and half Mexican, too shy to be tough, yet winning everyone with his sense of humor. The three musketeers went to local parties and started mixing cheap vodka with 7UP. Jenette was the homegirl with an attitude, someone the girls wanted to smoke with, and the boys wanted to fool around with because they could tell she was a "wild one."

"Hey, I want you to meet some friends," Liberty said. When Jenette looked doubtful, she added, "Don't we all just want real family again?"

"You don't want to stay a neutron." P-Wee pursed his lips and shot Jenette a confused look.

"What does that mean?" Jenette asked.

"It means you don't belong to any gang. We'll see what the Inca has to say."

"That's a great idea, P." Liberty leaned over and kissed him hard on the lips. "You know I love how you think."

"Yeah, you love my weed…"

"That, too."

Jenette looked on as Liberty kissed him. She wanted something, too.

"Who are these friends?"

"I know I said friends, but I mean *familia*. They helped me get through the worst of times. I'm in with Las Calaveras. I want to introduce you to them."

"This is for you," P-Wee said from the driver's seat. The music played loudly. "Damn It Feels Good to be a Gangster" by the Geto Boys, the pioneers of horror core rap in the twenty-first century. Liberty Love sat next to him in the passenger seat. Neto was in the back with Jenette.

She leaned toward Liberty's ear.

"Why do they call him P-Wee?"

"Because when he used to get high, he was obsessed with the old Pee-Wee Herman show. He's clean now, building his business, and never watches them, but the nickname stayed."

Liberty wore her tightest jeans and low-cut ribbed bodysuit with a sweetheart neckline. In the sepia of the streetlights and whirlpools of smoke, she could have been a caterpillar sitting on top of a mushroom. No worries and no rushing. Jenette couldn't help her eyes straying across the beautiful body, the sumptuousness of it.

Jenette had made out with boys before, and liked it fine, but the curiosity to explore a body like her own grew stronger the older she became. Desiring *both* felt normal. Lust was as amorphous and complicated as an uncharted galaxy, and depending what direction you find yourself floating, it was different for everyone.

P-Wee pulled up to the house on a residential street of large homes that bordered the blocks of Los Angeles projects in a neighborhood that once was called Downey—high-rise buildings with murals meant to inspire, but which had eroded over time. On the opposite side of the street were the blocks of tents where the homeless set up their own hood with whatever materials they could salvage. By day, do-gooders roamed the area, talking about Jesus and the perils of space while handing out clean water and energy bars.

Jenette waved off the residual smoke wafting from the blunt Liberty smoked in the front seat. The grassy scented eddies made her feel lightheaded. Ever since what happened to Roseanna, she hadn't been one for drugs.

"Hold this." Neto reached back and placed a small pistol on Jenette's lap. Her heartbeat ricocheted in her chest with an alien sensation, and she ran her fingertips across the cold metal, an instrument of life and death. There was a vibration of power, even if it was the type that stole innocence. Being in the car with the people she was supposed to consider family made her feel physically less alone, but in that instant the only thing that felt real, or had any weight, was the gun resting on her thighs.

When she was growing up, guns had been banned in their home because her mother always feared they would be stolen or used against them. Even Seraphin had complied.

Finishing whatever he was doing, Neto reached down

and took it from her, then aimed it out the open window. P-Wee slowed the car down.

"This is just a warning shot," he said. "Those cabrons better stop straying into our damn neighborhood. ¡*Las Calaveras, pendejos!*" he shouted out the window.

"Las Calaveras!" Liberty Love echoed loudly while throwing up a crown with her right hand.

The succession of pops made Jenette jump, then Liberty chuckled at the screeching wheels as they picked up their speed. It was an old car, so the engine roared. She extended the blunt to Jenette, who shook her head, so she pulled it back and took a deep hit. With heavy lids topped with thick black eyeliner and wispy fake eyelashes, she fixed her gaze on her friend.

"You know you're still a future," she said. "You won't be with us until you go on a mission of your own. It could be anything. Then you can shake up with me. Live and die for each other, familia. We can even go to the juntas together. It's mostly boring stuff, like what's happening in the neighborhood, dues, who wants to move up the ranks."

Neto placed the gun on Jenette's lap again. Poles of light and shadow crossed his face as they sped through residential streets then onto the freeway, where there was little traffic.

"Every gang requires some sort of sacrifice, a test," he said. "I remember you telling me you come from military. You think those boys don't do the same here or up there? A uniform or suit, fucking Dickies and tube top like Liberty over here wears, it don't matter. Dinero, territory, space, food, fucking medicine. Shit's only legitimate because someone with authority says so—and most of the time that authority is a weapon, or money."

"Then what makes Las Calaveras different?"

"Because we wear a crown with five points. Love, sacrifice, honor, obedience, righteousness. And every motherfucker will want to tear it off your head. Don't slip up. Respect your brothers and sisters. Respect your hood. Respect yourself. No cocaine, no heroin, no crack. P-Wee had to learn the hard way."

"Yeah, I had to take a neck down for five minutes from the meanest on the block," P-Wee said from the driver's seat. "Those bruises did not go away quick, but it sobered me the hell up. Can't make the hood look weak for nothing or nobody."

Jenette didn't say anything, rolled down her window to get fresh air in her hair, the beat of the music filling her head like the weed. She wondered where this life would lead.

"How much did you smoke, Neto?" Liberty Love joked.

Jenette turned to Neto. "You going to show me how to use this gun?"

He leaned back and kissed her on the cheek. His lips were slightly dry, but the softness on her skin made her neck go warm. Was it so bad to like both Liberty Love and Neto? The feelings were the same, because in her eyes both were equally attractive, just in different ways. Their bodies capable of different types of pleasure. They didn't cover those emotions in health class, or the few times she went to Sunday school.

He pulled closer and placed his arm around her shoulders.

"Of course," he said. "We're familia, and you need to know how to use a hood gun at some point. Us against the ugliness in the world. You think they want any of us to make it? If they did, we would see it. Nah, we fucking take it any way we can. They protect their territory like they the gangbangers. Believe that. Put that on your waist and in your piggy bank."

Jenette relaxed her body into the crook of Neto's arm. There was the faint scent of body odor and knock-off cologne clinging to his Dodgers jersey, but having the warmth of someone else was comforting. There was a sense of safety.

"I feel you. I believe that."

Jenette celebrated her sixteenth birthday by drinking at a house party while listening to twenty-first century hip-hop in the backyard. It was Neto's place, and a spread of vodka, Modelo, Coors, and tequila covered a card table along with cartons of fruit juice mixers. The music moved from old school rap to norteño. It wouldn't be a party without Los Dos Carnales belting out corridos. The stars were out, and they were all feeling good—either high or drunk or both.

Life was beginning to appear normal again for most folks.

Liberty Love and Jenette lay on a blanket in the bed of a rusted Toyota pickup truck without any tires. Whenever Jenette looked up at the stars, she thought of the last real conversation she'd had with her mother. She wondered what Carmen and Sandro were doing?

"I hope we don't get the cops called on us. It's getting a little loud."

"No shit," Liberty said. "Sounds like people moving into the streets, too. I think the end of summer has everyone going a little crazy, and after a year of bad news and dead bodies."

Liberty Love rolled toward Jenette and kissed her lips, the heaviness of her breasts pressing against Jenette's chest.

"I know you look at me," she said. "I like it. Figure this would be a good birthday surprise."

"You just doing me a favor then?" Jenette gazed into her eyes, then pulled away. "No thanks. Plus, don't Las Calaveras have some whack rule about this?"

"Maybe we can change that rule. Also, it's not like that. It's a present for me, too."

Liberty's tongue was soft. Her mouth slightly sweet and bitter from the alcohol and weed. Her body as supple as Jenette had imagined as she touched it with care.

Sirens wailed, along with the sound of screeching wheels.

"Fuck, I *knew* it!" Liberty put out the blunt hanging between two fingers she held at their side. "Let's go." They jumped from the back of the truck and ran through an alley to reach the street parallel to the one in front of the house. Others had the same idea, and there were other partygoers running down the street, hopping over fences, or jumping into cars parked curbside. Engines customized for noise roared to life.

Liberty hurled forward, face-first to the ground, when someone they didn't know crashed into her, running away from the police. Blood streamed from her nose and cut bottom lip as she lifted herself from the asphalt. She sat upright and began to cry as she looked down at her blood-soaked tank top.

"Damn it! My clothes, my lip feels busted." Jenette kneeled next to her and grabbed her upper arm.

"C'mon we got to go."

A police vehicle silently pulled up and blocked off one side of the street. They had to move fast between houses, or hide. To their right an officer came bolting through the alley, before they had a chance to run.

He pointed his gun at them.

"Don't you move."

Jenette put both her hands up. The last thing she wanted was trouble, even though she figured she already looked like trouble to him. All that mattered was getting out of here, and getting Liberty Love to a doctor.

"She's hurt. We didn't do anything! Help us."

"You shouldn't be here then."

Jenette looked up and down the street, then to the houses to her immediate right and left. People ran past, caring only about their own skins, desperate to not get trapped in the teeth of the law. Cars roared and shouts rang out around them. She hoped someone was watching between the blinds and recording it all.

Fear made her realize that, despite the people she ran with, she was still just a skinny kid no one wanted—except a sister who couldn't have her. She became conscious of her own body and Liberty Love's curves that might be too noticeable to this man who stood before them with a gun, taser, and badge. As a female in fight-or-flight, she realized her anatomy became acutely important.

True fear.

It was why her mother never wanted any of them to walk alone. Now she understood. She didn't know what to do.

From the house next to Neto's the screen door slammed open. A group of Las Calaveras charged in their direction with an officer chasing behind, shouting at them to stop. Two shots exploded between the shouting and sirens. So close, Jenette and Liberty Love ducked from the gunshots. Jenette glanced up at the cop who'd had his weapon pointed at them, pulling the trigger.

The body of the pursuing officer and a kid she had seen in the neighborhood thumped to the ground. Both were bleeding from the wounds to their torsos. Muffled moans faded with the flow of blood. Their eyes lost all life, until they stared back at her with the coldness of the merciless elements of space.

The cop looked at Jenette, then to the fallen officer.

His gun was pointing at her.

"You!"

"Fuck you, man. I saw what you did."

"Shh, don't say anything, Jenette," Liberty Love pleaded in a whisper through lopsided lips. "You'll make it worse for us."

The cop dashed toward Jenette, knocking her to the ground.

"Stop it!" she shouted. "Don't touch me!" She tried to push him off with her arms and legs. His bulk overwhelmed her and his limbs were those of a spider trying to wrap her into a web for later consumption.

"Help!" Liberty Love screamed, still bleeding from the mouth and nose. "Someone help us!" The houses were dark, with people minding their own, not wanting to incur the wrath of the law.

The officer pushed his weapon into Jenette's hands. She grabbed her switchblade from her back pocket and pressed the button hard to open it. Without thought of where it would land, she tried to slice him just enough to get him to move away. It only served to stoke his conviction.

"Now you'll really rot in prison," he growled.

He overpowered her by placing a knee between her legs and his forearm across her chest. The pressure made her breasts feel as if they might burst. His body weight made it difficult for her to move. Between sobs, Liberty was still screaming down the empty street. He grabbed the switchblade, tossing it away.

Liberty snatched it from the ground, closing it, then put it in her bra before grabbing the officer's neck to pull him off Jenette. Sirens made them all pause for a beat, then the officer started to hit Jenette in the face. A police vehicle and ambulance came to a screeching stop in front of them. Two more cops jumped out, and one pulled Liberty Love away.

The cop kept punching Jenette in the face, spittle spewing from his mouth.

"¡Mira! Stop him! It's not right!" Liberty shouted. "Why is it always us on our asses, having to fight up? *Why us?* Fucking do something!"

All Jenette could do was attempt to grasp his forearms as her head slammed right to left. She could see her own blood flying into the air, then felt it land back on her face. A paunchy officer with a thick straw-colored mustache stood next to her.

"What the hell is going on, Jason? Get up now."

The cop stopped his assault to look up. "This punk skank took my gun and shot those two."

"No she didn't!" Liberty roared. "He's lying!" She lunged from the officer holding her back. Her tank top was a mural of mascara black and blood red. "Look what he did to her!"

Paramedics from the ambulance rushed to the officer and young man lying dead in their comingling blood. They didn't look twice at Jenette with a swelling eye, or Liberty's broken nose and sliced lip. The mustached officer shook his head.

"You didn't have to take it this far. Go on. We'll take it from here."

The cop, Jason, rose from the ground, releasing Jenette. With one eye swollen shut she took a good look at him. He had a few pockmarks around a forehead topped with light brown hair that receded slightly. Only a few telltale wrinkles around the eyes and mouth to give away that he was an hombre who had worked too long in a job he probably hated, but couldn't give up. The only power he had—that gave his existence any weight—was this.

Did mutual hate cancel each other out, or did it just accumulate to create something more vicious they couldn't see? He looked down on her without any remorse.

"Take them both in, and check that one for a knife. She tried to stab me after shooting them."

Jenette remained silent, having no fight left in her as she stared devoid of emotion at the night sky. Not a scrap of fucking will left. Blood from her mouth dribbled down her chin and rested in the fold of her neck, staining the gold cross she wore. Each blow had done more than inflict pain—there was the fear that this is how she would spend the rest of her life.

How many blows are we supposed to take in one lifetime? she thought. If there was a God, why did it seem like the world she lived in was one big beating into submission. She sat there powerless, the one without a badge, a cock, a gun, money, family, hope. *Where is my hope, Seraphin? Where are the spirits of the soldaderas?*

I need them. I need you.

Before Liberty was taken away she screamed once more, but this time directly at Jenette.

"Whatever happens, homegirl, keep your head down and take whatever they give you. Don't make it worse. Just get out. Some of us have to make it. Swear to me!"

Jenette could barely open her lips to whisper.

"I swear it on the Vasquez name."

The judge had too much foundation and plastic surgery. Jenette could only see her through one purple-and-yellow-ringed eye. The other was swollen shut. Her bones ached even though nothing was broken but her heart.

"You were found with a weapon. A switchblade you gave your friend to hide after threatening the life of an officer."

"No, I did not give it to her," Jenette answered. "But yes, it was a switchblade, and the dead officer was shot. I told you it was another officer who did it, his name was Jason. Let me show you who it was. Please believe me. Doesn't he have a camera on him?"

"The officer in question stated that it was switched off because it had been quiet all evening. His shift was nearly over. There is no proof of what you have told me. It's your word against his."

Jenette's body tensed.

"My word isn't worth anything?"

The judge stared at her with little concern bordering on boredom. "It's very clear that you have no direction, so we are going to course-correct for you. You will remain incarcerated. You don't want to tell us details about the Calaveras? No problem, but this is the consequence for that decision."

"I told you I don't know details," she said. "I wasn't a full member. And if I was, I wouldn't snitch."

The judge didn't blink. "This matter is closed."

"Closed? That's it? How can you sleep, lady?"

The judge didn't give her a second glance before closing the case file and gliding out of the courtroom in her black robe.

Even at that age Jenette knew the world was divided between the people who carried the consequences of their actions and the ones who didn't. The hearing had been held behind closed doors, with her court-appointed lawyer making the decisions for her. There she was, stuck and totally fucked like one of those sad worms at the bottom of shitty tequila bottles the gringos like to take photos with in border towns, or corny fake Cinco de Mayo celebrations used as an excuse to get drunk.

Her lawyer turned to her.

"I did the best I could," he said. Then he added, "There's a program, but you're too young right now. You just might get out in a few years. Until then, do what you've got to do to survive. Your kind always do...

"I'd suggest doing research on the Marines."

With that the lawyer walked away. He wore scuffed shoes and a suit jacket that made his shoulders look like they were sliding off his body. The poor shit probably got paid peanuts for being a public defender, or he had done something wrong and this was *his* punishment.

The Marines.

Among the grief, partying, wanting to disappear, chaos, she'd almost forgotten about that small dream. Now she would have nothing but solitude to focus on it. Maybe it was a false promise he'd made to soften the blow. If there was any chance at a life outside of here, she would take it.

"You ready?" A guard with the most sympathetic look she had received since the incident tapped on the table to get her attention. "I don't think you'll give me any trouble."

Jenette nodded in numb shock. He guided her away without cuffs or excessive pressure on her body when she had to be guided from the courtroom to the van that was waiting to take her away. After he helped her into the vehicle, with his hand still on the sliding door, he looked at her straight in the eye.

"It doesn't have to be the end. Don't go in there thinking it is. Whole planets have been formed with nothing but patience. You feel me?"

"Thank you."

"De nada, sister."

The door slammed shut, and she was off.

3

Jenette lay on her single bottom bunk with her back against the concrete wall and her legs pulled close to her chest. She had tossed and turned most of the night. Her body felt so small, as if she took up no space in this world, and the cell amplified that feeling. Her right cheekbone still ached from the punches.

No wonder a gun had felt so good.

A voice came from above her. "You kept me awake down there," it said. "I know it's hard to sleep when you're new, but all you need to know is they're trying to maintain their image. We're as disposable as sanitary products. Too many people with not enough choices—no way will they admit it was friendly fire."

Jenette had been so locked in her own thoughts she forgot someone else shared her space.

"How do you know about me?"

"Gotta fill the time with something. Gossip is one of

the ways." A pause, then she added, "My name is Daisy Paxton."

"Jenette."

Daisy climbed down from the top bunk. "It helps to have a clique in here. You ran with Las Calaveras, so you should be alright."

"And you?" Jenette wasn't expecting a pretty white girl with freckles and brown eyes. "What are you in for?"

Daisy sat on the edge of Jenette's bed. "I caught my cousin stealing my dad's diabetes and pain medication. He was also taking my underwear. So I hacked his car. He got into a bad accident and almost died. I'm shitty at being a criminal, and didn't bother trying to cover my tracks."

"Shit, my sister was in a bad accident," Jenette said, "but she was trying to save the world, while doing everything she could to shut it out." She thought about it. "Damn. Small world."

"Yeah, too small. That's why there is a place up there called space. So many worlds to escape to, if you get the chance."

The metal door to their cell opened for her first breakfast in prison. The only daylight came from the small window that overlooked the staff parking lot, and farther off a sallow field. Knowing the sun and moon existed was a small comfort—otherwise it could be anywhere at any time of the day.

"With nothing else to do, you'd think they would at least let us sleep until a decent hour." Jenette rolled out of the uncomfortable bed, moving sluggishly. A shadow eclipsed the light coming from the corridor.

"Hurry up! Fucking cockroaches move faster than this. You're new and need to know the way of things in here. We run a tight schedule. You can't be lazy anymore."

The uniformed guard wasn't much taller than five feet nine, with black eyes and a puff of hair spilling from the neck of his uniform. He barged into their cell, stashing the personal device he'd used to open the door, and grabbed Jenette by the scruff of her blue sweatshirt so that her forehead bashed against the railing of the top bunk. Remembering what the cop had done to her, she fought the urge to kick and scream.

Who knew what would happen behind bars.

"I heard you're a cop killer," the man said. "A tough, gangbanging, murdering cunt. Well, you're nothing in here. Don't try anything on my watch."

"Leave her alone, Hanson!" Daisy shouted.

"Shut up, hoe. You can't protect your new girlfriend." He continued to drag Jenette to the door of her cell, controlling her movements with one hand on the collar of her sweatshirt and the other hand digging his thumb and forefinger deep into her neck. "When lights are up it *means* lights up. You hear me, girl? Don't even look like a girl."

He shoved her one more time toward the entrance. "Now stay, bitch." He sniggered before swaggering into the corridor to shout insulting profanity inside other cells. Jenette shot a glance in Daisy's direction.

"Can he do that? Treat us that way?"

The light in her cellmate's eyes dimmed as she looked off to the corner of the room.

"No one stops him."

"Damn. I feel smaller than before, weak." Jenette peered out through the bars. "Like a dead leaf being blown away, no way to tell where I'm going to land."

"Then don't be." Daisy took a step toward Jenette and gently rested both hands on her shoulders. "Fuck being small. Be the tree that don't move, with deep roots, and if you do get blown away, make sure you make some noise when you're falling, or take something down with you."

Jenette held back the tears mounting in her eyes and looked at her feet to hide her emotions.

"*Please make an orderly line outside,*" the intercom blared in a calm, inauthentic voice from the corridor.

"I guess we need to go. Thanks for the pep talk, roomie."

"I got you," Daisy said.

There was more than enough time to think about their crimes, but Daisy and Jenette lived out their desires in secret, finding solace at night in each other's arms. Daisy was real, solid, but Jenette still tried to hold on to her dream.

The Marines.

She wouldn't get lost again.

When she closed her eyes, she revived her memories of the soldiers in her family. As painful as it was to remember, she saw old Seraphin in his baggy jeans held up with a leather belt and large silver belt buckle in the center with an intricate design of a buck. He punched the air with his fist whenever Bruce Springsteen's "Dancing in the Dark" began to play, like it was his working man's anthem to a better existence, knowing it was there but just out of reach.

For a little dramatic effect, he added cumbia steps to the song and a twirl like he was spinning a beautiful woman in a dancehall. In her visions he always wore his red bandana and black ribbed tank top.

She imagined the soldaderas with their long braids, practicing their aim for their country, wearing big skirts and fighting to be a voice in a society whose fate was just as much theirs as anyone else's. She wanted to know *more*.

Nothing but time on her hands so why not learn something new, she decided. The meager prison library, smelling like moldy paper, was like a jumble sale with odds and ends of donations. The books she sought out explained survival techniques, military history, any type of fighting or combat. There were videos of rodeos and bullfights that kept her transfixed with the concentration the people had to maintain in the ring.

Then there were the books on physical training and anatomy. She touched the still-tender bone beneath her left eye as she watched. Who would look after her if she couldn't do it for herself?

When made to feel small, pliable, meek, muscle became a form of power, just like knowledge. Taking up physical space made Jenette feel as if her presence would be known. Lockup was a battle against a beast with no heart or eyes, only teeth. Not a goddamn thing was going to push her around or grab her by the neck.

Daisy taught art every Monday to a small group of interested prisoners. She was a tattoo artist, as well, and Jenette asked her to tattoo a single teardrop on the corner of her eye. Not for a murder, but if they wanted to think that, then let them. If the Marines panned out, she would become a cold-blooded machine with a weapon always hot in the most dangerous position.

She decided this would be the last tear she would show for her past, or for herself out of pity.

The gym was the perfect outlet to satisfy her need to take control of something in her life *and* fill the hours. Jenette wanted weight in this world that didn't come from her hips, tits, and ass. And if everyone thought she was a murderer, then she might as well play that part. The prison facility was mixed to accommodate everyone's gender— it was one of the few places all genders mixed.

The walls were lined with mirrors behind plexiglass that couldn't be broken, even from a weight hurled across the room. Cameras monitored from the four corners and there were two guards on watch at all times. It wasn't anything fancy, with only the basic equipment you would find in any budget gym.

A young gringo with dirty blond hair and skinny arms sat at the edge of a weight bench. There was a nasty scar extending from the corner of his left eye. He looked as lost as she felt as he scratched at the small pimples on his neck and next to his ears. His gaze passed her before doubling back.

"Want this bench? You need someone to spot you?"

Jenette looked around and realized he was talking to her. "I can't front," she said. "I have no idea where to begin. Mostly read a bunch of books."

"Yeah, this room is a little overwhelming, considering the terrible accommodations in the rest of this place." He gave her a crooked grin. "You ready to go hard? I'll spot you. Put that stuff in your cabeza to good use."

Jenette raised an eyebrow and crossed her arms. "What do you know about going hard?"

He shrugged. "I don't fucking know. Trying to figure it out myself. Look, if I'm not gonna spot you, do you mind spotting me?"

Jenette glanced around the room again. The other inmates either talked among themselves or seemed happy to be solo knowing what they were doing. Then she looked back at the gringo. He seemed decent enough.

"Sure, what do you want me to do."

"Cool," he said. "Put on another fifteen pounds." As she moved to do so, he added, "What's your name by the way? I should know before you have the power to crush me under a barbell."

"Jenette Vasquez. You?"

"Mark Drake. Thanks for partnering up. It's tough not knowing anyone, and not knowing who to trust."

"No shit," she said. "If this works out, maybe we can do it on the regular."

"Cool," he said again. The scar at the corner of his eye puckered when he smiled. Jenette wondered what kind of fight had made that. Didn't matter. The past had to be the past, otherwise she would remain in a mental prison. This one was bad enough.

If Drake showed her respect, she would return it in kind. And lifting heavier weights would require a partner at some point, anyway. No one would lay hands on her, ever again. Resilience in body, spirit, and mind—even if no one could see or feel it but her.

It worked out, so Drake and Jenette developed a routine. They met every day during recreation time. There was something she loved about the concept of tearing her body down to the smallest fibers, for the promise of building it up bigger and better.

Stagnation was a cell within the mind, she knew. Stay too long, and it was hard to leave. No, she had to keep up her regimen with Drake, especially on the days when the monotony of lockup hatched hundreds of monstrous larvae to tear apart her sanity.

One bash against the cell wall and it could be over.

Then she remembered the officer Jason, the judge, and in here, Hanson. No way would she give these motherfuckers the satisfaction. Sometimes one stand was all it took.

They alternated upper and lower body exercises day to day, with fasted cardio twice a week. After heavy lifting, the burn for one or two days gave her some sign there was change, movement toward a goal.

"Come on, dude." Drake lay on the bench press with his arms wobbling as he reached for the bar again. Jenette stood behind with her bandana around her forehead. "You got this."

"Well, technically, you do if I don't."

He was halfway through his reps when a familiar voice shouted toward them.

"The two pussies of the joint found each other."

"What do you want, Hanson?" Jenette didn't bother looking up. "This is our time. And your breath smells like salami. Back off."

"It's whatever I say it is, and you're whatever I say you are." Hanson walked over to the bar and placed an extra ten pounds on each side. The entire room slowed their workouts to watch. Some stopped altogether.

"Show us what you got." Hanson hovered over Drake with a malicious sneer. "Or are you only hanging with Vasquez cuz you're a little bitch, too?"

Drake leered back at him then gripped the bar. His arms

quaked under the strain as he took the bar overhead and lowered it toward his chest. His face changed from light pink on only his cheeks to bright red from the neck up as he began to lift it again. The veins in his lean forearms and biceps bulged as thick as his triceps. He gritted his teeth with sweat rolling onto the bench.

"C'mon, man," Jenette whispered. "You can make it. Fuck this prick."

"Who you calling a prick?" Hanson spat. "You're next."

Drake managed to just place the bar back on the rack. He exhaled loudly as he lifted himself from the bench. Those in the room clapped, with some whistling.

"Get on there." Hanson attempted to shove Jenette into the bar, but her frame didn't budge as she tensed. Hanson's narrowed eyes ran the length of her body when he couldn't push her forward.

"She's never lifted that high, man," Drake said. "Let me spot her." But Jenette slapped his midsection with the back of her hand.

"You want to be a bad man, Hanson? Just watch."

"You sure are cocky without a cock," he replied. "But with that hair and body…"

Jenette spat on the floor at his feet, just missing his shoe. She made her way to the bench then lay in the puddle of sweat left behind from Drake. One big breath, followed by adjusting her white bandana. It had to be white to avoid gang colors. She could hear the crowd murmuring, some placing bets of commissary and cigarettes.

Fuck you all, she thought to herself.

She wrapped her fingers around the bar, then wiped her hands on her sweatpants before taking hold of it again. She lifted it slowly until the weight of it was directly over her head. One second of wavering and it would give new definition to the exercise they call a skull crusher.

Stored in that bar, this was the culmination of the weight of the last few years, and the beginning of the years she still faced in lockup. If the weight fell, no one would be left hurting but her. Or she could try as hard as possible to make that one rep. Rise above the sorrow and disappointments. Slowly she lowered it toward her chest. God her arms wanted to give way, give up.

"Go on, Vasquez. Let everyone who didn't bet on you lose," Drake whispered. The bar reached just above her breasts.

Now was the real test, lifting it up again.

With every ounce of muscle, energy, and determination, she tightened her abdominals. There was a sudden awareness of the soft cotton of her bandana, absorbing her sweat. Then she pushed. Even if the metal melted from the heat in the palm of her hand, she would accomplish this—not for the crowd or Hanson, but for herself. She could do it. She continued to drive it upward, allowing one groan escape before placing it back on the rack. As metal hit metal, a cheer louder than Drake's filled the gym. Bets were won and lost.

Hanson stood over her.

"You still ain't shit," he growled. "It's just one rep. Don't mean a damn thing in the real world."

Jenette sat up, feeling every muscle in her body sigh in relief. As much as part of her wanted to break into tears from the exertion and humiliation, she knew this was the point of no return with Hanson. No more tears. She stood to meet his gaze.

"Let's see what you got, pendejo," she said. "You wanna play big dog, ese, then show us those big balls. This *pussy* has no respect or time for shrimp dicks, dickhead."

The room erupted into hoots and howls. He sucked his teeth.

"On duty. No can do."

There was sniggering from those still watching the standoff. More bets being placed if there would be a fight between the two. Hanson looked around, and found all eyes on them.

"Everyone get back to your own fucking business. Time's almost up." He turned his attention back to Jenette and Drake. "That goes for you, too."

When his back was turned to walk away, Drake held his palm up to Jenette.

"Hey, I didn't mean to doubt you. Just tryin' to look out. And damn, chica… mad respect."

She gave his palm a friendly slap. "I understand. No harm. I would have done the same."

"Think I'm done with lifting for the day," Drake said, trying to make it sound like a joke.

"Same. Let's just get on the bikes like we're somewhere cruising—but tomorrow back at it."

"You got it, sister. You want to stick with the bench press?"

She shook her head. "Nope, I want to do that." She pointed. "If I can lift my own body weight, I can carry anything."

Drake followed her pointed finger to the pull-up bar.

"Hell, yes," he said. "Mañana."

The next time she saw Hanson he hassled her less, opting for the hard stare when she passed. She could live with that and matched his glare. There was no harm or foul with exchanging a "fuck you."

Roseanna regularly sent her messages and money for her commissary. The notes always ending with her apologizing profusely. Jenette had no beef with her, or anger. How could she, when they were all they had left in this world, sharing blood yet destined to be worlds apart.

The world wasn't done with the Vasquez name. Jenette knew that for certain, but goddamn she needed a win. She had respect, puppy love, the body of Adonis with tits, read nearly all the books in their sorry excuse for a library that only existed as a charity. Prison libraries were never fully funded—it was so much bullshit.

With Daisy lying in her arms, she would stare at the

metal lattice of the bed frame or window, hoping for a way to slip through.

Rumors ran like wildfire through the cellblocks, and she ignored most of them for the bullshit they were. One piqued her interest, though—the Marines were recruiting. Something was going on out there, where new colonies were cropping up. Some said it was the different countries, each trying to snap up new territory before the others could get there. Others claimed it was the companies, always looking for new ways to take your money.

It didn't matter who it was. Not to Jenette.

Please let this be the day something comes through, she would pray, whenever the moon could be seen outside her small window. She wondered what had become of Neto, and Liberty Love. That lawyer had left her with hope, and she held on for dear life to it. *When life gives you limes, make a damn margarita and dance in the dark until it's dawn again.*

4

When the day arrived, it fell on a Monday—not that the days of the week held meaning, since each one was exactly the same as the previous. Only holidays stood out, and those only because of the dessert served at dinner.

Jenette stood in the middle of her cell tossing a hacky sack around with her foot. After that, she would use the hand grip to build up her strength further. A female guard opened the door.

"Vasquez," she said. "You got a visitor. Looks like the law."

A part of her panicked, wondered if it was bad news, because what else was there? *Please don't let it be Roseanna. Please, God. I'm asking for a blessing or a miracle.* She walked the corridor that seemed to be buzzing with a hushed excitement. There was extra movement and chatter. This gave her a glimmer of hope that it might be something besides another slap in the face from life.

"Hello, Ms. Vasquez." Behind the glass of the visitation unit sat the disheveled lawyer from her trial. She vaguely remembered him as Tom or Tim. He still wore a terrible suit, and had bags under his eyes. "Wow, you've changed. Do you remember me? Today is your lucky day. I have an offer for you."

"I'll take it." Jenette didn't bother to smile or offer any pleasantries. "I just want the fuck out."

He shook his head. "You don't even know what it is."

"I remember you, and I remember what you said about the military. I've been reading about it, in here. Working out. Keeping my head down. I'm no dummy."

He raised both eyebrows in surprise, then reached into the metal briefcase on his lap.

"That's perfect—I'm glad you remembered." He pulled out some papers, stapled together. "Here is everything you need to know about becoming a Marine. Just read through it, and if you agree, place your hand on the glass and I'll scan it."

He slid a contract through the small opening beneath the partition. He remained silent while Jenette read the letter, and the more she read, the more she wanted to cry— for once, tears of relief and joy.

This was her shot.

She was going to take it.

Jenette couldn't wait to share the news with Roseanna, Drake, and Daisy. She'd see Daisy when she got back to their cell, but wouldn't see Drake until just before dinner.

Through blurred eyes she scanned the small print. She could do all of this. Without looking up, she placed her hand on the glass. He took out a small device and used it to scan her palm print—just as the cops had done when she was arrested. This time, however...

"Alright," he said. "Looks like you're all signed up. You turn eighteen in a few months, and as soon as you do you will be a free woman—at least somewhat. Between now and then they'll perform a basic physical on you. Good luck." He looked as if a weight had been removed from his shoulders.

"Wait. Why did you come back to me? There are thousands of us."

He took a deep breath and exhaled. "You believe in luck or destiny? The number assigned to you in here was picked at random. I was given a stack of people to approach, and here you were. Get paid by each completed contract. So, thank you."

Jenette watched him leave, not caring about destiny. She was getting the fuck out. Freedom.

Grinning at everyone she passed as she swaggered back to her cell, Jenette was dancing inside to the mental beat of any Cypress Hill tune. Even Hanson got a wink and a smile, out of pure spite, as she passed him in the corridor.

"Adios," she said loudly as she flipped him the middle finger. She hoped he already knew. She was scanned as she approached the cell, the door opened, and she bolted inside.

"I have some good news!" she said, bursting with excitement. "I'm going to be a Marine. Once I'm eighteen, it's fucking *adios* to this place."

Daisy sat with her legs dangling from the top bunk. To Jenette's surprise, she stared out the window without a smile or hint of joy.

"Shit, they must need more bodies," she said. "After you left, I could hear a few guards talking about a big recruitment push. A bunch of you, it sounded like. I figured that was the news you were getting." She fell silent, then added, "A second chance."

"Be happy for me," Jenette insisted. "I'm not wasting any more time in this hole, all for something I didn't do. I'm not stupid, though I wonder whose hands are getting greased for recruiting people in lockup. What a racket it has to be—these places are a business like your local bodega." Then she shook her head. "Don't matter. I'm gonna do this. I *want* to do this. It's part of my family history. This isn't just a second chance, it's my chance to be a real soldadera."

Daisy looked at her with tears in her eyes. "You do what you have to do."

Jenette dialed it down, and stroked Daisy's leg. "You can't be happy for me? What about you?"

"I've got multiple sclerosis in my genetics. Chances are I'll get it at some point. They have all of our information, from when we were arrested. They only choose the ones that can make it—at least make it long enough for whatever war is going on." She looked out through the window again. "I guess I'll have a new roommate."

"What did you expect, Daisy? El riesgo siempre vive."

Daisy climbed up onto her bed and rolled onto her side, facing away. "Go hang out with Drake. He'll give you the high five you want."

Jenette didn't know how to react. This offer was the hope she had been waiting for ever since the seed was planted in her head. It had grown at the same rate as the strength in her body, the confidence she could still be who she wanted to be, or at least figure out who she was. Freedom.

Recreation time arrived, and it was a relief to get out of the cell. Jenette spotted Drake on the pull-up bar. He'd come a long way in their regular training. She jumped on the spot next to him. Without any words they synchronized their movements.

"Yo, I have some news."

"Me, too. I'll be damned if it's the same news." Through the exertion, he flashed her a mischievous smile.

"Marines?" She groaned as she matched his large grin.

Drake nodded, then jumped to the ground. Jenette did the same. He extended his open palm, and she slapped it harder than usual.

"¡Órale!" she said. "Good thing we already have the bodies for it."

He lifted both biceps and flexed. "We're gonna run that gun show, baby!" Drake's excitement got her pumped up again. This felt right.

"Maybe we can go in together," she said. "Fuck this place. I can't wait to see Hanson's face when we walk out that door. I swear if I ever see him on the streets…"

"Save it for training!" he joked.

Jenette felt free for the first time in a long time. She left lockup with the small bag of belongings she'd had when she went in—including the switchblade. It felt good in her hands and reminded her of her real family.

They had a week before the training began. Unfortunately, Roseanna couldn't leave her job to fly out to visit before Jenette had to report. All they could do was exchange smiles and tears of joy over a video call.

"Have fun," Roseanna said as her parting words. "Live your life. Sometimes taking a risk is the dream. Your dream as a kid was to be a soldier, and here it is. Things that are meant to be always come around."

Nothing would be off limits. The last few years had been pure discipline and teetering on the tightrope of hope, trying to not fall in the chomping maw of despair, its hot breath always licking her heels. Tonight, the new crew of Marine recruits was heading to The Rooster, a known watering hole for the Corps.

Everyone knew the drill, the uncertainty in wartime, which meant this was a guaranteed good time. There was no one to tell her to not drink until she blacked out, or smoke cigarettes until her lungs burned, or fall into bed with a stranger or three. There was nothing like a tight ass in fitted jeans.

The price she'd paid for this freedom was to sign the rest of her life away to the Marine Corps. She'd gone into juvie just a kid, and was leaving as a young woman. She wanted to pick up where she left off, but this time instead of throwing up a crown with her right hand to honor her gang, she would be wearing the USCM insignia.

Drake was already at the bar and two drinks in, messaging her to hurry the hell up, he needed his wing man. The place heaved with hot bodies ready for one last lay before heading to wherever they would be sent with the possibility of never coming back.

Bruce Springsteen's "Dancing in the Dark" played over the din of the crowd. It reminded her of Seraphin and when she was younger. Old Seraphin in his bandana tinkering with blades or reading one of numerous newspapers on his tablet. The nostalgia made her feel alive again. As she passed the bar and the long mirror behind it, she ran her fingers through her thick pompadour. Fitted Levis, Timberland boots, and a cropped black halter with thin straps tied behind her neck. The only jewelry she wore was the gold cross around her neck.

Damn, she looked caliente, if she could say so herself. Jenette wanted to listen to hours of oldies, and get drunk.

Drake stood at the end of the bar talking to two very attractive women. Jenette had to smile. He knew her type. Drake looked up, caught her eye, and waved her over.

Then *a stranger* moved next to Drake.

She caught his eye immediately—it was obvious. She'd worked hard for the muscle, and she liked to show off the chiseled lines of her traps, shoulders, and biceps. No more baggy, used jumpsuit. Jenette knew exactly the power that was the curve of the female silhouette. One advantage of having nothing but a jumpsuit for a Friday night was growing to love your skin for what it really is.

Jenette loved her body, what it was capable of. Her muscles may have been hard, but the soft folds of womanhood still as delicate as a newly sprouted petal. She looked him up and down to let him know she might be interested. Just depended on what came out of his mouth.

The two women were obviously into Drake.

"Vasquez, you finally made it," he said. "Meet Tawney and Pam."

Jenette gave the two women a short nod. They smiled with eyelids heavy from day drinking. The one named Pam ran glitter pink nails down Drake's chest like a territorial beast. Jenette wouldn't be a cock block.

"You three have fun," she said. "We can catch up later, Drake."

As Jenette turned to walk to the bar, the good-looking stranger was right in front of her.

"You look a little young to be hanging out here," he said.

Jenette smirked. "If I'm old enough to be sent somewhere to fight and die, then I'm old enough to have a drink." She let that sink in, then added, "I'm Jenette."

He raised one eyebrow and wrapped his thick lips around a bottle of Coors. "Lorenzo Sanchez. I'm a new recruit, finishing up courses at community college so I can jump to a higher position once my training is done. Only way to climb that rope is through a degree, or who you know—but let's be real, it's mostly who you know."

Jenette could feel herself become flush. The scent of his sweet aftershave when he moved closer to hear her better. The shape of his pecs and arms visible through his tight T-shirt. She wanted to reach out and touch his chest, then trail her hand lower. Before lockup she had only fooled around with Neto, who was two years older and gave her an informal education in weapons. Over beers counting ammunition he'd asked her to be his girlfriend.

Other than Neto, and making out with Liberty Love, it wasn't until juvie she met Daisy. They'd had a physical relationship and experienced young love together, until she broke the news she was leaving.

"Well, Jenette," Lorenzo said. "Can I buy you a drink while you tell me all your dreams?"

"Yes, you can buy me a drink. Make it a shot, because I'm celebrating."

"Really? I'm intrigued."

He finished the last of his beer and stared into her eyes. Jenette knew where she would lay her head that night.

* * *

By midnight the crowd had thinned. Drake was long gone with both women. She had given him the condoms she brought, because Drake always seemed short on cash.

She found herself slow dancing to Guns N' Roses "Knockin' On Heaven's Door." They were both drunk, already floating in the oblivion of space. Why put limitation on life, she thought, when the only outcome is death. She wanted Lorenzo, and wouldn't take no for an answer. Her mind needed a release...

He tilted her chin toward his mouth and kissed her. His tongue pulled more sexual greed from her longing body. One hand squeezed her hip.

"My place?" he said, then he pulled back a little. "But I am being deployed soon. Cryo for two years. This will be whatever it will be."

"Any place, as long as we have nothing on." Her hand crawled to his ass. "El riesgo siempre vive."

She all but moved in with Lorenzo until it was time for him to leave.

The days were spent running the perimeter of the base and challenging each other on the obstacle course. At night her body cracked in the darkness like the striking of a whip as she surrendered herself to freedom. Lorenzo handled her in the ways she and Daisy couldn't allow for themselves, what with the guards and cameras. In lockup, it all had to be under the sheets and hushed in the dark.

Jenette wanted to make up for time lost.

The present was all that mattered until his deployment to one of the brewing conflicts out in space. They both knew departure day would arrive, but the time passed too soon, and it came with both of them still wanting more.

They stood at the curb outside his place.

"I guess this is it?" he said, trying to keep his voice light. "Maybe we will meet up there, in the stars." Then he looked her straight in the eyes, and turned serious. "Thank you for making the last few weeks magic. *You're* magic. A real bruja. Don't ever forget that, and kick anyone's ass that tells you otherwise."

Jenette held back her emotions. Daisy had refused to say goodbye on that final day. That lack of closure still hurt, as if what they shared meant nothing. At least she could close this chapter with Lorenzo.

"Thank you," she said finally. "You will always be part of me. I'm sure of it."

He kissed her one last time before getting into the automated taxi that would take him to the base. Part of her soul was pinched with grief of what could have been. Then she reminded herself that people crossed paths again all the time. Grabbing her own duffel, she headed back to the base. Drake had been lonely and slightly jealous without his best friend for training.

* * *

"Wait, do it again."

Eight weeks later she found out she was pregnant during a routine drug test. In shock, Jenette sat in front of the nurse.

The nurse stared back at her.

"I did… three times. I'll have to report this," he said, almost apologetically. "In the meantime, you need to go for a scan. Now." He wrote down on a notepad what they needed to do at the base clinic. Jenette's mind was beyond that already.

How would she get in contact with Lorenzo, already frozen and floating toward a who-knew-what? She didn't want to tell Drake or anyone, not just yet. Her main worry was fucking up her one shot—and for what?

On the bus to the clinic, anger burned her to the marrow as she chewed on the skin around her nails. No way would she go back, serve the full term of her sentence. They *had* to allow her to terminate. It was still her body and her choice.

Sinking in her thoughts, she nearly missed her stop.

Whatever happened next was in the hands of fate.

She lay on the table with the red rectangular light moving across her body. The projection against the wall revealed two sacs. Twins. Her heart thumped harder than in any training session. She didn't know if she wanted to scream or cry, so she lay there while the tech made a call to someone. When finished he turned to Jenette.

"You can pull down your T-shirt and pull up your jeans. I was informed that you need to return to the barracks until an emergency hearing on your status is scheduled. You can expect it within a day or two."

Jenette just nodded—she had no questions or anything to say, given the severity of the situation. As she walked out, she messaged Drake and Roseanna. Whatever the outcome, she would need someone to lean on.

Drake messaged back.

Damn. Lorenzo?

I've got your back, whatever you decide.

See you at the barracks.

Twenty-four hours later Jenette stood in front of the judge, not wanting to look her in the eye. It's not like she hurt anyone or went back to running with the old crowd in the streets. Never touched drugs in her life. Yet the grief wouldn't stop.

"You just can't stay out of trouble," she said, her voice full of condescension. "All of you are products of arrested development."

Jenette's cheeks felt hot.

"Yeah, well maybe stop arresting and start developing." Her temper was a cluster of Roman candles set alight while still in her hand. God help anyone if she pointed it in their direction.

She wanted to explode.

The judge flipped through a file. "Now, do you understand what this means? This is a violation of your terms of service. We can't force a decision on you, but either way, once you reach the outcome you will be sterilized. History can't be allowed to repeat itself." While Jenette tried to understand what was being said, she continued. "If you choose to remain pregnant, then upon the birth your placenta will be claimed, along with your womb and eggs, for use by the government as they see fit. This will help to compensate for the cost of the procedure."

"What?" she said. "Sterilized? Taking my organs? For what purpose? So, I don't even get a choice later on? You want to take that away from me, too?"

"Given your position, you ask a lot of questions," the judge replied. "As I stated before, everything that's recovered will be put to use as the government sees fit. In terms of your military service," she continued, "by behaving as you have, you're taking away from someone who would be more appreciative of the opportunities."

"Have you ever been locked up, your honor?" Jenette asked. "And not just locked up—for something you didn't do? You got any clue what it's like in there?"

"I'm not going to dignify your first question with a response," the judge responded flatly. "As for your innocence… that is not for you to decide. If we took the word of every convicted felon, then *everyone* would be 'innocent.' So I suggest you be quiet, and take the offer that's on the table.

"You will find I am very generous," she added. "I have a soft spot for your kind."

Jenette took her advice, and remained silent.

If there hadn't been so much hanging in the balance—returning to jail, kicked out of the Marines—she might have spat in the judge's face and told her to fuck herself because she obviously needed it. Sometimes power didn't require any physical force at all. Rendering your opponent silent is enough.

"I want to think about it."

The judge gave her a fake smile. "Sure," she said. "You have twenty-four hours. If you are not back here by then, we will come and find you, to take you back to prison to serve the full term. You are in control of your future, Ms. Vasquez. I will place in the record my recommendations, should you decide to not terminate." The judge waved the bailiff over to hand Jenette a document. "These are the terms for keeping a pregnancy during training."

Then she gestured for Jenette to approach, and handed her a note. It was folded, indicating that it should be read in private.

Twenty-four hours to make this life-altering decision. Jenette needed to talk to Roseanna. Her sister had hit rock bottom before, had been forced to brave her storms, day in and day out. She also counseled people for a living. If anyone could provide some clarity, it would be her.

She went immediately to the barracks to make the call.

"That isn't much of a choice," Roseanna said bleakly. "Either way they will enforce their so-called 'right' to alter your body, just to suit them. Sterilized? Fuck them."

"I never thought much about kids," Jenette admitted, "but tell me I can't have them… Maybe I don't deserve them…"

Roseanna couldn't come on such short notice, so she had to remain an image on a screen. In front of the camera, she lit a white seven-day candle and placed it on her altar next to the photos of their relatives.

"I'm sorry, Jenette," she said, then took a moment to compose herself. "I know I have apologized to you more times than I can count, but I will never stop. And believe me when I say that I have had my own one-night stands and brief affairs. Don't you dare apologize for it."

"Fuck those clowns." Jenette ran her fingers through her hair. "I would terminate, if I knew I could choose later— but there won't be any later."

The candle on the altar crackled. Roseanna turned to look at it, then back to a fidgeting Jenette.

"I'll take them," she said. "I *want* them. If that is what you choose. I will also accept your decision, if you choose terminating. You…"

"What?" Jenette looked straight into the camera.

"*I want your babies,*" Roseanna repeated. "To keep them in the family. Should you ever want to see them… You can trust me. We all deserve options, the right to make choices. We aren't just our pasts. We learn and move forward, wiser… sometimes it's just with another scar or tattoo."

Jenette thought about what her hermana had said. Let it sink in.

"I know I can trust you." Then she added, "Are you sure?"

"You know me better than that," Roseanna responded. "I wouldn't say it if I didn't mean it. This is unfinished business for me, because I couldn't be there for you. But what will you do, when you can't train like the rest? What did they say?"

"The first trimester, I can train like everyone else," Jenette explained. "I'll be spending the second half of my pregnancy in the armory. I will be living and breathing big guns. Not a bad gig. Then after they are born, I get a few weeks to catch up on what I missed with the rest of the training." She paused, then said, "If I terminate, then it's business as usual, but I will never have a chance to have my own, if I want that later."

Roseanna shook her head. "I'm fucking sick of all these tests."

"Tests and timing, sister. These are the pieces we are given for the board."

The candle continued to crackle and burn bright. Jenette hung her head and clasped her hands. Teardrops fell one by one with the slowness of blood drawn from a pin prick.

"I want to go through with it, Roseanna. I'll tell the judge you have all the rights. But as far as seeing them… I have to make this sacrifice count. I have to make myself and the family proud. Make *them* proud."

"You will, Jenette. Keep that soldadera spirit alive."

Jenette raised her head. "After they are born, I'm going to the top, the stars. Nobody is going to stop me. They can take my children, and organs, they can't have my soul. I'll make it to the stars, you wait and see."

Roseanna nodded and brought her hands to a prayer position. "Rewriting our history in our own blood, by changing the future."

5

2179

It was now or never if they wanted to escape this hell of a planet and the demons who seemed determined to claim their souls.

Jenette reacted instinctively, pulling the trigger on her pulse rifle, filling the tunnel with gunfire as she moved backward, trying to follow Ripley and Newt. She fired until the pulse rifle was dead. Dropping to the ground she went for her pistol.

The Xenomorph continued its pursuit. Then from an open tunnel above, one of them lunged downward. She gritted her teeth and pulled the trigger. As it fell, she pinned it to the wall with her boot. Without hesitation she unleashed a spray of bullets until bursts of the Xenomorph's acidic blood burned through her ankle.

Jenette screamed out in pain. She had to make it out. With both arms she pulled herself through the tunnel, while releasing the clip in her gun.

"No, no, *no*," she cried out.

The pain shot through her legs, making it difficult to move faster than a crawl. She heard Gorman call her name, then he was behind her and grabbing her beneath both arms. From a distance they could see a Xenomorph trying to burst through a metal wall. Gorman shot in its direction until he ran out of rounds.

The sound of skittering on metal revealed Xenomorphs coming from all sides.

Fuck, she thought. *This is it. I wish I had more time.* For a fleeting instant, she thought of Roseanna.

Ramón.

Leticia.

Reaching behind, he pulled out a grenade.

"You always were an asshole, Gorman."

He held the grenade in front of them and flicked off the safety. As he hit the button, she clamped her hand over his. Despite what was coming, neither of them closed their eyes. They would both die with honor. Jenette would earn her place with the soldaderas who came before her.

PART 2

FAMILIA

6

The true cost of energy and habitable land could only be counted in blood, the cries of those left behind, and decayed flesh left to fertilize the hardened ground.

Dr. Brenda Moon never expected to accept a position in weapons, but it was one of those offers she could not refuse, that would create generational wealth in her family. Wealth, what everyone vied for on an Earth spiraling into decay, with people struggling to cover even the basic necessities of living.

Generational wealth equated to the wealth of opportunity.

That was why she sacrificed herself to this new Weyland-Yutani planet that had been in the making for years, with intensive terraforming and the harnessing of its immense geothermal energy, similar to Iceland on Earth.

The planet was so secret it hadn't even been given

an LV designation, a pet project launched by Meredith Vickers, who had died before she could create her own kingdom here. She had a great-grandson named Jacob who was only tangentially involved with the company. From what she knew, he lived in England. Brenda didn't know what Vickers' plan had been for the planet—no one did. She'd had a good eye for potential, though, because once the terraforming was complete, it became the perfect location for a scientific outpost.

The terrain was rough with sharp mountain ranges, plentiful water, and geysers to naturally surround the location of the facility. The landing station had been deliberately placed in front of a large swatch of brown and yellow sulfur fields filled with potholes of bubbling mud and burping water spurting plumes of sulfur into the air for hundreds of feet. It burned with the intensity of acid as it fell.

Large mud vents, some the size of a man, expelled smoke. Nothing grew there. Passing this section of the planet made her gag from the stench, even as her mind filled with possibilities for research. Only someone intent on reaching the facility would dare cross this unpredictable and treacherous road without special equipment, making it the perfect place to dispose of dangerous biological materials. The heat was enough to destroy anything.

Even the oceans on the planet were death traps with skyscraper-height waves and undertows powerful enough to drown a whale. Thus, the main facility was situated between the coastline and the sulfur fields. Perfect. Their research could be conducted far from the eyes of the competition, independent watchdogs, or government regulation.

The small group of scientists working here were a dedicated team who fully understood that they most likely would never leave the facility—nor would they want to. They would be tagged as the ones who had written a new chapter in humanity. Not everyone would understand.

They say the only constant in life is change, Brenda mused. *War should be added to that list.*

Brenda stood in front of the glass, half staring at her own reflection as it merged with the grotesque sight of a body that resembled a blackened charred log, despite the fact that it hadn't been exposed to a matchstick. Their synthesized bacteria was a different type of fire. Nearby lay a nameless human guinea pig whose chest had become a wide chasm of liquified organs and congealing blood.

Given what she had just witnessed, Brenda felt just as grotesque inside. The human hadn't felt a thing, with a powerful sedative cutting off their pain, but they did witness with their own eyes the creature that had emerged from their chest, tearing through organs and past shattered bones. A creature that had become the object of the weapons development efforts, and had died a painful death, never knowing what had killed it.

Her colleague, Dr. Gilda Patel, joined her as a team behind the glass removed every speck of blood spatter, vomit, and fecal matter from the walls and floor. No trace of the bacteria could remain, even if its origins were in part native to Earth—a variation on the once-rare "flesh-eating bacterium" known as necrotizing fasciitis. The original had been recorded as far back as the eighteenth century.

The other component was a black mold, the origin of which remained unknown to her team. She knew better than to ask.

Xenomorphs had a sophisticated immune system unlike anything she had ever witnessed. Nature was the mother of the cruelest creations, she supposed, depending on where one stood in the hierarchy of things. Creating the right combination of elements, getting past that amazing immune system, had been the greatest challenge of her career. They were still a long way off pinning their hopes on every experiment. Sometimes the experiments worked, and other times they did not.

"I hope this time it pans out," Gilda said. Then she enthused, "You're going to be rich—I can't wait to get my bonus! Our shares will be worth a fortune. I wonder where I'll buy my first property. And all it took was a deal with a living, breathing devil.

"What will you do with your share?" she added.

Brenda had to hold back the urge to vomit. Her stomach cramped as it pushed lunch up her gastrointestinal tract.

"I'll tell you when I'm paying the price in hell—but let's not get ahead of ourselves. We have to be careful. There can be no accidents, no data leaks. We're not there yet. We know the bacteria works on the creature while it's still in the host, but there's still a long way to go before we can collect that check."

Like I'll ever get to spend it, she added silently.

As she moved toward the area where they would conduct phase two, Brenda could feel the world contracting tightly around her neck, laying its evil eggs of self-doubt.

When she declared she was going into space, accepting a major promotion with a biological research team, her family in Guyana wanted to know where she was going. She'd had no answers, not because she wouldn't tell them, but because she *couldn't*. She'd had no idea where she was being taken.

Despite its lethal history, Brenda didn't fear the bacteria. During her time teaching at the London School of Hygiene and Tropical Diseases after leaving her home in Guyana, the CDC, and UNICEF, she had encountered all the worst bugs known to humans. She had seen firsthand what they were capable of doing. She was happy to flee Earth, to work in isolation from the chaos, and she didn't need to be there to make certain her family was still looked after financially.

The bacterium was only one of the projects they were developing. In this very facility they had created a newly engineered parasite based on the humble pork tapeworm.

They gave it real teeth. She would rather contract Ebola than have it inside of her. But her mother hadn't raised her to be a fool. Every product could be neutralized.

Except these other creatures. The Xenomorphs, as they were called, were unnatural things they had no business trying to harness—not in their natural form. The longer she studied them, the less she slept. She kept her doors to her office and apartment double bolted. She checked all safety protocols twice after each experiment and when leaving the research wing for the night. No one she hadn't personally vetted was allowed near the creatures, even the small ones, chestbursters. Pale phalluses with jaws, yet the damage they caused to their hosts was something she hadn't been prepared for when she first witnessed the viciousness of it.

There was no recovering from that.

Unlike humans, these things could not be manipulated with money, power, sex, drugs, contracts. Humans had nothing to offer these things within the concept of our world or existence. The exact opposite. All they saw was carnage and survival. Their life cycle was an act of destruction and death.

They could not travel on their own—their expansion depended on others passing them around with the same ignorance of a host coughing out a pathogen on a crowded train. These things had no inkling of time. They only existed for the sake of it. They seemed immune to everything.

Until now.

Brenda paced her steps as she made her way to phase two. Each research lab was separated from the next by walls that could not be destroyed by anything short of a tank or blast from artillery. She stood beneath the globe scanner until the door opened. Inside, Gilda stood by the glass waiting for her. Brenda checked a tablet that registered the growth of the Xenomorph. The dosage had to be precise.

"All checks complete?"

"Twice. Just as you like it."

Brenda removed a small fob from the pocket of her lab coat.

"Good. Do it."

Gilda swiped on the console inlaid in the glass. A light came on behind the clear partition, illuminating what lay beyond. A young Xenomorph thrashed around the polytetrafluoroethylene-insulated chamber designed to withstand their acidic blood.

Brenda knew that at some point she would have to allow a test subject to get bigger, but she would avoid it as long as possible. If she had called the shots and held the purse strings, they would not grow beyond this point. But she didn't. Before long she would be forced to allow them to grow.

If all went according to plan, this next five minutes would tell the tale. From the back wall, a small ball the size of an orange rolled from an opening just large enough to accommodate it. They didn't dare anything larger.

As soon as the ball entered the room the Xenomorph screeched and backed away. Its head lolled in confusion, with strings of viscous saliva pouring from snapping jaws filled with teeth.

The remotely controlled metal sphere continued to roll closer until the Xenomorph could no longer maneuver past it in the small barren room. Brenda pressed the fob in her hand.

The sphere exploded.

Projectiles sprayed from the orb to pierce the Xenomorph's armored exterior. The monster convulsed, waving its small arms as the bacteria invaded its body. The large mouth snapped at the air as if it was choking, until its body fell to the ground like the husk of a cicada from a tree. The bacteria caused toxic shock in the Xenomorph faster than in humans. It could lie there for hours in a delirium as the microscopic invader took over its system.

Today, however, they needed live samples.

She peered at the creature that could have been made of glass, a horrid Lladró from the depths of space. Brenda pressed another button on the fob. A man in full hazmat walked through a side door into the chamber, carrying a small rubber mallet in one hand. At the front of his waist were three small cylinders. Hoisted to his hip was a pulse gun, there in the event the test subject attempted to move.

Kneeling in front of the incapacitated Xenomorph, he extended a single finger to graze the limp inner mandible hanging out of its main jaws. The Xenomorph's teeth snapped, but not fast enough to catch the man's flesh. He stumbled backward onto his ass. That last movement by the Xenomorph caused another violent seizure before it slumped to the ground. Ashy blots bloomed on its exterior.

Brenda swiped her tablet to activate the intercom.

"What are you waiting for?"

The man remained sitting at a distance. *"Did you see what it just did?"*

She rolled her eyes, even though he could not see her. "It was an automatic response. The color exhibited on the skull tells me it's fine to proceed. We need the sample while it's still alive. Hurry. Unless you want to do this again."

Lurching back to his feet, he kneeled next to the Xenomorph and delivered a soft whack to the skull. Instantly the body cracked and crumbled. The inner tissue was deteriorating rapidly and that made it easy to destroy. He picked up the smaller pieces and placed them in the three cylinders on his waist. The last shard he brought close to the clear square visor on the helmet, giving it a few twists and turns before looking at the window, giving a thumbs-up.

Brenda smiled. The bacteria had neutralized the acidic blood of the Xenomorph, which led to its death. But so far it had only been tested on the young, the small ones. She didn't want to think about trying it on a full-grown Xenomorph... or a queen. One of the young queens they possessed she had named La Reina.

When fully activated, this bacterium could also be sequenced for use on humans. It would be lethal to everyone at any age. Yet even if the bacteria were sequenced to attack human DNA, they could be rendered harmless with the right antidote—currently under development.

For that matter, the bacterium might also be placed in a human without it being fully activated, and thus remain dormant. Humans could be the engineers of anything they wanted. Developing weapons like this could help mankind avoid long, protracted wars of tit for tat. One show of this weapon, and no one could stop you.

But Brenda hadn't been born yesterday, nor did she labor under idealistic delusions. She stayed as much for the money as she did to try to keep the Xenomorphs under control. The bacterium would offer some semblance of protection, even if it meant playing a shitty game to get ahead in the universe.

What was the old saying?

"Hate the game, not the player."

The humans they used in their research had "volunteered" to be a part of their program, and once they reached their inevitable end, they were dumped in the sulfur fields. No trace remained on the premises, and no one would go fishing in the fumaroles that were more than a hundred degrees Celsius. One of the scientists had suggested they toss the expired Xenomorphs into the treacherous oceans that were unsafe for anything or anyone.

"Absolutely not, not under any circumstances," she replied. "The only good Xenomorph is a pile of ash without anything recoverable from it." Even dead, the creatures came from unknown origins. She wouldn't run the risk that the remains might interact with any indigenous species.

Brenda prided herself on a degree of level-headed thinking, but where the creatures were involved, her imagination tended to run wild. Nature and science had taught her humility, but the world of men taught her how bad things could get when it was least expected.

"Dr. Moon, we're ready for you. *She* is ready."

Brenda didn't like this at all, but it was now or never.

"Take me to her majesty."

She walked along the narrow corridor and stopped to face a blank section of wall. A camera dome hidden in the ceiling scanned her, and a section of the wall opened into a windowless room known to a very select few. There was nothing inside except a single pane of reinforced plexiglass, filling the far wall.

"La Reina," Brenda whispered.

Her entrance alerted the team on the other side. In the middle of the sterile room lay an infant queen Xenomorph. She was one of three. Her hood was only starting to develop and wing back. She writhed with her arms, legs, and tail bolted to a PTFE gurney. Because of her blood, everything in the chamber was made from polytetrafluoroethylene. Above her head, a large heated glass sphere of black-and-blue bacteria particles floated in plasma.

As if sensing the threat, the queen paused in her struggles.

"Time to give La Reina her crown."

A scientist walked behind the Xenomorph, pushing a trolly that held five white bullet-shaped PTFE cylinders, each the size of a shotgun shell. He attached one to the top of a handheld drill, then placed it against the skull of the Xenomorph. With a hard jolt the first cylinder broke through the young creature's relatively soft cranium, leaving part of the cylinder protruding. The PTFE could avoid being absorbed deeper in the softer tissue.

La Reina shrieked loudly, thrashing and attempting to free herself. The scientist continued this process until each bullet was embedded, creating a circular crown. The Xenomorph increased her protestations with each insertion. Each bullet contained a chip that could be activated to release the bacteria.

Yet that wasn't the intent.

Time for the next phase.

A scientist to the right switched on a laser scalpel. The red tip burned through the bottom half of the creature's jaw, leaving the long inner mandible swinging side to side. The scientist then removed half her tail with a clean swipe, followed by both hands. The bottom half of each leg was removed at the knee joint. This left her utterly incapacitated.

The only thing they required of La Reina was for her to

reproduce. Brenda took a deep breath. Their queen would now be placed deep within the facility, in a new throne that would eventually be her tomb.

"How do we know this will accomplish anything in the long term?" Gilda said.

Brenda took another deep breath as she continued to look at the small queen. "We don't." Seeing Dr. Patel's expression, she continued. "Look how many versions of androids there have been. *Nothing* is perfect—including science. But science is what we have, and we couldn't have survived this long as a species without it. Hell, we wouldn't be up here in space without pushing the limitations."

"So you're betting on that she—I mean all the queens— will just grow to accept their chopped-off pieces? Giving up and giving us their limbs, their eggs, and their DNA until we kill them off?"

"I don't know," Brenda admitted, "but there's one thing I *do* know. If the slightest hint of a threat appears, before La Reina has a chance to do anything she will be executed, hence the crown. One press of a button and *poof*."

"What comes next?"

"We wait, and we see if she begins to produce eggs." Brenda and Gilda stood there in silence, watching as La Reina was wheeled out and a scientist removed the globe of bacteria. Its purpose had been served.

Gilda turned to Brenda. "Coffee?"

Brenda chortled. "Make it an Irish coffee, and you're on."

7

Roseanna Vasquez's small ranch in Texas, a few hours north of the restored Gulf of Mexico, had a pale blue, two-bedroom, one-story house on three acres of land dotted with pecan, oak, and mesquite trees, with its own small pond. The beautiful foliage and wide-open space from which she could watch the sunrise and sunset encouraged calm and gratitude when memory eclipsed her mind, sending her into dark corners of not wanting to live.

She had purchased it from a man named Robert Boone, a tall Black vaquero who had two children close in age. It had been instant chemistry when he opened the door, and even more when he showed her the property. This patch of paradise enabled her to stay sober and find a sense of purpose. A collection of wind chimes hung from the beams in the front and back of the house.

The wild spirit of nature was all she needed to put

her back into alignment so she could help others in their daily struggles.

In the final fight to live, as she lay on the operating table, she had wondered if she should just let go and let herself die. The world would continue to turn without her in it. Floundering in life wasn't enough. It had to have meaning, or she just wanted to go quietly into the night like everyone else in her life.

The din of the medical equipment, surgeons, nurses sent her to sleep as they fought to save her. She felt herself drifting off with one final thought.

Fuck you, God. You want me alive then make your move.

This is my white flag.

I'm exhausted.

To her surprise, she woke up wrestling between gratitude and anger. Perhaps being awake was a sign itself.

At that moment all she could remember were nightmares about the androids she had encountered during a visit to the factory with her father at about ten years old. Their life-like appearance frightened her, considering they were devoid of life. The coldness in their stare as she passed bordered on wicked curiosity.

In her nightmare, one chased her between rows and rows of their nude bodies hanging on what looked like meat hooks. It always ended with her seeing a group of them slicing open a screaming human with a shriek of something not of this world. But that was just a nightmare.

Roseanna's injuries seemed to have healed more than she would have expected. She asked a nurse how that could be.

"You've been in a medically induced coma for almost two months. The nightmares were a side-effect." The nurse's eyes shifted to her right and looked away—she wouldn't meet Roseanna's gaze.

"What is it?" Roseanna asked.

"I'm not authorized to tell you," the nurse replied. "When you're up for it, I suggest you read that." She gestured, then quickly left the room.

On the small table next to her bed lay a thick stack of paperwork with the city emblem on the top. After a time, she took it in her hands, not knowing what to expect. It was from the courts and the hospital giving her the options she had to choose from as a consequence for the accident.

Her mother was dead.

Jenette had been put into foster care.

As understanding sank in, Roseanna clutched her chest and heaved with hysterical mourning. Tears poured from her eyes. The pain in her body was nothing compared to the shredding of her soul.

Finally the grief passed, and exhaustion caused her to sleep again. When she woke, she mulled over her options, and realized she had none. She would have to relocate to Texas for rehabilitation and, hopefully, employment. Once there she would find a way to do right by Jenette.

That her sister was still alive told Roseanna something that buoyed her spirits—the one dose of vaccine she had stolen must have saved Jenette's life. She should have known Mama would refuse to take it herself. Every day humans made billions of choices—as vast as the canopy of stars—and each decision was connected to another. Francisca Vasquez had chosen her path, and now Roseanna had to choose, as well.

She had to stay alive.

Counseling proved to be as natural and fulfilling to her as walking around the pond on her property. She would tell the new members of the rehab program, "The accident took away my nursing career and the possibility of becoming a doctor—something I thought I would do until the day I died—but it led me to my true calling and to you beautiful people today."

Roseanna embraced the eccentric, getting into crystals and meditation. Buddha and Ganesh hung out side by side with La Virgen and Jesus on her windowsill in the kitchen. A gold cross always hung around her neck on a gold-linked chain. Unlike her sister Jenette, she practiced curanderismo, traditional healing and spiritual beliefs. They helped get through the bad days, to work through the remaining echoes of trauma.

Thanks to the car accident her right leg was held together with a metal rod, and she had a scar from her hip to the ankle. Like her favorite artist, Frida Kahlo, the accident left her physically unable to carry children, not that she had ever harbored an overwhelming need to have them. Now that the choice had been taken away, however, it hurt somewhere deep.

Then she received the most unexpected news of all.

She was going to be an aunt!

"That isn't much of a choice," Roseanna said, nevertheless trying to stay as positive as she could. "Either way they will enforce their so-called 'right' to alter your body, just to suit them. Sterilized? Fuck them."

"I never thought much about kids," Jenette said over the video connection, "but tell me I can't have them… Maybe I don't deserve them…"

As her sister spoke, Roseanna lit a white seven-day candle and placed it on her altar next to the photos of their relatives. This gave her time to think, as well. Then she turned back to the screen.

"I'm sorry, Jenette," she said. "I know I have apologized to you more times than I can count, but I will never stop. And believe me when I say that I have had my own one-night stands and brief affairs. Don't you dare apologize for it."

"Fuck those clowns," Jenette said angrily, running her

fingers through her hair. "I would terminate, if I knew I could choose later—but there won't be any later."

The candle behind her crackled, and Roseanna turned to look at it. She made yet another decision—one which would change her life forever—and her voice was firm when she spoke.

"I'll take them," she said. Jenette looked surprised, but before she could say anything, Roseanna added, "I *want* them. If that is what you choose. I will also accept your decision, if you choose terminating. You…"

"What?" Jenette's eyes were wide.

"*I want your babies*," Roseanna repeated, trying not to roll her eyes. "To keep them in the family. Should you ever want to see them… You can trust me. We all deserve options, the right to make choices. We aren't just our pasts. We learn and move forward, wiser… sometimes it's just with another scar or tattoo."

There was a long silence, and Roseanna worried what might come next.

"I know I can trust you," Jenette said, adding, "are you sure?"

"You know me better than that," Roseanna responded. "I wouldn't say it if I didn't mean it."

As she prepared for the journey to California, to collect Leticia and Ramón, Roseanna understood that she would have to love herself enough to love them. Only then would she be able to do what was going to be needed.

When she finally got to see them, they were cradled in small carriers. Fast asleep, both dressed in all white and looking nearly identical. Two little doves. Jenette was already back in the barracks, and any contact was strictly prohibited. It seemed unreasonably harsh, and Roseanna wondered if anyone else would have been treated that way.

They hardly made a sound the entire time, and once she was back in Texas, she dropped to her knees on her front porch, and looked to the sun.

"Please don't let me fuck this up," she said. "Of all the trials. Of all the tests. Guide me, ancestors and spirits. Guide them. Stay close to Jenette, as well, because where she is going, none of us can follow."

The wind chimes adorned with conch, oyster, and other seashells blew in the wind. The noise momentarily roused the babies, but they settled again.

Roseanna closed her eyes.

Thank you.

She would raise them the best she could. Most of their family was dead—as far as she knew, these were the last of the Vasquez seeds. Their little mouths, puckered in the shape of small butterfly wings, sucked instinctively. Roseanna didn't know how this would work, but she felt called to do it.

The Vasquez name had to be carried on.

Roseanna would tell them about Jenette, and do the best she could, one day at a time.

8

Leticia grew to inherit her mother's adventurous spirit, including an insatiable curiosity about space and mankind's push to colonize distant worlds. But before they were even ten years old, word came that Jenette had died on a distant world. All the children would have of their mother was a faded photo.

Roseanna wanted them to have as normal a childhood as possible. The money sent to her after Jenette's death was meant for them alone, and she would do everything she could to make sure it lasted. Each week, with pocket money in hand, Ramón and Leticia waited for the van that sold pickles, salt limon, and always saladitos—shriveled salted plums so sour it puckered their lips until they burst into laughter at the faces they made.

There were the usual birthday parties with a piñata and playdough. Summers meant raspa and colorful tongues.

They ate them fast before the ice could soften the white paper cone to mush. Roseanna taught them both to cook, preparing them to take care of themselves when they were older, but without any expectation that either of them would like it. Determined to raise them equally, she refused to treat Leticia like a doll, remembering the pressure that had been placed on Jenette.

Leticia adored the open space with chickens, a small pond, and more than enough trees to climb. Ramón, on the other hand, hogged all the Lego to create detailed, extravagant buildings and worlds where his mother and father had trained to go. La Llorona herself would have been scared at the screams that came from his little body if anyone dared destroy something that took him weeks to create.

There were the unsuccessful attempts to get them to play together, which would have made her life easier, but Ramón wanted Leticia to play *his* way. Frustrated, Leticia stomped on his creations with one foot while tossing other parts across the room. Fights would ensue, then they both would run to Roseanna for her attention and affection, demanding that she declare one of them right. The only fair solution was to send them both to their bunk beds until they could get along.

After the appropriate amount of time Roseanna would peek in.

"Look, we are all we have," she would say. "This is our little gang, and no one can break it up. If you give each other a hug, I'll make popcorn and we will watch a movie together."

Begrudgingly, they would agree. Leticia and Ramón hated sharing a room even when they were in a period of truce. Ramón claimed the space for his own by cluttering it with his things. There were his science experiments, posters, stacks and stacks of books on every subject. He knew how to manipulate and did his best to get what he wanted, especially from his sister.

Leticia retreated to the small bunk with her own belongings. Sometimes in the middle of the night she would climb into Roseanna's bed.

Finally one morning, Roseanna took Leticia aside.

"Stand up to him. Say no. What is yours is *yours*. Don't let him talk you into giving him the remote for the TV, or your pocket money, or the last bite of dessert. You deserve as much as him. Do you understand?"

Leticia nodded in understanding, and to Roseanna's delight she did as had been suggested. It didn't take long for Ramón to get the message, and before long a status quo was reached.

The same couldn't be said for Ramón's relationships at school. The students there didn't appreciate Roseanna's nephew for the brilliant child he was, and he was treated as an outcast of sorts. He announced at a young age that to have what he wanted, he would need to build his own worlds.

And be rich.

* * *

When the twins were twelve years old Roseanna built another bedroom and small bathroom with a shower for Leticia. She would need her privacy soon to have the freedom to blossom into the young woman she was born to be.

It was autumn again, and just before their seventeenth birthdays. The leaves on the property created a carpet of fire that offered a deconstructed reflection of the trees.

As above, so below.

Roseanna always kept an altar in the house to represent their deceased family members, including Jenette. There was a photo of their brother Sandro and his wife Blanca. They were gone, having died closer to God in space, but their eight-year-old son Cutter survived and was still up there somewhere.

From the beginning Roseanna made it a point to bring Leticia and Ramón into her Dia de Los Muertos ritual to honor the family, especially their mother. She taught them that physical death didn't have to be the end, unless it was what they wanted it to be. Through cloning, science had imposed itself upon the spiritual interpretations.

* * *

During the ritual there were white pillar candles and tea lights, fresh marigolds, roses, and a small red-robed figurine of Santa Muerte holding a cornucopia of gold coins. A small skull of obsidian rested next to a photo of Jenette alongside decorated sugar skulls. And finally a bowl of fresh strawberries because Jenette joked she was afraid she would forget what they would taste like traveling in space. Leticia, Ramón, and Roseanna stood before the altar, and Leticia's tears were hot as candle wax as she quivered inside like the crackling flames of the tea lights.

Dark shadows danced across the photos of her mother with the viciousness of dark beasts, she thought. The beasts invaded Leticia's mind, stripping her of everything but sorrow. Every year since she was fifteen years old, she had promised herself she wouldn't cry, and every year she couldn't help it. Ever since Roseanna had told her the whole truth about her parents, Leticia's birthday and Dia de Los Muertos had left her emotionally drained.

Roseanna had been honest, telling Leticia and her brother that lying wasn't the solution to easing the pain that came from loss. She didn't want any secrets between them, since they were all they had.

"It's okay to cry, mija," Roseanna said quietly. "The veil is thin. We feel everything, and we should. Let it pass through you and teach you something about yourself—it's the best thing we can do. I get the chills all day every year on this day," she continued. "They are close, I promise. When I first got the news about your mother, the two of you were the saving grace in my sobriety. She lived on with you."

Roseanna placed her arms around Leticia and Ramón.

"I appreciate your kind words of wisdom, tía, but there is nothing out there," Ramón said, ever stoic.

"Callete, Ramón!" Leticia barked, her eyes puffy. "You're so cold."

"No, it's okay." Roseanna patted her shoulder. "You're entitled to your beliefs, Ramón. All I can tell you is when I was battling alcohol, I was barely alive. It took dying to my old life and self for me to live again. Your mother wasn't perfect, but she lived without fear. She cut off all her hair to become the person she wanted to be, and not what she was told was right or acceptable. You both may feel you are dying inside sometimes, and that is okay. You need to grieve, and will go through personal struggles, but know that you have your lives to be lived."

Ramón broke away. "Whatever. She lived a textbook, stereotypical life that got her killed. A gang member? Prison? That is not for me. I have work to do." He moved toward the door. Leticia opened her mouth and moved to stop him. Roseanna gently squeezed her arm.

"Mija, let him go," she said. "We all have to work through things in our own way."

"He puts so much pressure on himself to succeed," Leticia protested, "like some sort of Atlas."

"That's because we are judged by the stories that came before us. He doesn't just carry his own desire for success, he also doesn't want to be written off before he has accomplished anything. Those are the limitations that are set for us, before we are even born. When that happens, we grow with them, believing them."

"Fuck that."

"That is exactly what he is trying to do," Roseanna said, "but it's eating him at the same time. Ouroboros, eating his own tail." She ran a hand through her hair. "Anyway, it's almost your birthday. What do you want to do?"

"I don't know." Leticia wiped her eyes. The longing faded, as it always did. "Just hang out with my friends. I'm getting old for a party."

"I guess no tres leches cake, either?" Roseanna quipped.

"No!" Leticia cried. "I didn't say that. Maybe we do cake, and a movie in the evening?"

Roseanna kissed her on the forehead. "You got it. Now go do your homework, too."

The Pleasanton Mall was quiet, with half the shops shut down. Most things were in short supply depending on which countries were fighting with each other, disrupting the supply chain. This made it difficult to keep stores filled with stock.

Leticia roamed aimlessly with Erika, Joslene, and Nadia. They were their own little clique, sharing secrets over sodas in the quad at lunch and sending text messages to each other in class without getting caught. Here they were dressed casually, in jeans and T-shirts, though Leticia wore some charcoal mascara.

"What are we doing, birthday girl?" Nadia asked as she took a short video clip of Leticia on her phone.

"Nothing crazy," Leticia responded, trying not to look into the camera. "Let's just get food and check out the sales. I could slaughter some sticky chili tofu and noodles. And put that away! My birthday isn't a big deal."

Nadia put the phone away. "It's a shame that hot brother of yours won't be joining us."

"Eww!" Leticia scrunched her nose. "I do *not* want to hear that. He's my brother, and I have to smell his farts and burps."

Nadia laughed with Joslene. "¡Cochina! So many girls like him, but he really doesn't care. Does he have a boyfriend?"

"To be honest, I don't know or care. He can be with whomever he wants—it's his business. The only female he hangs out with regularly is the mom of a kid he tutors. He never talks about boys or girls."

"Well give him my number!" Nadia said, and she giggled.

Leticia rolled her eyes, then stopped in front of a small boutique called Magnolia. In the window were second-hand and new designer clothes, cosmetics, and accessories.

"Damn, that's cute." She spotted a brown suede leather jacket with tassels hanging from the chest and extending to the back. *That would look good with the turquoise and silver teardrop earrings Roseanna gave me this morning.* The card with her gift also said from Ramón, too, but she knew better.

"C'mon, it's your birthday." Joslene tugged on her hand to drag her into the shop. The others were behind, so there was no use resisting. "We're all pitching in to get you a gift." Leticia gave in without any real protest.

The shop floor was half full, but the girls still browsed as if they had free run of the place, bantering without the care of disturbing anyone. It was a birthday after all. The only shop assistant, a girl in a straight bob and dyed cherry red hair, not much older than Leticia, gave them a long stare as they entered. Her sour face made Leticia feel uneasy, and spoiled some of the fun.

Trying to ignore her, they moved on, but she followed them. Leticia had grown used to Ramón and his hovering, with endless questions about her progress in school. It felt like that as they opened and closed different samples of lip gloss and pulled out the price tags of various items of clothing before tucking them back. In the back of her mind, anger began to burn.

With another slit-eyed glare, the shop assistant let Leticia know she didn't like them, and wanted them out.

An ember became a flame.

"You can't just try every lipstick," she said in a snarky tone.

This moment had been stalking Leticia in the shadows

of her mind. It was a bubble of teen angst, sorrow, and resentment that would burst and scald whatever was closest. There was still a rawness from Dia de Los Muertos.

"We can do whatever we want." She stepped closer to the girl. "It's a free country. At least that's what I'm learning in school."

The shop assistant gave her a sarcastic smile and squinted. "Fucking we—" she began under her breath.

"Don't you dare say it, pendeja." Leticia reared her head and narrowed her black-lined eyes. "The Rio fucking Grande dried up to a trickle. It doesn't exist anymore. Watch the news, or read a book."

"Whatever," the girl responded, refusing to meet her eyes now. "I saw you put something in your pocket. I'm going to call security."

Leticia squared up with her.

"I didn't take anything."

The pain of the moment reached deeper than the words. Flashes of memory blinded her. Images of her mother burst in her mind with the explosiveness of a grenade. Leticia lunged and grabbed a handful of the girl's hair, giving it a hard yank. Her ears were plugged with vitriol that made her oblivious to her friends shouting at her to stop.

She would be the one in trouble.

Another hard pull and a large clump of hair was left balled inside her palm. The assistant screeched in pain and fear, ran to the counter, and slapped a button next to the till.

Leticia's fist held her rage and sadness in a tight orb of cold space where her parents' souls now resided. She ran for the assistant again, and her friends attempted to pull her off, but she continued to pummel the girl's face that bled from the nose. Leticia screamed obscenities as tears left charcoal mascara streaks down her cheeks.

Two security guards rushed in, each grabbing an arm and pulling her back.

"Don't tell me who I am, bitch," Leticia shouted, sobbing. "Don't you fucking *dare*. All of you. Fuck you all!"

One of the guards pulled her to the side.

"Show us your pockets, miss."

Leticia didn't move, and looked at her friends who all wore fear on their faces. That brought her back to the moment, and she did it for them. They shouldn't get into trouble because of her. She complied and turned up her pockets, with nothing to be found. The other guard opened her small handbag, proving that there were no stolen goods.

"She still assaulted me," the assistant said, holding the crown of her head. "I want to press charges." Nodding, the security guard grabbed Leticia's upper arm again.

"Let's go," he said. "You can call your parents after the police arrive."

"I'm going." She snatched her arm away. "Don't touch me."

Joslene ran behind her. "We saw it all. We heard what she said. I'll stick up for you. Just tell us what to do."

The guard turned to Joslene, causing her to stop.

"Step away, unless you want us to take you, too."

"Go, Joslene. I'll be alright."

Behind her, Leticia heard Nadia knock over a stand with a box of bras. She glanced over her shoulder as her friend flipped the assistant the middle finger.

"I'll be talking to the manager about this, bitch. You just wait."

Walking through the mall with guards on either side of her, Leticia felt ashamed—not for sticking up for herself, but for what Roseanna would think. Her tía did her best for them, and now this. Roseanna didn't deserve the heartbreak or worry.

By the time they reached the mall entrance a police officer was waiting. Her pulse quickened. She didn't want to get in the police car, but what choice did she have.

9

Roseanna stood in the station entrance when they brought Leticia out from a three-hour wait in a holding cell. They made eye contact, but she remained silent while they walked out the front door into the night. The radio was on in the car, and Roseanna turned it off, then turned to her niece.

"I spoke to your friends," she said calmly. "They told me what happened, and I believe them. I also believe you wouldn't lash out unless you were feeling something... big. You want to tell me what's going on?"

Tears streamed from Leticia's eyes.

"I don't think I know myself," she said. "Just feel lost. Ramón has it all figured out. Most of my friends have some idea. I know there's something for me, but what? Where?" She paused to wipe her eyes. "I get good grades. Never had any trouble with the teachers—but for what? Where does it lead? Dorothy at least had a yellow brick road. Alice had a bunch of animals to guide her."

The tears came again, and she composed herself.

"Does Ramón know? It's just going to make him act like even more of a jerk."

"He doesn't know," Roseanna said. "Your friends agreed to not speak about it at school, either. If you don't want me to tell him, I won't. To be honest it's none of his business. How you were treated was unacceptable, but so was the extent of your reaction. But I know, you swallow that bullshit long enough, and all you want to do is *La Exorcist* that pea green shit back into their faces. I understand. When I was in nursing school and applying for jobs, I got it all."

Leticia stared down, feeling undeserving of Roseanna's understanding. Even that made her fall deeper into a chasm of grief. Roseanna placed a hand on her knee.

"We're going home, and I suggest you take some time alone to think about it. I'm not grounding you or punishing you. I think how you feel is enough. You know this behavior is unacceptable."

They spent the rest of the journey in silence. Leticia's mind and body were numb. She leaned against the headrest, watched the world pass by, and had an overwhelming desire to sleep. Where the hell in this world did she belong?

When the car came to a stop, Leticia threw open the door and rushed to her room to avoid making any contact with her brother. She flopped face-first onto her bed.

* * *

Two hours later a knock on the door roused Leticia from her self-pity and tears. To her relief, Roseanna was on the other side.

"You okay?"

She couldn't avoid her forever, and to tell the truth she wanted a little comforting. She knew it had been wrong to lash out violently, but something inside of her was begging to be expressed. She opened the door. Roseanna had two mugs of steaming manzanilla tea in her hands.

"Not really," she said. "I'm sorry and embarrassed. I don't want to be a burden. It just made me so *angry*, the way that girl treated me." The sweet aroma of the tea mixed with a little honey made Leticia feel slightly better.

"Thank you for the apology," Roseanna said, "but never say that you're a burden." She sat on the edge of the bed and handed a mug to Leticia before pulling a folded piece of paper from the front pocket of her brown flannel shirt. "I was supposed to give this to you when you were eighteen, but I think the time is now. You said in the car that Dorothy and Alice had guidance to find their way. So do you. It's already there... inside.

"You don't need to look outside of yourself," she continued. "Listen to it like a wind chime. Your mother was always going to be a soldier. Didn't happen the way any of us thought, but destiny had to be fulfilled. When the right words, or song, story, or bumper sticker speaks to you, it sets a little flame off in your soul. Then you will know. Don't let self-doubt stop you. El riesgo siempre vive. The guts to take a risk is the dream, even if your corazon must become as combustible as a grenade."

Leticia placed her mug on the nightstand to take the letter into her hands.

"It's from your mother. She was always a chingona, and in her defiance she wrote a letter for you and Ramón. She bribed a nurse to stick them in your baby carriers when you left the hospital."

Leticia began to open it, but Roseanna stopped her.

"This is for you alone to take in and to work through. If you need me after, then I'll be here. There is a box with items from your mother that goes with it, but I'll give that to you later. I'll leave you now."

Roseanna closed the door, and Leticia opened the letter. The fear of what it might say was greater than seeing the police officer. This was someone who had been a dream, a phantom all her life. Now Leticia had in her possession the words her mother had written with her in mind. She took a deep breath before beginning to read.

My dearest Leticia,

To you I am stranger, or some type of ghost if you share Roseanna's beliefs. You've probably heard things about me that aren't so great. Like everyone, I'm not perfect. Never been a saint, but I always tried to be real.

When you read this, you will be on your own journey.

Our family so many years ago traveled farm to farm, and my greatest hope was to travel planet to planet. I have always wanted to be the highest-ranking Marine in the Vasquez family. When you both kicked in my belly while I worked in the armory, I knew you both were fighters, even if you didn't choose the military. I hope the power in your choices will carry you through life and to your dreams, your destiny.

Even things we see as failures can be delayed blessings. Maybe you can be the first to do what has not been done. Life brought me you and your brother, and my plans took a little detour. I always felt insignificant to the point that I knew if anything should happen to me, that the world would keep spinning. Not many people would care or cry, and those who did would get over it quick enough and keep spinning in their own little worlds.

Know you are worth making an impact. Believe it more than I believed in myself. Don't forget, like I did for a little time, that we Vasquez women are daughters of soldaderas, Mexican fighters. You are the next generation of soldadera.

With this letter you will also receive a switchblade. It has seen me through the good and bad times. I'm leaving it here because I don't think there is anything I can do with this little thing in space. So I leave it for you.

Never think I didn't love you with all my soul, just because I didn't know you. Whatever anger you have, put it in your work. Do that with everything you feel. Create something spectacular with your life. I wanted it all because I believed normal people like us deserve to have it all. Be the best of the best.

Look out for your brother. I have written a letter to him and told him to do the same. Be there for each other even when you don't like each other.

And remember, real freedom starts with you. It doesn't matter what they call you, where they try to tuck you away, whatever barriers are in your way. See the light at the end of the tunnel and there will be light.

We are familia. Siempre.

Love,

Jenette Vasquez

Descendant of Soldaderas, Marine, Mama

Leticia pulled the letter to her chest. It answered questions and teased apart complicated emotions that hardened like smoky quartz when she focused on of them. This went beyond thought. It was a feeling.

Her mother didn't want her to settle for less than accomplishing her goals. This she knew and felt. It was the boost she needed, from beyond the veil. It came at just the right time, like Roseanna said. Despite the challenges, the barriers the world put in her way, trying to steal away every opportunity and make her buoyancy the weight of lead, Jenette Vasquez had followed her path.

Quietly Leticia left her room and went to sit in front of the altar with the letter in her hand. There was a patch there with the Marine Corps insignia, and she picked it up. Her fingers rubbed against the stitching, and she had the feeling of having tea with a ghost. Years ago, Roseanna had told them their mother's entire story.

Not much could be found on her father—who had died in one of the wars—or any information concerning his family. Maybe it would happen in time.

Leticia had researched the Marines, but casually, still with a hesitation. There were no guarantees in such a profession, not in the world on which they lived, and certainly not once you ventured past the stars. She had so many questions, coupled with not knowing the direction her young life might go. It had become like the fabled La Lechuza, an ugly creature with the face of a haggard witch and the body of an owl. It perched outside her room in the darkness waiting to pounce with spears for claws. Higher and higher it took her into the night before letting go as she tumbled to death.

That was what the uncertainty felt like.

The words *unfinished business* popped into her mind as she stared at the patch. Reading a letter written in her mother's own words had unlocked her fear of taking a risk. There was no reason, with all her advantages, that she couldn't succeed and go beyond what her mother achieved in her short life. Leticia knew then, the average challenge would not do.

She wanted to be admitted to the Raider Regiment, which specialized in special operations. Not an easy place for good girls to survive, or thrive. Their patch was a skull, like Santa Muerte, and no wonder.

It would be another year before she could enlist.

This was it, the flame, the heat that would melt the wax of doubt. She tucked the letter and the patch beneath the lace cloth on the altar and picked up a photo of her mother. One year. A sense of urgent purpose gripped her as she sat there with the ancestors, looked at the photographs of their Brown faces in uniforms.

There was one more thing—it had been on her mind since she was fifteen. Leticia wandered the rooms of the house to find Roseanna. Ramón had his door shut, but she could hear him practicing his Spanish. He was also becoming fluent in Chinese and wanted to conquer Japanese and Russian. Him and his "arsenal of languages," he called it.

Other times he played Pink Floyd. "Money" and "Wish You Were Here" were his favorites that played on a loop.

Leticia stepped out onto the enclosed back porch and found Roseanna in her armchair, reading on a tablet. The air smelled of the citronella candles lit to fight off the mosquitos at that time in the evening. Wind chimes sang their song along with the chirping cicadas and crickets in the long grass.

"Tía, can we talk?"

She raised her head, wearing the usual calm smile on her face.

"Of course."

Leticia took a deep breath and sat on the ottoman next to her.

"I read the letter."

"And? How do you feel?"

Leticia nodded. "I want to have her close to me, a reminder. I was thinking of getting ink." She held her breath expecting a no, or some sort of chastisement.

Roseanna's face didn't change. "Of what?"

Leticia raised the photo of her mother. "Her," she said, "on my left arm, and what is written on the back of this. What you said. El riesgo siempre vive."

Roseanna's eyes softened seeing the photo. She took it into her hand. "You will probably do it eventually, so why not now?"

Leticia jumped from the ottoman. "Really!"

"Yes, really. You want it done by hand or automated? I know someone I trust. When do you want to do this?"

"I prefer a human touch, the artistry of it. When can you make the appointment?" Leticia gave Roseanna a wide grin, knowing she might be pushing her luck again.

"I'll do it now."

Leticia's smile faded. "Why are you being like this? So cool about everything?"

"Don't think what you did was cool. You know how wrong it was. I know you. But instilling more shame in you than the world will try to do will only mix you up inside. Jenette told me about lockup. It does the exact opposite of what humans need. You need to learn how to manage yourself. People need tools and compassion."

"Thank you." Leticia wrapped her arms around Roseanna. "It won't happen again. I promise." She ran back to her room to get to the homework waiting to be completed. The Marines weren't just about physical strength. She needed to flex the biggest muscle of all to make it to the top.

Three days later Leticia walked into the tattoo parlor expecting pain. There was a heady smell of incense, and a woman wearing rubber gloves greeted her.

"Leticia? You ready? I received the scanned photo, and we are ready to start now."

She looked back at Roseanna, who had accompanied her.

"Thank you."

Roseanna chuckled. "I would say have fun and enjoy, but it hurts. You might regret asking for it."

Leticia sat down, feeling her heart begin to pound when the needle switched on. She braced as she stared straight ahead. Sure, machines could create a tattoo in half the time, but then it didn't feel like art to her. Her mother had her tattoos done in lockup, and it was a guarantee there was no machine service in there.

Roseanna sat next to her, holding the hand of the opposite arm. Leticia squeezed shut her eyes when the stinging hit her skin. Every line etched would be a tribute to the name Vasquez, all the women going back to the beginning of their bloodline.

When it was complete, she lifted her head to the side to look at it in the mirror. Mother and daughter, one face above and the other below. They shared the same high cheekbones and full lips. Roseanna kissed her on the top of her head.

"Wow. It's beautiful. You look very similar."

"I love it. Thank you both!"

When they returned home Ramón stood in the kitchen with a glass of orange juice in his hand and stared with a sneer at her glistening raw skin.

"You've got to be kidding me. This is how you remember her? By getting a tattoo? What will people think when they look at you?" He paused, and she hoped he was finished. No such luck. "It's unprofessional and doesn't do her any justice. She would be disappointed. It's a little desperate and pathetic."

Leticia could feel the same anger she had experienced at the shop. The spirit of La Lechuza inside of her, wanting to scratch him deep to match the way his words hurt her. Without thinking she slapped Ramón hard, leaving the imprint of a red handprint across his cheek.

"You aren't my father, it's not your body, and she wouldn't approve of your arrogance," she replied. "It will be your downfall one day, and maybe even your death. And don't get it twisted, I get grades just as high as yours. You can't call me pathetic!"

"Are you really that stupid?" His body twitched as he fought the urge to slap her back. "First a tattoo, and now you want to do the very thing that killed both our parents." Her eyes went wide. "I saw the Marine Corps letter printed in the kitchen. *Why?* Why would you do that? That's not making the most of your life, Leticia. It's called repeating the same mistakes. You'll die a broke soldier—you know how many vets are on the streets and never taken care of?"

"No, Ramón," she said. "I'm going to get it right. I'm going for special ops. I have the grades and the strength for it. Marine Raiders all the way."

Ramón's face changed after she said this. A small shock, and perhaps even respect, she thought.

Roseanna rushed in from the other room. "Stop it! Both of you. You aren't children anymore." They looked at her but didn't say anything. "Something has to change. Maybe you both need jobs to help you mature a bit." Before they could object, she continued. "Robert has space on his ranch—we were talking about it over dinner the other night. There are horses, and if you are serious about enlisting, Leticia, you can learn to shoot."

Ramón threw his hand into the air above his head. "I can't afford the time for a job right now, tía. Please. I'm on track to be Valedictorian, and the school counselor just gave me a list of scholarships. It could save you so much money, plus I could earn more with the tutoring on the side. I kind of already have a job." Roseanna placed her hands on her hips. "You know I don't like farms," he added.

"That boy's mother does spend a small fortune on his education," she admitted. "You're always helping out over there."

"She's doing it all alone." Ramón looked into his glass to avoid eye contact. "Sometimes she needs a second pair of hands to do stuff. If I'm already there, then why not? You're always telling us to help others."

For once Leticia could hear real pleading in his voice, and fear. It was so thick she thought he might choke on it. Sometimes she hated his guts, but at the end of the day they only had each other.

"He's right, Roseanna," she said. "And he always seems to have money—but I *do* want a job, and shooting sounds hella fun. Any extra experience might go a long way when I enlist."

"Thank you, Leticia." Ramón looked sheepish, that his sister had taken his side. "I'm sorry for being rude. It's just that these exams... I'm stressed." He started toward the door. "Anyway, I have homework."

"Wait," she said. "I'm sorry I slapped you. It was wrong."

He shook his head. "Nah, I deserved it. I was mean. Sometimes even I need sense knocked into me. You do whatever you want to do." When Ramón left the room Roseanna turned to Leticia.

"You slapped your brother? Leticia, you're on thin ice. If you continue that behavior…"

"He was being nasty about my tattoo," she said. Then, "I apologized!" Roseanna's gaze didn't leave Leticia's face.

"Leticia, you *both* need to channel your anger."

"I know and the farm sounds great. Thank you."

Roseanna was about to leave when Leticia stopped her.

"When are you and Mr. Boone just going to get engaged and move in together? You only have the hots for each other, and it's been years."

Roseanna raised an eyebrow. "This doesn't detract from your outburst, and I'm *not* talking to you about my private time. You're lucky I let you get that ink. But yes, Robert and I have been discussing our future together."

1 0

Lucinda and Avery Boone waited on the front porch of their home, standing with their father Robert Boone. Leticia had to admit that he was exceptionally handsome with dark skin and a square jaw covered with salt and pepper stubble, all beneath a tan Stetson that matched dusty boots. Straight Wrangler jeans accentuated his long frame.

He towered over Leticia and she could see why Roseanna was so hot for him. A millionaire rancher with one of the last horse farms in the country, apparently he was one of the best Tejano dance partners she'd ever had, too. He kept it quiet, though, and lived a low-key life.

The main house was a simple four-bedroom, single floor made from red brick, without flashy cars in the driveway or much to draw attention to it. There were a lot of desperate people on Earth, and there were also those choosing to live life without the technology that drove others to space. As people died or became severely ill, entire cities came to a complete standstill. Goods were no longer delivered at regular intervals, the demand for androids skyrocketed over the years, but with only skeleton crews to create more goods, prices increased.

The Boone family had always been farmers, and continued to live that way. There had never been a time when more people wanted to learn horse-riding, or purchase their own. He was also increasing his herds of goats and sheep.

Living the simple life was paying off.

"Welcome, Leticia," he said. "It's been a long time since you were here, and we're glad to have you back. Make yourself at home. Your aunt and I have a horse show later today, so Avery and Lucinda will show you the ropes. Help yourself to lunch with these two."

"Thank you, sir."

"No need for 'sir' just because you're at my house. You know this."

Leticia nodded. Usually when he came over, both she and Ramón made themselves scarce, feeling awkward exchanging small talk. Sometimes when they awoke in the morning, he was leaving out donuts and squeezing a fresh mix of grapefruit and orange juice. That, too, was weird, but strangely comforting.

Lucinda gave her a warm and welcoming grin. "How old were we when we last played together?" she said. "Why so long? It will be good to have another girl around. Between my dad and Avery, it gets to be pretty boring."

Leticia gave them a shy smile, especially when her eyes shifted toward Avery, who wouldn't stop staring at her face. He was just as good-looking as his father, and wore the same jeans and boots. Leticia and Ramón had spent time playing with Lucinda and Avery when they were younger, even staying over at the farm when Roseanna and Robert spent time together.

Once they hit middle school, however, they had to go to different schools and were no longer interested in "playing." They met new friends and drifted apart. Leticia was happy to meet up with them again.

"Thanks for having me," she said. "It feels like years since we caught frogs in the pond." She looked around. "Where do we start?"

"Wow. I almost forgot about that," Lucinda said. "Now it's swatting off frogs trying to kiss me. Roseanna said you have military in your blood, and plans to enlist—how exciting! You want to learn to shoot? We can do that after lunch, and start the chores tomorrow." She raised both eyebrows and grinned even wider while nodding.

Leticia had to chuckle. "I guess. Show me the way."

The memories Leticia had of the ranch were those of a child. Everything had seemed huge, an endless field of exploration from one of the older barns close to the main house to the creek at the edge of the property. She still had a scar extending from her left ankle to the knee from bouncing on two wires suspended between trees over a creek.

Lucinda had claimed they had always been there, probably some sort of property marker. They were rusted old things, completely unsafe but irresistible to a curious Leticia when she gave both a hard tug. A light rain was falling, but they seemed safe enough to cross. As she shuffled sideways, her foot slipped and metal cords ripped through denim and skin.

It felt worth the pain once they made it to the other side. She hobbled back to the main house, wincing yet feeling like a victor of sorts. Ramón had stayed in the barn that day reading a book and playing *Ages of Conquest* and *War Vol. II* on his hand-held game device.

One of her fondest memories was of Robert and Roseanna creating a large fire pit to roast marshmallows for Halloween. The scent of smoking meat from a grill had filled the air.

Today it was a normal farm, where play would be replaced with manual labor beginning at dawn on the weekends and once a week after school. She didn't mind. Only one more year before leaving Texas for what could be a very long time, especially if she traveled into space.

In the barn where they had played hide and seek among the hay bales, now there was a wall of reinforced locked metal cabinets roughly five feet high. Lucinda's eyes glittered as the doors opened to her handprint. The locker was filled with hunting knives, a crossbow, and several .22 rifles, 20-gauge shotguns, and a pair of pistols.

"It's nothing like the fancy stuff you'll get in the Marines," Lucinda said, sounding slightly envious. "We only keep what's needed to run the ranch. It's still good practice, though. Why don't I add you to the users? Put your hand here." Lucinda typed on the screen inside the cabinet then stepped aside for Leticia to scan her handprint. Once it had been recognized, she reached out to touch these weapons she had only seen, yet never held.

This was where her mother found her soul, Leticia mused, a sense of power and deep interest. These were also her companions in the final months of pregnancy, when she couldn't do rigorous training. Her expertise had blossomed, despite being shut away.

"Next weekend we should go camping," Lucinda suggested. "If you can survive with nothing but a knife and your wits."

Leticia shook off thoughts of her mother.

"Camping sounds fun," she said. "We've never done that. Ramón always had some bum excuse about needing to study or do this or that project, and Roseanna had to ferry him here and there to his different activities and study groups. But I thought this was a job," she added. "You're making it sound more like summer camp!"

"Damn, girl, we have a lot of catching up to do. There's something really empowering about going back to basics—and don't you worry about work. There's a lot to do all day."

There was a sound behind them, and Leticia looked to the open barn door. Avery stood there with a tray of coffees.

"Since it's the first day, let's take extra coffee breaks to get reacquainted," he said.

"Sounds good, as long as we can get to work tomorrow."

"Be careful what you ask for. We have to reinforce a temporary fence to keep the coyotes away, clear a patch of land for a new septic tank out by the horses, and paint the outside of an old barn at the far end of the main property. The horses have fancy new digs, and the smaller one will be converted to a type of studio. Pop is looking to hire someone to stay watch full time, to avoid thieves now that we're expecting foals and a few other new additions. He's finally broken down to put in a proper security system throughout the outer perimeter property. Those horses are as much his babies as we are. The coyotes are always trying their luck around the chickens, so the farthest ends of the fencing will be all electric. Will be good before lambing season, too."

"Let me guess," Leticia said, "he wants you guys to pitch in, just to teach you a little something he learned growing up."

"You got it." Lucinda rolled her eyes. "He says we won't appreciate what we don't work for. This is the 'legacy' he wants to leave to us. He can afford to hire a team to do everything, but he wants us to be 'involved.'"

Leticia nudged Lucinda's arm. "Well I'm not complaining, especially about getting paid."

"I'm glad someone is!" Avery chimed in. Standing there with coffee in hand, the three had a good giggle. Then Leticia took a sip, deep in thought.

"You mentioned coyotes. Do I need to worry about them? Will they attack?"

"No." Lucinda shook her head. "They're the least of our worries—but if you run across one, or a few, you have to give that animal respect. Same goes for wolves. It doesn't understand anything but territory, hunger, and survival. You make yourself as big as possible and maintain eye contact. No sudden moves as *you* get out of their way, very slowly."

"Good to know. If only people were that easy to understand."

Childhood memories of play fast forwarded to hard work. Each morning Leticia woke up to her phone alarm, and Roseanna drove her to the farm just as daylight was breaking. By the end of the day, she smelled of sweat, hay, splattered white paint, and horse feed.

At home the trees left blankets of leaves she had to blow into piles with the leaf blower strapped across her chest. This was something she also did on the Boone property.

It made her feel like she carried a flamethrower as the burnt orange and brown leaves flew into the air. Avery and Lucinda bagged them afterward.

It was peaceful on the farm. There was hardly any traffic on the road that ran along the perimeter. Occasionally she saw a truck go past, but it moved too slowly to be of any concern.

She loved visiting the horses, stroking their brown coats with taut muscles flexing and relaxing to her touch. When hauling and painting, her anxiety subsided and the future held less weight. Her mind gave way to the moment without worrying about what Ramón or other people in school were doing.

When they practiced shooting, Avery stood behind her and guided her aim at pumpkins, soda cans, and—even scarier—scarecrows. In the back of her mind, she knew that one day it might not be old clothing stuffed with hay standing before her. It might be a moving target of flesh-and-blood, intent on killing her.

At the same time, his breath on her ear and hands teaching her how to hit a bullseye affected her in ways she'd never experienced before. It caused inner confusion, because she couldn't tell if it was from the explosion caused by pulling a trigger, or the young man showing his affection for her day after day.

Good morning and *Good night* messages from Avery filled her phone. He gave her books on horses and shooting.

Leticia read at home, and practiced shooting at the

Boone farm, even when she wasn't scheduled for any work. Robert and Roseanna didn't mind. Ramón scarcely noticed, doing his own thing and making his money with his side hustle. He kept his bedroom door closed and a small whiteboard tucked away in his closet.

The small barn the farthest from the main house was looking good, given that neither Lucinda nor Leticia was a professional painter. Robert didn't want his place to be ostentatious, since so many had lost so much over the years. Keeping the farm simple was part of that plan.

Lucinda stepped out of the barn while Leticia rolled the last of the paint in her tray. Her body was tired from the work, satisfying as it was.

"I don't know about you, but I'm starving. Dad said Thai was fine, so I just put the order in."

Leticia stopped her rolling. "Will he be joining us?"

"Not sure. He said he was on his way home with Roseanna. I know it's early but damn it's getting dark fast." Leticia looked to the indigo sky deepening in hue by the minute, with a breeze kicking up without the sunshine.

"I know," she said. "It'll be the holidays before we know it."

Lucinda kneeled to replace the tops of the paint cans. "Let's get these inside. I'll soak the sponge brushes. Don't want to be out here when it's too dark, with the critters running around."

A single light in the barn provided illumination as they rushed through cleaning up.

"Right, looks like we're ready," Lucinda said. "Time for Thai and to see what's streaming on TV tonight." Leticia loved spending time with Lucinda. There was less pressure than with Avery, who made it no secret how he felt about her. She'd probably made a mistake by making out with him when no one was watching, but what could the harm be in a little fun?

"I'm not going to bother locking it," Lucinda said as she closed the barn door behind her. "Nothing in there anyone wants." They walked briskly with the half-moon overhead and stars coming in and out of view with the gathering clouds. "Hear that?"

Leticia didn't want to stop for the sounds of the nocturnal animals that lurked in the trees nearby.

"Foxes mating. There might be a few coyotes on the prowl, too."

Leticia shivered, only partly because she was wearing a thin long-sleeve T-shirt. The fall leading into winter in Texas was pleasant during the day, sometimes hot. The night brought cooler temperatures.

"I'm too chilly to stop and listen."

Lucinda was no longer by her side. She stood in the muddy road, patting her body.

"Shit. I forgot my phone. I need to run back. You go on ahead. The food will be here soon, and I'm hungry."

"You sure?"

Lucinda was already skipping backward. "I've never been attacked by a coyote! Not once."

Leticia shook her head and continued to walk. The sounds of the night were natural, had been there long before any of them. Still the unknown of the darkness, like deep space triggered fear. She looked back again, expecting to see Lucinda running toward her. Nothing. The light in the barn was still on. The longer she walked in the dark the more nervous she felt.

A coyote howled in the distance. Her mind began to wander. She glanced back again. The larger barn near the house was just a few feet ahead. She took out her phone and dialed Lucinda's number. After two rings it shut off. She stopped in her tracks to think about what that meant, and what to do. Then she broke out into a jog before sliding open the door and running straight for the gun cabinet.

A small pistol. Surely nothing more would be needed to calm her nerves or shoo away an animal, but that didn't make sense with the phone. She locked the cabinet and jogged back to the small nearly white barn. No Lucinda in sight, and her friend wasn't the pranking type.

Her heart began to beat faster than her feet. As she approached, the light from the barn showed dried tire tracks in the mud. She had noticed them the previous day.

Her head jerked to the side as she heard a crash from inside, and she knew something was wrong. She had to be smart about this, and approached the door with caution.

There was a muffled voice that was not Lucinda. With a heaving chest she threw the door open with one hand, then rushed inside with both hands back on her pistol.

A skinny guy with dirty jeans and boots was fastening tape around Lucinda's mouth. Her feet and hands were bound. Two paint cans were tipped over and oozing white paint across the floor.

Leticia swallowed hard. She had never been in a situation like this, real fear standing in front of her, shaking her to her soul. But to show that fear would only be used against her.

"Take your fucking hands off her."

The guy stepped away from Lucinda. His hands were dusty, with nails caked with dirt. He smelled of hay and manure... and horse feed.

"What are you going to do, little girl? Maybe I need to show you what you need, to be a woman. An extra lesson... for both of you."

Leticia's arms began to tremble. Part of her wished Avery was here, but at the same time, just because a man was by your side didn't promise safety. She had figured the intruder would back off, with a gun pointed at his face. Instead, he took a step forward with his left hand on his belt buckle. His greasy hair was tied into a short ponytail. His smile looked like he chewed tobacco.

What would Jenette do?

You're a Vasquez woman.

A soldadera.

"You want to try me, motherfucker?" Leticia cocked the pistol. "I said step away from her, and take your hands off your buckle. Nobody wants to see your pinkie finger. Not that there's anything to see."

"That's a dirty mouth, little girl. I'm gonna wash it out with my—" As he reached to the back of his jeans, Leticia fired three shots toward the ground. Two bullets hit his left foot and the other the floor. He cried out and collapsed into the paint, dropping the Bowie knife he'd pulled from his waist.

Her breathing and heart seemed to be in sync with the gunfire. The fear evaporated with the lightness of gun smoke. It felt like the most natural thing in the world to pull the trigger.

"Next time I'll aim higher."

He lifted his face, half covered in dripping paint, toward her as he groaned in pain. Both his hands clutched his bleeding foot. Half of the spilled white paint was now tinted to pink. Leticia kept her gun aimed at him while slowly making her way to the knife. With one foot she slid it closer to her and picked it up.

She kept her aim to his face.

"I'm bleeding bad," he said. "You have to help me. You'll go to prison for this. Who do you think they'll believe?"

"You'll survive, you piece of shit," she said. "I promise you that. You *will* pay for this."

He looked at her with a fury that filled her with fear and a matching animosity. Is this what the world would look like? Combat? Until now her world had been sheltered. It made her think of what her mother might have experienced.

Lucinda already had her hands lifted for Leticia to slice through the tape. The knife was sharp enough to cut through with ease. Once free Lucinda removed the tape to her mouth and cut her legs free. She reached for her phone. As they waited for emergency services to answer, Robert and Roseanna came running through the barn. Robert held a shotgun. His eyes went wide as he pointed his weapon at the bleeding intruder, still holding his foot.

Roseanna ran to Leticia's side. She still aimed the pistol. A single tear rolled down her face.

"Leticia, are you okay?"

"I'm fine, but it's a good thing you showed up, because he might not be."

Roseanna lowered Leticia's quivering arm. "You got him, mija. There are four of us and one of him."

Sirens wailed in the distance. Lucinda moved to Leticia's side.

"Thank you," she said. "You're going to be the best of the best."

Leticia turned to Lucinda and gave her a tight hug. "I'm glad you're alright."

"How did you know to come back?"

"I saw a truck passing by the farm for the past few days, but it's been going slow. Too slow. It held us up the other day on our way here. I thought I'd sound silly if I mentioned it. Then earlier in the day I noticed tracks outside the fencing. None of us have been driving around here. Something felt off when you didn't come running out. I called your phone. I don't know... I ran as fast as I could to the barn and back."

"Watch out, Marines, there is a new colonel in town," Lucinda said as she slapped Leticia gently on the back.

Leticia had to crack a smile. "We will see. I feel like I'm ready for anything, because I really don't know anything. There is a whole other world—and worlds—out there."

An officer entered the barn with his gun out. Something about him was strange. He looked at Robert, who wore a tracksuit and sneakers, then the intruder who lay on the floor bleeding. The guy shrieked with a cracked voice.

"That little whore shot me, and this big asshole would've done worse."

"Whore?" Leticia lunged toward the man "Who's lying on their back? Not me, cabron."

Robert lowered the shotgun to his side. "There was some sort of incident, officer," he said. "I'm just protecting my own. This is my farm, and I have no idea who this man is with my underage daughter and her friend. We arrived home when I heard shouting, then the gunshots."

The officer, who had no name tag, kneeled next to the intruder, removed a handheld device from his front pocket, and scanned the man's face.

"Sir, do not try to persuade me with any bias you may

have," he said. "I am an android programmed to uphold the law. According to this, you are a known criminal and match the description of someone sought in other robberies in the county. I will get you the medical assistance you need. However, I will not tolerate any more obscenities from you. You are under arrest, and I will now read you your Miranda Rights."

"The fuck?" The intruder moved his head from Leticia to Robert. "What is this country coming to?"

More sirens wailed in the distance. Another officer and a paramedic arrived.

"You may all go into your residence," the first officer said. "Once the criminal is secure, I will take a statement. Thank you."

Roseanna nodded and placed her arm around Leticia.

"Robert, girls. Let's go. I'll put on some tea and hot chocolate."

Two days later Leticia and Avery sat on the top of a round hay bale, watching the sun set. In the clear sky of lavender and pink the moon was a glowing crescent. The tree line of barren branches stretched toward the sky like claws attempting to choke the heavens.

Whenever Leticia looked to the sky, she thought of her family. It was a nice distraction from the realization that she had been prepared to take the life of another human, without a second thought. She still saw his paint-covered face and the fury in his eyes. That moment haunted her—the lack of remorse for injuring him after he threatened her. Then the sense of power welling inside, knowing she could. The deep sense of satisfaction knowing she could do whatever it took to survive. It scared her.

"So you are really set on going up there?"

"After I smash all my goals here, yeah. I'd like to go out there."

"I have to admit, going up there doesn't appeal to me at all. I don't want this place to fall into the wrong hands when my dad is older. He and Roseanna won't be young, or here forever."

Leticia knew this. It weighed on her, but she couldn't ignore the wind chime that blew her passion farther afield. Roseanna would never dream of holding her back, either. Still, part of her wanted to give back to Roseanna what she had given to her and Ramón.

When Leticia didn't respond, Avery spoke again. "No way I could convince you to stay in Texas? I mean why would anyone want to leave?" He chuckled and playfully pressed his arm into hers. "There are androids and machinery for everything now. I guess my dad wanted to teach us how to get on without any of that—you never know when the lights might go out." She still didn't answer, so he continued. "I like the idea of having my feet firmly planted on land I own. Hopefully grow the farm, then maybe grow some babies."

Leticia turned to him with a quizzical look.

"Not now!" he protested. "Later for sure… with the right woman. We'll work as a team in business and in life."

"I'm all about the team, Avery, but I want to play up there." Leticia shivered, now that the sun was nearly past the horizon.

"Why don't we go in, and I'll make you dinner."

"Avery…"

"No, I insist."

Leticia leaned toward Avery and kissed him on the cheek. His eagerness and attention were flattering, almost intoxicating. This sensation of young love was as soft as lamb's wool with the awkwardness of a foal's first steps. He was strong, yet tender with good looks and a good soul. She knew she had to tread carefully, to not break his heart.

"Hey, I just want to thank you for showing me the ropes with shooting," she said. "It felt good to have control over a situation that could have been very, very bad."

"No problem. It's all you—you're a natural. Guess that's why you might make a good Marine one day. It's in your blood."

1 1

An entire year passed with the slowness of a pregnancy. Her time helping out at the farm was done soon after the incident. Roseanna only worked mornings so she could be there in the afternoons for her and Ramón. Once a week she led an AA meeting. Robert paid for an android to stand watch and a security system throughout the entire farm, to be installed without delay.

Leticia was still welcome to shoot side by side with Lucinda, and they took camping trips out to Big Bend for hiking. When not at the farm she pored over the Marine Corps and Raiders training videos.

Her high school friends busied themselves with studying for exams and applying to college. They still took the time to gossip in class or wander the halls, but there was a sense of needing to have a plan in place well before graduation. Leticia took up any opportunity to push herself physically on Roseanna's three acres or on the Boone farm.

She felt awful about turning down Avery's advances, but she didn't love him. Sure, he looked impossibly cute feeding baby goats with a bottle, and attended to all her needs. He was one sexy vaquero. However, it was telling that in their many conversations he often led with, "Things don't always go to plan... but life with me on the ranch is a sure thing. You'll be safe."

He didn't mean it maliciously and maybe he was right, but safe wasn't what she wanted. She owed it to herself to find out in her own time and way what was truly meant for her.

The niggle to get more ink cropped up with every time she passed the altar, the statue of Santa Muerte catching her eye in the glow of the candle flames. Roseanna's response when she asked her was simply to put her hands up.

"It's your body, and you are nearly eighteen. You need to know how to listen to your inner voice and do what is right and good for you. Your choices are your own."

Wearing a black bandana like a head band, Leticia went to the same tattoo parlor that smelled of incense. It reminded her of the woody and fragrant palo santo Roseanna burned every full and new moon when she did her limpias. Lucinda followed her in.

The tattoo artist Brandy greeted her with gloved hands. "Good to see you again," she said with a wide smile. "I appreciate you going for the hand of an artist, instead of a machine. You ready?"

"If it's done by a machine," Leticia replied, "can it be considered art?"

Brandy threw up one hand. "Never was one for philosophy. I'm just doing what I love. Glad there's still enough work for me to keep going."

"And that's why I am here." Leticia removed her shirt, then leaned into a chair face forward. She pulled the bandana tight around her shoulder-length brown hair to create a ponytail, then used bobby pins to secure the rest in a bun. Settling in place, she put in her ear buds. Metallica would have to get her through the next few hours of patience and excruciating pain.

Lucinda found a seat along the wall, and did the same.

Brandy laid an imprint of Santa Muerte that covered most of her back. It was what Leticia wanted before joining the Marines. This tattoo was an act of faith, seeing and believing it would happen. Santa Muerte was the saint of death, depicted as a skeleton in long luxurious robes, associated with the afterlife and protection. The needle glided across her back with little pain to start, until Brandy had to double back and fill in the image. Then Leticia maintained her breathing, and the music helped her focus on thoughts of getting through bootcamp, the elation of reaching the goal.

It would happen. It *had* to happen.

Santa Muerte had her back, after all.

* * *

Leticia returned home with most of the tattoo complete. All that remained were the red roses at the feet of Santa Muerte, and they would be done another time. The Eagles played in the background and Roseanna took pizzas out of the oven.

"Hey, great timing," she said. "I have a few things for you. Have a look on the table, then show me the ink."

On the kitchen table sat a cowboy boot shoe box, with a rattlesnake on the front beneath a leather boot. Its fangs dripped with venom. The picture gave her the chills. She quickly removed the top and began to pull out each item with care, one by one. A collection of different colored bandanas, photographs, an old Bruce Springsteen *Born in the USA* T-shirt. "Dancing in the Dark" had been Jenette's favorite song, she knew. Leticia brought the T-shirt to her nose to detect any memory of scent. Nothing but fabric softener.

She still held it close to her chest.

"This means so much to me. Thank you."

"She would be proud of you. Your grades, your hard work on the ranch and dedication to getting into the Marines."

Leticia turned around. "Here. Careful when you lift the T-shirt. Lucinda laughed at me the entire way because I sat hunched over, not wanting to rub off the covering."

Gingerly Roseanna lifted the shirt, and gasped.

"Mija, it's beautiful. I can't wait until you get the roses done. Nobody better fuck with you. They would have to answer to a Vasquez woman with Santa Muerte on her back."

The doorbell rang. "Already? I thought we could shove a few slices down first."

Leticia walked toward the door. "I don't think this will take long."

A tall man stood in the doorway, carrying a large bag. "I take it you are my victim tonight."

Leticia couldn't hold back her laughter as she pulled out the pins and hair tie that secured her long brown locks.

"I am. We have hot pizza first."

"I love pizza."

After dinner Roseanna stood next to Leticia while she sat in their living room with Bernard, a friend of Roseanna's from the rehab center. Leticia held up a photo of her mother, from when she ran with the Las Calaveras. Bernard looked at the photo, then Leticia.

"That's pretty short, but you have your mother's bone structure," he said. "She's beautiful. You can pull it off. I get a lot of people chopping off their hair and regretting it. Takes time to grow back. Are you sure about this?"

"How else are people going to see all this beautiful art on my body?" Leticia replied. "And I don't want to mess with it during basic training. Do it. *El riesgo siempre vive.*"

The long strands fell to her lap with the ease of a snake shedding skin. Leticia felt lighter, a little closer to her destination, even if it was still uncertain. She had to do something to keep the faith in what she wanted more than anything. When the floor was covered with silky brown threads, he brought a mirror to her face.

"You're ready for what comes next," he said. "No hair to keep you weighed down or get tangled in some helmet."

Leticia ran her left hand across her head to the nape of her neck.

"Ready to settle unfinished business."

She showered to catch the rest of the remnants of fallen hair, then sat at the white desk she and Roseanna had found at Bussey's Flea Market one Saturday morning. Together they had sanded it down and painted it. That was a project she loved doing.

The application for the Colonial Marine Corps was open on her tablet, and nearly complete. This was it. She hoped it would be enough to get past the first hurdle— to not just be a grunt, but part of the elite. The Raiders. Leticia brushed her fingertips across the switchblade that had belonged to her mother. Perhaps the sharp end would point her in the direction of her destiny.

The front door slammed.

Leticia looked at the time. Roseanna was already in bed reading. She walked out to find Ramón appearing disheveled. He stopped as he inspected her new look. There was a startled sadness in his eye.

"Now they *have* to let you into the Marines. You look just like her."

Leticia could see something peeking from his T-shirt

collar. She walked closer to him and pulled it down slightly, but he jerked away.

"You and that boy's mother?"

He continued to stare at her haircut and face.

"What I do is none of your business."

"Ramón, we are the age of consent, and you can do whatever you want, with whomever you want, but that's evidence. Don't be leaving proof of the ways you make money, besides tutoring some kid."

His eyes went large. "Leticia…"

"No, I won't snitch, but keep yourself clean. And if you want to hide that thing, then I'll give you my foundation."

He touched his neck. "Thanks."

Leticia turned to walk away, hoping he could see the outline of her tattoo beneath her nightshirt.

"¡Mijo! Congratulations."

Ramón's face glowed as he wolfed down his plate of brisket, potato salad, cornbread, and pinto beans.

"You better eat up," Leticia said, "because I bet they won't have barbecue that good at the Harvard cafeteria."

"Early admission. Full scholarship." Roseanna beamed. "That's amazing, Ramón."

"Once I'm done with undergrad I'm not stopping until I have my MBA." For once his face appeared devoid of tension. He didn't seem distracted at all as he sat with them. "They have an amazing, combined program."

"You have it all figured out, bro." Leticia tried hard to smile and be happy for him, but the piercing switchblade of self-doubt stabbed at her from the inside. "That's excellent."

"Yes, I do. I'm going to be everything past generations could not or *did* not have the fortitude to achieve."

"Be nice, Ramón." Roseanna gave him a stern look. "You'll see what it's like when you get there. Life is not black-and-white."

"Whatever it takes, tía." His gaze, the dark determination, was more dangerous than the tip of a blade. It had an inky blackness that swallowed instead of pierced. Leticia couldn't prevent herself from feeling anxious.

"I think I'm done eating," she said. "Going to go check on the chickens and take a walk."

"Okay, mija. There is dessert for later." Roseanna gave her a reassuring look and smile. She always knew when to let her go, and she knew not hearing from the Marines yet was bringing her lower as each day passed without a sniff of news.

Leticia wandered behind the house to the pond. She loved it there. The body of water was surrounded by large reeds and hundred-year-old oak trees. Lily pads and ducks floated without awareness of anything greater outside of the pond. What always struck her, though, was the symmetrical reflection of the sky above—clouds, sun, or moon. The heavens were brought to Earth.

However, that was just an illusion, a reflection of what could be. She wanted to *be* up there, soaring with her own accomplishments and exploration.

Leticia was happy for Ramón, she really was, but it also stung, like a light drizzle of fire falling on her bare skin. Everyone was receiving news, except her. It was like waiting for food while starving, and watching everyone's order coming up. Her body was tense, ready to grab the brown bag and devour its contents. The aroma filled the air, making it even worse.

The waiting.

Then there was the fact that this was it. She had no plan B, C, or D. She couldn't imagine living the life on a ranch with Avery. Sure, he would be devoted to her, but she didn't want children. She wanted the stars and wonder, to push the limitations of her own being. Maybe up there she would feel the presence of the parents she never knew.

She wasn't "better" than ranch life, but deep inside she knew a different destiny awaited her. From the moment she had pressed *submit*, she'd lit each seven-day candle until it was a smoking pool of drool with nothing left to burn. Nothing to show for the waiting but empty glass tarnished with soot.

There was nothing worse than waiting.

Unfortunately, the next part of her journey was completely out of her control. She knew her ship would come in. But when?

And how to keep the bitterness at bay?

* * *

Graduation came and went. She sat in the crowd watching her brother accept top honors, beaming with pride as he gave his Valedictorian speech. Leticia *was* proud, though not as proud as a cheering and crying Roseanna.

As her friends and other students walked the stage, she continued to hold on to hope that the message would arrive soon—otherwise they would run out of seven-day candles. Joslene and Nadia were both heading to the west coast. Avery and Lucinda going to A&M in College Station for their agriculture program. Leticia stood in the waiting line for her name to be called.

And it sucked.

There was one unread message.

It had been there when Leticia woke up. Her finger hovered over it. It would be a moment of celebration, or a moment of she didn't know what would happen next. All the drive and passion in her soul was consumed with achieving this dream that was bigger than her.

During her research she had seen the faces of the women who went missing during military training, or during their service. Their families given bullshit excuses when they pressed for answers. Cases of harassment, abuse, rape, real horrors. But nothing ever changed if there *was* no change. The cost was high for those trying to make it happen, and those trying to keep it. That was the struggle for power.

Her mother fought to take back her power, and to a certain extent she did so during her short career. Now was Leticia's time. Her chest became tight as she could feel tears welling in her eyes. She sat up in bed and tapped the message.

Scanned the screen.

Her entire body trembled as she burst into sobs. The building energy of fear, worry, resentment, jealousy, the toxins created by waiting and impatience all coming to the surface to be released.

"Mama!" she screamed into the room still dark.

Roseanna came bursting through the door.

"Leticia? Are you alright? What's wrong!"

She couldn't speak. All the wind, the howling storms of self-doubt finally lifting. She handed the tablet to Roseanna.

"Oh my God! Thank the spirits! You! You did it, mija!" Roseanna wrapped her arms around Leticia. "Let me make you the best breakfast. I'm so proud of you. But more importantly, be proud of yourself."

"Forget cooking. I want barbacoa, chorizo, and egg, and bean and cheese tacos from The Donut Shop! Extra tomatillo salsa."

"You got it. Let me go put on a pot of coffee."

Leticia sat in bed, feeling as light as a paper lantern or ash floating into the sky. However, it was real now. It was the beginning of a long journey filled with trials and tests. As a

Marine she would be part of a greater cause, but there still would be competition. She had to prepare herself to lean on no one but herself. If her mother could do it, then she could.

As ecstatic as she was to start this new chapter, she couldn't help the clouds of sadness blowing inside. Roseanna had been a strong mother figure to her, the only mother she knew in the flesh. She had always been her rock. To get through basic training and survive becoming a Raider, she would have to be her own rock, all the pressure and time making her into a diamond.

Roseanna brought her breakfast on a tray and placed it on her desk.

"Here. I'll let you eat while you respond to the acceptance letter and fill out the rest of the forms."

Leticia gave Roseanna a tight hug, though to be honest she wanted to be alone. It was so overwhelming. After finishing her tacos down to the last piece of shredded beef, she made her way to the backyard. There she twisted and cut a fallen section of chicken wire in the fencing that surrounded the small vegetable patch. The work helped her untangle her emotions, and it would be something nice to do for her tía.

"Looks good. Thank you." Roseanna approached her while surveying the ground. One of her palms was closed. Leticia put the fencing down and wiped her sweaty neck with her T-shirt.

"It will be one less thing for you to worry about, or at least Robert," Leticia joked.

"I have something for you, mija. You weren't as excited as I thought you would be during breakfast. I know it's a big moment bringing up so many thoughts, fears, and emotions." Roseanna opened her palm. There was a gold cross on a gold-linked chain. She placed it around Leticia's neck. "Your mother died with the one that belonged to your grandmother, but this one belonged to our father, and it was passed on from Seraphin. It belongs to you now."

"Are you sure?" Leticia touched the chain. "You always wear this."

"Yes. Let it remind you that we are each one of those links. Our memories, pain, hope, and blood. In the end it all comes full circle because we are connected. Unfinished business in this life or the next. Where one generation cannot, the other strives for more and is capable of more because we *demand* more from ourselves and others. Hold your head high, mujer."

Leticia threw her arms around Roseanna. "I love you so much."

Her aunt returned the embrace. "Before you leave I was hoping you would do the temazcal with me, and a shaman I know. Just a little something to deepen your journey. The temazcal has been used by the ancestors for centuries, even before boats landed on the shores of what is now Mexico. Every time I step into that little limestone hut, I find clarity."

Leticia took a step away, giving her a suspicious look. "What will I see, you think?"

"I don't know. Whatever the spirit world or your subconscious is trying to tell you."

Leticia thought about it for a moment, then replied, "I'll do it. I want to *see*."

"Great. PJ has reserved an afternoon spot for us tomorrow."

Christopher Orozco lived half an hour away. He had been a curandero for fifteen years. Aside from his usual blessings, handmade candles, barridas, and advice, he had built a temazcal in his backyard. He brought lava stones back from Mexico and placed them inside the small, adobe hut to create the steam. His clients who tried it once always returned. It was better than any sauna. The guidance and re-centering they experienced was enough confirmation to reveal that they had to follow through.

Leticia and Roseanna sat cross-legged on a floor covered in sand, wearing their bathing suits and towels. PJ had to squat as he poured water on the stones.

"The best advice I can give you is focus on the moment you are in. If the mind is chattering, playing tricks on you, focus on your breath. Not just here in this place, but for any situation you find yourself in. You will be tested, Leticia. Be true to your breath because it comes from inside of you."

White clouds of hot vapor filled the small space. Leticia closed her eyes and could feel herself drifting as the heat of the steam took over her mind. Droplets of sweat landed on her folded legs, reminding her of the tears she had cried, not understanding why both her parents were gone.

"They say the ancestors are never far from us," the curandero said. "They act as guides to help us reach our full potential and correct broken generational paths, some predestined by the organization of the particles of dust that created everything. Each one a miniature dream that created a bigger one we lived in and on, and swam in."

Leticia's body lost all its weight as she was pulled through the darkness of space and back in time. High in the sky a cold disk, what looked like a planet, took shape. She could see the Aztec goddess Coyolxauhqui, her body in severed pieces slain by her brother, the god of war. It was a story she read about many times in the books Roseanna owned. The ancient tales of Mexico before it was called Mexico.

He shook a shaman's rattle, and the hypnotic rhythm bordered on a monstrous hiss as it carried her deeper into a lucid dream world.

Leticia shuddered, her joints ached. The hiss of the rattle and sizzling hot stones filled her head. The sweat falling from her body became viscous, no longer the tears of her mother but coming from the jaws of something waiting in the dark. In her mind she moved closer to the disk of the ancient goddess flung into the sky with veins, bone, and ligaments hanging from shredded flesh. Instinctively she brought her arms toward her face in protection as she crashed through a veil of blood and the thick atmosphere of whatever planet she approached.

Drums pounded, or was it her heartbeat thumping in her ribcage? Something wanted to emerge, to crack her wide open. She clutched her chest and opened her eyes. Lying on a stone altar below her was a large alabaster body split from the jugular notch to the bottom of the sternum. In her hand was a large blade. The open cavity of the body was a pool of black liquid. It wasn't human, even if the form vaguely resembled one.

Drums, the drums of war rang in her head.

Creatures cloaked in shadow and humanoids like the one in front of her fought at the foot of the pyramid where she stood. She watched the carnage of white flesh and creatures that resembled armored dragons moving with the speed of hungry locusts. Screams and shrieks rose above the fight to where she stood.

She looked into an obsidian pool of blood that resembled a scrying mirror. Within she could just see her reflection, but there was something else. The hiss. The hair on her body standing up and the shadow rising behind her in the reflection. Leticia slowly turned to face one of the creatures from the foot of the pyramid. It lunged toward her.

She screamed and lifted her blade to fight.

* * *

"Leticia! Leticia, it's okay. You're safe!" Roseanna wiped her neck and shook her out of her stupor. Leticia touched her chest, and then removed the bandana around her forehead. The cloth made her think of the Aztec warriors in their cotton armor. She wasn't the broken woman. She would survive, and do what others in her family could not do.

This meant something.

She could feel it growing inside of her, and only time would tell.

"What was any of that?" she asked.

"Facing your demon, yourself," the curandero replied. "All the parts no one sees, like the secret shame we all carry. Perhaps also signs of the future."

"I don't know if I can do it."

"You can," Roseanna said firmly. "Let me tell you a story. Before you were brought to me, I went out with a group of friends, ready to stay sober, but those old habits creeped up on me, the anxiety that sometimes wraps me up in a cocoon of death. I drank so much I fell asleep on my bedroom floor. I woke up in the middle of the night and vomited everywhere. Still drunk, I could feel myself choking on the undigested food.

"I sat there on the floor crying for help, beating myself up. All I could think of was if I died, where would that leave you and your brother when you arrived? Or myself? I wanted to live, and dedicated myself to change. That night I had let my fears get the best of me, so I drank until

I couldn't see my reflection. I fucked up, and put the hard work in to not do that again."

"I'm so sorry, tía," Leticia said, her voice low. "You have to know you have been amazing all these years."

"I was so ashamed," Roseanna answered. "Been sober ever since. Don't ever underestimate the power of unfinished business."

PART 3

OBSTACLES

1 2

"She wants us to do *what*?" Dr. Moon shook her head, her mouth open wide as she stared at her companion. "They really don't give a damn..."

Dr. Patel stared back, her gaze devoid of expression. "I mean, aren't you a little curious? Plus, we don't pay ourselves. This is what we signed up for—and I rather *they* be in there than us."

"So the science project will be in charge of the science project... great." She glared. "Why was I not informed before? This is *my* gig."

Her expression turning sheepish, Patel looked off. "Most likely because of this reaction," she said. "Look, we have to go now. It's happening whether you like it or not."

The two scientists walked from Brenda's office to the elevator on the opposite side of the hallway. They remained silent as they descended to the facilities reserved for the research requiring the most security.

The viewing room for Lab 10 wasn't far from the elevator. It was the largest and most secure research room in the facility—and they would need it. The large rectangular one-way glass was the only barrier that separated Brenda from the thing she feared and hated the most, yet was the key to everything she ever wanted to accomplish.

She hated the Xenomorph.

And the heartless creature that was Weyland-Yutani even more.

Three synthetic technicians stood beneath bright lights, observing two human bodies—one male, the other female. None of the androids spoke a word. One of them, Natasha, typed on a tablet, her eyes shifting periodically to the bodies.

Moon studied her own tablet. At first glance, the inside of the male appeared as if the cardiovascular system had morphed into a black overgrown tangle of jungle vines. Viscous slime seeped from every orifice, including the incision from the top of the neck to the pelvis. Sticky pools of the stuff formed on the floor. They quivered as smaller larvae and eggs began hatching.

The parasites had eaten through every morsel of flesh until the skin and skeleton were the only things left intact. The hybrids that combined Xenomorphs with *Taenia solium*—the pork tapeworm—squirmed and violently whipped their tails. Miniature jaws snapped at other parasites, competing for scraps of sinew, tiny fangs scratching into bone.

The other body appeared somewhat normal. However,

the female human was still alive, with her chest rising and falling as she breathed. One of the androids stepped toward the sleeping woman and took her temperature, then pulled down the sheet to uncover her distended belly. Her flesh rippled.

Though unconscious, she winced and one hand moved to her abdomen.

Brenda gasped. "What is inside of her?" She peered at her tablet.

Patel took a deep breath. "The synths suggested that the female body could carry the parasites for longer before expiring. We call them Xenosites. It also takes longer before any visible signs manifest."

Brenda clenched her jaw. She knew for certain she was going to pay for this and dreaded the moment that would arise, when she would be forced to make a decision between right and wrong. She glanced toward Gilda, who was staring at the mirrored window. The woman smiled, but it wasn't pleasant or friendly, and Brenda imagined it was sheer delight.

We are the experiment, and always will be, Brenda thought to herself.

2190

Ramón stood out of a crowd—especially here—and he knew it. Tall, with dark brown skin and thick black hair.

His teeth were perfectly straight because Roseanna led an Alcoholics Anonymous group that included a dentist she knew well. He gave her a huge discount. In middle school it was an inconvenience, but now whenever he smiled and spoke, people looked and listened.

Being the smartest and best-looking was always a plus when in a place where everyone had out-earned you for generations. Sure, Roseanna never struggled to provide, but he had never seen so much concentrated wealth, saturating everything from the cars driven by the freshmen to the accommodation upgrades.

Whenever he passed a watch shop, he promised himself his first would be a Rolex. Then a sleek Porsche. He would never be caught driving some hooptie around like a vato out of the hood. The shoes and suits would be bespoke Italian. Eventually the right woman to give him children to inherit the empire he would run.

His tía often talked about the power of intention, and his was crystal clear.

The Vasquez name would carry weight.

Ramón sat in the third row of the small auditorium. Not too close, but not in the back where he might miss anything. He'd lost any desire to look cool back when he was a freshman in high school.

"Hey." A young man slid next to him. "Nice to see you again." Ramón recognized him from the dorms—he'd moved in across the hall the day Ramón had arrived. The memory stuck because he brought in three monitors of the latest design, explaining that they were meant for trading. It wasn't unusual for corporations to begin cherry picking early.

"I'm Luke Grant," he added. "Since we're neighbors, I might be asking you for notes once in a while."

"Sure thing. Ramón." He knew an opportunity when he saw one. "I specialize in providing notes, helping people get the grades... the ones they deserve, of course." Luke's dorm was filled with the newest tech and his watch a Patek Philippe.

"Whoa." He nudged Ramón's arm with his elbow and pointed toward the entrance. "That's Mary Anne Kramer. What a body—and she's insanely rich. Banking family." The woman Luke indicated scanned for a seat, and caught Ramón's gaze. As she climbed the short steps, Luke leaned closer. "Damn, she's heading this way. Might have to try my moves... later."

Mary Anne chose a desk two seats away from Ramón. He gave her a shy smile and looked away to avoid appearing as thirsty as Luke. She *was* pretty, though with features that were pleasant enough not to be distracting, and dressed well. Hazel eyes and wavy strawberry blond hair cut to just above her shoulders. From this distance he could smell her light fragrance of vanilla and maybe cherry blossom.

Luke probably had a million Mary Annes, and she was probably used to a million Lukes trying to get into her panties. Ramón looked straight ahead, determined not to give her any more obvious attention.

For the next hour the professor droned on about grades, attendance expectations, and the breakdown of the Philosophy course he would be teaching. Before it was done, Ramón decided he wanted to know more about this girl, and he wasn't going to leave anything to chance. Halfway through the class he took a sip from his water bottle and placed it on the empty desk between them.

At the end of the hour, he got up to leave.

"I think you're forgetting something."

Ramón turned around, giving her his full attention.

"Oh, thank you. I'm Ramón," he said coolly. "And you are?"

"Mary Anne. It's nice to meet you."

"It's nice to meet you," he replied. "I'll see you next week."

He turned and headed toward the stairs. Best to leave her wanting more. Luke's reaction was of pure disbelief.

The following week she took the seat next to Ramón and smiled as she sat down. He'd already decided to ask her out for coffee, but not for a couple of weeks. Until then, he would give her just enough attention to keep her coming to him.

She wore a lavender mohair sweater that showed only a hint of cleavage at the top opal button. Her lipstick was pale pink, and she wore minimal mascara to cover her light brown eyelashes.

He paid for the coffee, but showing an impressive amount of class, she offered to pay her portion. Although she came from a wealthy banking family, and ticked all his boxes for the perfect partner, she had a mild-mannered demeanor and didn't appear to be overly ambitious.

She didn't need to be. The Kramer family's wealth had been there for generations. Mary Anne could pursue any career she chose without worry of pay, as long as it fulfilled her, and expressed the hope to raise the next generation of Kramers. But he wasn't looking to be the husband of a Kramer. He wanted a woman who would be the wife of a Vasquez.

After their coffee date they walked back to the entrance of her dorm, and he kissed her on the cheek. With both hands she pulled his face to hers and kissed him on the lips.

"Next time let me cook dinner," she said. "Sorry, though—it will have to be in the communal kitchen."

"I would like that."

He left, feeling settled in pursuing Mary Anne, and confident that he would succeed.

With that decided, he had to turn his attention to other, more tangible concerns. Although he had a scholarship that covered his tuition, and had saved a substantial amount in high school, he relied heavily on credit to pay for the costs of living. At times, the rate he went through the cash alarmed him.

The day was approaching when he would need to find a job.

Julia Yutani entered the Modern History class late, and showed no concern over how much noise she made. He was fascinated from the start—she was the opposite of Mary Anne. Julia's sharp tongue and dark eyes captivated him, though he couldn't escape the fear that he might end up "that guy with the famous woman."

Even so, a relationship with her could be very... advantageous.

He knew she was interested, as well, when they received their grades for an essay that would account for a large portion of class credit. Julia leaned over to peer at his tablet.

"Smart and sexy," she said. "You'll be first pick on my team, any day."

He pulled the tablet away and leaned in close, focusing on her eyes.

"Do you make it a point to be nosy?"

She matched his gaze. "I make it a point to be just what I am, and just what I want to be," she replied. "Why hide or fight it?" Then she added, "I'd wager you feel the same way. I'll bet you want to know what everyone in this room got, so you can zero in on the ones you'll have to beat for the top spot."

That captivated him all the more—here was a woman

who knew she wasn't a hundred percent good, but didn't care. She had teeth, and was willing to use them to get what she wanted out of the short experience called life.

Unlike the one with Mary Anne, his relationship with Julia wasn't entirely in his control, and it took months to move it to the next level—but he was determined to have them both. Each woman served a purpose in the grand plan he had for his life. A plan that included money and power.

Toward the end of the semester, a handful of students met at Julia's place—a nicely accustomed two-bedroom apartment near campus—for a group project.

"I have to throw you all out now," she announced. "It's ten, and I have to be up and out by six a.m. Believe me when I say I won't miss any of you after we graduate." With that Julia began to usher everyone out. Ramón gathered his things, but she motioned for him to stop.

"Ramón, I hate to ask, but do you mind hanging back and helping me clean up these bottles and delivery boxes?" She indicated the items that had piled up on her kitchen counter.

He could tell it was an excuse. They'd been exchanging glances all evening and she'd made a point of saying that she had someone coming the first thing in the morning, to clean the place top-to-bottom and pick up her laundry. It was an extravagance he couldn't afford.

"Of course," he said. "My first class is later in the day tomorrow, so there's no need to rush off."

"You don't need to run to… what's her name?"

He stopped in front of her, holding two Corona empties between the fingers of each hand. It shouldn't have shocked him that she knew about Mary Anne—he'd done his own research, and knew she currently was unattached.

"Where do you want these?"

She stepped closer, wrapping her arms around his waist. She was a full foot shorter than he, so she craned her neck to face him.

"I see. Come here, guapa." He dropped the bottles to the carpeted floor and grabbed her around the waist to pull her closer, kissing her mouth with a sexual aggressiveness she returned in kind. Both of his hands slipped into the back of her jeans to squeeze her ass beneath her panties. Her mouth released a sigh and a moan.

"Come to bed, Ramón," she purred between kisses.

Without a word he took his hands out of her jeans and lifted her up. She moved her arms to around his neck and wrapped her legs around his waist. Kicking the beer bottles and sending them spinning aside, he moved to the closed door of her bedroom, opening the way with one hand. When they reached the bed, he laid her down and she pulled off her thin, fitted jersey top. All night he had stolen glimpses of her body through the fabric.

Now he could devour all of her.

Their bodies fit perfectly together as they made love.

Each thrust was a push and pull of will, chemistry, and desire. In perfect measure they took each other's breath away. Whatever it took, he decided he would never let go of this woman for the rest of his life.

Walking home the following morning, Ramón felt pangs of guilt like a cheap, skulking sancho. Checking his phone, he saw six messages from Mary Anne. Each message wanting to know where he was and letting him know how much she missed him. She had a good heart.

Which made him feel heartless.

Mary Anne wanted a Ken so she could play Barbie. Ramón could live with that, as long as she didn't get any ideas of stealing the show from him.

Julia, on the other hand, was every bit his equal. Before he had left her apartment, she invited him for two nights the following weekend on her family's yacht. There was someone she thought he should meet. Julia Yutani understood him—body, mind, and soul—and what a break that would be, getting a foothold in the Weyland-Yutani dynasty.

On a yacht.

He'd always wanted a boat.

A short stout man greeted Ramón and Julia as they boarded. He was wearing a white linen shirt with the long sleeves rolled to his elbows. It was unbuttoned too far for Ramón's taste, as he could see where the red sunburn ended and his pale chest began. The blue eyes behind round clear-framed glasses appeared slightly bloodshot.

He handed Ramón a beer, and extended his hand. Despite the fact that he probably was worth millions, the man had the smell of a borracho who had been drinking for days.

"Benjamin Ross." His grip was firm. "I hear you are the star of Harvard."

Ramón knew that even if he could match this caveman display of authority, it wasn't the time. Not yet. He had to play the school kid who needed to be "educated," so he gave Benjamin a friendly smile, and allowed his hand to go slightly limp.

"Who would tell you that?" Ramón replied, chuckling. Benjamin puffed out his chest slightly before retracting his hand and grabbing a leather cigar case from the wet bar to his right.

"Julia and I might have asked some of your professors," he said conspiratorially. "Checked your background." Ross held out the case. "Want one?"

Ramón had never smoked on a cigar in his life.

"I'd love one," he said. "It's been a while." It took a bullshitter to spot a bullshitter, he knew. Benjamin guided Ramón through the ritual until they both were smoking.

"As you know, Julia works for the company," Benjamin

said, waving the cigar in her direction, "and I say 'work' very loosely."

"Careful, Benjamin. I know your boss," she joked. Or half joked.

"I know, and it won't be long before you *are* my boss."

Ramón suppressed a frown.

She would never be *his* boss.

Benjamin took his time with another puff. "As I was saying, there's a project I'm working on, and I need an extra pair of eyes, someone who would help with strategy. From what we hear, you're the best at anything you put your mind to, and—"

"And being a student, I'd come cheap and be easy to bury if I got a case of loose lips or blew the whistle."

Benjamin smiled, nodding his head. "True, true, but it won't come to that," he said. "This is a long-term thing, possibly your lifetime. It requires commitment, and loyalty. We need the best and brightest from the outset. People with vision. Truth to tell, I'm just a grunt who got here by kissing ass and doing whatever it took to get the job done.

"No," he continued, "we need someone who can take all the moving parts of a complex bioweaponry project, and put them together, make them sing—and in the process maintain strict confidentiality. Julia has been keeping an eye on certain students. You caught her attention, so I did a lot of digging. You might have fooled everyone in high school, but I found the sophisticated system you created to fleece rich kids out of their money for the grades they needed. You also rigged grades for teachers to get them their bonuses. From what I could find, you're doing the same now.

"People like you and trust you," Benjamin continued, a glint in his eyes, "even though you got ice running through your veins. And your class work is exceptional. I am confident that you can develop a program for the company that will take us to the next tier of weapons evolution—and the associated revenue stream. It won't be a cakewalk, though. Many have tried and failed. We have too many competitors to allow any of them to know what we're doing." He peered intently at Ramón, judging his response.

Ramón had to keep himself from shaking. It almost felt surreal. All his hard work, all his focus were on the verge of paying off. Everything he had sought, all his life, soon would be within his grasp. He just had to *take* it. Whatever it paid—even shit pay at Weyland-Yutani would be more than an entry-level gig where he'd have to slog to prove himself.

And the long-term payoff…

"You really don't care that I'm still just a kid in the midst of my education?" he asked, careful to sound sincere. "What is this project?"

"Sometimes, *kid*, the real education isn't in a book or in a classroom," Benjamin replied. "I can't talk about it— not here—but it's out there." He waved his cigar at the sky. "On an unnamed planet." Ramón couldn't keep from showing surprise. "Don't worry, no travel necessary… at least not yet. Tell you what, I'll send you some paperwork. Then come Monday morning, let's meet at the office and I'll show you what you need to know."

"Then we talk money," Ramón said.

Benjamin glanced at Julia with a smirk. "Now I know why you like this kid so much."

Julia looked away and blushed. "Enough for now—I need another drink. How about you, Ramón?"

He looked down at a full bottle of beer.

"You know, maybe I'll switch to scotch."

"Follow me." She took hold of one of his hands and led him to the bar. Collecting their drinks, they went to stand at the railing. The placid water reflected the setting sun, and it was the same color as bullion, Ramón noted.

"I could get used to this."

"I know." Julia touched his shoulder blade. "What would you say to being by my side?"

Ramón turned to her. There was a vulnerability in her gaze, and sincerity that made him want to reach out and kiss her, show her the same honesty.

"Is that an offer?" he said. "Second one today."

She giggled, something she rarely did in front of others. "Yes, it is, Mr. Vasquez. I'm looking for a partner. Not necessarily a husband, and I don't want children. Ever. The day-to-day rearing of small humans strikes me as tedious and unfulfilling. Most of the people I know who have kids regret it, or send them to boarding school. No thanks. There are worlds I want to explore, and build."

Ramón's smile flattened, at least inwardly. His heart ached. It had been on the top of his list to rebuild the family he'd lost, even if he had no real interest in the details of raising children. It was an open wound that never seemed to heal. Julia was perfect in so many ways, but he wanted a family, and he didn't want to be seen as Julia Yutani's lucky man.

It made him think of Mary Anne, the way she curled next to him feeling warm from sleep. *"All I want from you is to be my family, Ramón,"* she'd said. *"I have more than enough to live on… it will be wonderful, especially after the first little Ramón junior."*

He had turned to her. *"You know twins run in my family."*

"Even better."

He feared the demands Julia might have of him, whereas Mary Anne just craved his love and attention. She wanted babies, and a life outside of the one in which she had been raised.

Did he want to be a power couple, or a jefe of power in his own right?

He wasn't sure he had an answer.

1 3

Monday arrived and Ramón met with Benjamin Ross in the Manhattan offices of Weyland-Yutani. It was 6:45 a.m., well before anyone would be there except for the nightwatchman at the ground-floor reception. Having taken the first bullet train from Boston, he was exhausted as he exited the elevator on the twentieth floor, a backpack slung over his shoulder.

Ross was waiting for him.

"You ready?"

"Yes," Ramón answered. "Are you putting me to work already?"

"No, not today—not yet," Ross replied. "Later. First you need to know what's at stake. What you'll be committing to."

Ramón was confused, but refused to show it. Ross was talking in ciphers, still not letting on what they actually wanted of him. Julia probably knew, but no matter how he had pressed her, she just dodged the question while massaging his ego—and other things.

"Follow me," Ross said, turning to walk briskly through a long corridor of large executive offices. He carried a small valise. Gone was the jovial fellow with the white linen shirt, replaced by an expensive suit.

They continued along a windowless hallway until they reached what looked like a wall of dark expensive wood. The short man looked to the ceiling and centered himself beneath a small black globe. A portion of the wooden wall opened, but this was no ordinary door. It was a vault with large retractable locks, and the wall was at least two feet deep.

On the other side was a chamber with a wall full of monitors and a single rectangular table also made from expensive natural wood. The genuine stuff, not the synthetic materials most people had to use, and which never quite looked real. In the center a tray with six bottles of water, soda, an assortment of sandwiches, and a bowl of fruit. Ross walked to one of the monitors and flicked it on, his fingers tapping a tablet mounted to the wall.

"Since you've signed the NDA we sent," Ross said, "I can show this to you now. It's footage from the project you will live and breathe from this day forward," he said, "*if* you have the stomach—and the balls—for it." He stepped aside.

Ramón stepped closer to the monitor. His lips parted in disbelief as his mind tried to parse what he was seeing.

Once again he could feel Ross staring at him, to gauge his reaction.

All those years of Leticia, so eager to leave the planet of their birth to follow their parents into the void. Of Roseanna, talking her mumbo jumbo about the universe and space and not being alone. If what he saw on the screen was real, then she had been right, but she couldn't have meant this... this *thing*.

Who could comprehend such a nightmare?

"What is this, Benjamin?" he said, finding his voice. "And more importantly, *where* is this? Where on Earth—?"

"They're called Xenomorphs," Ross said, "and they are the future. They call this one La Reina, and as for 'where,' this is a planet that takes about five years in cryo to reach. Meredith Vickers began the process of making the planet habitable, before she disappeared. She had enough influence to keep it under wraps and claim it for herself. No one had this on their radar—it wasn't even given an LV designation. As a result, there's a small facility, and nothing else. She never specified what she wanted it for.

"One of her descendants, Jacob Vickers, has taken an interest in the planet," Ross continued. "He is being groomed, quietly, by a small faction who seek to steer the company in a different direction. Julia Yutani is being groomed, as well, but not so subtly. You know her—she knows how to play ball in *our* world."

Ramón was mesmerized. The thing on the screen was black, with a shiny carapace that resembled that of an insect. It had four limbs that could have been arms and legs, but had been cut off, leaving sharp stumps. There was a long narrow head with a crown-like hood, ending in an eyeless face and wicked jaws. The chamber in which it was secured was featureless, and the creature remained almost motionless. Yet he was pretty sure it was aware.

Horrifying, and yet…

"What purpose could such a thing serve?" he asked. "For that matter, what purpose could *I* serve in a project involving such a creature? I'm no scientist."

He turned, and watched as Ross reached into his pocket and removed a small metal capsule large enough to fit into a nostril. He brought it to his nose and snorted, then noticed Ramón staring at him.

"You want a bump?"

"No," Ramón said. Then, "No thank you. I don't do llelo." His mind was his greatest asset, and he refused to do anything that might jeopardize the one thing that gave him an unassailable edge. Ross shrugged, threw his head back, and lifted an arm toward the monitor.

"Just as well you don't do the shit," he said. "We have too much work to do. Sometimes I just need a little edge. There was a party last night I didn't want to miss." He shook his head as if to organize his thoughts.

"As far as 'why you,' you're brilliant—you know that—and you're a hustler. Perfect grades, and you don't let anything get in your way. Since high school, probably before, you've used your brains combined with raw greed to get what you want. Competition is phlegm in your throat, something to be cleared away. We like that.

"And regarding the 'what purpose,' people don't mind seeing guns and missiles being made and traded, but the idea of biological weapons scares them in ways that are unnecessarily irrational. We need a long-term strategy. The scientists are good at creating and replicating, but we need it to fit into our business model. We're selling our weapons to the highest bidders, private or governments, and that's where you come in."

Ramón swallowed hard and turned back to the monitor displaying the hideous thing Ross had called a Xenomorph. Glancing to the side, he saw Ross wiping his nose. In that instant Ramón knew that taking the man's job would be easier than he might have anticipated. From the look of it, between the drugs and burning the candle at both ends, Ross would bury himself without any help.

On the monitor, the room in which the monstrosity was being held made it impossible to tell the creature's true size. It appeared big, however, and a translucent, slimy tube attached to the lower body wobbled and contracted like a serpent digesting a large prey. It was pushing something out.

An egg.

"What are you... *we* doing here? What's the value in this?" In response Ross cocked his head toward the wooden table. He took a seat, and Ramón joined him.

"I need you to read all the sciencey stuff and come up with a strategy," the older man said. "How can we make money off the things we're learning here, and use them to bury our competition?" He opened a bottle of water, took a swig, and continued. "You need to think *big*, because the better the idea, the fatter the budget. Focus on the biological weapons program. It needs a refresh. There's a lot of profit there—I'm sure of it—but greed is only as good as the marksman taking aim. Again, think big."

"What do I have access to?" Ramón asked. "How deep do I get to dive?"

"You have it all, Ramón."

"Really?" There had to be a catch. Ross had to have something up his sleeve. They didn't just hand a newcomer the keys to the kingdom.

"Julia Yutani made sure of it," Ross said, and he made a face as if he'd tasted something he didn't like. "What Julia wants, Julia gets—even if she occasionally has to wait for it. Watch out when she gets tired of waiting."

Ramón thought of something.

"This might be a difficult find, but can you get me a whiteboard?" he asked. "My tía—my aunt—had an old one I used all the time to keep track of my, er, extra-curricular moneymaking ventures in high school. When faced with a particularly difficult challenge, I'd stare at it and come up with new ways to trick the school systems to access whoever I wanted, manipulate tests, find out dirt."

Ross looked as if he was about to jump over and dry hump him on the spot—exactly the reaction he was hoping for. He wanted this man to know *exactly* how valuable he was, and Ramón's confidence was growing stronger by the minute.

"I'll check the supplies list," Ross said. "No one uses those anymore, I don't think." He peered at Ramón, waiting for the next shoe to drop. "That's it?"

"I want a bonus," he said. "Think of it as a signing reward. Enough to cover the outstanding mortgage on my tía's house."

"Done."

"Paid by midnight tonight."

"Damn!" Ross slapped the tabletop. "You were born to work for us."

Ramón found himself beaming. "Benjamin… Ben, I'm really excited about this opportunity, but it's not the only thing I need to accomplish. I intend to complete my MBA, as well. It's not something I'm willing to leave unfinished. That will take time. I'll do what I can when I can."

"Ha!" Benjamin responded. "You won't need an MBA, doing this. Save your time and money. Stick with us, kid, and you'll get out of that dorm room. You'll have an apartment in a building owned by Weyland-Yutani."

That could present a problem.

"It can't be in the same place as Julia—"

"No, don't worry," Benjamin said. "You can still have both of them, in different places." Ramón opened his mouth to speak, but Benjamin raised a hand. "Don't," he said. "I've been there myself a few times." He gave Ramón a cheeky wink, drank the rest of the water, and stood, picking up the valise and pulling out a tablet. "This is an overview of the program—study it. Stay here as long as you want, and help yourself to the food. You know the way out."

Ramón watched Benjamin leave. This would mean strange working conditions and stranger hours, but he didn't think that would be difficult. He'd always done things his own way.

He lifted his eyes back to the monitor.

La Reina.

The Queen.

The Xenomorph was moving now, rolling its head back and forth as another egg emerged. Largest fucking huevos he had ever seen in his life. It looked grotesque, with a large tongue hanging to its chest. Stumps where there should have been hands and feet and a tail with an abrupt, ragged end. Whatever had happened to this thing, it must have been pure agony. There was something in its stillness that made him go cold inside. It seemed impossible that a creature like this had evolved just to hang there as a docile surrogate.

No, he needed to know every last detail of its existence. This was a thing that should inspire fear—though he felt none, considering how far away it was. God willing, he would never encounter one in the flesh.

Hunger made his stomach rumble, so he poked through the fresh fruit and sandwiches. Fresh ingredients, the sort that were in increasingly short supply, especially to the general public. Yet piled high, here in this secret room.

Just for him.

"A bonus… my first and not my last. Good going, Ramón." He smiled before beginning to read a file detailing the first encounter with the Xenomorph.

The door opened again, startling Ramón, who was engrossed in reading. He looked at his phone to see an hour had already passed.

"Ask and ye shall receive," Benjamin said cheerily. "Just in time, before anyone arrives. Here's a whiteboard and a few pens. Had to look through the storage log, and this was the only one. It was kept as some sort of prop—don't ask me. Right. I'll leave this here and see you when we're done for the day."

Ramón liked whiteboards for the same reason he liked notepads—the kind with paper. There was a type of wizardry when an idea went from the mind to the hand to the page. The same person could type the same sentence on a tablet, but handwriting was unique. It was a stamp. He loved that concept.

With black marker in hand, he returned to his research.

* * *

The whiteboard was full by the time Benjamin came back early in the evening, carrying two lowball glasses filled with whiskey.

"How was the first day?"

"Good," Ramón answered, taking one of the drinks, "but I don't know how I'm going to manage my schoolwork, too. There's so much information here, so many applications to assess, and a political minefield to navigate. Do the right things and we're rich. Do the wrong things, and we're sunk. I haven't even begun to scrape the surface of the weapons program."

"Don't worry so much," Benjamin said, waving the glass in the air, careful not to spill any of the contents. "You think everyone at those fancy schools gets there by merit alone? You're smarter than all of 'em combined."

Ramón nodded, unconvinced. "Well, I need to go," he said. "I'm meeting Julia for a little birthday celebration. She took the train down to meet me here, and I don't want to disappoint her."

"Oh, yeah," Benjamin said, beginning to slur his words a bit. "Tell her I said happy birthday. By the way, one day you'll have to introduce me to that sister of yours." Ramón shot him a quizzical look. "I stumbled upon her when I was researching you. Marines—impressive and a little sexy, if I may say."

As if, Ramón thought as he threw his belongings into his backpack and zipped it closed, not wanting to respond. No way would Leticia ever go near him. She could be a brat, but she was a damned *smart* brat, and he loved her. She was out of Benjamin's league. *What a parasite.*

The thought caused him to stop fiddling with his backpack and flick his eyes to the screen that showed the Xenomorph. *Parasites.* He'd read they were developing some nasty shit.

Water Systems.

Silent Coercion.

Isolated Displays of Force.

Ramón had always been careful in life, with so many of his desires under control. This project would allow him to indulge in all those tendencies. Even if it meant destroying someone else without conscience. His imagination was a jet pack with that thought, but it would have to wait until he was mentally refreshed.

With his new access to records, he also planned on scanning the files for information on his mother. Roseanna had told them her last message concerned a mission to a Weyland-Yutani colony. She had died there. There had to be more details, and if he couldn't find them he would ask Julia to pull some strings.

He downed the last of his drink.

"I'll see you tomorrow."

Julia stood at the bar looking the picture of poised perfection, as she always did. Her heels were high enough to warrant a car service to and from the restaurant. Ramón knew he was hopelessly in love with her, despite his misgivings.

"Hi, gorgeous," she said. "The table is ready."

She leaned in and kissed him on the lips.

"Show me the way, guapa."

He loved the way he felt when she was close. They walked through the half-empty restaurant to a back corner table. A bottle in an ice bucket and two full glasses of champagne waited for them.

"I reserved this table so we could have privacy," she said. After they had both slid into their seats, she removed a box from her handbag and pushed it toward him.

"What's this?" he said. "It's your birthday, and you're giving *me* a gift?"

"I don't need anything," she replied, "and I wanted to celebrate your new position with the company. I'm so excited you've accepted."

"Thank you." He wasn't surprised that she already knew. "Benjamin wastes no time."

"Benjamin *can't*," she said, raising an eyebrow. "He's been a cat with nine lives over the years, and he doesn't have many left." He wondered what that meant, but decided not to press it.

Ramón untied the gold ribbon and opened the box.

"A Rolex?" He tried to hold his smile, but he couldn't hold back the slight anger welling up inside. "This is too much!"

"You have to look the part," she said. "It's nothing. We're the same, and we want the same things."

"Thank you." Being careful to hold back his emotions, he leaned over to kiss her on the cheek. "It's very generous. I'm afraid I didn't bring your gift with me, though. Didn't want to carry it on the train."

She waved him off. "You can pay for dinner. I'm starving. You must be, too, after your day. I want to hear all about it over a steak smothered in béarnaise sauce."

"Sounds like a plan." He picked up his champagne. "Where do I even start?"

"Start with *her*." Julia put down her glass. "I'm told she goes by La Reina. That's 'the queen,' isn't it?"

Ramón could feel himself tremble with the thought of the Xenomorph. *La Reina*. Usually he didn't drink, or kept it to a bare minimum, but tonight he would. He lifted the glass and took a fast gulp.

"What I'm thinking, I can't share it with just anyone," he said, his mind racing again. "You're the only one I can trust with what I *really* think."

Julia licked her lips and took another sip before sliding a hand up his thigh the way he liked.

"And what's that, my love?" she whispered as she stroked him through the fabric.

"I think La Reina is checkmate."

Julia's red lips curled into a smile.

"My thoughts exactly," she said, "but we have to get it right."

* * *

When he arrived back at his dorm the following day, the cold metal of the new watch on his wrist sent shivers down his entire body. Is this how their relationship would be? With Julia always one-upping him? He had wanted to buy that for himself. But goddamn, she beat him to it.

He thought about how he loved her touch, the way her mind followed his thought processes without judgment—or asking for anything in return. Fuck the Rolex. He would buy a boat.

His desire for her fought with his ambitions and ego.

It wasn't that way with Mary Anne. She had zero desire to challenge anything—including herself. She was entirely satisfied with the status quo, and he liked that most of the time. It helped him shut off his overworked brain.

The brain Julia set on fire, nonstop, along with his body. Her ambition rivaled his, which both excited and frightened him. He had to remind himself that it was all about the Vasquez empire, not Yutani. Julia would be a Yutani until the day she died, that bonfire on the beach with hot embers flying every which direction. It was mesmerizing because it touched something primal.

Mary Anne was the glowing tea lights on a long sleek bar with jazz playing in the background. Soothing and safe.

She was out that night with her mother Laurel and sister Henrietta, choosing bridesmaids dresses for Henrietta's upcoming wedding. Mary Anne never asked him where he was, where he had been, just if he was "coming home." He could never tell Mary Anne the truth about this new job. With both of her parents on boards for various charities, the simple fact that it was Weyland-Yutani would probably send them into apoplectic fits.

The less she knew, the better, and truth to tell, he didn't want to tell her about it. She would remain his oasis. Eating meals with small talk and gossip would enable him to rest from himself.

In a few days' time he would be going back home to see Roseanna… and Leticia. That, too, might be turned to his advantage. When the time was right he might need a connection to the Marines, and to military intel. Ironically, Leticia's decision might turn out for the best.

Stack the deck before you need your cards.

1 4

Ramón arrived looking pale, as if he hadn't seen the sun in months but had packed on a few pounds of muscle. Leticia grabbed his arm.

"I have some competition?" she said. "Looking buff, mi hermano. You never seemed the least bit interested in fitness. What changed your mind—or maybe I should ask, *who* changed your mind?"

"No way," he protested, pulling free. "You'll get no competition from me. I'm not the combat type. Let's just say I'm stuck most of the time with research and studying, and my dormitory has a gym on site. It's given me an outlet. Helps me think." He stepped back. "But enough about me, how's it going with special ops. How does it work, anyhow? What's your plan for getting in?"

Leticia was taken aback by his questioning. It had been so long since he expressed any interest in her hopes for the military, and when he did, it wasn't positive. Then she shrugged it off. Maybe he *had* changed.

"At this point, the only plan is to make it through," she admitted. "It's tough going. I suppose if I get into the Raiders, though, I'll be going on whatever missions they send me to. So I guess *that's* the plan—I won't stop until I get there."

Ramón nodded. "You'll get there—I'm sure of it," he said. "We haven't always been as close as we could have been, but we aren't kids anymore. Who knows what the future holds for us, and what opportunities might come and go."

That piqued Leticia's curiosity even more. All this talk of the future, and she hadn't even set foot on the training ground. Whatever Ramón was talking about, she couldn't tell what was going on in that complicated brain of his. Better to let it go... for now.

"Thanks, bro," she said. "I appreciate the vote of confidence. It's all so far off. If I *do* get into the Raiders, though, it'll all be hush-hush. I wouldn't be able to tell you about it, anyway."

"No, of course," he said. "Being away from home has made me appreciate our family a little more. I'm just trying to be a better brother. We're familia. You never know what's going to happen—that's the way it's always been with us. If I can ever help... just say the word."

"We'll cross that bridge if we ever come to it. And thanks."

"Right, let's go find Roseanna." Ramón looked around. "I have a surprise for her."

"Really? What is it?"

"This place." Ramón gave her a sly smile that bordered on sinister, stretching his arms wide. "Who says generational wealth can't be ours?"

Generational what?

Before she could say a word, he dashed through the house. She knew something was up. Ramón had his hands into some cookie jar... just like in high school. There was no way a college student could be making serious money doing something legit. She just hoped whatever he had up his sleeve wouldn't come back to bite him.

Or any of them.

She heard a cry in the living room. Roseanna. Leticia took a deep breath and was determined to be happy. If it was good news, their tía might retire early, if she wanted to, or take a big trip without having to rely on Robert. She'd given them so much over the years, and never asked for anything in return.

Leticia found them in the living room.

"Did Ramón tell you what he did?" Roseanna said, excitement and pride in her voice. "He said the advance he got for a big freelance job covered the rest of the mortgage. The house will be paid off, and you two will always have this place to come home to."

"That's the best news," Leticia said, putting a big

smile on her face. "You deserve it, and Ramón deserves everything he gets for all his hard work."

"You're next, Leticia." Roseanna took one of Leticia's hands in her own. "I promise. Your hard work will make your dreams come true." Then her smile went wide again. "Why don't we go celebrate?"

A couple of days passed, and on the last morning Leticia found Ramón in the kitchen. He had made a spread of fresh breakfast tacos from The Donut Shop, and fresh orange juice to go with them.

"I wanted to do something nice for you guys," he said, "because I don't know when we will all be together again. I always liked it when Robert did this."

"Thank you, mijo," Roseanna said, and she gave Ramón a tight hug. "He has always wanted to get to know you better, but didn't want to push."

"Well, I appreciated it, even if I didn't say anything."

They dug into the tacos, making small talk and unwilling to admit that the visit was going to come to an end. After breakfast, however, Ramón rose and said that he had to jet off for classes and work.

"I guess this is it, then, brother," Leticia said. "Thank you for taking time from your break to come see us." She gave him a meaningful look. "Can you be careful? Watch your back."

"Trust me," he answered. "I'm fine—and you're only a

message away. Call me anytime you want. I really want to know how it goes in the Marines. And if you need money, with this side gig…"

"Or if I need an essay written?"

Ramón gave her a smile and chuckled. "Yes, something like that. Take care of yourself, and don't take any shit—not that you do, anyway."

"Wait, you can't go yet," Roseanna said. "One last photo for my altar!" Both Leticia and Ramón rolled their eyes.

"Go on, tía." Ramón beamed in his Harvard sweatshirt, and Leticia moved her body a little so the tattoo of their mother would be in the photo. Roseanna tapped her phone, then again, and a third time. "Right," Ramón said. "I'd better get to the airport—there's a lot to do before classes start again."

"And next time I want you to bring that girl you are seeing," Roseanna said. "I need to meet her, or maybe welcome her into our little family. Our home and land that I now own!"

"That sounds like a great idea." Ramón had a strange expression, Leticia thought, but he nodded. "You'll like her. She's very down to earth, wants a family of her own, *our* own, but doesn't need me to take care of her. Her name is Mary Anne. She comes from a great family, too."

"As long as she makes you happy and you feel at home with her," Roseanna said. "Really at peace."

Ramón paused before answering. "Of course. She is a

very nice woman." A car horn made them all turn toward the open screen door. "That's me. Love you both."

"Hey, don't forget, *el riesgo siempre vive*," Leticia said, giving him a warm smile.

He nodded. "And good luck with you. If it doesn't work out the way you want, you'll find another way, Leticia, or another way will find you." He grabbed the real-leather duffel bag with his initials monogrammed on the side, and walked out the door.

15

The drive to the Marine Corps recruit depot was long, all the way to South Carolina. The original Parris Island facility had long since been swallowed by the rising ocean, and it was now situated just outside of Fairfax.

Every exit and stoplight released more excitement and trepidation in Leticia. Roseanna kept the music low on the radio to allow her niece to think or talk. They had waited so long for this fated moment, she didn't press her to speak.

Basic training and leaving home; two rites of passage in a single day. Leticia didn't know what to say. Then she began to see the road signs, and knew it was close. They turned off on a dusty unmarked road, and the only way they knew the destination was the GPS code given to them by the Marines. Then a large brick wall topped with barbed wire seemed to appear out of nowhere, along with the signs.

DANGER!

MILITARY

TRAINING AREA

RESTRICTED AREA

NO TRESPASSING

USCM GOVERNMENT PROPERTY

There was a sound from overhead, and helicopters cut through the humid atmosphere. They could hear unseen jets, as well. They were getting close.

At the entrance were two outdated, ancient tanks from previous wars. She thought of her family members who had served, and wondered what her mother felt when she passed through these very gates. The thumping of her pulse was a twenty-one-gun salute marking the end of her old life.

They pulled up to an entrance with a large metal gate. Leticia and Roseanna had to stick their heads out of the car windows to be verified with a facial scan. Roseanna was only allowed to pull into the visitor drop-off lot.

"You have everything?"

"I do, tía. Thank you."

"You made the right decision, and stuck out the time that was needed. You will succeed in everything you do."

"I love you, tía."

"I love you, too, mija, and I'm already proud of you. Your mother and all the ancestors before us would be proud. You have gone further than any of them could ever dream of. Jenette did the same."

"I'll call you with an update as soon as I can."

"Don't worry about me. This is your time."

They leaned in for a long, tight hug. Then Leticia got out of the car to follow the path that led where Roseanna could not accompany her, farther into the bustling training facility. If she lingered any longer, she thought, she might burst into tears. From that moment forward, she was the only one who would determine if she succeeded or not—or more accurately, how far she would go without quitting.

First get through basic, service for three years, then nine months of Raider training. That was the plan.

People passed her by, some in civilian clothes, others in fatigues. Seeing the strange faces made her think of something Lucinda had said before she left.

"*I know you are set on doing this, you'll be great, but watch your back. Be careful. There are stories of young female recruits gone missing, or worse. The* I Am Vanessa Guillain Act *did a lot of good. God bless her soul and those who lost their lives, or were never heard from again. You can take any harassment or complaint to authorities outside the military, but still…*"

Touched by her concern, Leticia had hugged her.

"*I know. Believe me when I say I have researched it extensively. I know what I'm getting into. Keep in touch. This isn't the end.*"

Their final evening together had been wonderful, in

front of a bonfire beneath the stars with a pot of pork tamales made by Lucinda's grandmother, and arroz con pollo courtesy of Robert and Avery.

Before she knew it, the intake building stood before her. There was a line, and she made her way to the back, not knowing anyone. Some of the others talked among themselves as if they had joined together straight out of school. When she finally made it to the front of the line a Black woman in uniform greeted her.

"Here are your fatigues," the woman said brusquely. "I highly suggest you remove all jewelry during training. Any feminine sanitary products are provided for free at sick bay." She peered at Leticia. "Looks like you've already had a haircut, so we can skip that. Any complaints about the food will go unnoticed, so don't waste anyone's time. If you have dietary requirements, those can be processed through the mess hall. Your assigned bunk is on this card. All the items you have can be stored in your trunk. Any questions?"

"No, ma'am."

Leticia headed off to find her new home. The people she would meet would have to be her new family as they pulled together, eventually to work as a unit. If she wanted to be a Raider, then she had to forget that anything existed outside of the mission that was basic training, and completing the Crucible.

* * *

"You aren't a Marine until I say so," the woman said. "My name may be Mercy, but you will get none from me. They pay me the big bucks to get you fighting fit— and if anyone dares to sing *Mercy Me*, it's an automatic fifty push-ups."

There was a hushed chuckle in the room.

"Thirteen weeks," she continued. "You are my little babies for thirteen weeks, and then I will kick your scrawny asses out of the nest. Fly or die. Now some of you indicated that you want to go deeper into the Corps. Rumor has it some of you think you are Raider material. I will also be determining if you get a pass for such an honor. You know who you are, and know that I am watching you."

A white woman with the name "Frida" printed on her green T-shirt leaned to whisper into Leticia's ear. "Who's she saying has a scrawny ass. Definitely not me—and look at that one… Damn I might be in love."

Leticia glanced toward the man Frida was admiring. "Mohammed" was printed on his shirt. He had two large crow tattoos, one on each forearm, and a close-cut beard on his face. Arabic lettering on the left side of his neck. She had to admit, his black eyes were impossibly beautiful.

Mercy, the drill sergeant, began to walk their way again. Leticia and Frida snapped back to attention.

"I will only say this once—only you determine if you make it to the Crucible. If you think what you have to offer isn't enough, then it probably isn't. Your new life starts today. Now, time for the first hump across the training ground. Move!"

Another drill sergeant waited outside the entrance of the barracks, ushering them out.

"You heard Mercy, move!" The recruits all complied. Leticia's feet started off as a shuffle, then turned into a jog. They passed a large wooden obstacle course some distance away, with other recruits fighting their way through in full gear and holding their weapons. There was a gigantic warehouse that housed the training facility to prep for space travel, and again she thought of her mother. Her heart pounded faster as she picked up her pace.

There was no turning back.

The only direction she cared about was forward and up.

When they arrived back at the barracks nearly everyone was exhausted and shaking their feet from running in combat boots. Every shirt was ringed with sweat beneath the arms, around the neck, and chests. A table had large water coolers and MREs for the recruits to help themselves. Leticia's entire body trembled. She had exhausted the glucose in her system, and the humidity had pulled every last drop of moisture from her body.

She trudged toward the table.

"I wasn't ready for that." The voice next to Leticia came from the woman who had stood next to her in the barracks, Frida.

"Same," Leticia admitted. "I spent time on a farm and my aunt's land, but it was mostly lifting and hauling. Did a lot of shooting. Endurance—like running at a steady pace—I totally skipped."

"At least you had a head start. I was working android sales."

"No shit? What brought you to the Marines?"

"I want to know more about androids beyond selling them. I like the idea of special ops and using the technology out in the field. In sales, all the boss cares about are the bottom line, making the quotas. Everything was on a need-to-know basis when it came to the technology. I mean, have you seen the new Narwhals? Those things are fast on the water and capable of doing real damage with the grenade launcher on the front. Genius."

"Respect," Leticia replied. "That's a great reason to enlist. Hope you get the chance to ride one." She held out her hand. "I'm Leticia."

"Frida... oh shit. There's that guy. He looks even better all sweaty. C'mon, I can't go by myself. I really want to say hi."

"You want to be the best of the best, but can't talk to one dude?" Leticia said. "One very *attractive* dude?"

"What can I say, I hang around androids most of the day." Leticia chuckled. "Let's go."

As they approached, the man tossed water over his head and wiped it across his face. Frida grabbed an MRE and poured herself a cup of water.

"How about that run?" she said. "Where are you from?"

Leticia cringed inside.

"My dad warned me it was tough, but this will be something. I can feel it." He flashed a cheeky grin. "I'm Mohammed Faez." Another recruit joined them. Mohammed handed him an MRE. "This is my man Nathan Powell. We joined together because, what the hell is this world—or any of the worlds—coming to. The colonies fighting. So many damn wars. A lot of family and friends lost." He took a drink. "From Minnesota."

"I'm from Philly," Frida replied. "Go Flyers!"

While Nathan tore into his MRE, a Black woman from the barracks approached their corner of the table. She had been to her right before the run, and with the figure of a gymnast, appeared unaffected by the effort.

"Is this where the cool kids hang out?"

"Cool, not sure, but good-looking, yes." Nathan spoke up between bites. "And you are?"

"Desiree."

Frida brought her hand to her mouth. "Wait, I thought you looked familiar. Desiree Benson? The Olympian?"

Desiree nodded. "Retired and wanted to do something new. Got sick of the politics involved and wanted to make a difference, if I could. Sponsorships don't pay what they did back in the day, and this is a hell of a lot warmer than New York City in the winter."

She grabbed her cup and filled it with more water, before turning her attention back to Leticia.

"Cool tat on your arm. Relative?"

When she said this the others glanced at the tattoo. Leticia knew this wasn't a time to be shy or self-conscious. The Corps was all about teamwork, and honesty would be the best way to build trust.

"It's my mother. She was a Marine, and died during a mission to some colony. I'm from Texas, but *please* don't call me Tex!"

They all just nodded. Frida shifted the conversation.

"Is everyone planning on staying a grunt? Anyone want recon?"

Leticia spoke first, with confidence. "Raider all the way. For her." She tapped on her tattoo. Once again, all eyes were on her, until Nathan and Mohammed exchanged glances.

"What?" Leticia said. "You guys going for it, too?"

"Actually, we are." Mohammed placed a hand on Nathan's shoulder and squeezed.

"Been together since freshman year in high school. I'm the beauty and he's the beast."

"You two are a lucky pair..." Frida said, and Leticia detected a note of regret. She cocked her head and smiled. "I want to be more than a grunt, too. For sure."

"I guess this wasn't the spot for the cool kids, but budding Raiders," Desiree said. "We're all on the same page. Some coincidence."

"My tía doesn't believe in coincidences," Leticia said. "This is good—and Desiree, I'll be bothering you for training tips. An Olympian!"

"No bother, I started gymnastics when I could pretty much walk. If I know anything, it's the discipline required for training. I'll be glad to help."

Leticia lifted her cup of water. "To the Raiders. May we all have the ganas to do what must be done, in every situation. ¡Salud!"

"To the Raiders." They all followed her lead and lifted a salute to the stars.

The bond Leticia forged with her fellow recruits superseded any friendship she'd ever experienced in school, or even the one with her brother. When one dropped to their knees or wavered, another was waiting in the wings to show them back to the way of the warrior.

Mercy kept her eyes on them like the eagle on the Marines emblem, knowing they all wanted into Raider training. At the end of basic, her recommendations would be the difference between success and failure.

Leticia could shoot, but here she honed her skills and learned to take apart and put together any new weapon thrown her way. She studied harder than she ever had in school, learning everything there was to know about military strategy.

She watched Mohammed and Nathan with a secret envy. They had the kind of spark that was rare and undying. During training, their stolen glances of support radiated love and devotion. Their relationship was no secret, and

Leticia would have no problem fucking up anyone who dared show they had a problem with it. Then again, both Nathan and Mohammed were built like sentinels—step up to them if you had a death wish. Mohammed was a boxer, with his father owning a string of gyms. He'd enlisted to see the world, and then space. Nathan had taught piano as a side hustle to his main job as a mechanic.

Though she hadn't wanted a commitment with Avery, she hoped there was someone out there for her. There were her dreams as a soldier, and those were her priority for now, but she still possessed those desires of a woman. Was there a man who would complement her life in ways that could only be described as a bright constellation to light her way for the times life went dark?

Maybe a distant star would bring them together.

In her footlocker she kept the photograph of her mother as a Marine. Desiree spotted it one morning.

"Your mom is… damn. A gorgeous machine. She would have been a Marine Raider."

"I know." Leticia instinctively smiled and ran her fingertips across the photo. "I want to get into that shape. What comes next is no joke."

"Where do you want to start?"

"The pull-up bar," Leticia said. "Running with a pulse rifle in hand, and all the rest of the gear, brings a special kind of pain."

"Sounds about right. Why don't we start fresh tomorrow?"

"Thanks, Desiree. You got it. Las lobas." When her companion gave her a look, she added, "The wolves."

If she wasn't practicing her marksmanship, Leticia was in the gym with Desiree, preparing her body for what would be the most grueling weeks of her life. Her goal was to fight the biggest motherfuckers and do so with her bare hands. Basic training was designed to create quitters, she knew. The more that dropped out, the easier it would be to find out who had the stuff to succeed, to become a part of the elite.

She would be one of them.

Their hard work—on the range, in the gym—began to pay off.

Combat water survival made her think of the first time she jumped into the pond back home, all her clothes on and without considering how deep it could be. There had been the biggest frog she had ever seen, and she wanted to touch it.

Water filled her mouth and ears. When she couldn't touch the bottom, her first instinct was to panic. She grasped at darkness with her hands and feet, and felt the bottom scrape her big toe. It wasn't far. Leticia allowed herself to sink a little farther to touch the bottom with her feet, then pushed toward the surface. Her arms propelled her through the water, pumping against the heaviness of her jeans and T-shirt that added weight to her frame.

She grabbed the roots of the reeds at the edge of the pond and pulled herself out.

Training required her to swim fifteen feet, wearing fatigues, and keeping her rifle out of the water. The main thing that was missing, though, was the panic. She swam with confidence, and tomorrow she would do a drop into the water blindfolded.

All of this with Mercy's eagle eyes still watching.

Every day, on the way out and on the way back, they passed by the gigantic warehouse. There were no windows—she couldn't see what was happening inside, but one day she would be in there, preparing for her destiny.

When the time came for the group to tackle the fifty-four-hour test called the Crucible, they were prepared for the lack of sleep, physical exhaustion, meager rations, and grueling demands. More importantly, they were working as a team.

Leticia held the two MREs that would have to last for the entire exercise, but food wasn't the only thing that would be in short supply. They would also only have eight hours of sleep for the entire time. She knew she would need all the ganas of her mother and all the Vasquez ancestors to make it through.

"How the hell are we supposed to wake up at three a.m. to march ten miles." Desiree playfully elbowed her as she packed her own backpack. "I'm wound up—how about you?"

"I think I'm more gassed for the leader stations once we get to the Crucible site." Leticia shoved the MREs into her backpack, happy she had eaten more than her fair share at breakfast and lunch.

"You're going to be great. And don't you mean 'warrior stations'?"

Leticia smirked while securing a red bandana around her forehead.

"Soldadera station for me. Ooh-rah!"

Getting to the Crucible site, they each carried fifty pounds of equipment and alternated between marching and running. Upon arrival, each squad went to a designated "warrior station" named for a hero from the history of the Corps. As she considered the bravery of their predecessors, Leticia thought of her mother.

Mi madre, Jenette Vasquez, should be here—but if she can't, then one day I will. That thought sharpened Leticia's focus and made her forget any hunger or physical exhaustion. This was so much bigger than her. This was the beginning of leaving bootprints for others to follow. Leticia completed her task as squad leader knowing the spirit of her mother, the ganas to persevere, would be her guide.

What followed was a series of complex problem-solving exercises, after which they moved to hand-to-hand combat, then an obstacle course. She and Frida had to squirm like larvae on their bellies in mud beneath the sharpened teeth of barbed wire while pulling a "wounded" Mohammed to safety. Leticia gritted her teeth and thought of her mother's photo glowing from the candlelight on Roseanna's altar.

When the obstacle course was complete, they marched and jogged back to the base. The Crucible ended when she stood before the Iwo Jima flag-raising statue. She wondered what wars lay ahead for her.

What was she willing to die for?

Setting aside those thoughts, she focused on the here-and-now. Her crew made it to the end, earning their Eagle, Anchor, and Globe. For the graduation ceremony, Leticia marched in her uniform feeling as if the ground didn't exist. She was already floating, that much closer to her mother.

Roseanna and Robert were somewhere in the watching crowd. Ramón had a deadline he couldn't miss, but he had sent her an email congratulating her. In formation she marched with her best friends toward what she hoped would become a pass into Raider training.

When the graduation ceremony was over, Mercy found them all standing together.

"Thought I might find you together," she said, an unusual warmth in her voice. "It's a good thing you built a tight crew and fought hard during your training. You've all received my recommendation for Raider training—after you finish your three years in the service. Don't go slacking or quitting, and make me look like a fool."

"Thank you, ma'am," Leticia said. She resisted the urge to jump up and down and kiss her friends.

Mercy gave them a short nod and turned to leave.

Frida and Desiree squeezed each other's hands as they squealed. Nathan and Mohammed shared an embrace. Leticia had never felt pride like this.

"Three years," she said. "We have three years to be on our shit, guys." As they were allowed to find their guests, Leticia found Roseanna and Robert at their agreed upon meeting place, a bench overlooking the space facility.

"I did it!" she said, breaking into a jog.

Roseanna nearly jumped out of her dress as Leticia approached.

"Of course you did!" she said. "Look how sharp that uniform is. Wow. I am so proud." She and Robert both gave her hugs.

"Lucinda and Avery both send their congratulations," he said. "You're welcome at the farm anytime. Roseanna has moved in, so my home is your home."

"Thank you, Robert. Congratulations to you both!"

Roseanna brought her hand to her mouth, and looked as if she might cry. "Remember when you were so worried. Everything worked out as was intended." She gathered herself, and added, "Do you know where you go next?"

"Not sure. Service is service, and you go where orders take you—but I also received a recommendation for Raider training!"

"Oh, that's wonderful! I knew it. See. You were always meant to fly." She glanced at Robert. "Well, you can always come home, whenever you want. We're keeping the house. Your room will always be yours, and Robert has space, too."

"Thank you. I know you will always keep a room for me, and that gives me the freedom to reach for more. I will carry the Vasquez name with pride wherever my boots take me.

"I promise you that."

1 6

Julia stood in her kitchen chopping vegetables. It was her favorite way of passing time as she organized her thoughts. Handcrafted in Kyoto, the Japanese knives were the best and the only ones she used. The handle was mother of pearl and wood.

"Are you feeding a vegetarian army?"

She glanced up long enough to take a sip of red wine and lean in for a kiss from Ramón.

"Looks like the Vickers school boy is gaining more support," he said, "after that media leak about one of the colonies going boom and killing a bunch of people, including kids. Then we have another story about weapons being smuggled to rebels in one of the colony wars. Of course, all Vickers can do is spout nonsense about philosophy, and what a reluctant leader he is."

"It used to be said that even bad press is good press," she said, returning her attention to the knife.

Her chopping became faster, but no less precise.

"I hear rumblings that he is also interested in Meredith's pet project, the planet we have been using."

"Exactly!" She lifted her knife in exasperation. "He wants to call it Olinka, or some such nonsense. What does he know?"

"So far, he has just been shown the small facility. He thinks it's a surveying outpost." Ramón leaned his back against the counter and crossed his arms as he tapped his foot. "What does he want to do? I'm a little behind on the politics, the weapons program has taken up all my time."

"He wants to build some mega facility for people to create… I don't know… art? Innovations that will bring peace? For people to live in harmony. In his idyllic world, there are no borders whatsoever."

"Then let him," Ramón suggested, and she shot him a look. "Rather, let me. I'll build his utopia—above the facility. Let him play for a bit, then we will take it back. And not just take it back; make sure Vickers is never in the game again."

She slowly stopped chopping.

"To make way for Vasquez."

"No, for us." He moved behind her to place his arms around her waist. "The Xenomorph, taken to the world stage in the hands of Weyland-Yutani, could be a game changer in all aspects of the business. If we have something no one else has or can control, the company will remain untouchable—even from governments, not that they matter anymore. Circus states run by clowns honking each other's noses in one big circle jerk as worlds including Earth continue to burn."

Julia placed her knife down and turned to face Ramón.

"This is why I love you," she said. "You're not just a big cock. That cunning brain of yours is such a turn on." She looked off, with her smile fading. "There's one issue, though. The scientist in charge is incredibly paranoid. I'm worried she might blow the entire project, if she can't keep her lunch down. Not literally, but she should be watched closely."

"Dr. Moon," he responded. "I know. At some point one of us, maybe both, will have to go out there. But I have a handle on her. Eyes everywhere."

Julia raised her eyes to Ramón. "I won't settle for anything less than the both of us." Her expression sent a shiver through him. "You either make a commitment to me, or it's over. You have to prove that you know when an investment just isn't good enough."

Ramón took both of her hands in his. "Leave it with me. You deserve a commitment, and I don't want to lose you. Ever. The idea of you with another man isn't something I can bear, let alone allowing it to become a reality— and I know you can have any man you want. I've had children to carry on the Vasquez name and my legacy. All Mary Anne wanted was to play house, and she had that opportunity. Can you handle being a stepmother?" He gave her a look. "They will always be in my life."

She wrapped her arms around his waist. "If that is the compromise then yes…" She raised an eyebrow. "What is that look, Ramón. Now?"

He broke away from her. "You know. Since this chopping is all for nothing you plan on cooking, how about you order dinner and come find me." Ramón left the kitchen to a smaller room.

All four walls were whiteboard, with nothing else in the room except a single chair on wheels. He sat down and stared straight ahead. He entered the space in his mind where all things of his creation came together. To his right a row of pens stood at attention on a magnetic square. Ramón rose and plucked one off. In the center of the wall he drew a large pyramid.

An hour later Julia entered. He sat on the chair with the whiteboard pen still in hand like a smoking gun. She began to rub Ramón's shoulders, and kissed his temple.

"I guess all our pillow talk has been recorded for posterity."

He craned his head to the left and kissed her hand.

"Benjamin Ross wanted all the fucked-up biological research pertaining to the Xenomorphs to have the same fear-inducing effect as a large planet-busting missile and to be as compact. The delivery of the weapons must be efficient. No waiting years and for the weapons to reach a location. No. They must be stored from day one on planets of interest, kept on ice. Either the Xenomorph eggs or humans carrying the engineered pathogens.

"They could be activated by the touch of a button," he continued. "Humans infected with the Xenomorph-spliced parasites could be sent anywhere undetected. We will hold the key—the bacteria used to neutralize the Xenomorphs and anything containing Xeno DNA. Unmanned ships could be sent to any location. Grim Reapers, I want to call them. They will have the ability to land and unleash silent hell without anyone knowing." He gave a wry grin. "My sister might put her faith in Santa Muerte, but I will be the Reaper."

Julia moved to Ramón's side, took the pen from his hand and walked to the whiteboard. She scribbled in her messy cursive.

Ramón's lips spread to a wide smile.

"Consider it done," he said.

"I want to see La Reina right now. In the flesh."

Dr. Patel screwed her face. "Usually you are so paranoid," she said. "Why? We can get up close with a drone."

Brenda didn't reply—she had slept just three hours the previous night, instead combing through correspondence from Weyland-Yutani for any clue as to why she had been kept from key information on the project. As she did, there seemed to be a precision to the requests from Weyland-Yutani beyond the scope she found acceptable.

She stared at her companion. The synths had seemed to be increasingly observant, taking more time with tasks assigned to them. Was someone using one to spy?

What Brenda wanted now was for La Reina to make the slightest move, provide the slightest provocation that would allow her to press the button. That would release the bacteria stored in the crown on her head, sending enough into her system to end her existence. She possessed a fob that would do the trick, created with the help of a human assistant she'd paid out of her own pocket to keep it a secret.

"Always keep watch," she said finally. "Make certain she doesn't move against any of the androids sent in there to retrieve the eggs."

"And if she does," Patel replied, "what are your orders?"

"I trust you will do the right thing." Brenda knew better, however. "Now let's go see our captive queen."

"Why are you doing this now?" Patel said. "We have the other project to oversee."

"The more we do here the less I understand," Brenda muttered. "Or sleep…"

They reached the chamber door, donned hazmat suits, and entered a complex series of security commands. The barrier slid open with a hiss, and Brenda stood in front of the huge, misshapen Xenomorph, feeling like an ant. Thanks to the amputations, and the scab-like growths that had formed where they had hacked off pieces of her body, she was the worst nightmare from the deepest parts of hell.

Normally only synths were allowed in here—she was the first human to face the monstrosity.

The upper part of the Xenomorph's jaw remained fixed with large, daggered teeth suspended in the air. Strings of mucus that might have been tears, had she possessed eyes, slid down to her glistening black body. Eddies of the humid atmosphere surrounded her, giving the lowest part of the facility an otherworldly sensation. Damnation according to Christianity, and while La Reina's scream might be silent, Brenda could imagine the hideous sound it made. No wonder humans had created the concept of hell.

Look what they were creating here.

Why did the queen remain so still? What was happening in this stasis? Brenda's thumb rubbed the fob as she looked at the slimy eggs strewn across the floor. They would be removed by remote-controlled machines to be cut into pieces, used in research, or frozen.

Brenda had prayed to Yemaya, the goddess of the sea, to send a mighty wave this way, or a storm that would destroy it all. The oceans here were as treacherous as they were beautiful.

"What are you planning?" she whispered as her eyes strained to take in every inch of the La Reina.

"*Planning?*" Patel said in the earpiece of the suit.

"Nothing. I..."

They stood in silence for what felt like an eternity.

"*We should go,*" Patel said. "*There's a lot to do in preparation.*"

Brenda nodded and turned to walk away. Keeping an eye on the Xenomorph, she reached out to touch one of the eggs. Then she stopped.

The long string of liquid dripping from the elongated inner mouth had begun to congeal, taking on a barbed aspect. Similarly, the scabs where her arms and legs were removed, had adopted much the same shape. Brenda moved her hand away from the egg to focus on La Reina. They needed to begin measuring these changes—which none of the androids had seen fit to report.

A scan would be sent to her every day.

She turned and left La Reina to the darkness of the Weyland-Yutani abyss.

"If we don't take preventative measures, one of these test subjects is going to make us all part of a sick experiment," Brenda said, free of the confining hazmat suit. "Yet we aren't permitted to destroy them—they're placed in cryo and shipped out—and why?"

Too much was being kept from her.

Several human technicians just nodded, but an android stopped what it was doing and addressed her.

"This is a research facility," he said, taking her words literally. "To destroy what we have produced would be counter-productive." The android's dead eyes and programmed smile sent a shiver down Brenda's spine.

Her own eyes went wide as more androids approached, wheeling bodies from Lab 10. As one of the gurneys came closer, a woman—perhaps the same one as before—moaned. A black viscous liquid leaked from one nostril.

"Stop!" Brenda shrieked. "Take her back *now*. We don't have enough of the antidote for everyone!" As she tried to control her panic, the other human techs moved to the exit, forming a clot in the doorway.

The woman on the gurney began to struggle against the straps across her chest and thighs. Her belly was still swollen, and more of the black liquid came out of her ears and one eye.

"I'm sorry, Dr. Moon." Patel appeared at Brenda's side. "I thought we had given her enough of the sedative to ameliorate the risk. It has always been enough."

The woman groaned and gnashed her teeth while her eyes rolled to the back of her head. An irrational part of Brenda feared an orisha, a deity of old, was about to speak through the snarling woman and tell her she had to answer for this.

"Do something!" she shouted at the android who had spoken before. When he made no move, she reached to her back and the small opening she had left in her lab coat—just enough for a pistol to fit through.

She aimed and fired.

The synth moved in front of the female subject, taking the bullet. He turned and lifted a taser to stun the test subject, who was still thrashing to free herself. Her body convulsed from the shock, then relaxed again onto the gurney.

"You shouldn't have done that, Brenda!" Patel said loudly.

"The fuck I shouldn't," Brenda responded. "We can't let any of the Xenosites get out. All we have is simulated data on the speed of infection, and not enough antidote for everyone in the facility." Her voice rose as her anger spiked. "What if one of the infected found their way onto a ship? We'd be—"

Something sharp bit into her back, where she'd pulled out the pistol.

Patel held up a syringe.

"You have been overworked, doctor," she said. "Rest now." As she fell into a chair, Brenda wondered if any of this had been an accident.

PART 4

LETICIA

1 7

The Rooster was quiet for a Thursday night. Leticia's core crew sat around eating a greasy dinner of burgers, curly fries, beers, and a pitcher of margaritas. They had just returned from a freezing-cold mission, and the heat of the south was a welcome change.

Before Peter Weyland's efforts to address climate change, the rising seas had swallowed entire shorelines, including some cities. Some called it the Great Rising. The United Americas had secretly used a small island just inside the Arctic Circle as a port for three submarines carrying nuclear weapons. When it was abandoned, the subs were thought to be secure, and were left behind.

Intelligence reports indicated that they had begun drifting, and were settling to impossible depths, but pirates had struck an agreement to claim them. If it was known which government was behind the scheme, Leticia wasn't privy to the intel.

She had been among the Marines sent to reclaim the submarines and guide them toward Alaska. As the systems were turned on remotely, it would pinpoint the location of their targets.

Their reinforced rib bounced on the arctic waters. Outfitted with an advanced propulsion system, it moved with an increased speed and remarkable maneuverability. A single sleek Narwhal jet ski was attached to the side. Droplets that hit their faces had the cold sting of rapidly falling hail. The only way they could communicate was through their helmets.

As a lance corporal, Leticia led a group that had managed to remain together through training and military service and hadn't lost a single member of her crew in all that time. Before every mission she instilled as much confidence as possible.

"Who are we?" she said over the comms.

They responded in unison, *"La Loba Pack! Ahhooooh!"* Mohammed gave three extra barks into the cold air. His breath releasing eddies of steam.

Nathan studied his handheld tablet.

"Right," he said. *"The sub's systems have been activated. We should be nearly above them."*

"Desiree, what do your eagle eyes say?"

"According to the drone, there's nothing on the approach. We just might get away with an easy peasy day."

Doubting they could be so lucky, Leticia still scanned the water and stark white snow along the shoreline. As more people had ventured into space, that left behind some of the less desirable elements, and piracy had become an epidemic.

Nathan gave a thumbs-up, and Frida slowed the rib.

"Don't let your guard down," Leticia warned them. "These guys are acquiring more and more sophisticated tech all the time."

Despite the hail, the water was relatively calm as they waited for the subs to rise far enough that they could be guided toward US waters. Mohammed leaned back against the railing. Without the sound of the engine, they could hear one another without needing the headphones.

"If this wasn't a job, I'd love to do some ice fishing out here. It's so—"

A large splash erupted to their left, accompanied by a *boom* that violently rocked the boat. Nathan had to grab the rail to keep from falling over the side. An engine roared to life and another rib approached, cleverly camouflaged to fool their drones. Three figures were inside the rib, and one had a rocket launcher.

Frida raised her rifle and sent a round in their direction, causing the trio to duck down below the edge of the inflatable hull. Tucking her rifle into a holster on her back, Leticia jumped onto the Narwhal and smacked a button on the side of the rib to detach it.

"You get those damn subs into friendly waters," she said. "Our aircraft carrier isn't far."

Desiree nodded. "We have firepower waiting in our airspace, as well. Be careful, Leticia."

"I will," she replied. "I'm getting tired of chasing these vermin, and we need to make sure our presence here stays off the books. I can buy you some time to get into friendly territory."

"We will wait for you," Mohammed said. "Wherever you find yourself, we will find you."

Leticia nodded and peeled off as their rib came to life again, to follow the subs toward the aircraft carrier that would be waiting. Tapping the control panel, she shot a grenade from the Narwhal at the pirate rib's engine. Behind her, Frida continued to fire to keep the pirates at a disadvantage.

As she approached, Leticia could see scuba gear on the deck of the enemy craft. These pirates didn't have a Narwhal, but they did have a jet ski attached to their rib. With one hand she pulled her rifle out of its holster, while controlling the Narwhal with the other. She wished this was one of the android models Frida had told her about, with its own AI.

A woman in white combat gear jumped onto the jet ski. Leticia fired, hitting the side of the rib, then with the butt of her rifle she hit the grenade launcher. She missed, and the grenade exploded uselessly off to the side, then one of the pirates popped up and aimed their rifle at her.

Veering to the right, she revved the Narwhal to move out of range. It was a minute late, though, as their shot hit the back of the propulsion system, nearly causing the Narwhal to topple over. Leticia veered left, and then right, conscious that if she fell into the frigid waters they could kill her within minutes. Ditching the rifle, she used both hands to maintain control of the jet ski.

Losing speed and with her maneuverability badly compromised, her plan would be to plow into the shoreline and run for the snow-covered forest until she could be extracted. Gripping tightly with both hands she braced for a bumpy impact. It wouldn't be long before whoever shot her would follow.

She amped up the speed as much as she could, with the smell of smoke filling her nostrils. The Narwhal, which had limited capabilities on land, skidded across the shore and, without missing a beat, she jumped off, rolled, and ran hard into the tree line.

Desiree's gymnastic instruction sure came in handy, she thought. From a short distance to one side, she could hear another vehicle approaching.

She ignored the branches hitting her face and body. Her only concern was the ground beneath her feet—and then she stopped.

Something growled. Something *large*.

The wolf's eyes seemed to glow in the shadows of the trees. It was all white except for a large strip of black fur on the top of its head, and a few smaller patches falling from the crown trailing down its neck. It was as if this creature had been anointed with some dark oil. It appeared to be a female, and judging from its protective stance, there must have been a litter somewhere near. Leticia knew she had to stay away, and keep calm.

"I don't want to hurt you, loba," she said, keeping her words steady. "I'm backing away. This is your turf. I respect that."

The crunching snow beneath her feet and the soft powder falling from the branches was the only thing that separated Leticia and a creature that could tear her to pieces, unless she shot it on the spot. She didn't want to do that. It wasn't the wolf's fault—she shouldn't be there, and neither should the nukes they were trying to retrieve.

The wolf stared intently and continued to growl but didn't attack her. She backed away until the animal seemed satisfied, and melted into the shadows of the forest.

She entered a clearing that was a cold haze. White crystals glittered on barren branches. Crouching in the trees she began to send her coordinates to Desiree, tapping them into a pad on the left arm of her all-white cold-weather camo fatigues. She still had a firearm strapped to her right leg, and a blade. Those should be enough.

Footfalls caused her to look up.

A woman dressed in a similar fashion to Leticia held a pistol in her hand. She hadn't yet spotted her target, but she had a scanner in the other hand. That would detect her—it was now or never. Leticia raised her weapon to shoot.

A crack in the snow caused her to shift her gaze to their right. A deer stopped, turning its head toward the woman and then in Leticia's direction before darting away again. The woman followed its gaze and swung her head toward Leticia.

"Fuck," Leticia muttered, and she ran toward the enemy to knock her off her feet. Hoping she wouldn't have to kill her. She always carried double flex cuffs to avoid going down that path if she could.

The woman fell backward. Her weapon flew into the air and sunk into the soft snow nearby. She gave Leticia a hard punch to the face, knocking off her reflective glasses. Leticia attempted to turn her face down.

"You don't want to do this!" the woman strained to say as Leticia put her in a head lock. "Instability creates opportunity. I don't expect you to understand, but you serve kings who keep you as a peasant. Soon governments will cease to exist. Take away that square patch with a skull, and you're just like me. Continue, and you'll piss a lot of important people off. The Weyl—"

"Tell them to file a complaint with the Marines, pendeja," Leticia spat as she grabbed the cuffs out of her left cargo pants pocket.

Then they both stopped struggling.

More growling was coming from the trees—more

than one of them, this time. She slowly lifted her head, remembering what Lucinda had said, a lifetime ago.

"It doesn't understand anything but territory, hunger, and survival."

This wasn't a fight for her. She let go of the woman and silently backed away standing as tall as she could make herself. La loba—the wolf from before—was there. Leticia maintained eye contact. Her fingertips gently touched the pulse gun on her leg, just in case.

The other woman scrambled on the ground to look for the gun, her head moving violently toward the wolf pack that continued to growl. Then one howled, and another, and another.

Leticia continued to move back and away until she felt confident enough to turn away. Behind her, the sounds of snarls and barks turned to high-pitched shrieks from the woman who had been one of the pirates.

She sprinted through the trees, careful not to lose her footing. That would be the end of her. When she made it back to the shoreline, a USCM team was already flying overhead. In the distance the pirates' rib floated in the icy waters, overturned and smoking. Two bodies bobbed with the waves.

"For a minute there I didn't think I would taste grease ever again," Leticia said. "You guys are the best."

"The pack is only as strong as each wolf," Mohammed

said, "and every wolf is only as strong as their pack. You should know that more than ever now."

"To my lobas!" Leticia responded.

Frida raised her beer, looking slightly tipsy. "Don't forget yourself," she said. "An alpha with fangs! Gang, Gang, Gang, *jefa*!" She even pronounced it right this time, Leticia noticed.

"Don't worry, I haven't forgot myself," Leticia said, licking cheese from her hand. "That is why I want it."

"What? The promotion?" Nathan put his Corona down.

"You should." Desiree raised her glass. "Your marksmanship is hot, you're a decent leader, and judging from that last mission, the animals love you."

The table murmured in agreement as they continued to consume their meal. Leticia was proud of what she and her team had done, but she didn't want to be chasing pirates for the rest of her life. None of them did.

"Yep," she said. "We've been doing this, how long now?" She took a drink. "There's a way to get on the fast track, and I'm going to take it. Once I've completed the written test, according to the rules I'll need one other person to accompany me."

She left it there...

No one volunteered.

"I'd rather do the Crucible over again, than the twenty-four hours you're looking at," Mohammed said. "No sleep or rest. Even less food, if you eat at all. It's in the field and not in a simulated environment. Plus I need a break." He shook his head. "I hear Haas is interested…"

Leticia replied, "I don't trust her, or whoever she might take as her number one."

"Nothing against you, boss," he said, "but they should probably consider just handing her the promotion, considering her family. All military, all the way. Why go to the trouble, when you don't stand a chance?"

Desiree turned to Leticia. "Don't listen to Crow. He'll be eating his words. Give it a shot. If it doesn't work, then at least you'll know what your next move will be. I got you." She turned to their companions. "And the rest of you… you've all seen some shit up close and personal."

"Yeah, but I'm tired," Frida said. "The side gig is killing me."

"Yeah, same here." Nathan placed his hand on Mohammed's. "I'm tired of hearing about the pay and bonuses you get for going private, as long as you have the right military experience. You take your pick of a country, corporation, you name it, there's a job in the stars and your name on a big check. Desiree, can you say that you aren't tempted to go back to New York for some private sector job? Big city means big pay."

"It's tempting." Desiree hung her head. "If I do go back, you all have to come visit."

Leticia understood where they were coming from, and she shared the frustration. That was why she had to do this. She wanted more responsibility, *needed* more—and a bigger check. Maybe even get involved in policy.

The only way for her would be up.

"No hard feelings," she said. "I feel you, and thanks, Desiree. We can start on Monday. For now, let's just enjoy being alive."

Leticia stood next to Melissa Haas, who held the same rank as Leticia and wore a permanent haughty sneer on her face. Leticia wanted the satisfaction of wiping it right off when she was the one getting promoted.

Colonel Smith stood before them.

"You both know the rules. It was your responsibility to read the brief, and you got your one chance. Anything you can't remember, anything you do outside of what's been laid out, will count against you. Your number one will be taken to a pre-determined location, where there will be further instructions. You'll be taken to a different set of coordinates off the coast and dropped off.

"It will be dawn," he continued, "and you'll have twenty-four hours. Now go and get ready."

Haas turned to Leticia and offered her hand. "Good luck," she said, and she seemed to mean it. "We both have military in our blood, so may the best woman win."

A short time later they sat on the Narwhals, ready to drop into the water. From there they would make their way into a swamp that teemed with alligators, snakes, and who-knew-what other dangers. Clouds obscured the dawn, prolonging the darkness. By this time Desiree would already be waiting in an undisclosed place.

Leticia revved the engine on her vehicle. This exercise was all about speed and precision. There was a slight resistance on the controls, but there was no time to do a full diagnostic. Haas watched her from the corner of her eye.

Leticia didn't like that.

In their helmet earpiece they heard the CO.

"*It's time*," he said. "*Go!*"

Both of them were propelled forward into the air. Using her right thumb Leticia pulled hard on the acceleration to get her onto the water smoothly. As the surface approached, the propulsion jets activated and she felt good about the distance she'd achieved.

She didn't bother looking to her side. All that mattered was the goal in front of her. The Narwhal glided with ease across the open water, and she pressed the acceleration again.

Nothing.

¡Pinche tu madre! Fuck!

Leticia tried again, and a sick panic formed in her gut. The Narwhal remained in neutral as it coasted and began to slow on its own. What the fuck was happening? Had it been sabotaged? Haas passed her by, leaving a large wake in the shape of a V.

Victory.

Dead in the water, she had to think. The shore was close, but so far away. The only option was to swim, and given the distance she would have to ditch everything. Leticia looked to the sky and screamed her frustration, until she remembered the shaman, Orozco.

Just this moment.

No time to blame Haas.

She removed her backpack and waterproof jacket. To make up time she had to be as light as possible. Reaching down, she made sure the switchblade was secure inside her boot. The helmet she kept on, to remain connected to the comms system. Her scanner and map were waterproof and would fit inside her cargo pocket on the side of her fatigues.

Jumping into the water, she swam hard. One arm at a time with her feet kicking. Forward, with each breath taking her closer. There was nothing else to do, and no point worrying.

After half an hour she made it. The sun was beginning to break through the clouds, which was good news. In this heat she would be dry in no time. Removing the water from her boots, she gave her T-shirt a quick wring. The scanner gave her the coordinates for the next rendezvous. As she began to jog, she could see Haas' footprints in the sand.

Anger gave her the fuel to pick up her pace.

* * *

Leticia's thighs burned with the increasing amounts of lactic acid building within the muscles, but she had to carry on through the mud. There had been heavy rains, so the water level in the swamp was higher than usual. The ground pulled on the soles of her boots with every step she took.

It had been hours, and hunger began to gnaw at her stomach. She had been forced to abandon her provisions, but there was enough in the swamp to keep her going if she needed to eat something. No sign that any people had been there, though, and nothing on her scanner to alert her to Desiree's presence. She continued on with eyes and ears on full alert, despite a niggling desire to crawl into a ball and sleep.

The sun was low in the sky, and nocturnal animals would be out soon. Her compass watch beeped, picking up Desiree's vitals, and Leticia stopped in her tracks. Sweat dripped from the bandana tied around her forehead. She was close, but the device didn't specify where.

The sunlight was filtered through the swampy canopy of trees, making it hard to see. Listening for sounds that couldn't be attributed to the environment, she scanned the area, taking in an inch at a time.

Then she saw it.

In the distance, the green wasn't the same as the other trees or foliage. It didn't move like it was of the swamp, either. Leticia moved forward cautiously, looking at the ground for footprints. No, they wouldn't have come this way. Too obvious.

As she got closer to the greenery that looked off, she saw that it was a camo canopy, and pulled it off. Nothing. A decoy?

A water snake slithered across her boot. She kicked it off. A chunk of mud flew into the air. That's when she saw a black wire that could have been mistaken for a vine or root. Following it, she tossed aside foliage and muck until her hands and fingernails were caked with dirt. The wire trailed into more water, murky so she couldn't see the bottom. Bright green scum floated on the surface.

With no visible signs of predators, she dipped both hands into the water and pulled on the cable. It wouldn't give, so she pulled as hard as she could, her shoulders flexing until they cramped. Still no release, and the water was getting deeper—she would have to go under. Holding on to the cable, she plunged her head beneath the surface, steadying both legs against the inner wall of a hole that was not natural.

With Haas' face in her mind, she pulled with both hands, giving it five hard yanks. It finally broke free. A loud hiss and beeping made her turn around.

"Amiga!"

It was Desiree. One of the wide swamp trees wasn't a tree after all. Leticia felt lightheaded from the hours of exertion.

"The instructions?" she said eagerly.

"What instructions?"

"They should be with you?"

Desiree frowned. "There was nothing inside, and no one told me anything. They blindfolded me during transport and I wasn't allowed to remove it until the door closed. I've literally been sitting in there, staring at darkness the entire time."

They searched the compartment in which Desiree had been kept, looking for a secret drawer or container, but the space was empty. Leticia wanted to sink to the bottom of the swamp. She looked at her watch. Haas had a running start, and now this. She climbed out, not sure how to proceed.

She told Desiree what had happened with the Narwhal.

"I can't believe those motherfuckers sabotaged you," Desiree said. "Was there anything else in the initial brief?"

"There's a second marker," Leticia said. "According to my map, it's not far, and there should be a vehicle there. Haas will have it by now." Leticia shook her head. "It was all a set-up. They cheated—I *know* it. Haas pulled strings, and I'll bet you a bottle of whiskey they'll claim it was all a big joke, or just deny it."

"You're probably right," Desiree said. "But what do we do? Stay quiet?"

"No. Turn over every damn fact until there's enough proof piled up to climb to the top. That's what we do." She wiped away the sweat and peered around in the fading light. "Tell you what, though, I wouldn't mind being paired with one of them in another exercise, so I can knock them the fuck on their asses."

"How far are we from base?"

Leticia glanced at her comms control watch. "Not far. Fifteen short miles. I never realized how wild it was this close to the base, ever since the Great Rising. No wonder the base was relocated here. It's great for training."

Desiree kept her eyes on Leticia. "You have it in you for one big push?" she asked. "I know it's probably too late."

Leticia looked at her muddy boots and hands. She had to accept the "L"—everyone did at some point. Losses were a part of life.

Quitting didn't have to be.

"Fucking race you. I have unfinished business."

Desiree slapped her on the back and they began to jog. It quickly turned into a sprint.

They made it back to base looking as if they had run through every test of Mictlan. It felt like hell, too. She glanced at her compass watch. Everyone would be in the mess hall for supper.

"Where are you going, Leticia? Showers are this way."

Leticia ignored Desiree and headed toward the mess hall, marching with purpose. She burst through the doors, allowing mud to fly from her stomping feet. From the distance she could see Haas and Martinez. Her strides became longer, leaving muddy prints across the white floor.

With one swipe of her hand, she tossed Haas' tray across the table, then the Coke Martinez had in front of him.

"You have something to say to me, puta," Leticia screamed. "That little sabotage wasn't fun or fair. Both of you should be ashamed of yourselves and kicked the fuck out."

Haas stood to face Leticia. "I don't know what you're talking about."

Leticia continued to stand her ground with a snarl on her face.

"¡Mentirosa! Yeah, right."

"Haas and Vasquez! To the main office. Now."

A CO approached them.

"We will see, Haas," Leticia spat.

Leticia stood next to Haas in front of Colonel Smith.

"I realize you are disappointed, Lance Corporal Vasquez, but we have no proof that Lance Corporal Haas committed any wrongdoing. For all we know, you could have done it yourself. There are no cameras in the field, and for good reason. Candidates must perform without artificial distractions."

"Sir," she replied, careful to control her reactions. "It was clear someone had sabotaged my vehicle. And it clearly states in the rules that this is not permitted. 'No candidate is permitted to come into contact with the other candidate's equipment.'"

"But do you have proof?"

"With all due respect, sir, what proof do you need? I left the vehicle in the water. It should have been recovered."

"You could have done it yourself, to gain sympathy," Smith persisted, giving no ground. "This could be *your* way of sabotaging Haas." He looked at his tablet. "I see your mother is Jenette Vasquez. She died with dignity, but had a nasty track record."

Leticia stood there, trying to hold back the pounding waves of tears and anger hurling themselves just beneath her skin. She wouldn't cry. Not in front of them.

Colonel Smith shook his head.

"Just accept that you lost the promotion."

"Send someone to check the Narwhal."

"I have, and until then this matter is on hold. Haas will receive the promotion. I'm sorry. Maybe next time, but if you continue with this attitude, it will be highly unlikely." He tapped the screen and put the tablet on the desk.

Leticia stood there, feeling her cheeks go hot. Left out in the fucking cold, and for what? The part of her that resented Ramón for playing the game rose to the surface, whispering in her ear like a little devil.

Give up.

As much as she wanted to, she had to continue to hope. Hope for change. Hope could be buoyant, but carry it too long without anything in hand, and it could leave you exhausted.

"You both are dismissed."

Haas and Leticia saluted Colonel Smith, turned, and left his office.

Desiree was waiting outside of the building. "So? What happened?" She tried to keep up with Leticia who didn't slow her march.

"I have to let it go."

"That's bullshit, man. You know who her father is?"

Leticia stopped and looked at Desiree. "No, but I *want* to know," she growled. "They brought up my mother."

Desiree shook her head. "Her dad is an ex-major general who does private security for Weyland-Yutani. A big-time government contractor."

Leticia felt her entire body go slack. Every muscle losing the will to move. What was the point of all the stress, the striving to be better, to take a stand, when others had it all mapped out already? In that moment she understood the flares of anger she saw in Ramón's eyes, and how easy it was for determination to grow into something insatiable. The desire to win could make you do what you never thought you would.

Yet part of her couldn't sever that rope to the hope that she was on the right path, as much as it was a journey wading through tits-high muck.

"I'll catch up with you later tonight. I'm going to go for a walk."

"Yeah, I actually have a job interview," Desiree admitted. "Private security. Pay is great, and no threat to my life, except maybe falling in love. You better come see me."

"I hear you," Leticia said. "Good luck, Desiree." She gave an ironic smile. "So much for big dreams to change the world."

Feeling like a foolish, bitter idiot, she left her friend. The best remedy to resistance was not to resist it. If this was truly the way it was meant to be, then where the fuck was everything she hoped to accomplish?

Leticia remembered when that spineless pendeja in high school accused her of shoplifting. Then her mind raced to the long time it had taken to hear from the Marines, while watching everyone around her get their responses. Back then, all she could do was smile and keep the faith.

Where would she put her faith now? How could she have been so sure of traveling to space, and becoming an elite soldier?

Fuck this place and fuck waiting. Destiny didn't exist.

It was time to think about writing a resignation letter.

Find another way, Leticia, or another way will find you.

1 8

"This Dia de Los Muertos is extra special," Roseanna proclaimed. "Congratulations, Ramón. The youngest chief financial officer for the Weyland-Yutani Corporation!"

"Thank you, tía. I couldn't have done it without your support."

"And Mary Anne—she stopped working after the twins were born. You can't discount her contribution."

"Everyone is good. Lara Jenette and Lorenzo are growing up fast." Ramón turned toward Leticia slumped in a dining chair staring vacantly at a tray of condiments that went with dinner. "How about you, Leticia? Any good news? I was sorry to hear about the promotion."

Leticia rolled her eyes toward Roseanna, who turned the chicken flautas in a shallow pan of hot oil. Leticia could feel her temperature rising like sizzling grease. She didn't want to talk about the promotion. Any minute frustration would send her popping out of the frying pan.

"I'm taking night classes, and doing the Marine thing in the day—at least until my paperwork is processed," she said. "Who knows how long that will take. Not much else to report."

"I know we have not always been on the same page," he responded, "and this isn't charity, but I might have something for you."

"Like when you wanted to write my essay?"

"Nope. Not like that at all. I think you are being wasted, your *skills* are being wasted right now. Our mother left us letters, and mine said we had to look out for each other. Well, that is what I want to do."

Leticia played with a spoon, stirring it in a bowl of homemade salsa. She knew he wasn't lying because that was in her letter, as well.

"I'm listening."

"Thank you," he said, and he took a deep breath. "Weyland-Yutani has a new CEO who is trying to clean up past mistakes and create a new, ethical way of doing business. There's an opening for a prominent security job. It would be a big payday. You could buy your own home, or travel to another world. The point being that you would have the only kind of freedom that matters."

"I'm supposed to believe a company like that has grown a heart, like the Grinch? That's about as easy as making a U-turn in a vacuum." She shook her head. "Nah, I'm good. Our mother's last mission was for them."

"And why was she there in the first place?" he countered. "I'm talking real freedom, Leticia. I've accumulated more wealth than anyone in the family history, probably more than all of them combined. But not just money—what I'm *accomplishing*. Real wealth gives you a lifestyle to create more wealth and more opportunity. Real wealth spans across generations. My children will learn from me, and be bigger and better. Everyone will know the Vasquez name." When she didn't reply, he added, "Come on, don't be stupid."

Before she could respond, Roseanna spoke up. "Don't fight or be unfair with each other," she said. "It was bad enough when you were kids, but you are grown-ass adults now." She pointed tongs at them before turning back to the cooking.

"Will you at least give the executive a chance?" he persisted. "I'm talking one hour."

Roseanna stepped between them, placing a plate of flautas and rice on the table. She turned to Leticia. "It's just an hour," she echoed. "That's less time than it takes to get a tattoo, and maybe it's what you two need."

"Fine." Leticia grabbed a hot flauta and dipped it into the salsa, then the bowl of guacamole. "One meeting with Old Man Weyland."

"He's not a Weyland, or an old man."

"Whatever. Set it up. Let's eat, before the ancestors get pissed."

Ramón placed his hand over hers. "Thank you. After

we eat, I will book a flight, hotel, and reserve a meeting in his calendar."

As usual, Ramón went above and beyond and chose a hotel in the tallest skyscraper in Manhattan. She craned her neck as she stared up at the enormous building, and wondered how many secrets those windows shielded the world from. Before this meeting she had dropped in on Desiree at her new job.

They met in a fancy coffee shop on the ground floor. Ramón ordered only the best for them, though it was too early for champagne, and he didn't drink much.

"Coffee?" the barista said.

Ramón took the paper cup. "Thanks."

The java came from a nearly extinct animal found in Indonesia that ate the coffee beans, then shit them out. That was what gave the joe its unique taste. It was the only brand Ramón would drink, he explained.

Rich folks.

"Don't worry," he said, "this is going to be super relaxed. Jacob is a little… different." Leticia decided not to press him. She would see what he meant, soon enough.

"Lead the way."

They walked through the lobby with the security team nodding in recognition. Ramón walked with confidence and importance, as well he should. He was a man with the good looks of the old film star Esai Morales, and the smarts beyond anyone he knew. Smart to the point that he was dangerous, which was precisely why he rose through the ranks. The company didn't want its *consigliere* floating around with its secrets, or worse, going to the competitors.

Ramón fiddled with the zip on his fleece as they stepped into the elevator that led directly to Jacob's personal office.

"Be cool, don't ask too many questions, and for God's sake smile," he said—the only words spoken on the ride to the penthouse. Leticia opted to give him a scowl. There was real worry on Ramón's face, though. He was always more concerned with appearances than she. The secretary sitting outside of Jacob's office greeted Ramón warmly, her smile a little *too* warm for Leticia's liking, but that was her brother.

"Go on in. He's waiting for you."

"Thank you, Sara. Your hair is lovely today."

Leticia ignored the comment. She could feel herself go tense, however, as if to put on invisible armor. She had one of her mother's bandanas in her back pocket.

The office overlooked the main hub of the MagnoRail train system. As busy as it was below, not a sound could be heard. There were windows from floor to ceiling, and it gave her a little vertigo, her mind and body tricked to thinking they were hovering above the real world. To her surprise, there was no old decrepit man speckled with age spots and trembling hands. The only occupant was a guy who looked of a similar age to her, dressed in head-to-toe Patagonia.

We're going into space, not Everest, she thought wryly.

As he stood to greet them, she wondered who this pencil-pushing chump was. Probably a lawyer with a million papers for her to sign, releasing the company from any knowledge, culpability, recourse, or anything that resembled responsibility. The world was built on this bullshit. She was ready, but truth be told, it was these kinds of people—men like her brother—who she feared the most.

"Hello, Jacob," Ramón said. "Please meet my sister Leticia."

Jacob? Her eyes slitted a bit, then she recovered.

"Hi, Leticia," Jacob Vickers said. "Your brother has told me a lot about you. I especially liked the stories about the frogs in his bed."

Leticia thought this guy might be okay, after all. That *was* a great story.

"Well, while he's been telling tales, he hasn't told me much about you," she replied. "I thought I was meeting 'Old Man Weyland.'" Then she remembered. *"He's not a Weyland, or an old man."*

Jacob smiled, extending his hand. "Old Man Vickers at your service. It's great to meet you. You're a Marine Raider, aren't you? That's very impressive."

Leticia felt slightly embarrassed. So sometimes she got it wrong. He moved closer to her without looking at her brother. She slipped her hand into his to shake it. Leticia didn't know if she imagined it, or if the weight of his hand possessed a gravitational force of its own.

He was anything but an "Old Man," and he wasn't just young—he was very attractive with blue eyes and light brown hair just long enough to tuck behind his ear. His gaze continued to hold her.

Avery was nice, sexy, and solid—a cowboy.

Vickers was electricity with a British accent.

"I don't know how much Ramón has told you about the job. You would go in as a contractor, to establish a basic security force for the colony. Nothing too 'military,' nor like we're trying to police the place. There should be some security presence to make people feel safe, but not to exert force."

"It sounds like more than a desk job, but without fighting or danger," she said, beginning to get her feet under her. "That should be no problem—the Raiders do a lot more than combat."

"Well, it was actually Ramón who suggested a specialized force," Vickers said. "He knows how much this project means to me, and made the point that if we ever faced an outside threat, we should be prepared. Special forces could remain low key if nothing overt is happening, yet react swiftly to anything unexpected. I agree with his thinking.

"Olinka isn't meant to be of any military value," he continued. "I want to gather the best and brightest to live there, to create wonders for humanity outside of the threat of war. With all of the conflicts currently flaring around the galaxy, I want to create a planet without borders or petty squabbles over resources. Everyone will have equal access to what they need to thrive.

"It's about bloody time humans learned how to govern and live a different way." His voice carried the strength of commitment. "It's time for us to evolve. You will be paid very well, and watch history as it's being made… I hope."

"I see." Leticia didn't hide her reticence.

Vickers must have recognized it. "Hey, I'm gambling, too, and doing my best to get people to take a chance on me. I can't make any promises how boring it might be, or not."

Leticia liked him, and found that strange, given his last name. Maybe he was the one in his family who *would* make a difference, and change the course of his industry. Hell, a Weyland had cured cancer. She supposed anything was possible.

"Send me more information," she said. "I want as many details as you can provide."

His eyes brightened with the light of a kid asked to play on someone's team.

"You'll have the essentials this afternoon," he promised. "And if you're available, there is a wine tasting tonight— an extracurricular activity sponsored by the company. You can meet the rest of the board. Will you join us? Your brother is invited."

Ramón spoke first. "You know I wouldn't miss it for the world. I'm not sure it's Leticia's thing, though."

She shot him a dirty look. "I'm available, and it *can* be my thing. I'll be there."

Ramón suppressed a frown, but Vickers didn't notice.

"Great," he said. "I will see you both at the Waldorf at eight."

Leticia didn't want to look away from him.

Once in the elevator Leticia felt comfortable to confront her brother.

"Why do you always have to try to speak for me?"

"You don't understand these people," he said. "They aren't simple. These are snakes, Leticia."

"I guess it takes one to know one?" she responded. "And are you calling *me* simple?"

Ramón rolled his eyes and forced a smile. "You're not simple, Leticia—you're just not devious. Your enemies tend to meet you head on."

"Only in combat do you see the whites of your enemy's eyes," she replied. "There's a hell of a lot to deal with before that." Once again, Haas' face appeared in her mind. It just made her angrier.

Ramón ignored her last comment, looking at a message on his phone.

"Hey, since you aren't booked into the hotel for another night, why don't you hang at my apartment. It can be like old times. It's not far. And go buy yourself something *nice* to wear tonight."

"When did you get a place in the city?" she asked. "I thought you worked from Boston. Everything okay at home?" She felt herself caught off guard. Was his mood related to something happening with his family? She'd always thought his good looks would get him in trouble one day.

"Yeah, as fine as it can be." Ramón blew air out of his mouth and looked to the top of the elevator until it stopped and the doors opened. "Look, I can't get into it now. Here are the keys, I'll text you the address." Then he dashed through the lobby. "Something nice!" he shouted over his shoulder.

Leticia smirked. She would wear something nice, all right, and he would pay for it. Mary Anne had told her they had an account at Saks where he got all of his suits tailor-made, and she bought her outfits for company events. Today Leticia would be a lady who lunched and shopped.

When she arrived at the apartment she was carrying an armful of bags. In addition to an outfit for the evening, she had bought a new pair of red-and-black sneakers and pretty underwear, just for fun. To avoid alarming Mary Anne, Leticia had texted her from the shop, sending photos of her haul.

Mary Anne texted her back a picture from the playground where she had taken the kids.

Next time I will join you!

Leticia thought she looked sad, but maybe it was just running after the twins. Her firm had made her redundant while on maternity leave, and she never bothered to go back. Neither she nor Ramón wanted a nanny.

"Our tía was the one person who pushed me, not a stranger she paid. No, our kids need a parent," Ramón had told her, making his feelings clear, and Mary Anne had complied.

The apartment was beautiful, with a view overlooking a small gated park kept exclusively for the tenants of the building. It struck Leticia as odd, though, that there were no family photos, not even of the children. It looked more like a bachelor pad, with nothing but sparkling water and beer in the fridge and a separate wine fridge that was fully stocked.

It had the feel of a show apartment.

Damn, I could get used to this, she thought.

Ramón rarely drank, and she wouldn't have been surprised if half the wine bottles were empty and only there to look good. Ramón's overriding vice was his ego. He couldn't resist indulging himself, and that left very little for others.

She tried to resist the urge to snoop, though it was in her nature. That had been how she found out Ramón was stealing tests for other high schoolers. When Roseanna wouldn't buy him a car, he bought one himself, saying the money came from odd jobs. Of course, she believed him, and Leticia hadn't wanted to snitch.

It would catch up with him one day.

The bedroom looked as unused as the kitchen. Her instinct got the better of her and she looked in both side tables and the bathroom cabinets to check for condoms. Nothing. There was plenty of time before she would have to be ready, so she propped her tablet on the coffee table, then sprawled out on the L-shaped green velvet sofa and slept until she needed to shower and dress.

In her gut Brenda always knew she couldn't trust Gilda Patel. The woman had literally stabbed her in the back, then insisted it was for her own good.

The incident reinforced the need to have the detonator fob, and for her to monitor the slightest physical changes in the three queens—who were only meant to produce eggs and Xenomorphs for further experimentation in the biological weapons program. There was still so much they had to learn before they could fully control them.

Especially La Reina.

While the queens remained in stasis, however, the other Xenomorphs were becoming more aggressive.

Now a poor soul appeared on a screen in her office that took up half of the wall behind her desk. He had been infected with the activated bacteria, and was to be sent into the holding pen with one of the monsters. Blinded, he would not see what he would face, and in its own way that was a mercy. His skin was streaked with black veins and his eyes were completely white. Sweat rolled down the side of his face.

The Xenomorphs were kept on a corridor one level above the queens, along one side of the pyramid. A steel acid-resistant door separated each from the rest. Along a corridor adjacent to the wing were the rooms where humans were kept. With the swift opening of a retractable door, the two would meet in a shared space.

Upon hearing the door open, the sightless man moved toward the sound. It shut just as quickly behind him, and he whipped his head around as it locked with the metallic *clang* of a death knell. He froze in place, until the silence was filled with a hiss.

"What are you doing to me?" He waved outstretched arms. "What have I done?"

The Xenomorph's head rolled left to right, but it did not move toward the intruder in its space. As the man slowly walked around the room in confusion, the Xenomorph kept its distance, yet snapped its jaws into the air. It let out a shriek, and Brenda felt every muscle in her body jerk.

The other Xenomorphs along the corridor screeched in unison, rearing their heads and pounding on the doors that separated them.

In the test chamber, true fear was displayed by both species. They only wanted to live, albeit for different reasons. She wondered how long this tango would last—they had seen what they needed to see. The bacteria did, indeed, fend off the monsters.

"That's enough," she growled. "Pipe the bacteria into the room at full strength." At least then the blind man would know peace.

"But we are not done." The android who had opposed her before flashed that same menacing smile. He swiped and clicked on a tablet. To Brenda's surprise, another door opened into the chamber, and another test subject—a woman—stepped through. This one had the same black streaks.

Wasting no time, the Xenomorph launched itself forward as the doors began to shut.

"No!" Brenda bellowed. "It can't get out!"

She tried to grab the tablet from the android.

The clang of metal hitting metal was as loud as the screams of the woman as her arms flew into the air. Her wailing stopped when the Xenomorph's tail arched like a javelin before tearing her head from her neck. Red and black spewed everywhere, covering the walls, and the blind man crumpled into a ball crying in the corner.

The Xenomorph ripped into the body, coating itself with her blood. Every sickening blow caused the blind man to jerk tighter into a ball.

"It knows the bacteria isn't active."

"A very smart pet indeed." Brenda would have sworn the synth was smiling smugly.

Caught up in a killing rage that must have overwhelmed its survival instincts, the Xenomorph used its tail to spear the crying man through the skull. Instantly blots of ash began to appear on its carapace, shrinking as they disappeared beneath the surface.

Brenda succeeded in jerking the tablet from the android and shoved him as hard as she could, sending him to the floor. His programming would prevent him from retaliating—at least she hoped as much.

Typing in commands, she gave the tablet a swipe and the entire screen became a black fog. The Xenomorph let out a guttural scream that sent the others into a renewed frenzy.

When the fog cleared, the man's flesh was disintegrating to crimson and obsidian ash. The Xenomorph appeared as if it were made of charred wood. Her hands trembled, despite a surge of power and relief. Certain she had headed off a disaster that could have consumed the entire facility, she handed the tablet back to the synth.

"Get that room sterilized and cleared out."

Brenda left her office to retire to her room and write a full report.

She had to take a stand.

1 9

She arrived purposely looking out of place, mostly to stick it to Ramón. It would be a pleasure to see those corporate stiffs sweat, too. Just because she was a Marine didn't mean she didn't know how to hold her own in stilettos.

Anything could be used as a weapon in a pinch.

A backless dress made from shimmering black chainmail and held up by spaghetti straps revealed her tattoos and strong thighs that brushed each other when she walked. Bright red roses bloomed at the base of her spine, echoing her lipstick. The cowl-neck revealed just a hint of cleavage and the hem stopped mid-thigh. She carried a small purse—also a potential weapon.

Ramón waited by the coat check in the lobby of the Waldorf Astoria, which had only recently completed renovations.

"Wow," he whispered. "I said nice, not sexy." Then he added, "Saks called, thanking me for my continued support. Then Mary Anne messaged me saying she wants more time to go shopping with you."

"You can afford it."

"The attitude… I swear." She couldn't tell if he was being serious. "Never mind, anything for my sister. Why don't we go in."

She opened the door for Ramón. "After you, brother." He shook his head while walking past her.

The restaurant was filled with round tables and dark leather booths. The lights were low, even over the long bar. Jacob stood alone sipping on a lowball glass, dressed in what he had been wearing earlier in the day. He appeared relaxed as he watched the crowd, then he spotted Leticia and Ramón. Her eyes met his across the crowd of diners, and it felt like there was something there. Without giving Ramón a further thought, she walked straight over.

Jacob's eyes widened, accompanied by a smile. She could tell he was trying hard not to gawk.

"What happened to the black Nikes?"

"Well, Ramón told me to dress appropriately. I chose something fun."

He opened his mouth to speak then closed it again. Leticia cocked her head, knowing she looked good. Felt good, too. The flirtation was entirely inappropriate, but she had been lying low for a long time. She'd thought she might have imagined the tension between them in the office, yet it still lingered.

Ramón interrupted. "Guys, the tasting is in the private room." She shot him a look, but he continued. "We can hang out another time. We have business."

"Yes, you're right," Jacob said, and she caught a hint of disappointment. "By the way, Ramón, did you hear about Benjamin Ross? Terrible news. Isn't he the one who brought you in, while you were still at Harvard?"

Ramón looked off-balance.

"I heard," he said, "and I was shocked. I mean, to be found in a bathtub with llelo up his nose and on his chest? I've always kept it strictly professional with him, and it looks like that was for the best. He seemed to have a problem with the white stuff, but it was none of my business."

"Smart, Ramón," Jacob replied. "Alright, let's get this over with." Ramón led the way, and Jacob and Leticia trailed behind. As they did, Jacob leaned closer to Leticia's ear, close enough for her to smell the cologne he wore.

"I really don't like these things. Even though I went to good schools I grew up around pubs with sticky floors, pints, and packets of crisps. Football matches on the telly."

Goddamn, she loved a good accent.

They walked into a large room and found a long table topped with wine. There were spittoons, and well-dressed people wearing expensive clothing and even more expensive watches. Ramón did his best to talk to a variety of attendees, but he kept one eye on Leticia as she stood next to Jacob—who gave her all of his attention. Neither of them spat out the alcohol like they were supposed to when tasting fine wine.

She could feel the heaviness of her brother's watchful eye but ignored it. Jacob was captivating.

"So, you want me to get a team together," she said, trying to focus. "I got your email, and briefly looked over the details."

"Yes," he replied, "and the sooner the better."

"I'm not sure if Ramón told you, but I was passed up for a promotion—one that was important to me. It was a set-up, but it taught me something important. Maybe to change the game we're playing, even when we're made to think we've failed."

Jacob's gaze was one of understanding.

She thought it was sincere.

"That's exactly what I think," he said, "and it's what Olinka is about, and it's the way I choose to live, as well. I'm a Vickers. The politics that brought me to this position weren't pretty, and I have many opponents who would just as well like to see me strung up by the neck.

"Living life in England protected me in many ways," he continued, "and kept me sheltered from the business. Peter Weyland did many great things, but somewhere along the way the company became something else. He dealt with climate change. He saved the planet, and now we need to save the soul of humanity. I want to get back to his roots."

"Roots are important." Leticia looked around the room,

at the crowd talking among themselves, and realized that she didn't belong here. Ramón was distracted for the moment, and she wanted to get to know Jacob better—without a chaperone. She touched his forearm.

"How about we leave this place and you come with me?"

He nodded. "Let me just say some—"

She interrupted him. "No goodbyes. Let's go before anyone"—*Ramón*, she thought but didn't say—"realizes we're gone." He shot her a strange look.

"Show me the way. I'm all yours."

Leticia gave the room one more glance then took Jacob by the hand. They took the elevator to the lobby, exited through revolving doors, and jumped into an automated taxi waiting in front of the hotel.

"Where are we going?"

"The bad side of town," she whispered in his ear.

Leticia scanned her watch and typed the location into the vehicle's keypad. Jacob laughed at her comment and watched the direction the taxi was moving. Traffic was steady, but not at a standstill.

They turned onto a block with very few streetlights and pulled up in front of a club that looked dark. No sign to indicate its name. There was a bouncer in the front who could have been a giant—he probably injected growth hormone.

"Leticia! Good to see you again."

"Hey, Jack." She gave him a wink. "I'm here to see Desiree."

"No problem. I know you, so I'll let you both in."

Jack opened the door to allow them to enter. Leticia held out her wrist for the cash band to be scanned by the receptionist. Jacob held out his wrist to swipe, but Leticia placed her hand on his arm.

"I got it." She turned to the receptionist. "Two please."

"You didn't have to pay," he protested.

"You paid for that fancy thing before," she said. "Now get ready for the best mozzarella sticks and wings. I'm starving!"

"So am I." Jacob followed Leticia down an aisle of half-naked women dancing behind slot tipping machines blinking with numbers. Leticia ran her wrist across every screen on the left side of the aisle as she walked. A whooping of cheers erupted in her wake, even above "Love Is Strong" by the Rolling Stones. They stopped in front of a woman who hung at the top of a pole, ten feet in the air. She had a robotic leg. One hand held on to the pole, and her metal thigh was magnetically attached. She circled down with her real leg splayed out. Clear platform heels glittered beneath the spotlight. A large grin spread across her face when she saw Leticia standing in front of her stage.

The number 100 blinked across her screen where Leticia had just tipped.

"Well, if it isn't my favorite bad bitch and Raider!" she shouted as she slapped her metal thigh to detach from the pole. "Come to see Desiree again? And who is this?"

Leticia glanced at Jacob who must have been blushing—
it was impossible to tell in the low purple lights of the
room, punctuated by lights over each small stage.

"Hey, Taffy. Can you grab us a couch in the Champagne
Room? I'm here to see Desiree."

"Sure, she was in the back office organizing the bouncer
roster. I'll tell her you're here."

"Feel free to join us for food. Jacob here arranged for
wine, and all they had were these little things that were
supposed to pass for a meal." She turned. "Sorry, Jacob."

"I would have been happy for a Cornish pasty or
ploughman's lunch," he replied. "The company arranges
all that poncy stuff. Appearances…"

Taffy stepped off her small stage. "I'll be sure to reserve
you a table and let Carl know to let you in to see Desiree.
Your name will be a hologram above the table. New tech
and it's getting fancy around here."

Leticia led Jacob through the rest of the darkened club
until they reached a back office with another bouncer
standing at the door.

"Here to see Desiree."

The bouncer just nodded and opened the door. As they
entered, Desiree turned and gave Leticia a huge smile. In
sharp contrast to the dancers, she was dressed in a black
suit and white shirt unbuttoned to the top of her sternum.
Her shoes were black-and-red Nike sneakers.

"This is unexpected." She looked Jacob up and down
before giving him a nod, then went back to Leticia. "I guess

I'm happy you brought your latest fling to meet me. Nice dress by the way. Your style expensive, now that you're a civilian."

"Actually, I'm here on business. Taffy was setting us up a private table in the Champagne Room. You free?"

"I'm always free for business. Let's go the back way."

Another door led to a narrow hallway, and they entered the Champagne Room from there. Each table was private, hidden behind silver drapes. The occupied spaces were drawn shut. Their table was open, with Leticia's name blinking above it. They ordered from a console in the table—two orders of mozzarella sticks, faux chicken wings, and a bottle of bourbon.

"You wouldn't be impressed with the wine they serve here," Leticia said. "No offense."

"None taken." Desiree made herself comfortable on a soft silver couch. "Right, so why are you here? Usually you call before."

"This came up kind of suddenly," Leticia said. "I'm not going to bullshit you, Desiree. The government didn't exactly take care of us like they promised, what with new cuts and a new administration. We don't owe them anything. Jacob here has a job, and yours truly might be the director of security. If I'm going to take it, I'm going to need a team—the best."

Jacob looked surprised, but kept silent. The bottle of bourbon and glasses arrived before the food.

"How much we talking?" Desiree asked.

Leticia flashed a persuasive smile. "Gimme your arm, bonita." Leticia pulled a pen out of her purse, and wrote a number.

Desiree looked at her arm, then Jacob, then back to Leticia. "You're shitting me." She frowned. "I don't do assassinations or overthrow governments."

"Nothing like that," Jacob interjected. "We're just securing a new settlement. As far as we know, there is no life there. Leticia's brother has built a grand facility over what was a small surveying outpost."

"Nice accent," Desiree said as she poured them drinks. "God knows I can't do this forever, and dashing into danger is getting to be old." She took a sip. "One last odyssey I suppose."

The food arrived. Leticia grabbed a mozzarella stick and greedily devoured it. Jacob couldn't help himself from chuckling.

"You seem to do everything with abandon," he said. "Unlike your brother. He has, how should we say, a more rigid personality."

Leticia took a sip of bourbon.

"You don't know the half of it."

"Tell me more." He grabbed a mozzarella stick and ate it as quickly as Leticia. "You have me all night."

Looking into his eyes, it felt like being caught in a pool of whiskey. Another glance was another shot of not giving a damn. It was always a risk to take attraction to the next level, but…

Taffy had slid next to Desiree and they spoke with their voices low. Desiree got up and left. Leticia moved closer to Jacob as he poured more bourbon for her.

"Can I ask you a personal question?"

"Sure," she said.

"Will you be leaving anyone behind?"

"Nope," she said, maybe a little too fast. "Don't think I have ever really been in love. And relationships... well when the time is right, I guess. You?"

He shook his head. "No one. I've yet to meet someone I connect with, who doesn't really want to connect with my name or money. And I want to build something. When I'm old can we sit on a boat and watch the sunset, knowing it could be our last. To me that would be a life well lived."

"Tell me about Olinka."

"Olinka is inspired by the real concept from the 1950s by a Mexican artist and philosopher, Gerardo Murillo— also called Doctor Atl. It was his idea of a utopian city for scientists, intellectuals, and artists. There would be vast resources that would be given to scientific and spiritual research, for humankind to reach their greatest potential. Philosophy was my minor in school."

He took a drink and continued. "In the summer between my junior and senior year I went to Peru. It got me thinking. The body count from company-sponsored secret missions was as great as the number of files on each misdeed and sin. Past generations made killing and murder a science, literally. I spent weeks poring over the files until I could read no more, feeling sick to my stomach.

"Yes, there is the money—billions," he said, "but I began my career in urban planning. Decided to join the Weyland-Yutani Corporation when politics got messy. Members of the board approached me, and it was the perfect opportunity. The planet was unnamed, but there is a close resemblance to Earth."

Leticia was... impressed.

"You know how Ramón made his first little fortune?" she said, maybe thanks to the bourbon. "He hacked the school and stole tests, as well as altering some grades."

Jacob frowned.

"Is that how he got to the top of his class?"

"Hell no! He's more psycho than that. He did it all himself, always had to prove he was the best. It was okay to help others cheat, but he needed to know he was intrinsically better than everyone else. No, he earned his place."

"I've never seen drive or dedication like his."

"I think we both got parts of our mother. We don't know much about our father, but she would definitely find some of her in us."

"For that I am grateful," he said, "and glad to have had the privilege of getting to know you, have you on my team."

Leticia fluttered inside. She wanted to kiss him. Feel his saliva on her mouth.

"What's the hardest lesson you've ever had to learn?"

Leticia drank the last of the bourbon in her glass. "To be alone."

He nodded. "Same."

"I guess we're both following our forebears' dreams, but attempting to do better than they did." Her mother's dream had been to get into the Marines and look where that got her, Leticia thought darkly. Where it got both of them.

"All we can do is try," he said, breaking her out of it. "I'm tired of war, greed, and destruction infecting generation after generation. On Meredith Vickers' final mission she encountered a place, and something ancient. There's little data available. Who knows what or who they were, but it scares me to think what course we have set for ourselves."

Desiree returned to the Champagne Room dressed casually in jeans, heeled timberlands, and a leather jacket.

"My shift is done. Let's head to The Rooster."

"Yes," Leticia shouted.

2 0

The Rooster was crowded. Heads turned as Leticia walked in, seriously over-dressed, but she didn't mind.

They grabbed a place at the bar and were waiting to order drinks when she noticed a guy with a robotic arm and robotic leg staring at them. His face was deeply grooved, likely from the sun, and there were blooms of purple spider veins across his cheeks and nose. Judging from his bloodshot eyes, he'd had one too many.

Leticia didn't say anything, but kept an eye on him. Desiree excused herself. Jacob and Leticia were alone when the man moved to approach.

"I recognize your face, you know," he said, his voice like gravel, "but you wouldn't recognize me. None of us grunts are given a second thought when we go up there, or have to survive down here."

Jacob looked baffled, and unsure how to react.

Leticia stepped in to defuse the situation.

"And how are you doing, sir? What can we do for you today?"

He pointed a fleshy middle finger toward Jacob. "That rich piece of shit can get the hell out of this bar. He's probably never worked a day in his life, or even paid taxes. No, he sat at home in a shitty diaper waiting to have his ass wiped while I had this done to me."

"Excuse me, but I am a qualified teacher and have spent years nurturing the minds of young people," Jacob said before Leticia could stop him. "Taxes were always deducted. Now, can I buy you and your friends a round?"

"Hey, Jerry!" the guy said, raising his voice. "This Weyland suit wants to buy us drinks. As if it can make up for all of it." Spittle from the man's mouth landed on Leticia's bare arms.

He was too damned close.

A large man with hair cut close to his scalp approached. The people at the bar began to move away from the escalating argument.

"The hell is *he* doing here?"

"He's with me," Leticia said, "and I lost both my parents up there. You don't see me acting like an asshole."

Both men looked her up and down. "You his hooker for the night? Must be, dressed like that." At that moment Desiree returned, standing at Leticia's back and watching the rest of the room.

Jacob started to speak again, but Leticia placed a hand on his chest without taking her eyes off of the two men.

"Could a hooker do this?" She grabbed a bottle of beer from a woman standing next to her, then a shot glass Desiree was holding. Leticia downed the shot in one gulp, then smashed the bottle into the chest of the larger man. She grabbed both of his shoulders then kneed him in the groin. As he bent over, groaning in pain, she put him in a head lock, digging the heel of her stiletto into one of his sneaker-wearing feet.

"You're lucky you're a woman," he moaned with spit falling from the side of his mouth.

"Tell me something I don't know, pendejo," she replied. "Now leave us the hell alone. You and your drunk-ass friend." Releasing her grip on his neck, she pushed him away and he stumbled before regaining his balance.

With a humiliated look, the two men skulked off.

Leticia turned to Jacob. "Now we can have fun. El riesgo siempre vive."

"Damn, bitch." Desiree stared at her friend. "Now I have to buy another shot. That took me ages!"

"Buy a bottle on me," Jacob suggested.

"I can do that."

Around 11:30 the lights lowered and the music turned louder. In the back of the bar Leticia ground her hips to the beat of the music. Desiree chatted to a woman who had caught her attention.

Jacob's hands found their way to Leticia's waist. He

couldn't dance for shit, but the way he licked his lips and his hands touched her body told her he knew exactly what to do with his tongue and fingers.

"I have a confession."

Leticia tensed. If he had a girlfriend or wife, after he said he didn't, she would sock him in the mouth.

"I told your brother to join us."

Internally Leticia breathed a sigh of relief. Ramón was the ultimate cock block, but at least Jacob could still be hers for the taking. She brought her mouth closer to his as an invitation. He kissed her hard, with authority. She matched his power with her tongue, hands wandering to touch his chest.

"You still haven't given me an answer," he said breathlessly into her ear. "Say yes, Leticia. Be by my side."

She kissed his neck and dragged her lips across his flesh before giving his earlobe a little nibble.

"Yes, I'll take your job, and you will pay my crew a decent wage to set them up."

"Done," he replied, though she was pretty sure he would have promised her anything at that moment. "If the company can pay for bullshit that only ends in death, then let me spend some of their profits on real people."

"My own crew?" she said, pressing her advantage. "That includes Desiree, and a few others still in the Corps."

"If you can't trust the people with guns to have your back, then what the hell are you doing?" he said, looking painfully serious. "I will try. It might be an uphill battle.

I won't promise you anything right now, but this… the politics…"

"Understood. I'll give you a list of names, and there's equipment we'll need."

"I already can't wait to hear from you again."

Their bodies were close—any closer and they should have been beneath sheets. Desiree tapped her on the shoulder.

"Attention, soldier. Your brother is here."

Ramón walked in with his usual air of confidence. He looked over the crowd until his gaze zeroed in on Leticia and Jacob. Everything about him looked tense, and *definitely* less than excited about the surroundings.

Leticia moved quickly away from Jacob. If Ramón stared any harder, smoke would be coming out of his ears. He was always the superstar, not her. Well, fuck him. She could hear his gripes before he even started.

"Leticia, you put me in a very awkward situation back there. Everyone wanted to know where Jacob went."

"I'm sure you're exaggerating, Ramón," Jacob said. "People pretend to like me, but I've called out too many of them on their shit. Half put up with me, and others want me out, one way or another. And Ramón, Leticia is… well I don't have to tell you."

Jacob gently touched the back of her arm.

She imagined what it would feel like for it to be her back, followed by her ass, instead of her arm. *Not now, not here*. But she wanted to know. She responded with a touch to his arm, and a small smile crossed his face. Ramón was too occupied with wanting to get out of the bar to notice. This would be something they would have to revisit another time even if it bordered on the unethical.

Then again, when did love or lust follow anything but the rules of biology? It was a creature that could only be satiated with flesh.

"Ramón, we need to talk Olinka," Jacob said. "Your sister is on board, but only if she can pick her own crew. I told her if there was one person who could get Satan into heaven, it would be you. You're the best with strategy. I will need your thoughts on Monday."

"She said yes to you." Ramón gave her a hard stare. "Then I guess, Leticia, you have work to do." Then he had a smile of his own, but it wasn't pleasant. "Don't stay up too late."

Leticia woke up the following morning alone with a dry mouth and pounding head, but no Jacob next to her. It was better that way. She would pop a couple of pain relievers before sending out messages explaining the proposal to Frida, Mohammed, and Nathan.

Desiree already knew the deal and wanted in.

The hope was they would all say yes because money talked, and none of them wanted to die young.

It didn't take long for her to hear back. Not a one of

them could say no to the zeros on offer. Next she would contact Ramón with a figure, and let him work his sorcery to make it all happen. In the back of her mind, she wanted to contact Jacob again and see him. Camping out in Ramón's apartment was nice, but it didn't have the same rewards.

No, she had to keep it professional. Fought the urge to keep it strictly business, knowing Jacob could be at the front door in minutes.

Three days later her phone rang, and Leticia rolled over in her bed. The empty space with an unused pillow made her think of Jacob for the umpteenth time, and the sensation of his heartbeat beneath her hand as it had been slung across his bare chest.

The phone continued to ring.

It was him.

Even though it was probably business, a jolt of excitement pinched inside her belly.

"Good morning."

The sound of his voice increased the longing.

"Must be important for this early."

"I had an early night," he said. "Stayed in… alone. Anyway, your brother has one hell of a reputation. I don't know how he did it, but you got your team. He'll be joining us, too."

Leticia sat upright in bed. "Really? No wonder he's

shot up the ranks." As usual, she didn't want the specifics of what Ramón had done. "Thank you. I'll get started on a plan—and travel, it seems."

"Contracts will be drawn up shortly, and we'll want to begin as soon as possible. Does everyone you want to include know that we leave on short notice?"

"They do," she said. "Leave the rest to me." There was a pause. Neither wanted to say goodbye. "Um, I guess we'll talk when there's an update."

"That would be great," he replied. "Feel free to drop by the office. If you need a space here to work, I can arrange it very easily."

Leticia smiled with that giddy schoolgirl rush of talking to a crush. She wanted to be close to him, too.

"I'll let you know. See you soon... I hope."

Leticia hopped out of bed, marveling at how it all had worked out. By not getting that promotion, something bigger had been reserved for her. *And* she had stumbled across Jacob. As she began to compile a checklist in her head, she pulled on a pair of jeans. Her soft brown belt with flowers and bees hung next to them, a gift from—

Roseanna.

She had to call Roseanna. Her tía would be sixty soon. Depending on what happened up there, she might never see her again. The price of travel throughout space, a place thought to be devoid of life, was time. Cryo bought you time, but it cost years for those left behind on Earth.

Leticia didn't know how long they would be up there,

or what they might find themselves facing. The unknown wasn't just above their heads—it was also in her mind.

"*Mija, it's so good to see your face. You look well.*"

"How are you, Roseanna?"

"*The same. One day at a time. I have my plants and clients. Me and Robert have our horse shows. But you didn't call to talk about that.*"

"I said yes."

"*I knew you would,*" Roseanna said. "*There was no way you wouldn't. You could have left a long time ago, both of you, but you stayed. I trust your decision. You have my blessing, and I will light a candle for you every day.*" Leticia could tell that she was genuinely pleased, but also a little wistful. It hurt her heart.

"But I may not see… I don't know… We will be in cryo for five years, and after that who knows what awaits. It's not dangerous, at least." Leticia could feel her voice wanting to crack from the emotions of saying goodbye to her beloved Roseanna.

"*You might not see me, but you will always feel me, just as I still feel your mother. I'm still fit and healthy.*" She took a deep breath, and continued. "*None of you know what lies ahead, but you can't live your life wondering. Don't go walking around like you're already in cryo. Go.*"

"I love you, Roseanna. Thank you for… for everything. I wouldn't have made it this far without you."

"*Yes, you would have. You're a Vasquez woman, a born soldadera. El riesgo siempre vive.*"

Leticia touched the tattoo of her mother on her arm.

"I'll send you a message as soon as I can. By the way, I don't know if you have spoken to Ramón, but he is going, too. Not sure what that is all about, with his kids and Mary Anne."

"*I did speak to him. He just said they would move when the time was right. It's not my business. You can't tell him anything, anyway.*"

"Very true."

21

Departure day was unlike any she had experienced during her military career—or even before. All her life she had worked toward a goal, had objectives along the way. It felt strange signing on for a project that had no real directive. They would be reacting to the needs of the moment.

Leticia still requested a cache of weapons to be taken on board. It was her job to anticipate the worst, even in the best of conditions. One of the items had been a Narwhal. Jacob stood by the sleek vehicle, inspecting it intently. He motioned for Leticia to come over.

"It's not that I mind paying for it," he said, "but what is it?"

"I couldn't believe it when Ramón had that beast approved. It's a Narwhal. It's called that because it's small, like a jet ski, but lighter, and it has a long launcher attached to the nose. Inside there's a revolving chamber with a harpoon, a spear, grenades, and as a last resort you can blow the whole thing up to create a powerful explosion. It works best on the water, but the propulsion system can be used in short bursts for an air-to-water landing, or even to go a short distance on ground that isn't too rough."

"That's brilliant," he said, then he faced her. "How are you feeling?"

Leticia ran her hand across the amphibious craft, remembering the incident with Haas.

"If this job is as easy as the description then fine."

"If the job isn't, then I'm in trouble," Jacob countered, his gaze lingering on Leticia. There was an awkward moment caught between staying professional and wanting more.

"I better get back to work," she said. "I *am* on the clock."

"Sorry, yes," he said. "See you on board."

In addition to the soldiers directly under her command, there were people from the fields of science and anthropology—some at the top of their fields—and their assistants. Her crew seemed to be in good spirits as they prepared for a long sleep with no threat to face once their boots hit ground again.

Nathan and Frida showed each other pictures of family, bringing them up on their watches. Desiree and Mohammed inspected the weapons waiting to be loaded with their bags and other supplies. Leticia watched them, hoping this job would be good for them financially, and present opportunities not available to them otherwise. Not everyone had a hot-shot brother with good connections.

Speaking of Ramón, he was late. She looked at her watch. A missed message said he was nearly there.

Ramón arrived at the spaceport appearing sleep deprived, with dark circles beneath his eyes. He also seemed cagey and irritable as he snapped at peripheral staff, including a few of the scientists brought along by Jacob. His grumpy demeanor had to have been tied to his wife, and Leticia wondered what was going on with them.

"Hey, Ramón. What gives?"

He dropped his duffle. "Mary Anne isn't too pleased. She knew what she was getting into when she married me, but it's still been a long time coming."

"You don't have to go." Leticia patted her brother's bicep. "Why are you doing this, anyway?"

He looked at her as if he wanted to spit something out.

"Because I *want* to go."

That was all she was going to get out of him. Ramón was too deliberate. In the back of her mind, she wondered what or who waited on Olinka.

"Your call, bro, but please think of the twins."

"Oh, I am." He leaned in close to her ear. "And us, the Vasquez name." That left her bewildered, but a shout from Desiree broke her train of thought.

"We gotta go," Leticia said. "Get ready, and sweet dreams, hermano."

PART 5

OLINKA

2 2

Julia Yutani left her heart—and—scruples on Earth. Glory always required leaving something behind, she knew. Sometimes those things returned, and other times they only survived as rays of light reaching the Earth from a star long dead.

This project was her glory in the making.

Dr. Moon had perfected the bacteria, and it was time to introduce it in various scenarios. There was also promise in the engineered parasites spliced with Xenomorph DNA and the lowly pork tapeworm from Earth. Under the microscope the ugly things ate through tissue with a quiet viciousness. The hook on their tails cut with the sharpness of a razor's edge as they burrowed into tissue. They reproduced rapidly like the Xenomorphs, were easy to transport, and could invade an entire water system.

But no parasite would be complete without a cure.

Dr. Moon's paranoia made her diligent in finding a neutralizing agent.

Julia had made this journey for another pressing reason. There had been an unexpected change in the three Xenomorph queens, and by Brenda's exacting protocols, nothing could be left to chance. For years the incapacitated queens had lain like sleeping giants, growing to their true size and reproducing with little overt movement except to generate eggs.

With the missing lower jaw, the inner mandible hung black and heavy like the tongue escaping from a drowned corpse's mouth. Saliva pooled directly beneath. Year after year it gathered and thickened. Ridges spiraled with bony thorns around the smaller inner mandible, the teeth lengthened across the top jaw—only by centimeters, but still a change—until they were longer than ever recorded.

Where the arms and legs had been amputated, barbs were beginning to sprout with the slowness of spring buds on a barren tree branch. Evolution. Given the environments in which they had been found, Xenomorphs were likely to experience hibernation, and Brenda postulated that their years of hibernation were a form of silent evolution. With these new, subtle changes, Brenda petitioned that they should be terminated as soon as possible.

No fucking way would Julia have any of that.

She had convinced the board to send her out to oversee the final decision. No hard feelings for the good doctor, but this was way above her pay grade.

As an unexpected bonus, the man who gave her everything and nothing at the same time would arrive on Olinka not far behind her. Ramón had promised a commitment, and with this relocation he had kept that promise. No more sneaking around or stolen moments. Now they would wake up and work side by side. Their story generated among the stars, because *they* were the corporate stars who would shape worlds.

Getting rid of Ross had made it all the easier. His use had run out, as did his ability to get things done the way Ramón could. Her body trembled when she thought of Ramón's hands on her waist again, the way he whispered that he wanted to make love to her before opening his eyes. It was always the subtle moments that created craters in the heart and soul.

She had been chasing him since college and meeting him in secret during the entirety of his sham of a marriage. His desire for a family was perfect as a Hallmark movie— something he couldn't let go of because of those old abandonment wounds. Part of her hated herself for always holding space for him. Year after year, her resolve had eroded away, knowing he was playing happy family with a woman who wasn't his true match, or the one he loved. Mary Anne had to know he wasn't faithful. Something in her roving eyes, when she accompanied him to corporate events, betrayed this truth.

"Who is it?" they said. *"Which one of these women am I sharing my husband with?"*

Julia did her best to give her a pleasant smile. Mary Anne ignored her as she clung to the crook of his arm with that pretty face, minimal makeup, modest dress, and kitten heels. The princess-cut diamond ring on her left hand blinding as it reflected the light in any room. And it was always, *"the twins this"* and *"the twins that"*... It was as if they married each other for nothing more than a photo opportunity.

Eventually his children would join them here. She didn't mind, because that was what staff was for, and there was something to be said about birthing your heirs as opposed to appointing them. Julia was an heir.

Ramón had been given an ultimatum, to confront what would he do, knowing he could lose her—or more importantly, lose a lifetime of wealth. Finally, he had come around and decided to leave his wife, under the convenient guise of work and an empty promise of sending for her once settled. His children would be placed in the best boarding school in the country, and he justified leaving them because in the end they would have it all. They would see it as training to be proper heirs.

It had happened to Julia.

When she had first relaxed into cryo for the journey, she smiled knowing that in five short years they would have their own empire. An instant, really, when spent in deep freeze. It would be easy to push out Jacob, who was unfit for his position.

Julia loathed Jacob and that the board had chosen

a British-born Vickers to take the top spot. Weyland-Yutani had a long way to go before they could clean up their image. He was nothing like his great-grandmother, Meredith. His office was filled with photos of his trips with humanitarian projects, with students achieving high honors, and accolades from non-profits for his continued support to charities in the places with the most need.

God knew why he really took the position. She would have held more respect for him if he was hiding a secret agenda, and ended up poisoning the entire board who had voted him in. Altruism in its purest form only got you killed, or dying broke. Out here he would be isolated, though, chasing an illusion that was rays of light from a dead star. A half smile spread across her face.

Accidents happen all the time.

She stepped through the doorway of Brenda's office for the formal review.

"Julia, it's wonderful to finally meet you," Brenda said. "I know how busy you are, so I have everything already set up. Whatever we decide to do, it should be swift."

Leaning in closer to the screen on Brenda's wall, Julia played her fingertips across the screen and brought the image into closer focus. A queen Xenomorph sat upright with the stiffness of a sphynx. No riddle here.

"What's the problem?" she said brusquely. "You have her under control. You've managed to do what we need, tamed the bitch."

Brenda looked startled and pursed her lips. She pulled up another image.

"Look here and here." She pointed. "There is growth. It's as if they have matured into full-grown Xenomorphs while evolving or adapting to the… changes. The inner mandible is thicker. It doesn't move much, but it is changing. Here. Where we inserted our little bullets of insurance, they have grown out into sharp horns. Ironically it looks like a crown on their large hoods—and look at the tail and hands. See those barbs?"

Julia swung her head from one image to the other. "But has she moved an inch? Have any of them? All that matters is they continue to create more eggs for our research, and for the end results we need."

Brenda remained silent for a beat. "No. However, I still think we should terminate all the queens now. No waiting to see what happens next."

"You will do no such thing." Julia snapped her head away from the screen. "All the other Xenomorphs will be allowed to grow, as well. No more euthanizing them—*any* of them—while they're still small. What's the status of the eggs you're freezing? Have you figured out the optimal temperature for keeping them on ice, so they can be used as biological grenades?"

Brenda's mouth hung open as she struggled to regain her composure.

"We don't know enough about fully grown Xenomorphs," she said finally. "I don't trust this many queens changing in ways we can't predict and keeping full-grown Xenomorphs all in the same facility. What if they can communicate? What if these queens—"

"With all due respect," Julia said, "and I *do* respect everything you have done in your career, the sacrifices you have made; however, this is not up to you. You want to destroy something huge based only on a scientific hunch… or rather, on your own fear."

"Yes!" Brenda snapped. "You *should* fear these things, and respect them. They are hideous. She is a monstrosity." Brenda gestured toward the screen. "And another thing— we don't have a proper security team, or much of *anything* to defend ourselves in the event of an emergency."

"Is she hideous because of her latent power? Because you are afraid of how much we don't know about her yet, if we allow it to bloom?" Julia countered. "There could be so much more. You don't fear the bacteria or parasites you created. Those will be used in warfare, and against other humans. Where is your fear for those?"

Brenda stared, unable to answer. Julia could tell she had crushed the woman and her irrational arguments.

"As far as security is concerned," she continued, "that's being taken care of. The bacteria is all that should concern you. You've prepared safeguards, and the dosages have been calibrated. They're ready to go, should we need to wipe them all out.

"But it should *not* come to that," she said, making certain the scientist understood the implications. "If that happened, we start back at square one. Continue your work, or send me a letter of resignation. If you choose that route, however, you will forfeit the generous bonus you were given—or has that already been spent? Your sister is out on one of the colonies, isn't she, with her own business? It would be a shame for her to have to give it all back."

Brenda straightened her back.

"You're the boss, Ms. Yutani," she said. "But no matter what you decide, she is hideous." She looked at the abomination on the screen. "I know much of what they are capable of, and I fear everything we *don't* know they are capable of accomplishing—like these changes."

"Acknowledged," Julia said. "I'll expect a report about the frozen eggs, by the end of the day."

With that Julia walked out of the office, holding in the elation she felt. Spontaneous evolution. The queen would indeed be terminated, and then picked apart to find whatever was causing it. Imagine harnessing the power of evolution.

Her watch beeped. She had to move quickly for her next appointment, deeper in the facility.

The elevator doors opened to a wide research room from which all projects were monitored.

"Are we ready for the specimen?" Julia demanded as she stepped in front of a large screen showing a live feed.

"It's not fully grown, and should prove to be easy."

Human trials were always bogged down with red tape, money, and a little thing called ethics. Peter Weyland had changed the world and done what people labeled "good," but the path to it hadn't been paved with cobbles of altruism. Every human possessed an ego.

This round of trials would begin before any approval had been granted. The lab was far from anything or anyone who could get in the way. The participants had been recruited from floundering colonies, or people stranded in space who had been brought here with the promise of work, a fresh start.

The poor guy, Dylan, didn't even know he was part of an experiment, but this was how it had to be. There had to be that element of surprise. In times of war the chain of events couldn't be anticipated. If they were lucky, this thing would never have to be used—the threat of it might be enough. There also might be applications that hadn't yet appeared.

Xenomorphs proved that humans were not alone.

"Dylan, I'm Dr. Yutani." Julia maintained her cool, even tone as she gave the young man a reassuring smile. He still appeared to be filled with dread. "It's time for you to take the samples."

"*Is it safe?*" he said over the intercom, his eyes wide. "*I mean, what is the stuff. Th-this isn't what I was expecting. Could you use an android, instead?*"

He had no clue.

"You signed up for this," she said, "and we can't rely on androids for everything. As humans, that would make us obsolete. Do you want to be made obsolete?" Without giving him a chance to answer, she continued. "You're being paid well, and a lot of people wanted this opportunity, so you should be grateful." Her smile remained, but her eyes were a squeeze to his balls.

"*I'm sorry, Dr. Yutani,*" he said. "*I... I'll do it. I trust you.*" With that, he picked a vial off of the table in front of him and swallowed the contents.

"Good," Julia said, trying to sound reassuring. "That will offer you the protection you need as you collect the samples." It was a lie, of course, but the young man seemed to take it at face value and calm down a bit. He dressed hastily in a hazmat suit. An assistant behind him secured the back of the suit and latched the helmet.

"*All set.*"

Dylan approached the airlock carrying a tray holding the instruments he had been given, ostensibly to slice off pieces of the pulsating egg. When the door opened, they could see black weeping streaks shooting from the base to the top. Flakes of dead flesh lay on the floor. He glanced back at the camera where he knew Julia and the others would be watching.

Stretching out a shaky hand, he gathered pieces of curled dead flesh on the ground and placed them in a plastic vacuum bag. The egg continued to pulse, causing Julia's own heart rate to increase in pulsating beats. Her eyes widened. If only Ramón could be standing next to her for this. Afterward they could celebrate with champagne and sex.

As he hovered over the egg and reached out with the scalpel, the spider-like face-hugger came shooting out of the top, shattering the mask. In an instant Dylan lay on the ground mottled with black blooms spreading across his face. If all went as planned, the dosage would be just enough to transmit the bacteria. The assistant entered the room, lifting off Dylan's helmet.

"Looks good," he said. "Both the host and the *Manumala noxhydria* are still alive. Transmission appears to have been successful."

"Great," Julia replied. "We need to let the bacterium continue to do its work before the face-hugger falls off. Get him out of there."

Dylan was the last of five infected hosts. All of them would be kept in secure hatching rooms. Dr. Moon should have been there, watching with the same intensity she reserved for her objections. But she had made some bullshit excuse, and Julia would not forget.

Brenda's time was limited.

2 3

The long sleep was over. A soothing voice greeted the crew while the sounds of chirping birds was piped into the cryopod. The light was bright to give the effect of curtains being drawn. They hadn't arrived at their destination, but they were close.

As Leticia's pod opened, Jacob was already up twisting his body in various yoga poses. Tennis and yoga. She chuckled to herself how different they were, despite the chemistry being so magnetic. After five years the thought of jumping his bones was also strong. The word that came to mind when she thought of Jacob Vickers was *caliente*. The scent of coffee filling the cabin distracted her from her fantasies.

This was a job.

Leticia tossed her legs to the side, feeling hungover without any of the fun. Hunger pangs pinched her awake, enough to move her feet to the floor. She'd kill for chorizo and egg breakfast tacos. Extra salsa, of course.

"When do we eat, I'm starving," she croaked.

Jacob answered her still doing his impromptu yoga session. "We meet in an hour for breakfast and debriefing."

She didn't want to wait an hour; patience was one of the virtues she'd never mastered. She looked around, but no Ramón. The rest of her crew were pulling on track suits or had wandered to use the hygiene facilities. The civilians on board were dressing in their own clothing while talking among themselves. Leticia quickly pulled on her own track suit and followed her nose to the mess cabin. She heard Ramón's voice as he spoke to a scientist.

"Good morning, director of security," he said cheerfully, turning as she entered. Five years must have done him good because the man who stood before her wasn't the man who lay down in his cryopod and immediately shut his eyes.

The spread was a lavish buffet, unlike the vacuum-sealed crap she was used to having dispensed by a machine or pulled from a backpack during a mission. Something was going on here. He was buttering them up for something. Fluffy pancakes with lashings of syrup, crispy bacon, fruit at its peak of ripeness, muffins, real coffee.

Man, this is mala, very, very bad.

But at least she could eat well, before he revealed whatever mission of death was in store. As her crew filtered in they showed the same astonishment as she.

Not knowing Ramón so well, though, they didn't seem the least bit suspicious. Each one grabbed a plate, the others crowded in around. Jacob was the last one into the mess, and he joined her in the back as he watched the feast.

"Your brother really is generous," he said. "I wasn't sure about a celebration breakfast like this, but look at their faces." He turned to Leticia and smiled. "Why aren't you eating?"

"Why aren't *you* eating, Jacob?"

The smile left his face. "Nerves. Like being in love for the first time."

"C'mon, mi amigo. You have to eat something. I'll join you."

Leticia left it at that. This would be Jacob's moment to address them all. After a satisfying breakfast, the group of fifteen turned their attention to him as he stood in front of a white wall. Her stomach cramped from a mixture of overeating and excitement.

"I want to introduce you to planet E2," Jacob said. "We call it E2 because it has been terraformed to almost resemble Earth's long-lost sister, but its formal name will be Olinka. From our observations, it seems to be in a stage similar to what Earth was before humans. Anyone been to Iceland? Half of the planet resembles that country, with its vastly different landscapes, some dangerous. We lost a few rovers to geothermal activity, and at the very far reaches, the cold.

"There is also water, but not a place for wading or sunbathing. Until Ramón became involved, there was only one facility that had been established for Weyland-Yutani to stake their claim. Most of it existed beneath the ground. We will be going over virgin terrain because all prior work on Olinka One was completed on-site. No one was allowed to explore outward."

Jacob clicked on another photo. It was the pyramid Ramón had built.

"This will be our center of operations," Jacob said, "and these are the raw materials from which we will build our masterpiece." The enthusiasm built in his voice as he continued to run through drone photos taken from above. It was a beautiful, rugged, unspoiled version of Earth. Where other worlds were being terraformed by working-class families that had run out of options on Earth, people were going to pay big money for this place. Leticia could envision her brother living in some high-rise penthouse in the middle of unspoiled land, with an infinity pool overlooking his empire.

Her musings were interrupted when she heard her own name.

"… Leticia Vasquez, the director of security." All eyes turned toward her. Leticia smiled and lifted her hand to give a wave, and immediately felt self-conscious. Then she caught Ramón's eyes. If they hadn't been twins, she wouldn't have seen the shadow that lurked within.

"Whatever happens here—I don't care if you've found

the one thing that will revolutionize mankind—if Leticia says move, you move," Jacob continued. "We don't expect anything dangerous to occur, but for the moment please stick together. No wandering, because while we have extensive footage of the planet, it's still a mystery of sorts. Some of you are here under Ramón's direction"—he nodded to a group standing with her brother—"and others are with me, but we *all* answer to Leticia if there is any sort of emergency." He paused and scanned the room, but all he got were nods and words of assent.

"Alright," he concluded, "let's get ready to land."

Jacob sought her out after his speech. Before she could get a word out, Ramón stepped in.

"Excuse me, Jacob, may I have a word with my sister?"

"Absolutely. We can catch up later, Leticia?"

"Whenever, you need me, come and find me." She watched him walk away without caring what her big brother might think of her wandering eye.

"Hey, sis, just watch it, okay?" Ramón said. "I see how you look at each other. It never hurts to have a little something on the side to keep you occupied, but he isn't some private you can hop on and off for fun. He's the company, and a little lip gloss isn't going to impress him."

"It's called trying to leave a good impression," she said, wondering why the hell he'd chosen this moment to bring it up. "And it's not lip gloss. It's Carmex."

"Just be professional, and keep your distance unless it's genuinely important. We have a lot to do when we arrive at the Olinka One facility. Neither of us needs the distraction. Maybe after some time passes, you can do whatever you want." When she didn't say a word, he added, "Just trust me and give him some space."

She still didn't know why he was bringing it up now—he had to have figured it out before. What, was he going to ask if she was on birth control? All she could guessed was that he didn't want competition.

Desiree arrived just in time, before her exchange with Ramón could become any more awkward.

"Looks like we're close enough to start heading down," Desiree said. "I'm thinking three dropships."

"Sounds good," Leticia replied. "You get the crew suited up and I'll tell Jacob to make the announcement. No more waiting."

The first team of scientists and assistants went down in two larger dropships, along with supplies to set up camp, including the rovers they would use to cross the terrain to the Olinka One facility. Jacob wanted to do it this way for everyone to see the planet with their own eyes and begin the surveying process for another facility.

Leticia, her crew, Jacob, and Ramón strapped themselves into their own ship loaded with what she had requested for their security detail. The ship disengaged and began its descent. As always, she began the mission with a little pep talk. This would be her first time formally leading her own team in space, a small band of soldiers, too restless for civilian life but too tired of and broke for service.

"Alright, my people. You know the drill. There's been no strange activity reported, so this should be a walk in the park—but when was that ever the case? Thanks to Ramón, we've had an amazing last meal that wasn't freeze-dried." They all smiled and sniggered, knowing exactly what she meant. This made her feel good. She wanted her crew to feel comfortable.

"We work as a team. Sounds like this is a nice payday for everyone, so we don't want any fuck-ups. Tell me everything. If a beetle shits the wrong way, I need to know. You know I will take everything you say under consideration.

"Let's do this."

It was an odd sensation, being the boss on the most unlikely of missions, like new boots on a marathon-long hike. Leticia attempted to read everyone's mood. Jacob had a permanent smile on his face, and the demeanor of a big kid about to have his first real visit to an amusement park.

Whereas Ramón looked straight ahead at a red sign reading WARNING. ONLY PULL IF AN EMERGENCY. Gone was the casual, even cheerful person who had woken— his grumpy and anxious demeanor had returned now that he didn't have to be on show for a large crowd. She couldn't help but feeling he wasn't being totally honest with her. When she looked his way, he avoided eye contact. His mind was elsewhere. But where?

Supposedly he knew everything there was to know about the Olinka One facility and this planet. Maybe the idea of leaving Mary Anne and the kids was hitting him again. Whatever it was, it would be revealed in its own time.

Leticia felt the dropship slowing down. They would land soon, and she found herself smiling with the same giddiness as Jacob.

Landing would be the easy part. Next they had to follow a drone through a hot and humid sulfur field that would eventually give way to lush meadows, an ocean, and a pleasant temperature. The cargo bay door opened, and Mohammed pulled a bandana over his nose and mouth. A skull with vampire teeth.

"Holy shit, that smell," he said. "There must be the biggest pile of manure under our feet."

Even so, Jacob and Ramón emerged from the dropship with the posture of kings. Jacob breathed in deeply and stretched his arms.

"Fascinating, isn't it?" he said, not seeming to notice the stench. "I can't wait to set up a research facility here. I wanted to see for myself the geothermal flats. The facility out here will expand the natural energy grid across the planet, making way for future habitation."

Mohammed patted him on the back before walking away. "Enjoy and good luck with that, buddy."

The sulfur yellow and burnt orange hardened fields of rock and dirt smelled like giant exploding rotten eggs.

The breeze blew the stomach-churning scent from the smoking vents across the landscape. Ponds of bubbling mud of all sizes pockmarked the surface. Nothing grew here because the planet burned from beneath and belched out its contents for miles. There was no sign of animal life, either, though previous drone and satellite scans had shown it to be plentiful elsewhere.

"So Ramón, where you putting the casino?" Frida joked.

"Very funny," he said, but he didn't look amused. "Some respect would be nice. I *am* your superior."

"Sorry. I forgot—this is a super serious mission." Frida lifted her hands and eyebrows in surrender before walking off. Leticia joined Jacob, who scanned the area, taking it all in. The terrain had a sparse amount of foliage along the border of the hot mud springs.

"So this is it? Your big dream?"

"It is," he replied without a hint of irony. "If everything goes well on this trip, more scientists and civilians will follow."

The scientists had already organized themselves and their equipment and were exploring the area without concern for the smell or the dangers of the geothermal vents. They were too engrossed in this new world and its undiscovered secrets.

"Right," she said, "I have work to do. Have to make sure nobody gets sucked into one of those mud pots or steps into a sinkhole. I guess I will see you later." She jogged toward the civilians. "Yo! We don't have time for that now. Get into your rovers. You can eyeball the area from a safe and tracked path. In a rover."

She looked to the sky. So far so good. The fog was clearing as the heat from the sun sent its radiation into the atmosphere. This was good, because the vents emitted smoke that could disrupt their visibility. They would rely on the drones to safely guide them as they traversed the terrain.

They had a head start. It had been previously mapped via satellite, but with all of the geothermal activity, it was always changing. A tracker alerted them to unstable pockets that might lead to boiling ponds of mud. Jacob wasn't lying when he said this had been a work in progress.

Eventually their route would become a proper road. Their destination was located on the border of a forest with fresh water close by.

For two hours they sat in the rover with bandanas or other masks over their noses, looking out on virgin terrain. Halfway through the journey the wind changed direction and the air smelled less toxic. It felt light with the incoming breeze from the coast, not too far off.

As they approached Olinka One, Leticia stood in the open roof rover. She wondered what her mother had thought when she stepped on her first planet among the stars. She couldn't help but feel proud in this moment.

Maybe it was the virgin air or feeling the ground beneath the vehicle's wheels, but out here was the best thing to happen to her.

Small tufts of grass cropped up before there were small shrubs, and the ground became stable. It seemed like the obvious place to set up camp, or possibly the first settlement. They would build the colony's power supply on the sulfur fields, and Jacob also wanted to be close to that point.

The rovers came to a stop and the technicians began surveying. The group looked like they had stepped off the island of misfit toys, with a tiny crew of soldiers and civilians. Jacob and Ramón were the only "suits."

Leticia walked the perimeter in absolute wonder at the sight of the outline of two moons. There was no sign of anyone, or anything, on this part of the planet, though it seemed likely there were some indigenous faunae hidden away. Its beauty made them all stop and stare at times, then sadness would appear on their faces at the grim reality they would face going back to Earth.

A short distance away there was a patch of large trees that appeared nothing like anything she had seen on Earth. The shape of something you might see in the Serengeti but the needles like those of a pine. From what she remembered from the photos, they extended all the way to the Olinka One facility and the cliffs overlooking the ocean. Leticia wandered closer. The faint hint of pine was refreshing, comforting.

At her feet lay a branch with a smooth surface. She reached down to feel it. It was heavy, roughly the size and weight of a baseball bat. It would be a souvenir to help her remember this first day of what could be the start of something exciting.

Her watch vibrated. It was time to get back to the business of securing the camp, setting up sensors and cameras, exploring the outlying area, then preparing for a night under the stars that would be brighter than on Earth. No flashing lights or pollution to dim their shine. Jacob and Ramón had gathered the civilians. Leticia needed to know their plan before she began hers.

"What are you thinking for today?"

For once Ramón didn't make a move to dominate. He took a physical step back to allow Jacob to speak.

"Surveying. I want the next facility to be between the sulfur fields and Olinka One. My architect will take notes to come up with a concept."

"Anyone going beyond the grass line needs to take a scanner with them," she asserted, "to alert them to hot spots and sinkholes. No one ventures alone. Tents are being set up where it's stable. As the light dims, all work beyond the perimeter stops."

Neither Ramón nor Jacob protested.

As much as Leticia appreciated the ease of this job she would reserve judgment until proof presented itself. She and her crew joined the staffers who had been brought in for labor to get the camp up and running—they would never be above getting their hands dirty. That was a quick way to lose the respect of people upon whom her life might depend.

The sun, roughly the size of Earth's own star, dipped toward the flaming horizon and the sky morphed from a pale blue to deep indigo. She and her crew walked the perimeter to make sure all civilians came back to camp. There would be no stupid accidents that could have been prevented. The civilians moved to the mess tent, gathering in groups, keeping to themselves, discussing their findings and paying rapt attention to Ramón as he tapped away on his tablet.

He probably loved having that kind of control, she thought, then she shrugged it away. Whatever had bothered him before appeared to have been compartmentalized.

She and her four ex-Marines set up a small pop-up table as more and more stars appeared. Rather than starting a fire, they set a glowing globe on the table. That, combined with the glow from above, provided plenty of light. Frida was singing a Stevie Nicks song to herself, and on a small speaker "All Along the Watchtower" by Jimi Hendrix began to play. A light breeze blew in the air.

Nathan leaned back in his canvas chair and broke the silence.

"What I wouldn't give for a beer right now," he said, peering upward. "This place is really something. Look at that sky." Her Las Lobas crew gave a collective chuckle in agreement.

"Well, don't bother to ask for more, because we need to be on guard." Leticia pulled a small flask of Fireball out from the thigh pocket of her fatigues and handed it over with a mischievous smile.

"Hell, yes!" Frida said. "You get boss of the year award."

Leticia drank first and passed it around. Jacob joined the group and exchanged glances with Leticia before speaking to the crew.

"I want to know what brought all of you here."

Without missing a beat, they all said, "Dinero." The table erupted into collective laughter.

"I can't argue with that."

She thought he looked a little disappointed.

After an hour of Jacob getting to know the soldiers better, Leticia excused herself. Before leaving she flashed Jacob a smile. He also rose to leave.

The tents provided were spacious, made from the most advanced textiles. Compared with what she had endured in the military, the cot seemed as if it could easily fit two. Everything new. Then again, with Ramón in charge of supplies, it would only be the best. That breakfast on the ship had been something else. Everyone ate until the food was ready to explode from their bellies and chests. In the field and on missions she had become accustomed to sleeping rough, managing hunger, braving the elements, and getting whatever supplies that were available. The only new tech had been the weaponry.

She looked forward to getting cozy in these new digs, and felt as if she could get used to it. By the looks on her team's faces as they set up camp, they could, too.

Peeling off her makeshift uniform, she opened her tablet. There were complete backgrounds on the civilians who were on board with them, plus files upon files of research on the planet. Concerning the already established facility, however, they didn't have much in the way of detail. She wanted to know why.

"Director of security," she whispered while smiling to herself. After what seemed like hours her eyes began to ache from reading. At least the sleeping bag on her cot was comfortable.

"Leticia, may I speak to you?"

Her heart fluttered. It was Jacob. She looked around the small space for something more appropriate than panties and a thin white tank top that she wore without a bra. He had already seen her like this in cryo but that was different, with others around and in the same state of undress.

"Uh… One second."

"I can go. This is probably—"

She stood up straight and alert. "No, no. Don't go!" She regretted sounding entirely too eager and tapped her forehead with her palm. From her peripheral vision she spotted the corner of a green towel robe sticking out of her backpack. It would have to do.

It's only business up here.

Be professional.

She couldn't help how irresistible she found him, and it wasn't some manufactured gravity between them. When their eyes met, it felt like a homecoming. Leticia took a deep breath before pulling back the canvas flap that served as a door. He held a pair of bottles, and looked good in the shadowy light of the two moons.

"You know, you need to stop impressing me," he said. "You're quickly making yourself indispensable." When she didn't answer, he continued. "I hope you don't mind me showing up like this. Do you want to join me under the stars for a drink?"

Leticia glanced at the bottles, and allowed her eyes to glide over his body. He was holding a bottle of Zacapa rum and Hibiki Japanese whiskey.

"What is this? Very nice stuff."

"This was already on board, as a gift from Julia Yutani wishing me well. Which is odd, because she hates me with a flaming passion. If you prefer wine or beer, though, I can go back and—"

"It's okay," she said. "I'm an equal opportunist with booze. Come in."

He paused before looking over his shoulder. "You sure? I don't…"

Leticia's heart pounded, but she didn't want to play this game any longer. Her resolve to keep a distance was gone with the night breeze. She felt like a nocturnal animal come to life. She licked her lips and flashed him a smile.

"I *want* you to come in."

"Whatever you say."

He looked around the tent and settled on a spot on the floor in front of her cot. Leticia grabbed two metal cups from a green canvas bag, then handed him one of them. He poured the rum first.

"I wanted to talk privately," he said, "about my plans for the colony, and your place in it. You chose a good group of solid people. I like them all. Despite their protests that they came here for the pay, it sounds like they want a place to settle down. That's what I'm looking for, individuals invested and valued in their community. I know I've told you bits and pieces, but we will need a permanent head of security. This has the potential for being more than a temporary job."

He handed her the rum with puppy dog eyes and an inviting mouth as he sipped on his own drink.

"Is that the only reason you stopped by?"

His gaze shifted to his hands, then back to her eyes.

"Why else would I?"

She leaned closer to him, taking the cup from his hand. "I'm about to do something really stupid."

He stretched out his legs and leaned his back against the cot.

"Do it."

Now *that* was a surprise. She liked it. Direct. Not a bullshitter or a time waster. Get to the good stuff fast, because it was occupying too much space in her brain. Maybe the looks she'd been trying to hide hadn't been so hidden after all.

The sooner they fucked, the sooner she could forget wanting it to happen.

Leticia straddled him and pulled off his Patagonia water-wicking T-shirt. Would the fantasy live up to the reality? He slipped her signature bandana over her eyes while his mouth found its way to her neck.

Fuck that, she thought. She didn't want fifty shades of anything. Leticia liked to watch. He needed to know exactly what to do, just in case they didn't have this opportunity again. Their bodies connected and it felt like the most natural place to be.

His saliva trailed across her flesh like comets across the universe, bringing her closer to God and death. When it came to sex, she was an unapologetically greedy woman. Tonight, her hips were the drums, his thrust the guitar, and the pleasure he was giving her was every instrument in between. For a man in control, he let her take the lead, remaining still as she did whatever she wanted. She leaned in and kissed his lips while riding him, and he felt as good as the fantasies she had played in her mind, early in the mornings and late at night when her desire to be touched was at its peak.

The ripples of their lovemaking kept her wanting more, heated like the tall vents in the sulfur fields, steady and unrelenting.

* * *

After sex that didn't seem to end but ended too soon, they lay on her cot inside her sleeping bag, sipping on rich boy brown liquor. Leticia felt comfortable enough to press him for more information.

"You really haven't seen anything suspicious down there?" she asked. "When people aren't honest, that's when shit hits the fan. This place is amazing on paper, and from what I have seen, it definitely beats some of the places I've seen on Earth. It's almost too good to be true."

"I promise you, there is nothing that we know of," he said. "I trust Ramón. This place means everything because, as we speak, there's a bidding war among the wealthiest for who gets first dibs at development. That was out of my hands, but I did manage to ban anything except geothermal energy, and there will be no formal borders—anywhere. This did little to dissuade anyone. Most of them just want clean air and a safe place to call their new home among people like themselves." He frowned. "Bunch of elitist assholes. I want this place to enjoy a new sense of freedom... for everyone."

Leticia looked at him, wondering if he knew who he was. Jacob must have read her mind or felt her body tense. He kissed her shoulder.

"I plan to live here to make sure this place isn't turned into a billionaire's playground. They don't know it—not even the board—but I've got a secret lottery going to bring everyday people here. Young families from the worst parts of the Earth, bright students needing a boost in life, even orphan kids, once it's safe. The ones who are paying will hate it, but what's the use of all this power if you can't wield it. Teaching opened my eyes to so many things. They all think I'm a little trust-fund professor playing tennis on the weekend, with my nose in a book, who knows nothing of real life."

Leticia ran her hand across his chest and burrowed her nose into his skin. He smelled good. She hoped the scent would linger on her flesh.

"I guess you've found your empire, Caesar," she said. "You're right, though. I don't think the other billionaires will like your plans. Watch your back."

He turned to his side, placing his hand on the inside of her thigh. "Well, my Cleopatra, they don't have to like it. If they want borders, mediocre air, and sandy beaches for vacations, they can stay on Earth or terraform their own planet. Don't get me wrong, I don't plan on running the place like a dictatorship. I believe in democracy."

She slid his hand farther up her thigh. "Baby, you're smart enough to know that utopias don't exist. Humans are incapable of such a thing. Believe me, I know."

Those perfect blue eyes wavered.

There it was.

A little tell that she was on to something. Her job, as a soldier in the trenches, seeing the gnarliest shit had had a way of giving her a sixth sense. Her second sight developed from experiencing the real Heart of Darkness, yet also seeing extraordinary acts of kindness in the most desperate of situations. Soldiers weren't welcome most places ravaged by war and corporate exploitation, but Leticia had been fed and sheltered when she didn't think she had a hope in the world. In turn she did whatever she could to bring her helpers whatever they might need in this village or that, even if it meant breaking the rules.

Bullshit archaic rules that were meant to be broken enough times until they exploded so the new way could be ushered in.

"I accept your challenge," he said while caressing her. "Did I not surprise you tonight?"

"Not there," she said, "here." Leticia liked him before— well, liked his body, his eyes, that geeky shy boy smile—but now she wanted to know more. She liked a rebel, and if his ability in the sack had anything to do with his yoga, maybe it wasn't so bad after all.

"You must know the feeling is mutual." She kissed hard. It was easy to ignore the blinking on her watch, lying on a small pop-up side table next to her cot. Ramón had been messaging Leticia.

His last one was direct.

Jacob is nowhere to be found.

Now you are not answering.

Be careful sister. Don't be getting too close to him.

Trust me on this. I don't want to warn you again.

2 4

Dylan imagined that he floated downstream on an inner tube, with the motion of being suspended. Bright lights that might be sunshine escaping through tree branches passed over his closed eyelids, causing them to flutter. Then his perceptions shifted.

A heated blanket covered him to mid-chest. He had the worst heartburn he'd ever experienced in his life. It had to be the thing that leapt out of the egg and crawled into his suit just before he blacked out.

They told him there was nothing inside.

Desperate to impress and despite his intuitive fear he gave them the benefit of the doubt. Julia Yutani did this to him. Her reputation wasn't just whispers among the low-level workers. Coming from a colony on the verge of war, he should have known that the offer extended to him was too good to be true. They always were.

He was tied to a gurney, and it was moving. Dylan

flexed both hands to test his strength. Would it be enough to break free? He knew where the dropships were located, if he could somehow escape. First, though, he needed to discover where *he* was.

The motion stopped. The sound of a metal door opening, followed by more movement. He could feel the straps easing off his chest and legs.

Now.

His eyes snapped open and he threw his entire body weight into knocking the assistant in the face and ripping the key fob off their wrist. It would be needed to open the myriad of doors in this maze of a facility that had felt like an emperor's tomb from the instant he saw it. The recruiter had said that Jacob Vickers—one of *them*—was establishing a place of peace and opportunity for everyone.

To his surprise, when he arrived in a group that disembarked from the same dropship, Julia Yutani herself had greeted them. He had a sense of relief when he saw the half-constructed building, thinking how it would mean steady work with good pay. Then when the facility was complete, he was given the opportunity for a new position.

Now here he was fighting for his life. It was a slim chance, but one he had to take. If he survived, everyone would know about this.

Dylan bolted out the door while the assistant scrambled to get to their feet. Before they could reach him, he secured it shut. Turning, he found another member of staff in the corridor, staring at him in shock, not knowing how to react. Dylan wasted no time in driving him into the wall and hitting him hard enough to knock him out.

Wrestling in high school came in handy.

Grabbing this person's fob, as well, he glanced through a round window in the top half of a door on the opposite side of the corridor. A man he didn't recognize sat upright on a cot rubbing his chest and neck. They got to him, too. Using one of the key fobs he opened the door.

"Let's go!" he shouted. There was another door in the corner, with a blinking disk. Dylan touched the fob to the keypad, then handed it to the fellow on the cot. "Open as many doors as you can."

The man's eyes went wide in bewilderment, but he eased off the cot and stood on shaky legs. Dashing out again, Dylan hit the corridor as the lights switched off, then went blue. A loud alarm blared, and he pivoted to run toward the elevator that would carry him through the residential space and to the dropships. Perhaps he could free more prisoners.

With the fury of vengeance, Dylan ran through to find more like him as alarms wailed throughout the facility. He spotted a row of sealed windowless doors, and swiped the fob. The heavy doors began to slowly lift, but he didn't wait to see who would emerge.

* * *

Julia sat in her office making last-minute preparations when the lights dimmed and turned blue. She spun around at her desk and pressed the keypad on her chair.

A feed from the research area lit up the wall. She jolted upright before slamming her palm against the desk, then scrolled until she found the office of Brenda Moon. The doctor appeared, already speaking to someone not visible in the frame.

"Julia!"

"Are you watching this?" Julia demanded. "Fuck! Get him—but do *not* under any circumstances unleash or activate the bacteria. And do not terminate *anything*." In spite of herself, Julia could feel the fear taking over.

"I'm on it," Moon responded. *"We'll do what we can to neutralize any immediate threat of Xenos breaking free, and resecure the facility. The fob he's carrying shouldn't open any of the Xenomorph holdings... Wait. I think I hear him. Stay where you are."*

Julia paced as she watched the chaos on the wall. The experiment was supposed to remain under control, as were the test subjects, *all* of them. The company was counting on her. All eyes in the family scrutinized what she did here, to prove her worthiness to take her place on the Weyland-Yutani throne. The Weyland name would be reduced to a prop, and Yutani would wield the power and influence. No matter how many people had to die, they were just numbers.

Dylan What's-His-Name, that low-level piece of shit, would not ruin it. No way in hell.

She was still pacing, trying to make sense of her limited point of view when the alarm indicated that sector XIXI— also called "the Pen"—had been opened. Red lights flashed in unison with the blue. She slowly turned her head toward the door to her office. A fear she had never known slithered down the length of her neck until pangs of disbelief stabbed her in the stomach and chest. The flashing lights added to her panic.

Julia pulled up a screen that would locate Brenda's watch.

Nothing—no indication of anything.

She tried again, and again with no luck. With one last scrap of hope she called Brenda's office through the video comms. The connection opened, but it wasn't Brenda. A sweating Dylan appeared, with black blooms on his skin.

"*Wrong number, Julia.*"

"Dylan, stop this. I have an antidote. Money. We can make this right. I was wrong."

"*Nope. Wrong, bitch. Your friend here had all her files open for you. You. Are. Lying.*"

"Dylan, what are you doing," she said. "Do you know what you just did?"

"*Yes, I do now.*" He laughed with a crazed look in his eye. "*Checkmate. You die.*" The video link went dead.

She threw herself into her chair and began to type as fast as her fingers would move on the surface of her desk.

Her hands were shaking. The Throne Room was still secure, a small miracle at the very least. She took a deep breath to calm her thoughts long enough to follow protocol, perhaps salvage the situation. It was time to do what she had never wanted to do, following Ramón's ability to see an entire chess game being played out.

If the Xenomorphs got out, she knew what was coming.

Then she dropped to her knees and crawled beneath the desk to a hatch door in the floor. Her handprint in the center unlocked it. This panic space might be her only hope of survival. Once safely inside, she could send an alert and continue with the chain reaction she and Ramón had designed.

Before closing it above her head, she wondered if Ramón had anticipated, even *hoped* something like this might happen. Maybe not on this scale, but it was certainly enough to ruin Jacob for good. She pushed those thoughts away.

The panic room was scarcely a room, more like a pod. She looked around hoping there were enough supplies. She wouldn't be climbing out until she was met with boots and proper weapons.

Underground and at the corner of the pyramid was the space where two worlds met. Dylan Graves opened the gateway to hell with the swipe of a fob. A still-young Xenomorph cried out, then paused, surveying its surroundings before moving through the opening.

Behind it, a succession of locks clicked, and walls opened. A cacophony of shrieks filled the corridor with the power of an ancient steam engine traveling at full speed through a tunnel. Every human on the adjacent wing could hear.

The small Xenomorph skidded across the floor of the corridor. A synth was there, and her eyes were wide as she scanned the intruder. In one quick slice her torso went left and bottom half to the right. White liquid erupted from her body. Strings of cables flopped uselessly.

The humans that had been freed saw what happened and screamed, their cries echoing along the corridor. The hallway turned, then turned again until it met itself, a serpent eating its tail. Larger Xenomorphs emerged and charged ahead toward the running test subjects.

The synth stared at the ceiling, expressionless, and whispered a command.

"Send all files."

"Yutani."

"Vasquez."

Julia woke up to a wet tapping on her bare foot, and something sliding off. She jumped up and looked around in fear. A few hours of sleep had passed, filled with nightmares. Wet streaks like tears slowly crawled down one of the walls with another single drip where her foot previously rested.

"Fuck!" she said, and the sound echoed in the tiny space. "This is supposed to be air and watertight. Fuck!" She wiped her toes with her hand, not wanting to think what was happening out there, but needing to know if the Xenomorphs had unwittingly caused damage to the guts of the building.

Turning on the monitors she half expected to see chaos and their snarling faces. What she saw scared her even more. On every screen view it was deserted and silent. Not a single body or flickering light. There was no way of knowing where they could be, or who was still alive. How long could she stay down here? And what about this leak? The monitors only showed a fraction of the cavernous facility.

She turned the monitor off again. Someone had to come. She was too important to be left behind, and Ramón should have landed by now. The alert on her watch indicated that he was here.

It was ironic. All her life she had never had to rely on any knight in shining armor—she was both the knight and queen. For the first time she had zero control over a situation, a circumstance she had, in part, created. Brenda Moon had warned her, and she didn't listen.

If anyone could get a handle on this situation, it would be Ramón. She curled back onto the soft padding in the small space she had designed for herself with a few more comforts. For the moment she would wait, and dream.

2 5

The morning arrived with the warmth of the sun brightening the haze swept in from the sulfur fields, mixed with a descending fog. The wind direction had changed again. The slight smell of rotten eggs made most of the crew push their freeze-dried scramble to the side.

Leticia and Jacob kept a distance but could not prevent their gazes from finding each other again. She knew it had to be kept quiet, for now. However, whatever was happening between them felt part of the plan, whatever it was. Desiree slid in next to Leticia with her plate in one hand and a steaming cup of coffee in the other.

"So far so good, jefa," she said. "I could get used to this treatment—and what a planet."

"I agree," Leticia replied. "In fact, my exact words. Would you consider staying out here long-term, if the money was good?"

Desiree put her fork down. "We are a good team," she

said. "I would go to the steps of hell with you to kick the devil's ass. This is practically paradise. After you left last evening, the rest of the crew couldn't stop talking about a future outside of the Corps."

Leticia started to speak, then stopped.

Her eyes shifted overhead. From a distance came the sound of an incoming air vehicle. Desiree picked it up as well. She looked around at the others, who were eating without care. Jacob approached.

"Did you send anyone out this morning?" he asked. "I thought we were leaving together?"

She shook her head, then scanned the mess tent again. "No, but Ramón isn't..." Her brother darted through the flaps of the tent, accompanied by Nathan, who was on watch.

"There's a dropship with an emergency beacon approaching us," he said. "We can't contact the crew, and no video link."

Ramón's eyes were wide with pure terror—she had never seen him look like this. After an awkward silence, he spoke again. "We have to get to Olinka One, and *now*. How quick can we move, and more than move, be prepared for combat?"

Everyone was watching them now, with their ears silently pricked. Whatever situation was developing, her crew could handle it, but she had to keep the rest of them calm to avoid dealing with more than one fire—if indeed a fire was approaching.

Leticia stood and grabbed Ramón by the elbow, then made eye contact with each one of her team. When her gaze met Desiree, she tapped her forefinger twice against her chest. The signal to get combat ready. The others would know to follow. Then she leaned close into Ramón's ear.

"Keep your voice down. Let's go outside." Before leaving the tent, she said in a firm voice, "Keep eating, everyone. Nobody leaves here until we come and get you." One or two might not listen, but she had to still say it. Otherwise they would all go in different directions. If a threat loomed, that would be bad. She couldn't spare one of hers to babysit the entrance of the tent.

Jacob, Leticia, and Ramón left the tent without meeting anyone's stare. Her crew followed behind.

The large dropship weaved back and forth as it approached in the distance. By the size, it was meant to carry quite a few people and cargo, but there was no way to tell if it was filled with many, or just one person. Whoever manned the ship didn't know what they were doing, or some sort of damage had occurred to the navigation system.

Ramón spoke first. "I can get into Olinka's system and manually control the dropship—there's nothing I can't access. We blow it up. We have no responsibility to answer that emergency call. Jacob, you have every right to get rid of it without any legal issue. You are Weyland-Yutani."

Leticia shot Ramón a look as swift as a switchblade to the jugular, even though fear fluttered in her bowels. Judging from his expression, however, he felt the same.

"How did we go from an emergency call to blowing it up?" she demanded. "That makes no sense, Ramón. Whoever is inside could be in real trouble."

He paced their surroundings, distracted as if he fought off multiple demons screaming in his head. Sweat ran down his temples and gathered above his stubbled lip. He was usually a man who found success by keeping his cool. This was not that man. Leticia walked in front of him, following his roving head, so he had to look at her, give her some sort of straight answer.

"What aren't you saying, Ramón? If you know something, any lost lives are on your head." He still retained the look of terror. His usual steely determination returned, however, when he stopped his imitation of a caged beast.

"Get combat ready. I'll explain later."

Leticia turned to Jacob. "Get into our dropship and seal it shut."

He looked confused and slightly hurt. "But I—"

"Now," she said in a stern voice. "This is what you hired me for. You can watch from inside. Ramón will secure you." There was a heavy silence between them, a tie that neither wanted severed.

He complied with his jaw clenched.

"If I see anything—"

"I know," she responded a little softer. "I feel the same. Stay safe, and just do as I say. Go."

Ramón placed his hand on Jacob's shoulder to lead him to the ship. Leticia ran toward her crew, who waited together for their next orders. Nathan was hefting a flamethrower. Frida already had Leticia's helmet, with a bandana tied to the chin strap. Leticia grabbed the red strip of cloth and placed it around her forehead before securing the helmet.

"¡Oye! You will be my medic," she said to Mohammed. "Frida, get everyone out of the mess tent and into the ships. We don't have much time. Then join Desiree and Nathan with me, and be ready for whatever is on that ship. It's coming in hot. *Vámanos.*"

"*Shitty eggs, and now an unannounced visitor,*" Mohammed growled. "*I thought this was going to be easy.*"

"Same, brother." Leticia grabbed his forearm before leaving. Then she spoke into the mouthpiece attached to her helmet. "I want a perimeter, the best we can do right now. Be ready as soon as the ship touches down." She raised her head to the sky. The fog was turning thicker and smoke was blowing from the sulfur fields in claw-like gossamer wisps. Visibility was poor at best.

Perfect fucking timing.

The ship arrived skidding and bumping before coming to a halt.

"¿Qué es esto, Ramón?" she said into the comms, shouting over the clatter of the landing. "What aren't you telling us?"

Then Ramón stepped up beside her, but remained silent as the ship powered down. Soon there wasn't a sound, except for their heartbeats. The back hatch began to open. Leticia's crew stood in wait with their weapons aimed and fingers on the triggers.

A barefoot man in a medical robe emerged from the ship, appearing ashen-faced with a tinge of jaundice and a black rash. His hair clung to his skull from sweat and dark circles tinged his eyes. He looked around in confusion before lifting his hands in the air.

"I need your help," he called out. "I didn't know there were others out here. I have valuable information." Mohammed wasted no time rushing toward him, but Ramón ran to block his way.

"Don't!"

Leticia didn't take her eyes off the man. Jacob's voice crackled in her earpiece.

"*I'm coming out*," he said. "*I need to see this. Dammit, this project has my name on it.*" By the time he finished, he was standing with them.

"Jacob, get back into the ship," she shouted. "Ramón, stop him. People, expect the unexpected. This don't smell right."

"*No, I'm staying*," Jacob protested. "*Ramón, what the hell is this?*"

"Nobody go near the ship, or him!" Ramón shouted as loud as he could without a helmet and mic. "Leticia, he's a dead man. You have to trust me on this."

The newcomer continued to stumble closer, coughing and clutching his chest until he fell to his knees as his body seized up. Every vein in his neck and forehead protruded, his fingernails were black, and there were bluish-black lesions on his skin. These were getting darker the more violently he convulsed. He pressed both hands against the middle of his chest as he shrieked in agony and terror.

Ignoring Leticia's instructions, a few of the scientists and crew had come to see what caused the commotion. She shot them a quick look before turning back to the man. There was no time to deal with the bystanders.

There was a *crack* with the *pop* of a busted piñata, and a slimy creature exploded from the dying man's sternum. Bone, blood, and viscera erupted from his body with the speed of an active volcano. He clawed at his chest, trying to hold the sharp-toothed monster biting at the air as it whipped around to escape the ruined chest.

Leticia pulled her trigger, shooting with perfect marksmanship and causing the small thing to let out a high-pitched screech as it took a bullet to the head. The man fell to the ground, dead before he landed. His blood oozed into the dirt, an unusual shade of red—as dark as blood in the moonlight as it congealed into a tar-like substance.

A louder hiss and a screech echoed from the ship. Mohammed dropped his medic bag and pulled the pulse rifle from his back. He ran to Leticia's side.

"*What the fuck was that, and what's still in there?*" he demanded. "*I trust you, sister, but I don't trust whatever the hell they were doing here.*" He lifted his weapon to aim it at the hatch. "*Some fucking vacation.*"

"*Holy shit,*" Desiree shouted.

Two full-grown Xenomorphs crawled from the ship on all fours, with their barbed tails weaving in the air like cobras ready to strike. Recognizing them from the records, Leticia nevertheless couldn't believe what she was seeing. Her bandana, saturated with sweat, released a single drop, managing to sting the corner of her left eye. This was no time to flinch.

Their bodies were as dark as pure obsidian and their razor fangs as sharp as that black glass when it had been fashioned into a blade. Obsidian was used by their ancestors to see the future—they would stare at their reflections until the truth was revealed. It was also called Itzli, after the god of stone, human sacrifice, and rock blades.

One of the scientists who had disobeyed her orders let out a screech and tried to run off. Before he could, one of the monsters leapt into the air and punctured his back with its tail. Talons swiped across the scientist's skull. Fragments of bone and chunks of flesh burst into the air amid fireworks of blood. These beasts were killers of men and showed the only truth they could bring—certain death. Frightening enough for Leticia to believe that dark gods existed, to craft such perfect harbingers of destruction.

One of the hissing gargoyles opened its jaws to reveal another mouth that punched in and out like a battering ram.

That was the last straw.

"Now!" Leticia bellowed. They fired off a volley at both Xenomorphs. The one ripping into the scientist was hit multiple times and sent writhing to the ground. Pieces of its body blasted into the air, flinging chartreuse blood toward the soldiers. Frida cried out as a drop landed on her exposed left hand and forearm. The ground where the rest of the grotesque body lay began to smoke from the acidic blood scorching the earth.

The second monstrosity turned to flee.

"Don't let it get away!" Leticia shouted. "Blast this bitch now! Do whatever you have to do." She followed the second Xenomorph's path with her rifle and continued to shoot, but it gave new meaning to the old phrase "bat out of hell." Desiree and Mohammed followed her lead.

The other bystanders ran to wherever they thought would be safest cover, stumbling and scrabbling as they did so. Dropping his rifle in favor of the flamethrower, Nathan ran toward the Xenomorph, but too late. The creature leapt *through* the flames with slimy jaws open and the energy and terror of Satan himself. With one swipe of its hand it cut his body in half. Leticia could hear the rest of her Marines scream and meet the creature with everything they had. She didn't have the heart or time to look at Mohammed, who screamed into the comms.

Finally the Xenomorph fell to the ground, a smoking liquified corpse. The acid leaking from its body burning into the ground. Tears streaming from his eyes, Mohammed continued to shoot rounds into the creature. He didn't stop until his weapon ran out of ammunition.

Frida touched his shoulder.

"He needs you. This doesn't."

Mohammed's chest rose and fell along with the smoke coming from his expended rifle and searing acid. He turned to Nathan's remains, and fell to his knees.

"I can't," he said, his voice small. *"Someone... please."*

Jacob ran out with a foil heat sheet and placed it over Nathan's body while Frida led Mohammed to his tent. As he walked away, he spat at Ramón's feet. Leticia patrolled the scene of horror that was not meant to be. Part of her couldn't believe this was real, and not a nightmare. El Diablo had manifested before her eyes for a dance to the death. It had happened so fast and without warning. The sense of betrayal overwhelmed her, combining with the nauseating odor from the sulfur fields mingling with burned flesh.

Then the wind stopped—the air went still, leaving them surrounded by the aroma of death. She couldn't bear to look at Ramón, yet she knew she had business with him, and it wouldn't be pretty. She didn't care who heard or saw, or how high his pay grade. One of hers was dead. She approached Frida who was having her burns attended to by one of the scientists.

"What's the damage?"

"Not too bad," Frida replied. "Kinda like being splashed with a million-degree hot grease. It didn't get my throwing arm, though, and Jim here has this crazy numbing cream."

"Good," Leticia said. "And thanks, Jim. Please get back into the ship as soon as you are finished. We'll let you know if we need you." She turned back to her Marine. "Frida, after you're patched up, cover the corpses until we have a plan." She moved along to check on everyone else.

The dropships were open again, with the civilians wanting to get a look at what happened. She could hear gasps and hushed conversations as they craned their necks.

"Desiree, you make sure no one touches a thing. Not Nathan, or those things. Threaten them with a bullet to the knee if you have to. Get them back into the larger ships. And check on Mohammed, will ya?"

"On it, jefa."

Leticia pivoted to find her brother. "Ramón! Where the fuck are you?" she bellowed. No one dared look in her direction. Jacob stepped out of one of the smaller dropships.

"We're here."

She was ready to unleash hell, and could see that he was just as enraged, but more than ever she didn't know who she could trust—especially if they hadn't dragged themselves through the trenches of basic training back on Earth.

Leticia had to be sure.

"Start talking, man."

Jacob had a manic glint in his eye. "Leticia, I promise I didn't know… The entire planet could be at risk. I don't want another world destroyed because of the bullshit greed and politics of my own company. This isn't me."

Leticia had to feel this out. Every part of her wanted to believe Jacob, yet…

"He's telling the truth, Leticia."

Ramón appeared behind Jacob at the bay door of the dropship, looking like a sad sack. Hearing those words, Jacob's face sank into an abyss of betrayal.

"Let's talk inside." Leticia looked over her shoulder. Desiree and Frida had everything in control—of course. So they entered the ship and closed the bay door for absolute privacy.

"We have no time to waste," she said, struggling to control her words. "You waste any more of my time, or more of my people get killed… We have a big problem, brother. I don't give a fuck who you are, I will see to it that you get what's coming to you. Your types never see a day of time for the dirty shit they do, but there are ways. You better come clean, hermano." As she and Jacob faced him, Ramón stood as if he were on trial.

"I know this is bad," he said. "Very bad, but we have to stay calm. Think about the investment, and—"

"Fuck!" Jacob screamed as he ran his hands through his hair. Leticia jumped at the sound. "You *know* this is going to fall on my ass. Or was that your plan all along? An inside job to bring the Vickers boy down. How much did you get paid?"

Ramón paused a beat.

"Julia Yutani is at Olinka One," he said. "There are Colonial Marines two days away—she sent an alert before she messaged me. They may be too late—and if there is a Xenomorph infestation, they will need more muscle and firepower."

"The fuck, Ramón?" Leticia threw her hands up and began to pace, her boots echoing in the enclosed space. "Xenomorph infestation? Is that what you call it? These are not a nest of cucarachas we can squash with a boot! You better tell me everything. First, I need to know if that sick and dead man was contagious. He didn't look right."

"He wasn't… isn't. Not yet, but we should dispose of everything as quickly as possible. Jacob, those scalding hot fumaroles aren't just valuable because of the geothermal energy here. We've been using it as a biological waste disposal system."

Leticia saw Jacob's hands shaking. "I'm not a violent man, Ramón," he said, "but I could knock you the fuck out ten times over right now."

Leticia stepped between the two men.

"Both of you get the hell out of here—and Ramón, you're on clean-up duty. You want to shit chaos, then pick it up."

Ramón jerked his head toward Jacob who stepped back and put his hands up.

"Don't look at me," he said. "She's in charge now. You take orders from the director of security."

Ramón's lips tightened. "Where do you want me, *jefa*?"

Leticia felt guilty for the small satisfaction she got from watching Ramón heave and gag with a bandana around his nose and mouth as he assisted with the clean-up. They didn't have proper disposal gear, because none of this was meant to happen in the first place.

Ramón lowered the corpse of the man into one of the bubbling hot mud pots roughly the size of a small pond, to dissolve it quickly. The brown liquid hungrily dragged the figure below the surface. He then had the honor of lowering the Xenomorphs into the same vent, with help from Mohammed, who wore Nathan's dog tags around his neck.

He requested to lower Nathan's body alone in one of the fumaroles. Leticia allowed him to do what he needed to do.

Unlike the humans, parts of the Xenomorph skeletons remained intact, dissolving slower. Both skulls rose to the top.

"This could be the nastiest game of bobbing for apples," Frida said, shaking her head with a scowl of disgust on her face. "Where are these damn things from?"

"Yeah, not even the planet wants these things." Leticia couldn't help to throw Ramón another dirty glance. "My tía, Roseanna, would say it's a sign. Take them both out before they are gone for good."

"I was joking," Frida said, "but you're the boss."

"I want to inspect them."

"Me, too," Jacob said. "This is insane, and it's not like we can get close to a live one. Have you seen what their guts do? They're pure fire inside." He turned to Leticia, who had a vacant look in her eye as the Xenomorph skulls smoked on the barren dirt. "You alright? What are you thinking?"

"I had an experience with a shaman," she said. "Like what you may have seen when you went to Peru. It was almost a premonition, now that I see these things. I mean, Roseanna would say it was the ancestors or even my mom guiding me, but no way…"

"What's the plan, Leticia?" Jacob asked.

"What do you mean, what's the plan?" Ramón pulled down his bandana from over his nose and mouth. "We go get Julia now. The clean-up is done. We pack up and leave."

"No." Leticia turned. "Fuck no, Ramón. We are *not* going in unprepared, Yutani princesa or not. I will send in a drone first. Our parents died somewhere out here. I'm not risking the same fate, if I'm in charge. They didn't have a choice, but I do."

"I know this place better than anyone," he protested. "I'm telling you we need to move now. You said yourself we can't waste time."

"On lies," she said. "No more wasting time on lies." They stood face-to-face. She met his gaze in silence, without any giving in.

He broke away.

"Fine."

The Xenomorphs continued to run the perimeter of their level of the pyramid, crashing into every possible weak point, causing damage to the communications and electrical systems.

Four of them gathered, hissing and with their heads swaying toward the floor. Lights flashed in intermittent bursts like the Fourth of July fireworks of red and blue. Without warning the sprinkler system let out steam and water.

Tossing anything that might be heavy enough to break through to freedom, the humans also scrambled to find any way out, only to be eviscerated by the Xenomorphs. The youngest of the creatures managed to slip through a door Dylan had opened. Going its own way, it roamed and shrieked as it attacked any sudden movement. It did not care nor understand the damage it continued to cause.

A larger Xenomorph hissed above its head, and slinked into an open office.

2 6

Julia couldn't put it off any longer. The pool of water was growing larger, and the stack of sodden towels and blankets stored in the small pod were useless now, yet streams of water continued to flow. She looked at the monitors again.

Nothing. Not a soul. She hadn't seen a single human or Xenomorph. The feed appeared exactly the same as before. This room was soundproof, so maybe they were all dead and she hadn't been able to hear what was going on in the spaces not covered by the cameras.

Taking a deep breath, Julia tucked a flare gun into her lab coat pocket. Her quivering right hand reached for the center of the hatch to unlock it again, and the door rose in silence. She poked her head out to look at the entrance to the office. It was open, but she couldn't remember if it had been left when her colleague ran out. It should have shut automatically and locked.

Her eyes narrowed when she saw the source of the

water. "Shitty contractors," she grumbled to herself. The water cooler in the corner of the room had fallen over. A stream from the external pump still drained into the square glass container on the floor. Barely visible to the eye was a small seam in the floor where the tiles met.

It must have been someone looking for a way out. She had conjured up all kinds of outrageous scenarios of those things burrowing closer to get to her. Surely if a Xenomorph had been inside of here, though, there would be more evidence of it. She exhaled a sigh of relief. It would be an easy and quick fix and she could return to her pod.

Her eyes darted around.

Nothing but sweet silence.

Twisting to exit the hatch, she stood upright and stretched, then stepped over to her console. She hit a control and the display lit up. A banner blinked.

LIVE FEED

At the sight of those words, her entire body shook. The images on the monitor she had been seeing all this time hadn't been live. It was a still. What she saw now defied what she thought the Xenomorph capable of accomplishing.

The bodies...

Brenda...

The rooms and passageways were unrecognizable, covered in a bizarre resin that was clear in places, opaque in others—transforming crisp, squared-off walls into rounded, uneven tunnels. Here and there she could see masses along the walls, each roughly the size of a human body. That sent shudders through her again. In a short amount of time they had managed to reshape the facility to create their own world. These mindless beasts wanted a home.

Well fuck them. As much as she hated to destroy valuable assets, they would all have to be terminated when backup arrived. For now, she would go into the system and terminate the queens remotely. *What a waste.*

Julia returned to the hatch and grabbed the door to close it. Her hand came away wet... and sticky. She brought it back to inspect it. Before she could, her eyes caught something else. A hole in the ceiling that hadn't been there before. She would have to open the door to her panic room completely to see the extent of the damage, and couldn't bring herself to do it.

Returning to her computer, she called up a list of the security breaches. Her eyes fixed on a specific one.

THRONE ROOM

The view was obscured—just a vague blur of light and darkness. Most likely the creatures had covered the camera in that weird organic material. But she knew what was in each of the holding chambers, and she knew what to do about them.

One click, and the crowns would explode.

She reached out to tap the command.

Black, bony fingers with long talons filled her vision. Her head was snapped back, and she lost consciousness.

Leticia, Jacob, and Ramón sat in Ramón's tent watching the live feed from the drone as it appeared on the control tablet. Desiree operated the brand-new machinery with skill and expertise—at least *this* part of the investment could be used to their advantage.

She slowed its approach as it arrived at the entrance to Olinka One. No one uttered a word. The dark, semi-transparent pyramid showed no damage to the outside, and no sign of life.

"Have you heard from Julia again?"

"No. Nothing." Ramón stared at the building without looking at Jacob. "But she made it into the panic pod." He spoke to Desiree. "Focus on the lower levels, where the labs are located. It wouldn't make sense for most of the inhabitants to be in the residential quarters, given when I received the alert."

She brought the drone close to the ziggurat. Due to the reflective energy-efficient glass, there was no visibility from the outside.

"I'm switching to scan for bio readings, movement, and heat."

The readings pulsed across the screen as the drone continued to whizz at speed around the perimeter. Every second was another breath none of them inhaled or exhaled too loudly. Abruptly words blinked yellow at the bottom of the screen.

HUMAN LIFE DETECTED

"See!" Ramón whipped his entire body toward Leticia. "Can we go in now? There are survivors. We *have* to go in."

Desiree shifted her eyes to Leticia, and nodded. "As much as I hate it, I have to agree with him," she said. "We don't leave anyone behind."

Leticia continued to watch as the drone circled the facility that was as still as a corpse. She didn't like the look or feel of the situation. Surely people with any ability to get out would have tried, or showed signs of trying.

"What if they're like that guy who was infected with one of those things?" she said. "Alive but *not* alive. Ramón, what kind of weapons do you have stashed inside?"

"Not much," he admitted. "Just enough to control the more dangerous projects like the Xenomorphs. If there are humans being used as hosts, then we have to put them out of their misery as we encounter them, find Julia, and shut it down."

Leticia nudged Ramón's shoulder. "Are you saying *there are more* like him?"

"Probably." He waited a beat before continuing. "But we can't be certain without knowing what has happened inside. The exterior was meant to withstand a lot, in the event of an attack. The interior is intricate. The upper floors store dropships, with a single exit. That's how that guy must have escaped, taking the Xenomorphs along without knowing it. Once he was out, an electromagnetic field sealed the exit even before the physical doors closed.

"The middle floors are residential units, leisure facilities, and communal spaces," he continued. "The lower floors and those located beneath the facility are where the research is conducted. We figured if anyone needed to escape, it would be out the top to leave by ship, rather than on foot out the front door.

"There's a ventilation system at the bottom that could be used for an escape, I suppose." Ramón pointed. "The bars couldn't be opened or penetrated by a Xenomorph— they don't have the intelligence or the strength. We coated them with PTFE—polytetrafluoroethylene, a synthetic polymer that's super strong. There is one lift from the basement that goes directly to the top. The basement and lower floors should be completely locked down, unless someone overrides the security system.

"Only the ones considered not expendable have access to that."

As opposed to the ones who are *expendable*, Leticia thought bitterly, but she didn't say it. There wasn't time.

Jacob turned to Leticia. "I don't like Julia, but we have to attempt to get her. Otherwise it will be very bad for the company… and she *is* a human being. If our competition gets wind of this…

"We have to try," he added. "This is bigger than her or me."

"Alright. Let's go." Leticia placed a hand on Desiree's shoulder. "Move to the dropship, but keep an eagle eye on every corner with the drone. Report the most insignificant thing you see, if it seems the least bit out of the ordinary. Keep the entire perimeter scanned."

"Got it, jefa."

Leticia turned to Ramón and Jacob. "You two, follow me. We have a lot to discuss before we crack open Olinka One. Ramón, are you sure reinforcements will be on the way?"

"I'm certain," he replied. "Julia would not leave herself in any position without an escape plan. Her family would not have allowed her to come here without one."

Leticia stepped outside. Ramón and Jacob followed. Soon it would be dusk, and the majority of their party was sticking close to the vessel in case another unexpected danger reared its ugly head. She spoke loudly enough for everyone to hear.

"I need everyone to gather around," she said. "If you know of anyone in their tents or the mess tent, then go get them. I'll give you five minutes."

"What are you doing, hermana?"

Leticia ignored Ramón. The small group of civilians and even smaller Raider crew found their way to her. She tried her best to not appear frightened or angry about the place in which they found themselves. It made her think of when she had been forced to swim to shore when her Narwhal was sabotaged.

She had to focus and move forward the best way she could.

"Okay, people—listen up," she said. "My crew are used to dealing with the unexpected. Well, not with blood-thirsty monsters from space, but it's still what we were trained to do. The rest of you are probably frightened and I understand." She paused, and added, "Reinforcements are on the way."

There was a murmur from the crowd. She could hear sighs of relief.

"But all of you—everyone except my crew—will remain here with the dropship until they arrive. We are leaving to make an extraction, and all of my team will go with me. I can't spare any of them to stay behind."

The civilians grumbled as they whispered among themselves.

Leticia raised both hands. "I know it's not ideal," she said. "Worse than that, it's shit. But we can't babysit. You will be safer near the two dropships, until you can be flown out and picked up by the Marines. Those of you who know how to use a weapon will be given one, until we run out. Frida will be waiting by the mess tent. Make your way to her. Absolutely *no* wandering beyond camp." She looked around to make sure they understood. "There are enough supplies to last until backup arrives. We leave as soon as you're all secured."

Leticia felt terrible, as if she was abandoning them, but this was the decision that had to be made. She just hoped it wasn't like a parent who said they were going out to get cigarettes and never coming back. This was the safest option for everyone.

She turned to Ramón. "Happy now?"

He didn't reply and couldn't meet her gaze.

The Raiders wasted no time preparing weapons, double-checking supplies, and securing the civilians they had to leave behind. They silently gave her the thumbs-up as she passed. This was why she loved her crew. They worked as a team, and without question. A true wolf pack, Las Lobas. When satisfied with their progress she called Ramón and Jacob over and climbed into the dropship. Frida and Mohammed followed soon after, and they all buckled into the passenger compartment. Desiree was already in the cockpit.

"Ready?" Desiree said over the comms.

Leticia took one more look at the screen on the tablet. Those they had to leave behind remained in their tents, and the hatches for the other two ships remained open in the event they needed a quick escape.

"Let's do this. Take her as fast as she will go."

As they lifted into the air Leticia noticed that Jacob kept his eyes on Ramón, one leg bouncing in place. He sat across from him without any of the passive or relaxed nature he always exuded.

"Before we get there," Jacob said finally, "you better

talk fast. How the *hell* did the Xenomorphs get here? It was your job to make sure this colony followed my vision. A vision I thought we shared!"

"You really want to do this now? In front of others?"

"Yes," Jacob said. "These people are putting their lives on the line for something you and Julia did."

Ramón shook his head, vitriol in his eyes.

"You delusional trust-fund school boy. The perfect little niño," he said. "You have no clue how many people despise you. No matter which way you present yourself, the company used you to look good. Fake and meaningless gestures to trick everyone into thinking they were changing direction, and get regulatory bodies and the press off their asses. You're nothing but a corporate tourist who needs to be running a charity on Earth."

He looked Jacob straight in the eye. Leticia had to give him credit—he had cojones.

"This has only been a success because of me," Ramón continued, not giving Jacob a chance to reply. "You are ruining the company with your stupid ideas of 'peace.' The math didn't make sense, and we had to generate revenues to keep your little project alive—all to satisfy those in the company who shared your views, and to justify it to the board of directors.

"Yes, we have been using Olinka to study the Xenomorph… and other things. They have been here since long before you became involved."

Jacob was silent for a moment.

"After the news breaks of what has happened here, are you hoping to save your skin by saving Julia?"

"You don't have a clue," Ramón said. "Julia was meant to be there all along. We need to salvage Olinka at all costs. The Yutani family is heavily invested in everything we are doing."

Leticia shifted her eyes to Jacob. Ramón's words were stinging. She could tell because she lived with him long enough. Part of her felt hurt for Jacob. No one wanted to be a puppet.

To her surprise, Jacob's demeanor remained calm.

"The difference between me and you, even me and the company, is that I know who I am without any of this. I want something greater than myself. I can survive stripped, and widdled down. Same with your sister. Her biggest concern in all of this was for her team. That's why she said yes to me." He leaned in. "Be hurtful all you want, but right now you have to give us every last detail concerning the shadow operations—this is a life-or-death situation.

"When we get through this crisis, I'll expect your resignation."

Leticia believed every word he said, and even felt bad for her brother—almost. He'd just got a taste of his own medicine.

"Whatever," Ramón spat out. "I don't care anymore."

"Of course you don't. You're probably already set for more than a lifetime."

"Niños, you've said your piece," Leticia said, cutting in. "We will arrive soon. If it won't help the mission, I don't want to hear it. Not now. This is the only moment that exists. We survive one minute, then survive the next."

Ramón cleared his throat. "Perhaps you should know that, like an Egyptian or Mesoamerican pyramid, the facility has been created with smaller chambers. It's not just the levels I mentioned before. There are the secure spaces where the team worked with the Xenomorphs—and other pathogens in development—but they're sealed tight. Julia's distress call would have ensured that.

"When I unlock any of those doors," he continued, "it will probably unlock the other large entrances or exits, including the dropship bay. I can't isolate the front entrance. And whatever damage has been done..."

Leticia slowly reared her head toward him. "This just gets better and better. We're walking into a tomb, then, and might let out the fucking mummy at the same time. Is that it?"

"I don't know, sis," he said. "I'll bring up the blueprints and see if I can find a hack." Ramón buried his head in his tablet, and Jacob turned to Leticia.

"Hey, can I ask you a favor—not that you owe me one."

"You can ask."

"I'm a bit embarrassed, but that won't matter if I'm dead." He scratched the back of his head. "You mind showing me how to use a weapon?"

Leticia could see the fear, and his desire to contribute in

some way. She suspected that given the chance he would do anything to save Olinka. She had to give it to Jacob, he had heart and soul, even if he was naive. And she couldn't blame him for being taken in. Ramón had been a charmer all his life. He and Julia had created an elaborate plan with everyone else just bricks in their building.

Ironically, it was a pyramid they would enter. How many economic disasters had been built on such foundations?

"Alright, I will give you a crash course," she said. "It could save your life, or someone else's." She lifted her pulse rifle. "La Loba" was written in white across the body of the weapon.

"La Loba." He smiled as he said this. "The wolf?"

"Yeah, my roots are in Mexico." Leticia ran her fingers across the writing. "But if I were to be anything, it would probably be jaguar. In the Raiders we have our pack, and we fight like a pack, but the pack is only as strong as each wolf."

"That makes sense," he said. "So can we start that training now? Run through the basics. I don't give up easily on the things I want." A ray of hope glinted in his eyes as he said this. Part of her hoped she was included in the things he wanted.

Of course, if they were dead, romance didn't matter.

"Sure," she replied, and she showed him the basics of using the rifle. Mostly just made sure he could point and shoot. "When we land it will be dark. We'll need to create a perimeter of sensor mines, even if the building seems secure. Contain the threat as much as possible. And we need to stick together at all times." Remembering how well he'd obeyed orders before, she put extra emphasis on her words.

Then as the dropship got closer, they went silent. Leticia gave Mohammed and Frida a glance they would recognize as a sign to prepare for anything.

"*We have arrived*," Desiree said from the cockpit. "*I'm landing us.*"

As soon as they touched ground, Leticia unbuckled herself from her seat. "Mohammed, get those sensor mines ready. Program them for anything bigger than you." She moved to the hatch to be the first out, rifle in hand.

A two-hundred-fifty-foot pyramid of reflective solar glass stood before her, utterly black in the approaching night. The main research facility, Olinka One. What different stories she heard from Jacob and Ramón. There were no visible lights, mayday signals, or *any* signs of human activity. Still not a trace of destruction to the outside.

Frida was next to her. "I don't know what's worse, a ruined war zone where you can guess what your opponent has in their pocket, or something like this. It's so silent, we could be entering another dimension." She nudged Leticia. "Good thing we aren't virgins—otherwise we would all be dead within minutes."

"No shit, and that's what worries me. The silence, I mean, and the dark. We're going in blind until we get the drone inside. Those Xenomorphs are big fuckers, they won't escape any radar, but they're predators, too, and will hunt like it. I'm not dealing with those things in the dark. We wait for daybreak." She looked up. "It won't be long—this ain't Earth, as much as it may feel like it.

"Seeing those things, it's made me feel farther from home," she added, "but closer to my mom. If Julia is in her 'panic room' then she can wait a little longer. To tell the truth, my gut says there are no survivors."

A voice from behind startled her. It was Ramón.

"I know whatever I say won't be heard," he said, "but we should act now, and pray it's enough."

"Go on in, be my guest, Ramón."

He could pout like a child, because it wasn't his show anymore. She scanned the area in the encroaching night. There was more vegetation here, and the cliffs backing into the ocean weren't far off. The faint scent of saltwater wafted in the breeze. The two moons in the shape of crescents glowed above the dusty indigo sky turning dark. The stars would be out soon, and in a few short hours the sun.

"Finish up prep and get a little shut-eye, Frida."

Jacob joined her, but didn't show any of the pride he'd held when they arrived on the planet.

"It's even more impressive than the photos," Leticia offered.

"I know," he said sadly. "Since I started this project, I had high hopes for how this first meeting would go."

"Let me go check on Desiree and Mohammed, and I'll come back to give you another short lesson with the pulse rifle."

"Anything I can do?"

She smiled and touched his cheek, remembering how good it felt to make love to him. Might have been the last time either of them experienced ecstasy.

"Pray."

Leticia left Jacob to check on their small band of lobas. Frida and Mohammed unloaded and took stock of the cache of weapons and ammunition. Desiree still scoured the perimeter with the drone. In covert operations they sometimes only had six, now they would have to make do with five.

The feeling of being diminished cut into her confidence, especially when she remembered how the Xenomorph towered over Nathan. It was her responsibility to keep him alive. To keep all of them alive.

Fuck the facility. Let it burn with the same acid fury as the blood of a Xenomorph. She turned the situation over in her mind, trying to see it from different directions, like trying to figure out the best place for a sniper to make the cleanest kill shot.

Desiree rushed toward her.

"We have incoming communication, and I think you'll want to take this." As they ran back to the dropship, she added, "They're already in orbit."

The fuck?

Leticia hit the comms. "This is Director Vasquez."

"*Vasquez?*" the voice said, sounding strange, and… "*Yeah, so we received a distress call. We're in orbit, but not over your position, so we can be ready to roll in a few hours. What's your plan?*"

"First, how long have you been in orbit?"

"*Stand by,*" he responded. Then, "*Been here for a hot minute, on orders not revealed.*"

"Well, that's damn good news for once," she said. "First light we head into Olinka One—I don't want to risk going in the dark with this one."

"*Smart. We will be there as soon as we can. How hot is it? Our satellite shows things pretty quiet.*"

"Believe me when I say this threat isn't quiet. So far it's contained inside the facility. When we go in, that might open the door—no time to give you all of the details. There are civilians not far from us, with two dropships. They need a place to dock. Also be aware, we have created a perimeter of sensor mines for anything bigger than your largest soldier. Just be ready to use all the firepower you got. It's an alien species."

Leticia expected a snort, or silence. She received the latter.

"*Gotcha,*" he said. "*See you soon. Stay alive.*"

"Thanks. Desiree will connect you to our personnel comms, so we can stay connected once we go in. God speed."

"*Roger that.*"

Leticia exhaled. The heaviness in the front of her skull lightened and the stinging that rimmed the inside of her eyes—where she held back her tears—burned less. She walked out of the dropship to let the group know the news.

"Everyone, try to get some sleep, or at least pretend. As soon as the sun rises, we move in." She jerked her thumb toward the cockpit. "That was backup. They're a few hours away, but they will be here soon."

Frida and Mohammed slapped hands—it was the closest she'd seen to a normal response from Mohammed. That was reassuring. Jacob sat on the ground, staring at Olinka One.

Leticia stood there, looking up at the burgeoning stars. In that instant she felt closer to her mother than she had ever before. Somewhere in the gases, meteors, icy comets, radiation, dark matter—all of it—Jenette Vasquez lived on. Leticia took a deep breath.

Keep us safe. Guide me, por favor.

She touched the gold cross around her neck and took the bandana out of her pocket, placing it across her forehead. It didn't matter much where her father was, because he hadn't faced the same battle as her mother— the battle that was Leticia's. Still his face flashed in her mind, and she said a prayer for him, too. Theirs had been a star-crossed brief affair that brought her and Ramón into existence, and ultimately to this moment in time for a destiny now out of their hands.

Leticia would never understand the machinations of humans, but she did understand herself and the desire to survive like the soldaderas during the Mexican Revolution, the pachucas in the 1950s LA riots, the migrant farmworkers, the boys who couldn't afford college and were drafted to fight in Vietnam. All the way back to her indigenous ancestor warriors suiting up in brightly painted cotton armor as they fought the conquistadors.

Their souls resided here and now she called on their power to survive this fight.

Ramón approached. "I have something I need to say, but in private."

"You have five minutes," she said, leading him a short distance away. "I'm teaching Jacob how to use a rifle. Is it more important than a man not wanting to die?"

"In my research, I uncovered all the files relating to the Xenomorphs and all previous encounters. Our mother died in one of them. They were there to neutralize the threat on a small colony. LV-426."

"And you brought them here," she said. "You're fucked up, Ramón."

"I suppose I wanted to know that I could change the course of destiny, and harness whatever destroyed her. That I was smarter and death could be... something I owned. It wouldn't hurt me because it was my possession."

"But instead, it's just doing what it does best," she said. "You can't cheat the stars, and death belongs to no one, but comes for us all."

"She was a hero," he said. "According to the files, she gave everything until the very end." He looked into her eyes. "I was wrong about all the things I said about her as a kid. She would have been proud of you."

Leticia wiped her eyes and touched her bandana. "You have a way with timing, but at least it gives me even more reason to fuck these things up. I hope you do what's right when we get in there. You need to make her—and yourself—proud."

Leticia walked away. She couldn't process this right now, but she could use the vengeance coursing through her veins. Those things would see who had acid for blood. She approached Jacob.

"You ready for a fight? Let's go over that weapon for you."

He rose from the ground then kissed her hard. She didn't care who saw.

"I'm ready," he said, "and I did that in case I never get the chance again. You're an extraordinary woman, Director Leticia Vasquez." She kissed him back.

"I have one helluva story, that's for sure."

2 7

The onyx pyramid reflected the morning light as it absorbed its radiation. The two moons were still present, remaining on watch until they would have to relinquish themselves to a mightier foe, a sun.

Leticia had planned to remain on watch, but Mohammed couldn't sleep and took her spot. "We need your leadership, which means you need rest," he said. "This is one job you can't sleep on. For Nathan."

"Mohammed, I'm sorry," she said. "This was not supposed to end up like this."

"I know." He closed his eyes and touched Nathan's dog tags. "I feel responsible, thinking there was anything more than war in the universe. Nathan and I saw the money, too. We get through this, the rest is a tale yet to be told. Now go sleep." Leticia reluctantly left, and drifted off quickly next to Jacob on top of a sleeping bag on the floor of the dropship.

Ramón could fuck off if he didn't like it.

It was the nightmare of her experience in the temazcal, years ago, that alerted her to the breaking day. The dark hands of the Xenomorph had her by the neck, and there was nothing she could do about it. Then she woke up. When Leticia emerged, Frida was already distributing energy bars to the rest of the group and pouring hot instant coffee.

"Last one for you, jefa."

"Thanks." Leticia took the coffee that went down hot and soothing. She raised one hand to get the group's attention as they prepped themselves and checked ammunition. "Las Lobas, are you ready?" They saluted in response, giving a *whoop*. "Desiree, do you still have the drone stationed on the dropship port at the top of Olinka One? I need eyes, in the event something wants to escape."

"It's already in place," Desiree replied. "Other than that, we are locked, loaded, and ready to fuck shit up. Still no update from the Eagles above, though."

So much for good news, Leticia thought darkly. "Mohammed, you're on party patrol. Keep the scanner looking for any movement that ain't us, and especially bigger than us."

"On it, jefa, but why do I feel like I'm living the song 'Hotel California'?"

"Ándale, then." Leticia finished her coffee in a gulp of heat that burned her mouth, then tossed the cup into the dropship. "We listen to the Eagles drunk as fuck when this shit is over." Mohammed nodded in agreement, and hefted a flamethrower—the one Nathan had carried.

Ramón had the tablet in his hand, ready to override the facility's main computer to open the doors.

"Open sesame…"

Leticia turned to Jacob, who now wore fatigues. He had stripped himself of his old life of the Eton boy, Oxford grad, and CEO. He held his pulse rifle, looking ready to fight and die. She admired him for that. He had no high horse, or if he did it wouldn't last long. The first time she saw a man die it looped through her brain with the same motion of an old movie in a projector. The silence in his eyes, with his brains splattered across a wall, made her aware of the illusion of time.

He had been talking to her one second and gone the next. The unknowing was the worst part of it. The inability to face an adversary head on was as close to death as she could get. When the anxiety built to an unbearable level, was life worth living?

You have to push through those illusions of shadow and imagination, past the difficulty of the moment to move forward.

The entrance that was as wide as three people, but felt like the mouth to hell the size of a pinhole. Leticia raised her arm and waved everyone to move forward. They all carried pulse rifles—all except Ramón. Just as well. She had no desire to die from friendly fire. He wore Raider-standard protective gear, though, and a helmet to stay connected.

Looking to the clear sky one more time she remembered sitting on Roseanna's back porch, barefoot with a book in her hands and the wind chimes serenading her. She hoped Santa Muerte was bringing their backup closer.

The inside of the facility no longer resembled anything created by a human hand. The simplicity of the interior—with clean lines, minimal decoration, and modern art seen in the photos taken when first built—was nowhere to be seen. Viscous slime crawled down the walls. Some sort of hardened resin morphed the entire space to a level of an inferno only captured in fiction, from the writings of a wild imagination. But this was real.

The grooved walls resembled carved wet stone as they glistened beneath the pulsating emergency lights. This was no haunted attraction at Halloween. It was a temple garden for dark gods, the Xenomorphs. Those creatures had taken over.

Despite the heat and humidity of the interior, matching that of the towns close to what remained of the Gulf of Mexico or the re-established jungles on Earth, she felt her body go cold. The monsters had wasted no time creating a hive. If this happened in a confined space, in such a short amount of time, what would happen elsewhere? What might an entire world look like? Only a fool could think they could be tamed, made into bioweapons.

No one spoke, their breathing heavy in their helmets, shared with one another via earpieces. The farther they ventured, the hotter it became.

"This way."

His voice startling, Ramón guided them through the facility that could have been the guts of an organism. It was the anatomy of alien life taking hold doing what it did best, surviving. They continued on with slow deliberate steps, through an open thick vaulted door with triangle locks. The archway had been transformed to a trellis of onyx pumice dripping in precipitation and slime. The path spiraled deeper into the facility until it opened up again to what had been a large lab.

Cylinders contained small things, almost spider-like with legs that looked like the fingers of a bruja and a tail that could be the cousin of a rattlesnake. Four other containers held clear water that appeared harmless. The fourth had a powerful microscope attached to an extendable robotic arm, amplifying the contents. It showed what lurked invisible to the human eye.

"Híjole, Ramón," Leticia said. "What the hell?"

"We've linked Xenomorph DNA with the common pork tapeworm," he said, as if it was a perfectly natural thing. *"It's meant to contaminate water systems."* Writing coiled parasites swam in unison. Mouths snapped open and shut and were lined with jagged teeth. Barbs edged their bodies.

"I want nothing to do with any of this," Jacob said, not disguising the disgust in his tone. *"We've fought so hard and long to bring clean water to humans everywhere, and here you are creating a weapon that will do the opposite."*

He growled. *"No wonder half of my family isolated me in England. The other half is pure poison. While I'm trying to spur human evolution to move ahead, they're finding more cunning ways to murder each other."*

Clear chambers hung along a wall, tinged with frost that indicated refrigeration. In them were multiple Xenomorph corpses in various states of decay. Their bodies were deformed, the shiny carapace mottled.

Leticia's anger has risen above her fear. "I just need to know one thing," she demanded. "Why are you doing this? Why are you studying something like that? You can't bring it back to Earth, or take it to any world. These aren't dogs you can train, and they kill without mercy."

Ramón remained silent.

"Answer, Ramón," Jacob said. *"I want to know, too."* He gave her brother a look of disgust. Ramón shot him an equally acrimonious glare.

"I'm doing what we do best," he said. *"We manufacture life and death, and sell it to the highest bidder. It's always been that way. You can't build better worlds if you are fighting over them. These will stop the fight once and for all, because no one will doubt our superiority."*

Leticia could tell he was still holding back.

"Ramón, if we don't know what this is we can't fight it."

He stopped and pointed to a row of smaller tubes, a size that could be held in the hand. Something black shimmered inside.

"We've been engineering our own weapon for use against the Xenomorphs," he explained. "It's a type of necrotizing fasciitis—flesh-eating bacteria that passes quickly between the creatures. When activated, it can also be lethal to humans. With a high enough dosage, these samples can be used against the aliens. Their immune systems are tough, but we managed to crack them.

"The true test will be to infect a queen," he continued, "then for her to pass the bacteria to her eggs. You should see the early footage of their reactions when the bacteria is introduced into their environment. With just the proximity, the Xenomorphs can sense the danger."

"What does it do to humans?" Desiree asked.

He didn't answer.

"Burn this fucker down," she said.

"Are you joking?" he responded, his voice rising. "We've worked too hard to lose all this valuable research, all this time, effort, and investment. None of our lives are that valuable."

"Heads are going to roll."

"Whatever, Jacob," Ramón spat. "Yours has been on the chopping block for a long time now, you know."

"You think I'm just a stupid boy scout? Of course I know. Hell, Julia Yutani is probably the chairman of that board."

"Boys, callete!" Leticia said. "Holster your balls." She turned to her brother. "Where are we going, Ramón?"

"Here." He pointed to his tablet, then moved on.

Though she didn't want to show it, her skin was crawling. There was nothing secure about this place, and according to Ramón some bubonic plague-level bacteria just waiting to be let loose. Nothing about this was right. Leticia moved closer to Desiree.

"I want you to cover Jacob." Then she addressed Jacob. "You can expose all of this, but only if we manage to survive. If those things hate the bacteria, our only way may be to take it with us. So grab a vial. In fact, everyone grab one."

"*Say what?*" Frida said. She stared, but didn't move.

"There really is no other way," Leticia said. "We already have one foot in the grave. Better to take our chances where we find 'em. Once we get away from here, we can drop that bacteria shit into one of those steaming mud holes. Ramón, you said it had to be activated—how does that work, anyway?"

"*Um, aerosol, water supply, even a puncture wound, like the source fasciitis.*" He moved with the others to take a sample, stopping briefly at a desk. "*Now can we get out of here, and find Julia?*"

"Lead the way, Ramón. I want to get out of here as quickly as you do."

"*This way,*" he said, but he looked perplexed. "*We are… getting close… but it doesn't seem to be the panic room.*"

The path that had led them to the lab carried on spiraling down, with the heat intensifying. They turned on the lights that were attached to their rifles. The walls became thicker with the Xenomorph-made onyx insulation, and the floor a sodden mire of something she didn't want to know. Leticia looked behind them. It was as dark as the hand of the Xenomorph and the souls of the men who created them.

They moved into a larger space that could have been any place in the facility, with no discerning markers. Their lights strobed to illuminate bone and viscera. The open chests of the inhabitants resembled the remnants of a chorizo con huevos taco regurgitated by a drunk. It was an alien cathedral of gore, pain, and reproduction.

Some of the bodies were trapped in icicles of sludge and hardened mucus. Human waste covered the floors from the suspended bodies. The ammonia stung Leticia's eyes. Shards jutted in every direction, preventing any possible escape. The room breathed humidity, giving the facility its own atmosphere to help the Xenomorphs thrive in an inferno paradise.

To their horror, some of the poor souls attached to the walls were clinging to life. They wheezed and gasped for air, not realizing they no longer needed it—every life-form sought survival above all else. While it was as natural as breathing, now it only fed what grew inside of them. The sound was a hymn of desperate torture.

If Santa Muerte walked anywhere, it would be here. Her robes would bless this unholy ground and eat this torment.

"We need to take their pain away," Mohammed said.

"I agree." Leticia turned toward Desiree, and her gaze was met with rows of gooey eggs pulsating with their own tempo of weeping slime. "Oh, shit," she breathed, "this is one cascarone fight I do not want to be in."

"*I can't believe...*" Ramón began. "*I knew they were dangerous, but this.*" His face showed nothing but terror now, as he continued to walk while trying to hold his vomit at the sight of the bodies. In the corner was the decomposing corpse of one of the queens. The hood on the roof of her had exploded from the inside.

"Ramón, what is that?" Leticia asked. "It doesn't look anything like the ones we encountered before." She shone her light directly on the dead creature.

"*That may be La Reina,*" he said, and she gave him a weird look. "*We raised more than one queen. See that metal halo above the fanned crown on her head? It shocked her with electricity that fried her from the inside out. It could have released the bacteria, if we chose, but we relied on her for eggs. It's good news that she's been killed—whoever did that must have got them all. We can't be sure, though, unless—*"

He stopped abruptly and turned his light toward the wall.

"*No,*" he said in a hoarse whisper.

Leticia froze.

2 8

Ramón couldn't help but feel his own ribcage throb and give way to the sharp-toothed bite of grief as he saw Julia's pale face. She moaned as her eyelids fluttered, and winced with the light on her face. Next to her was Brenda Moon, and the other people involved in the initial stages of the experiments. Some appeared to have been dead for some time, with decay setting in. Flesh flaked away in the natural cycle of things.

"Ramón…" she said, her voice a croak. "You came for me." To see her like this made him want to climb into the cocoon with her. It was a greater love than he even felt for his own children.

"Yes," he said. "I'm here. I love you. I left everything behind to be with you. We are going to get you down, right now." He frantically looked to Leticia. "Help me get her out of here. Please!"

Julia spoke again in a voice barely audible.

"Ramón, look at me. It's too late. Don't bullshit." She coughed, a dry, hacking sound. "I love you. It was always you… My files… Nothing. Don't let them get out. We only managed to destroy one. Destroy them all. Yutani has a plan… we talked about, already in motion. You'll have everything you need."

He darted his head toward Leticia, but Julia moaned in pain and he turned back as her head lolled. She looked toward Jacob.

"I'm sorry, Jacob, but this involves you. You'll be blamed for all of it, and Vickers will be forced out. Those who supported you… also discredited. Run. No other choice for you."

Her head slumped forward.

"Julia!" Tears flooded from Ramón's eyes. He had known death intimately all his life, but now it stared back at him for the first time. Coming here had been his way of course-correcting. This was his way of leaving Mary Anne and his children for Julia. This was supposed to be their own garden of Eden, a world they could build together with more money than could be spent in several lifetimes.

It was also his way to make it right with Leticia and give her a big payday. He didn't want her to fall into any of the traps of his aunt Roseanna, his mother, or Cutter's family. Leticia was his only true family, after all.

Julia's body began to convulse—the chestburster was trying to emerge. Pink foamy saliva oozed from her mouth. The unbuttoned portion of her blouse revealed the flesh between her breasts, and it was bubbling.

"*Ramón, look at me now!*" Leticia screamed.

He reared his head toward her. His eyes went wide as Leticia raised her gun, and she shot Julia in the chest four times. The chestburster shrieked a shrill cry before falling dead from the gaping hole. Ramón's entire body jerked at the sound of every bullet that echoed in the chamber of life and death, a birthing suite and cemetery at the same time.

"*I'm sorry, Ramón, but it had to be done, and you weren't going to do it,*" his sister said. "*I wouldn't want you to. If you want to make it right, then do as she requested. Get all of her information about these things—and we better move fast, because if they didn't know we were here before, then they know now.*"

Wordlessly Ramón nodded. "For Julia," he said, finding his voice. "We need to go to her office, adjacent to the lab. It isn't far."

Jacob squared off with Ramón again, holding his pulse rifle high to his chest. "*What the hell was she talking about when she said I had to run? What did you two do to get rid of me, and apparently any Vickers?*"

Without any emotion on his face or in his voice Ramón answered. "We were going to discredit you with these projects, and take over the entire planet but still keep the experiments going while you were the one being indicted. Or an accident would happen. Your death would uncover all the Vickers misdeeds, and anyone who supported a Vickers."

Jacob shook his head with a disgusted snarl.

"Lead the way. I'll deal with you later."

Ramón couldn't look at him. He refocused on his tablet.

"In here. Leticia, I don't know if you heard Julia, but we had a plan. A chain reaction of sorts in the event of any emergency. All her files would be transferred to me, then to you. You need to do the same. There's no time, in case we don't make it out." He said this while typing. "Right, who is your backup?"

She looked around. *"Jacob and Desiree of course. You think I'm going to let you and that bitch frame an innocent man? And make me part of it. Were you going to bribe me, or bump me and my team off eventually? We are done, brother. I fucking swear."*

"No," he said. "You would have believed it, too. And no offense, but Desiree? She has no power in the scheme of things. Jacob I can understand, but the files might not help him. It's all designed to point to his guilt."

"No offense taken," Desiree said sarcastically.

"Oh, she has power," Leticia said, *"and she's not part of the Weyland-Yutani gang. How can I trust you after all that has been said, all your lies from day one?"*

"You don't have a choice, and I'm trying to help you," he insisted, focusing on the moment. "I need both of you to press your thumb here. You will have a code for an electronic lock box."

Jacob and Desiree exchanged glances, but didn't move.

"*Do it!* I have nothing to lose or gain anymore. She's gone, and I don't want this anymore. There is a chance you might find a way to clear yourself. It's everything here. You see, humans aren't perfect, and our little scheme a failure. It's all you got."

Jacob pressed his thumb to the tablet, while maintaining eye contact with Ramón.

"*We will see.*"

Desiree followed.

"*Is this episode of* Family Feud *over?*" Mohammed craned his neck as he scanned the space for movement. "*Fuck. Where the hell did they come from? We got company, wolves. There are a few of them. Everyone keep quiet, get your weapons ready.*"

Then the sounds began. A cacophony of monsters in the form of hissing like a valve of steam being released. It was the same as when the dropship opened with the dying man.

"*Eyes in all directions, people.*"

The small band put their backs to each other.

Ramón took a bag slung across his chest and handed it to Jacob without looking at him. "Consider this an apology. I snagged it from the lab with the bacteria. You can run, space is big, but maybe you need to clear your name, because this is only a small portion of what is going on."

"*What's this?*"

"Your lucky day and lottery ticket. Activated bacteria, and a chip with the formulas for activation and neutralization." He turned. "Leticia, go with Jacob and get him out of here."

"Why aren't they attacking?" Frida said.

It was exactly as she said. The Xenomorphs hissed and snapped at the group without attacking. Leticia maintained eye contact with a beast that had no visible eyes, but she damn well knew they saw everything.

"It's the bacteria," she said. "What Ramón was carrying. Fucking go! This is your chance. I'm not leaving—this is my mission. Backup should be here soon. Desiree, turn on your sensors and get Jacob out of here."

"Leticia, we can all get out of here. Let's stay like this."

"No we can't. Look at them." Three Xenomorphs were gathering just beyond Jacob, who was holding the activated bacteria. "They will attack, even if we pass the bacteria around like a blunt at a party. No, they'll pick us off one-by-one and use the confusion to strike the rest. Desiree, go now with Jacob."

Desiree frowned, but then she braced herself.

"Will do, jefa," she said. *"As soon as we are clear I will try to find out where the fucking backup is."* She squeezed Jacob's bicep to draw him away.

"Leticia!" he shouted.

Then they were gone. Laying down fire to cover

them, Leticia ignored his desire to stay and fight these things head on. Now she had to get Ramón out. He knew weapons, had brokered arms deals, but didn't have any combat experience. Without her backing him up, he was as good as dead.

"It's time to use your good arm, Frida."

Frida grabbed a timed grenade from her waist band and aimed for pockets in the wall of human cocoons and open bodies. The more of the facility they could take down, the better. She made three perfect pitches. She had the fourth in hand when a black claw came from her right and grabbed her ankle.

"Leticia!"

Her scream made them turn. She hit the ground, and one of the monsters hovered over her. With the grenade still in her hand she grabbed the Xenomorph back. As it lifted her into the air, Mohammed took another one from his pocket. Frida looked back and gave them a thumbs-up.

The inner mandible pushed out between the hideous jaws.

Frida's body and the Xenomorph shattered together.

"Move!" Leticia bellowed. "Which way, Ramón!"

"*Back! We go back!*"

They ran up the spiral corridor. Leticia fired behind them, at times eliciting a shriek, until they were back into the lab.

"*It's a risk, but there's a ventilation system here,*" he said. "*Only one way out.*" Ramón typed fast. A square vent opened at the base of a wall at the far end of the lab. Behind them, Mohammed tossed a grenade toward the entrance. Leticia's watch vibrated.

Desiree and Jacob had made it out.

All the sensor mines were hot and ready to blast anything bigger than a human. She felt a small pinch of relief before slipping into the shaft with Mohammed and Ramón. The heat went from manageable to choking, and she blessed the bandana around her forehead. It was a source of comfort and protection, like Santa Muerte inked on her back.

"Ramón, lead the way as fast as you can. We're going to suffocate if we don't move." The bandana around her forehead leaked sweat as she hunched, wading through muck that smelled like the sewage system had been damaged. She did the best she could to calm herself and use as little oxygen as possible. No amount of training or physical strength would get her out of this trap if she couldn't be strong in mind.

The mind and soul are muscles. They were what determined success or failure. What propelled the soldaderas in war and got her mother through an unjust lockup. As the leader, the solution fell to her shoulders.

She closed her eyes and thought of her niece and nephew, toddling with their chubby legs in diapers, the aroma of Roseanna's borracho beans—without alcohol—cooking for hours.

Only Santa Muerte could save them, because some

ruthless god had created these things in their image. Faith had fled Leticia the day she was arrested for assault. But now…

"*Where's Vasquez?*"

Leticia stopped. The voice was in her ear.

"Here—I'm here. What's good, backup?"

Something was familiar. It couldn't be…

"Who is this?"

"*It's Major Haas.*"

"Listen to me," Leticia said. "We're practically in a fucking mine shaft. As hot as balls in a polyester suit on prom night. Can you register our location?"

"*Depends how deep you are. Some of these facilities are built with tech to block scanners. They don't want their private business exposed.*"

Ramón shook his head.

"Good," Leticia said. "No tech. Give us some time to get out of here, and then blow it. This place has to be torched."

"*Holy shit.*" Haas' voice broke with static.

"What? Talk to me!"

"*I don't know what the hell is going on down there, but it looks like you got lice. There's an open escape hatch. The fuck is crawling out of there?*"

"Blast them!" Leticia shook her head. Rolling sweat made her neck itch. "Kill them all! Don't let a single one off this building. Circle them like vultures!"

"*Roger, that. Get out of there, because blowing it all might be the only way. Holy shit! One just—*" The sound of grenades echoed through the building and in her earpiece, followed by the hideous shrieks.

The facility above them shook.

2 9

"*Jefa, I have a launcher at the base of the pyramid, below the hatch.*" Desiree's voice piped through her earpiece. "*It will do what it does until it runs out of grenades.*"

"*Fuck,*" Ramón said. "*You have to see this. This… wasn't supposed to happen. Not like this.*" He shoved his tablet in front of Leticia.

Two heavily weaponized dropships circled the top of the pyramid, blasting the Xenomorphs that were scaling the walls, trying to find a way out. Two of the monsters leapt and reached one of the ships, where they began tossing out soldiers. Then the entire thing was going down in flames like a paper plane.

Haas was having none of it. Her crew blasted the Xeno-morphs and the ship that could not be saved. The sight gave Leticia some hope they just might make it out alive. Haas could be a cold-blooded bastard, if this was *the* Haas, but as long as she didn't do Leticia the dirty again, she was okay.

Leticia turned to Ramón and Mohammed. "We get out now. Move. We're not going to worry about the maternity ward back there. We have backup."

They picked up their pace with renewed vigor. Toward the end of the shaft blue and red lights flickered and it seemed to slope upward. Ramón tapped on the tablet.

"I've opened the other side."

Mohammed forced his way to the front with his pulse rifle aimed. *"I want the first taste of whatever is there, for my Nathan."* He touched the second pair of dog tags around his neck. Then they entered another space that could have been anywhere.

"Ramón, where…" His eyes moved above her head. She turned with her pulse rifle ready to be fired. Mohammed followed her actions.

The amorphous shadow against the wall stretched across with a menacing reach until she came into sight. The queen was a violated monstrosity. Her missing body parts had been replaced by a rage as she shrieked with only half of a mouth. The gaping hole poured saliva, with the long inner mandible swerving and striking at the air with a cobra's speed. It had grown to compensate for its changed anatomy.

La Reina had no hands or feet, but she used the thorned bony bayonets to move across the floor. She heaved and jolted forward, the umbilical-like cord quivered in her wake. With a sickening realization, Leticia saw that she was still producing eggs. Tarantula-like face-huggers followed in her wake and scrambled toward them on the floor. The ground was a carpet of the slimy creatures that possessed only one instinct before they gave their existence over to the perpetuation to their species. They were willing to sacrifice without knowing they were the sacrifice.

"Mohammed, now would be a good time to use that flamethrower."

"*This way!*" Ramón shouted.

Both Leticia and Mohammed unleashed fire on the face-huggers as they began to run in Ramón's direction. With a gurgle the Xenomorph queen regurgitated a greenish liquid. It fizzed and bubbled, and the onslaught of liquid flowed with the speed of magma. A river of acid. Mohammed unleashed a round on the cord containing the eggs.

"How far, Ramón?"

"*Keep going. Almost there.*"

Leticia turned to shoot more rounds at the queen. As Mohammed took aim to do the same, the monstrosity grabbed him by the waist and tossed him in the air as it coiled what remained of its tail around his body. Her inner mandible was a barbed vine that had unnatural dexterity. His weapon fired in the air as the barbs pierced his flesh to spew blood with the power of a sprinkler system. Leticia screamed and fired through a shower of blood.

The queen released his body as she convulsed from the shots. She collapsed to the ground in a pile of chartreuse-

and-black pulp. Mohammed didn't move as his body smoked and sank into the acid.

"How the fuck is this happening, Ramón?"

"*I don't know,*" he shouted back. "*Dr. Moon is the one who named her La Reina. Said she was acting funny, that she would evolve to escape.*"

"Funny?" Behind them in the tunnel, she heard a scabbling on metal. "There isn't anything funny about this."

He pointed. "*Through there. We should be close to an exit.*" Ramón tapped the tablet and opened a metal door that would have been invisible to the casual passer-by. "*Get ready to jump.*"

They managed to make it through. Leticia pressed hard on the trigger on her rifle, and as more face-huggers leapt, the door slammed shut. They fell a short distance and landed with a splash in the semidarkness of a larger chamber. Though a ruin, it didn't have the coating of resin. Instead they stood knee-deep in water thick with slime and blood.

The only sound was of trickling water. The reassuring blasts from Haas' crew had stopped, and there was no choice but to move forward. They dragged their legs through the muck.

"*It should take about ten minutes,*" he said, still gripping the tablet, "*then we can find our way out.*" She tried to pass him, to be the first out to secure the area, but Ramón matched her pace.

"Let me go first, hermano."

He ignored her and pushed ahead through the opening. She could see light from where artillery had blasted through the exterior.

Abruptly he stopped and looked up.

A Xenomorph rose from the water to spread its arms and legs wide enough to display its true size as it towered over Ramón. It whipped its tail in the air and darted it toward them with the anger of a threatened scorpion.

"Move, Ramón!"

But he was transfixed. *"So you are what we all chase, but can't seem to tame. Perfection…"*

"I said *mueves*, dammit!" she bellowed. "I need a shot and it's going to ricochet in here." As he turned, the tail speared him through the chest. His eyes widened and blood dribbled down his mouth. Ramón stretched both arms out toward Leticia.

"Do it," he said. *"I deserve it. Don't leave unfinished business, sister."*

Leticia brought her gun up. There were tears in her eyes that she refused to allow to fall until this was done. Before she could pull the trigger, however, a blast shot through his forehead. It also hit the Xenomorph. Flesh and blood mushroomed in her direction as they fell. She screamed in pain at the sight of losing Ramón and of her skin being seared, but she kept to her feet and looked to the blasted entrance.

Desiree stood with pulse rifle in hand.

"*I'm not losing you, too.*"

Her emotions released, Leticia screamed through tears. After what seemed like an eternity, but was only a few moments, she closed them off again.

"Gracias, mi amiga," she said. "Give me a report."

"*Haas is ready to land. Looks like we got 'em. I'll meet you in the front of the facility.*"

Leticia ran to Desiree and embraced her. "Thank you, hermana. Las Lobas."

"We ain't done." Tears fell from Desiree's eyes. "Fuck this joint. We need to turn it into a bonfire."

"Give me a minute."

"I'll cover you. Hurry."

Leticia turned to find Ramón's body. She used her pistol to shoot through the Xenomorph tail and release him from its spear. The backfire of Xenomorph blood still sizzled her skin to fajita meat, but the sight of her brother made her forget any physical pain she felt. He was not a good man. The worst, this had been his plan, with that cabrona Julia Yutani.

But he was still blood.

Her boots splashed through blood, water, and viscera. There would be no salvaging this facility. She would only take Ramón's body, and torch the rest. Mohammed was in too many pieces to be carried out, and it was too hot to go back in.

May Las Lobas rest in power.

When she emerged from the building pulling her

brother's corpse by the arm, Jacob raced toward her, stopped short, and placed one hand on her hip.

"Leticia... I'm so—"

"I know you mean well," she said, switching off her comms as she laid him down, still holding his hand. She unhooked a chain from around his neck, and stowed it in a pocket. "He brought it upon himself. He knew he was dancing with the devil—Julia, too."

"What do you want me to do?" Desiree asked.

Leticia couldn't look her in the eye. Even though there was no way Leticia could have saved the crew, the guilt remained. That was the gig, though. She let go of Ramón's hand and let it fall, before raising her eyes to Jacob.

"We have to torch the entire premises. We have all the information we need." She looked back. "That place is not even a tomb, it's a slaughterhouse. I know it means a lot to you, but it has to be done. We won't get answers from those things, and we won't get them from the people who were trying to fuck with a beast built to not be controlled or studied."

"Smoke and mirrors," he said, following her gaze. "Everything we do is just smoke and mirrors. I feel like a fool. Maybe Julia and Ramón were right. All of this has left me questioning everything." He looked at her. "Do whatever you want."

"Smoke and mirrors, eh," she replied. "That is all we are, so it makes sense that it's what we build—but we can choose to be the light reflecting on that mirror. You can't give up. My mother blew herself up to keep these things from getting out. She took her own life for a world that had locked her up, made her abandon her children, and gave her no other choice but to be battle fodder. You have power, Jacob, and so do I.

"We will blow this facility up and bring down more boots to make sure none are left. Then you rebuild here from scratch and do it your way. So people like my mother can have a real chance."

There was the sound of engines and a fighter ship landed. The hatch opened and Leticia couldn't believe her eyes for the who-was-counting-fucking time. It *was* Haas, who had stolen her promotion.

"When I heard Vasquez I wasn't sure if it was you."

"Same. I want to say it's not a pleasure, but you showed up. That counts for a lot." She gave a grim smile. "By the way, you stole my promotion, and now it looks like you stole my hairstyle."

Haas didn't answer, and looked at the body beyond Leticia. She had heard everything on their connected communication link. Then she ran her hands over her scalp.

"Take it as a high form of flattery," she said. "I'm glad I could come through here."

"It would have been nice if you could have arrived a little sooner, but me, too." Leticia extended a hand. "Teamwork from here on out."

Haas took it, giving it a solid shake. "I'll give them the word to place explosives inside, to destroy everything."

"As long as there's nothing left to scavenge, including the Xenomorphs," Jacob said, and Haas looked as if she was noticing him for the first time.

"I agree," Leticia said. "Can we get as many of them as possible to the mud pots? That seems like the only guarantee."

Haas took a moment to think. "I got a net we can load them into, then drop them from the sky."

"What about the ocean?" Desiree said.

"No." Jacob shook his head. "We don't know what has evolved on the ocean floor, and I haven't seen all the files of what they were doing here. Keep this planet as clean as possible."

"We start with cremating Ramón, then scattering his ashes in the sea. He should remain here with the results of his work."

"You do what you need to do, Vasquez," Haas said. "You can count on us to start the clean-up. And for what it's worth, I'm sorry about your brother."

"I appreciate that, Haas. Thank you."

"And another thing," she said, and it was her turn to smile. "I'm an asshole. I got that job and had to grow up a bit by doing it day-in and day-out. It took me down a notch. Some of the shit I saw, had to do, humbled me in ways I wish I didn't have to experience. Glory for ego's sake is a bitch."

Leticia opened her palm to receive a light slap. "I appreciate that, too. I think we can call it even."

3 0

The waves were larger and more violent than any she had ever seen. The crests far from the shore looked powerful enough to obliterate a skyscraper. They were walls of water and beauty as they hit spires of basalt. The energy from the waves created a mist that hovered in the air. Leticia could smell and taste it when she licked her lips. But the sound… If her soul could scream it would sound like this. The water did what it did with little care of anything else. It was strange, though, to not see gulls in the air or any creatures leaping from the water.

She couldn't help but feel that everything came full circle, or was recycled if not resolved. Leticia had accomplished everything she had, as a young girl, set out to accomplish, but in the moment, she felt just as lost as she had before receiving the letter from her mother.

Once again, she needed to find her internal compass.

When she raised an upturned palm, fat drops of water splashed against her skin.

"It also rains here."

"It does indeed," Jacob said. "Didn't pack any umbrellas, though." The droplets became larger and fell more rapidly, soaking them both.

"This is pretty majestic... wow," she said. "You know if anything lives in those waters?" She could feel his hand on the small of her back.

"No, not from what I've been told. Then again, that seems unlikely, and there aren't many things I can trust anymore. To be honest, after all this I don't care to find out—but all that unbridled power..." He looked out to sea again. "We could harness that. At least that was the hope."

"I'll bet that's exactly what they said about the Xenomorphs, time and time again. It's in people's deceptions that you see their truths. Now you know the truth of Weyland-Yutani. I know the truth of my brother."

"It's not the same..." he began. "I guess you read the files."

"Yes, I did, and this I know—humans always want to control what they don't understand, in order to be less fearful of it. Then they are surprised their actions lead to chaos. It's like squeezing a lemon and expecting orange juice." She let out a sigh. "I guess part of me thought this would be an escape.

"I've seen razed villages, known people who lost their

lives because of a choice I had to make on a moment's notice. I can't forget seeing bloated bodies torn by God-knows-what weapon. If the soul is made from anything, then I would say hope, or maybe love. See enough tragedy, and a piece of your own soul ignites, and sanity floats away as ash until nothing is left."

"Why did you want to scatter his ashes here?"

Leticia looked at the rum bottle acting as an urn, and chuckled. "He loved his damn boat, *Sail La Vie*. What a dumb name, but goddamn I loved some of the times we had on there with his kids, when I was on leave. Didn't mind that all he did was quiz me on my work. Now I understand why.

"What I wouldn't give to be listening to Christopher Cross's 'Sailing' and drinking a vodka and soda. Extra lime to go with the wind in my hair. A little sunburn on my cheeks. At least we had a few good memories. I figured this would be the best place to send him off. And his kids... Twins like us."

Leticia curled into Jacob's body as sobs began causing her chest to hitch. He squeezed her tighter, allowing his own tears to fall.

"They have their mother," he offered. "They are safe. I'm so sorry... If I had known—" He stopped, then added, "You have me."

Leticia broke away from him and wiped her eyes and nose with the back of her hand. She walked toward the steep cliff edge that filled her with dread. The grayish

blue current churned with the ferocity of Neptune blue.
There was no surviving these waters.

"Adios, hermano. See you next lifetime."

She took a few steps back, then dashed three steps
forward to throw the rum bottle filled with Ramón's ashes
into the gigantic waves. Leticia felt ready to die, because
clearly death had plans for her and her bloodline. Might
as well embrace it, and fuck it all the way to the afterlife.

Jacob stood behind her with another bottle.

"Tell me what to do." He placed a hand on her waist.

She grabbed the Hibiki from his hand and took a long
swig. "Come to my bed in an hour, and don't leave."

He kissed her neck. "Whatever you need."

She looked back at him. "I need you to be a Vickers. You
need to clear your name. Remove the deception and start
your own company. Fight, Jacob. We *fight*, goddammit!"

"I'm not a warrior. I don't have what you have."

"Really? Because what I saw today says you are. We
all are—we just have to have fucking guts to earn that
title and claim it. I don't have any trust fund or a name in
lights, but I *am* the motherfucking light. My mother was.
My grandmother… my grandmother Francisca sacrificed
her life so her daughter, my mother, could live."

"Then I'll follow you." Tears streamed again from
Jacob's eyes. "Weyland-Yutani wants a war? They have it.
I will clear my name even if I forfeit my fortune."

* * *

By the time Leticia returned to their position just outside of the Olinka One facility, Haas had left to find the civilians left near the sulfur fields and reassure them that help had arrived and to get them on the ship orbiting above.

"It's just the three of us now," Leticia said, looking around. "You think we're safe? What about weapons?"

"From what the scanners say... probably," Desiree said. "To be honest, that building is pretty complex. It's like a puzzle cube inside. Plus, those mines are still active. Haas will blow it all to hell when we move out at first light. Then this place will be empty again, except for the elements.

"As for weapons, there's nothing left," she added. "We took it all in with us. Jacob and I used all our rounds shooting at anything that moved, to keep our way clear. Flamethrowers, but you gotta get kinda close to hit one of those things. There's the Narwhal, but that would be tough to... Wait, I have a pistol!"

Leticia smirked. "Switchblade, and the launcher on the other side of the building, if it's still intact." She gestured back toward the ship. "Before you get any shut-eye, we need to bury the bacteria, insurance for a later date if we need evidence of what we witnessed. Ramón gave Jacob a live sample, plus the formulas for activation and neutralization. Those we keep on us." Another sigh. "Guess he developed a conscience, just a little too late."

"Got it, jefa."

Desiree wore a mask of grief. Her eyes red from crying on and off.

"Let's do it, and get some rest," Leticia said. "You fucking earned it."

"So did you, jefa." Desiree left to seek out the package with the bacteria, and to prepare a roll-out mat inside their dropship. Jacob was already on board, falling in and out of sleep as he read the files Ramón had given him. Leticia looked to the facility one last time before turning and walking away.

The first explosion rocked the dropship.

Leticia jumped from the floor and grabbed the flamethrower by the hatch. Desiree followed suit, but ran to switch on the flood lights attached to the ship. The rain had stopped and in the semidarkness two Xenomorphs lay twitching on the ground, blown to kibble from the sensor mines but leaving a space without protection. She and Leticia exchanged glances.

"We can get the bacteria," Desiree suggested.

"No. It stays buried."

"I'll call Haas and get the launcher."

"No time…"

Out from the bombed maw of the Olinka One facility, another Xenomorph emerged. It had a large hood that extended behind its head, and horns that were as sharp as its fangs protruding from its skull. This was her crown. The black mangled tail her scepter of death. She was larger than the other two.

This was La Reina.

Her missing jaw had only served to make her evolve into a more lethal creature. Her body had become a grand phoenix worthy of rising—she commanded respect. Where the ends of her legs and arms had been amputated, there were thick spikes lined with spirals of thorns. Free of the confining limitations of the tunnels, she walked on the spikes with the agility of a ballerina on her tiptoes.

The spikes on her arms helped to move her forward. The inner mandible had the same thick ridges and could now reach to the top of her hood. The mouth at the end snapped with a powerful crack to compensate for her missing lower jaw. Leticia had never before seen fangs the length of a human head.

La Reina screeched and hissed, then began to move toward them with determination. From the corner of her eye, Leticia noticed the Narwhal. It wasn't ideal, but...

"Go!" she commanded. "Take the ship and get out of here!"

"No!" Jacob said, standing at the hatch. "We stay."

"I agree with, Jacob. You need backup."

Without bothering to argue Leticia hopped onto the vehicle and switched on the launcher. The vehicle wouldn't be nearly as effective here on land, but she'd have to make it work. It was all they had.

"Adios, pendeja. Your reign is over."

She accelerated as hard as she could. With one hand she guided the Narwhal and the other she slapped the launcher. It blinked and as La Reina leapt forward, the grenade shot forward. Leticia swerved with both hands to a hard right. She could smell the flesh on her fingers sizzling. The Narwhal skidded into the ruins of Olinka One, and she looked back.

La Reina had barely been fazed.

And now she was *pissed*.

Desiree kneeled, firing a small pistol and doing minor damage to the large creature. La Reina charged again, but this time Leticia revved the Narwhal and released the harpoon into the leaping form. La Reina shrieked as it pierced her chest.

If only the Narwhal had enough power for what she was about to do next. Her thumb pushed the propulsion system to max, and she flew from Olinka One toward the sulfur fields not far off. She had to risk falling through the surface or flying into a fumarole. Either way, La Reina would be going, too.

The grotesque Xenomorph screeched as Leticia dragged her past the dropship. Jacob crouched in wait and blasted flames toward La Reina. Desiree had stopped shooting and held a tablet. Then Leticia was past them and couldn't look back as she raced toward the sulfur field at best speed.

It was just coming into view.

Smoke blocked her vision, and the Narwhal began to slow. La Reina must have dug her spiny arms and legs into the ground.

"Santa Muerte, ancestor soldaderas, Jenette Vasquez—see me through!" She revved the engine one last time as a large mud pot bubbled ahead. In an instant she felt herself jerk backward.

The Narwhal skidded left to right.

Leticia held on to the handlebars and looked back. As she dug with her arm and leg talons, La Reina's bulk had disturbed a sinkhole. Smoke rose from her body where the flames had licked her hardened exterior, but to no effect—that was what her mutation had accomplished. It hardened her exterior until it seemed able to survive anything.

The harpoon remained embedded, and it was dragging Leticia down with her foe. She scanned the unstable ground, not knowing what would happen if she jumped. Closer and closer she slid.

Her watch vibrated. Leticia glanced at it.

Santa Muerte still has my back!

Desiree had sent her a tracked map of the sulfur fields. She detached the harpoon and the cable snapped back as La Reina's head began bobbing up and down as she attempted to use her spikes to lift herself out of the hungry ground. The long, serpent-like mandible waved in the air, still snapping with the fury of survival.

The engine of the Narwhal finally died and Leticia jumped off, keeping an eye out on her watch. As she did, a large belch of gas exploded beneath the Xenomorph, piercing her carapace, charring every inch of her body, then dragging her once and for all into her sulfuric grave.

The perfect funeral for a demon that should not exist.

The sky began to lighten, with both moons and sun becoming visible. Jacob and Desiree stood in the distance.

Leticia looked up. "Thank you."

Her watch vibrated again. According to the map the ground beneath her feet was unstable, so she began to jog to make it to the edge. She raised her arm to keep an eye on the map as the ground rumbled behind her. Hot mud and water landed to her side as geysers began to spew their hot spittle from the depths of the planet.

Picking up her pace she began to run hard, pumping arms that wanted to fall off from exhaustion—but she couldn't call herself a Vasquez, soldadera, or Marine Raider if she didn't see this through to the bitter fucking end, even if it ended in blood and fire.

The other side was just there.

Desiree and Jacob had terror in their eyes, which was all she needed to know with the ground continuing to shake at her heels.

"Now!" Jacob bellowed. Leticia dove and tumbled onto solid ground. Instantly they were next to her and pulling her farther back. A large hole had opened. She made it with moments to spare.

"What you just did, jefa, it's fucking miraculous. One for the books."

"Get me the fuck out of here please." Leticia's chest heaved as she grabbed Jacob's arm. She needed to feel him close, otherwise she might think this was just a dream. "And get me some of that rich boy liquor, while you're at it."

Jacob chuckled. "You can have anything you want. There is only one La Reina now."

3 1

None of them wanted to stay there. As Haas flew in to bomb the facility to hell, Desiree, Jacob, and Leticia were picked up to be taken to the main ship that orbited overhead. There they would decide what the next move would be.

Still lost in the numbness of her twin being dead, Leticia stared at the burning wick of a white candle on the altar she had created using small wildflowers, Olinka soil, a photo of her mother, and some of Ramón's ashes not thrown into the sea. She had located two sheets of paper and a pencil. Technology was wonderful, but sometimes it wasn't enough. While she would send letters electronically, under these circumstances it felt right to write them down first for Ramón's children.

She still had a few of his personal items as well, including the dog tags she had made for him as a joke. When the opportunity arose she would send the letters and mementos back to Earth. They would get there when they were meant to, at the right time.

The handwritten words would be her vow to continue the work of her mother and their bloodline. The frigid emptiness of space expanded within her heart as she thought of her mother's letter and what she said about a switchblade not being enough out here. She was right. On the floor she had Xenomorph teeth she had taken from one of the skulls. She also had a large branch shaped like a club. With the switchblade she would whittle the wood to create what she needed it to be.

Like a jigsaw she arranged the teeth to surround the wood with which she would create a weapon. It was a weapon used by the Aztecs, a macuahuitl. Historically, it was a handheld club with obsidian points embedded in the wood along the sides, but this one would be embedded with the teeth of the very enemy she would use it to cut down.

Sorrow was a drowning man's acknowledgment of defeat, she knew, but rage could be a life raft until feet found dry ground again. Leticia was filled with new determination. At the foot of her altar was the other Xenomorph skull she had kept from the sulfur fields. The strange shape of the bone still didn't register as real. The universe was so very different from what she ever imagined.

At least she knew they were not indestructible. This was proof of it. They had fought like true warriors against this thing. On the top she carved "El riesgo siempre vive" and the names of her fallen crew, including Ramón. A token and reminder. Her mother would be proud. A life for a life.

Because in life we experience many deaths. There were the deaths of relationships, of dreams, of the illusions she held of herself and others. Life was full of many transformations, and there could be no beginning without a death. The Xenomorph egg gave way to the face-hugger, which died, but not until after it had found a host. The host only lived until the chestburster was ready to break free.

Embracing death was the only way to live without fear.

May our mother's spirit live on inside of me.

If she had her way, she would destroy an entire plane—or as many of them as she could find—to defeat the enemy. Then go after the men who sought to tame such things. Those creatures didn't end up out here on their own, and they would be taken somewhere else or unleashed. They took her mother, and now her brother.

Leticia remained still in the dim light of the candle.

Jacob entered their room. "I wanted to come check on you. If you still want to be alone, I can go."

"No," she said. "We should talk." He looked startled at that. "What are we doing?" she continued. "We blast a few, then what? I don't know how I can go back, knowing what I now know."

Jacob sat on the floor next to her. "I've been drinking and thinking the same thing. How can I set up a utopia, here or anywhere, and turn a blind eye to what others are doing out there with the Xenomorphs and the bacteria? Those parasites? Miniature Xenomorphs meant to be ingested? I thought we were fighting for clean water, a pure life. If these things are supposed to be some sort of weapon, eventually my vision won't matter because we will all be dead."

"Then we need to find where they are, or if they have some home world," she said. "We blow it."

"Genocide. Even if the Xenomorphs contribute nothing to the universe. And what about the people who will die in the process? You want to hand them that sentence? How will they be remembered in history? Or us?" He gave her a moment to think about that, then asked, "Have you read through the files?"

"A few, but I couldn't concentrate."

"Well, they seem to be everywhere. There are floating labs… Weird shit you only read about on conspiracy sites. This is far from isolated, and it's only a matter of time before something hits Earth. We like to posture about the apocalypse, yet we are actively engineering it. Messing with things we can't possibly understand, or control, is our own apocalypse." Anger filled his expression. "Fucking Weyland-Yutani."

"I hear you, but you of all people should know that history will repeat itself, and these monsters have no consciousness or values within their blind bloodlust. As well, there will always be men who will seek them out for gain."

Jacob took a swig of Hibiki before extending the bottle to Leticia.

"I needed that for what I am about to say. How about instead of making a grand—and high-profile—gesture by destroying an entire planet, we locate the monsters wherever they are, and infect them with the bacteria. We become the pest control."

"And Olinka? Your paradise?"

"Do we ever know what any of this is about, or where we stand? I can promise you one thing—those things don't. What an advantage. They are the epitome of 'ignorance is bliss.'"

"You're talking like a drunk philosophy student now."

"Student... More like fool."

"Aren't we all fools, looking for signs, misreading information, overthinking?"

"There's one thing I don't overthink or misread."

"What's that?"

Jacob scooted closer. "How I feel about you. The moment I laid eyes on you, I knew my world would never be the same. You would be mine or I would have to give you up forever. All I know is, I choose forever with you, and try to stop this. You are the most amazing woman I have ever met. Now we have the rest of whatever time we have left. If I'm going to die it might as well be next to you.

"I know without any doubt you are the one to do whatever it takes," he said. "You love hard and you fight hard. And you must know… in this short time we've spent together, I've fallen hard. Olinka can be my retirement. For now, I let it go and see what happens. No one will be allowed on the planet. It's mine."

"Letting go and allowing yourself to be carried by the whims of this universe," she said. "I've had to let go of my parents, Roseanna, and now Ramón. It ain't easy. Guess I'll have to trust what comes next."

Leticia leaned in and kissed Jacob tenderly. He gave her peace and a sense of home.

"I choose you, too, this mission whatever it turns out to be, and however far or long it takes. For now, let's go to bed. Forever begins tomorrow."

Jacob's hold on her body was tighter than before. The warmth of his hand on her hip was an anchor to what it meant to be human. This could be it for her, for both of them. They might be each other's last lovers. As much as she didn't want to know anything about romance, there was something poetic about their relationship. He made every other man's kiss and touch feel lukewarm. It made her think of when she asked Roseanna advice when it came to love.

"I have had my fair share of lovers and fuckboys," her tía had said, *"and my best advice is don't give yourself away cheaply, and settle. You didn't stay with Avery. On the flip side, if a dude can't afford to give you all of his heart, then you are too damned expensive."*

Here Jacob was, giving her his all.

Breaking away from his embrace she pressed the front of the drawer on the side of the bed. A small light illuminated. As she sat up she caught a reflection—in the full-length mirror on the closet door and the smaller mirror on the desk—of her Santa Muerte tattoo. The image writhed in the low light, and as she twisted and moved it took the form of a Xenomorph.

She snapped her eyes away.

That wasn't what she wanted, not right now.

One of the red bandanas that belonged to her mother always remained close, whenever she slept. She placed it on a plank jutting from the wall that served as a side table. Leticia kissed three fingertips and touched the faded cloth.

Looking at it made her think of "Dancing in the Dark" by Springsteen and her new relationship with Jacob. There were only so many strangers she could sleep with, or friends to meet for drinks, but here she was a hired gun. Dead or alive, she would be dancing in the dark for years to come.

ACKNOWLEDGEMENTS

I want to acknowledge Christopher Golden who sent an email on my behalf to Titan for an introduction. Steve Saffel is a shining star when it comes to editors. He has believed in me from day one and has never waned in his support. Working with him is fun! I will be forever grateful for this opportunity and the joy it has given me. I hope it will bring joy and entertainment to those who read it. For others, I hope it will inspire them to tell a story of their own even if it has never been told before.

From Titan: Nick Landau, Vivian Cheung, Laura Price, Michael Beale, Louise Pearce, Kevin Eddy, Katharine Carroll, and Julia Lloyd. At 20th Century Studios: Nicole Spiegel, Sarah Huck, and Kendrick Pejoro.

Beth Marshea from Ladderbird Lit. She has been a wonderful advocate of my work!

Clara Čarija who makes sure all the details are correct and in order.

ABOUT THE AUTHOR

V. Castro is a Mexican American writer from San Antonio, Texas now residing in the UK. As a full-time mother she dedicates her time to her family and writing Latinx narratives in horror and science fiction. She has been twice nominated for the Bram Stoker Award. Her most recent releases include *The Queen of the Cicadas* and *Mestiza Blood* from Flame Tree Press. *Goddess of Filth* from Creature Publishing and *Hairspray and Switchblades* from Unnerving. Connect with Violet via Instagram and Twitter @vlatinalondon or www.vcastrostories.com. She can also be found on Goodreads and Amazon. Don't forget to leave a review or rating!

ALIENS™

BISHOP

T. R. NAPPER

Massively damaged in *Aliens* and *Alien 3*, the synthetic
Bishop asked to be shut down forever. His creator,
Michael Bishop, has other plans. He seeks the
Xenomorph knowledge stored in the android's mind,
and brings Bishop back to life—but for what reason? No
longer an employee of the Weyland-Yutani Corporation,
Michael tells his creation that he seeks to advance
medical research for the benefit of humanity. Yet where
does he get the resources needed to advance his work.
With whom do his new allegiances lie?

Bishop is pursued by Colonial Marines Captain Marcel
Apone, commander of the *Il Conde* and younger brother of
Master Sergeant Alexander Apone, one of the casualties
of the doomed mission to LV-426. Also on his trail are the
"Dog Catchers," commandos employed by Weyland-Yutani.

Who else might benefit from Bishop's intimate knowledge
of the deadliest creatures in the galaxy?

TITANBOOKS.COM

For more fantastic fiction, author events,
exclusive excerpts, competitions, limited editions and more

VISIT OUR WEBSITE
titanbooks.com

LIKE US ON FACEBOOK
facebook.com/titanbooks

FOLLOW US ON TWITTER AND INSTAGRAM
@TitanBooks

EMAIL US
readerfeedback@titanemail.com